The Spare

Jules Hayes

Jules Hayes lives in Berkshire, UK with her partner, daughter and dog. Before writing, she was a physio therapist.

She has a degree in modern history and is fascinated with events from the first half of the 20th century where her historical fiction is set. Her work has been longlisted in Mslexia Novel Competition and short-listed in the prestigious Bridport Short Story Competition.

Jules Hayes is a pseudonym for JA Corrigan who writes contemporary thrillers. *Falling Suns* by JA Corrigan (Headline Accent) was published in 2016.

You can follow her on
Twitter: @JulesHayes6
Instagram: juleshayes6
Facebook: juleshayesauthor
www.jules-hayes.com

This edition first published in Great Britain in 2021 by Orion Dash,
an imprint of The Orion Publishing Group Ltd.,
Carmelite House, 50 Victoria Embankment
London EC4Y 0DZ

An Hachette UK Company

A CIP catalogue record for this book is
available from the British Library.

ISBN (Paperback) 978 1 3987 0810 5
ISBN (eBook) 978 1 3987 0396 4

Printed in the UK

www.orionbooks.co.uk

In memory of Miguel Soto ~
14th December 1925 – 29th November 2015

&

Dedicated to Isabel Carmen Adame Hernandez

Quien bien ama, tarde se olvida

True love never grows old

Prologue

A farmhouse near Sabadell, 18 km north of Barcelona, Spain

The Skinny Boy

DECEMBER 4TH 1937

The skinny boy turned away from the broken window and snagging his sleeve on the jagged glass, he lost his balance, fell off the barrel, crashing hard onto the muddy ground. He puked and then wiped his mouth in one swift movement, more concerned a Nationalist soldier might have heard him than about the vomit seeping inside his shirt. Taking a deep breath he steadied himself and climbed back up.

And watched.

The screams made his heart hurt. They came from the girl lying prostrate on the wooden table inside the farmhouse.

'Scilla, I'm here,' he whispered. 'Here, by the window.' He thought if he used her nickname that she would hear. But she did not. He could barely hear his own words. Pretending he stroked her sweat-drenched forehead, with gentleness, the boy rubbed the window frame's peeling paint.

The terrified-looking woman who had been forced to stay in the corner of the room, was allowed to step forward. Under the officer's orders, she cut the cord with a rusty knife and snatched the baby from the soldier. The boy didn't know if the child was alive or dead, but then it whimpered. The woman covered the baby's face with her hand and all became quiet, and then the boy looked towards the man who had ordered the murder – because this was murder.

Studying the officer, he etched every detail, line and furrow into his memory. The boy then jumped off the barrel and hid behind it. The same woman was pushing open the farmhouse door with her foot. She held the baby tight to her chest and ran down the dusty track, through the sea of yellow winter jasmine, never looking back.

He waited and watched. The two soldiers appeared from the house and together they carried Scilla outside. Her eyes were closed but her lids flickered. She was still alive.

Dear God, please let Scilla die soon.

They carried her down the track which led away from the farmhouse. The officer sauntered behind, kicking up damp lumps of dirt to cover the trail of blood.

The boy guessed they were taking her to the roadside ditches where previously he'd seen renegade Nationalists disposing of bullet-ridden Republican bodies. But the three men carried on.

Following behind unseen he realised they weren't heading for the road after all. Instead, they walked towards the hill where the neglected olive grove was, like the rest of Catalonia, slowly dying.

It was when they, and he, reached the old twisted Freedom Tree – a place where with indulgence Scilla had played hide and seek with him – that the boy would feel true fear. He could have run away, back down the hill. It would have been the most sensible action. But he couldn't; he had to watch. It was all he could do. So the boy stayed with his fear.

And it stayed with him.

PART ONE

I

Bilbao, Spain

Isabella

MAY 1976

Disorientated, I flipped over, pulled my arm from under the cover and touched the gash that travelled from elbow to wrist. A loud bang outside and I was properly wrenched from a sleep that had been too difficult to find. The previous night's events surged back and in the blanched early morning light I still smelt burning rubber, still saw the civil guard striking the young student protestor and the boy's eyes closing, never to open again.

Another blast but this time more violent and causing the pension's thin walls to shudder. I threw off the sheet and leapt up, stumbling towards the grease-covered window. A vibrant orange fireball on Bilbao's main bridge where the boy had died lit the dawn sky. I rubbed the glass with my palm. A car was ablaze; its petrol tank must have exploded.

Wiping my hands on a towel, I grabbed a jumper from a chair and shivering, made my way to the next room and knocked on the door. No reply. Had my guide already gone? We'd agreed the night before that it would be better travelling out of Bilbao separately. I'd hoped to catch him before he left, and thought I would – because every morning for the past two weeks of our assignment I'd had to wake him. Like all teenagers Tomás loved his sleep. I stared at the closed door in mild agitation; there were questions I wanted to ask Tomás about the man we were meeting later. Forewarned was always forearmed. Background information key.

I pulled the jumper over my head, opened the door and stepped inside the room.

A scrap of paper lay on the unmade and empty bed. I picked it up.

Isabella,

I'll meet you in Balmaseda, at the clock tower. I'll wait. Rafael is expecting us before nightfall.

Do you have my cigarettes? Bring them with you. I didn't want to wake you.

Tomás.

The Ducados were still inside my bag. In the chaos of the night before I'd told my young guide to give them up; it was the same advice I'd have given to a son.

Familiar loneliness bit into me as I made my way back to my own room. I peered in the mirror above the grimy, chipped sink, and was horrified at the image reflected back. At thirty-eight, lack of sleep was having its effect. Grey shadows were visible in the hollows of my cheeks, my face narrow, sucked in. After splashing my face with cold water I rummaged around in my bag for perfume, which I sprayed liberally over smoke-infused skin and clothes; the pension's plumbing didn't stretch to a shower. Leaning across the bed I pulled my necklace from the bedside table and as I did every day, opened the heart-shaped locket and stared at the two photos embedded in the tiny frames. On the left was an image of my adopted mother, the right, the birth mother I'd never known. Her eyes were so like mine, almond in shape and bluebell violet. I touched the tiny photo on the right with the tip of my index finger and experienced the familiar thump of unexplained sorrow in my gut. Snapping the locket shut, I put it around my neck.

Half an hour later I was on the main arterial road leading away from Bilbao.

Pushing down too hard on the Citroën's brake, everything on the passenger seat landed in the car's footwell. My knuckles turned white as I gripped the steering wheel, my eyes fixed on the roadblock. Everyone had turned off their ignitions and the only noise I heard came from my own sprinting heart.

A civil guard was weaving his way through the lengthening queue of cars, his leather belt pulled tight around a waist that heaved for freedom. I'd been working as a journalist in Franco's Spain for twenty years but fear of the Civil Guard still crawled through me. He stopped at the small truck in front, opened the driver's door and yanked a man from the seat, throwing him against the bonnet. Slight in stature and wearing what looked like farmer's clothes, the man was well over seventy I guessed. He'd begun to cry. I adjusted the rear-view, looked at myself, and was glad I'd put on lipstick. I undid the first three buttons of my blouse, and then a fourth for good measure, pulled my platform sandals from my bag in the footwell and quickly put them on. I got out, the bag slung over my shoulder.

'*Señor*, might I ask you a favour?' I said to the guard's back.

He swung around, his face a picture of confusion. I straightened up and leant against the Citroën, glad too that I'd gone braless.

'Step back in the car, *señora*,' he said, making his way towards me.

I grabbed Tomás's Ducados from my bag. Took one out. 'Do you have a light?' I planted what I hoped was a provocative smile on my face.

He didn't reply but lit my cigarette. I tried not to cough as I inhaled and tried not to look at the old man who was staring at me. 'Is there a problem, señor?'

The guard watched me for a few seconds and then his hand moved to the buttons of my blouse, a fat forefinger snaked up my chest. 'A very big problem today, as you will know if you were in the city last night. You were, I think? Name?'

My throat constricted and I wasn't sure if it was the cigarette or the anxiety. 'Daria Martinez.' Daria had been my alias for five years. I'd never had a problem with my papers and hoped today wouldn't be a first.

'Where are you travelling to?' the guard asked.

'Balmaseda. I'm visiting from Barcelona, to see family.' My unbuttoned shirt was stuck to my back and it wasn't hot.

His hand dropped away from my neck and cupped my left breast. I didn't flinch. Finally after too many minutes and too much pressure on my nipple his hand snapped away, and he fondled the gun sitting at his right hip. 'Papers.'

I threw the cigarette onto the dusty ground, delved inside my bag and handed him my documents. He didn't even look.

'Off you go.'

I nodded at the old man's vehicle. 'His truck's in my way.'

The guard turned. 'Get back in and on with your journey,' he shouted to the trembling man, who did as he was told but not before looking at me, gratitude in his expression.

To me the guard said, 'Have a good trip, *señora*. And next time you travel, I suggest you wear a bra.'

I got back in the car and as I accelerated away I gave the bastard a wave, which he ignored, already tormenting his next victim.

The old man's truck ahead gathered pace, tyres dislodging the damp dust in his haste to escape. I took my hand off the wheel, threw the packet of cigarettes through the window and buttoned up my blouse, my thoughts already in Balmaseda, and the meeting with Rafael Daguerre.

2

The lush, emerald-coloured hills surrounding Balmaseda's valley were in stark contrast to the dust of Bilbao's outskirts. The town's clock tower told me it was exactly noon. Above, the sky brimmed with clouds that fractured vertically as they disappeared into a bright blue midday horizon. It should have been pleasantly warm but a slicing wind was finding its way from the North Atlantic, and through the Citroën's open window.

I turned off the radio but carried on humming the tune of Abba's 'Fernando'. And waited. Tomás should have been there by now. I thought of the roadblock, the Civil Guard and hoped Tomás hadn't given them lip, something he was apt to do. The block would have been set up long before I'd got there. Attempting to dampen my fretting I flipped the radio back on and fell asleep listening to Bowie's 'Golden Years'.

A knocking on the Citroën's window woke me and I turned to see Tomás's smiling face. Groggy with the snatched sleep, I wound the window down.

'Hey, glad you made it,' he said, poking his head inside the car, his long dark hair falling fashionably onto his shoulders, his yellow shirt encasing his willowy frame like a well-fitting glove, although the ridiculously wide collar was tucked inside. I adjusted it for him. 'Thanks!' He ran around the car, opened the passenger door and got in. 'You have my cigarettes?'

'Sorry, gone. I bribed a civil guard with your Ducados. Did you get out of the city okay?'

'I did.'

'Good.' My hand found the locket, caressing it in thought. 'How well do you know Rafael Daguerre, Tomás?'

'Well.' His chest puffed. 'He's taken me under his wing.'

'You mean he's recruited you?'

'I didn't need much persuading.'

'There are other ways to achieve freedom rather than brute force. It makes the hard-line Basque nationalists, like Daguerre, no better than the Civil Guard.'

'Your mother was hard-line during the civil war,' he said in a hushed tone.

I didn't reply, my eyes fixed on the windscreen.

'I shouldn't have mentioned your mother. Forgive me, Isabella.'

'It's okay.' Tomás was a great guide but came without a censor button.

Responding to my green light, he pushed on. 'Rafael says her body was never found.'

Breath caught in my throat. 'Daguerre knows about my mother?'

'It's Rafael's uncle who knew her.'

'During the war?'

'I think so, yes.'

The man I was going to interview, or his uncle, had known Sofia. I couldn't believe it, but it wasn't so outside the realm of possibility. My mother had been born in this region. All I possessed to give me some essence of Sofia, my mother, was the image inside the locket, two other old photos, and a tin box full of dried Spanish bluebells; the flowers were ones that she'd kept from her childhood in Bilbao, so Calida had told me. The only reason I still had these keepsakes was because Calida, *mi segunda madre*, my second mother, had risked her life to save them.

'Have you tried to find out what happened to her?' Tomás asked, breaking into my thoughts.

'Of course I have.'

He dipped his head. 'Sorry.'

'What are you studying at university?' I said, changing the subject, because talk of my mother had thrown me.

'Law.'

'Good. You should stick with that and not get involved in nationalism or with men like Daguerre. Safer.'

'You'll love Rafael when you meet him. Everyone does.'

'I don't think so.' I shivered, repulsed at the idea of everyone falling in love with a man who used violence to achieve his aims.

'Whatever you say, Isabella.' He pulled the rear-view, got out a comb from his shirt pocket, groomed himself, and then pushed the mirror back. 'You follow me in the Citroën. Rafael's base is about a mile from the centre of town.'

Daguerre was a myth, with no photographic images of him, although rumour had it that he was charismatic and intriguing. I huffed quietly to myself; although in fairness my French editor had intimated it wasn't Daguerre who perched at the top of the tree these days, and that he wasn't happy with the separatist movement he'd helped form. I had to bury my prejudices and place my personal opinions to one side before interviewing him, because personal opinion would impede a genuine response to my questions. And, if what Tomás had said was true, I might find something out about my mother, if I played the meeting right.

Tomás stretched like a cat, yawned and got out of my car, jumping back into his own.

I followed him, passing the town's church that sat grandly on the main street. I caught sight of a robust bloom of vivid pomegranate flowers that surrounded the ancient building like an enormous garland. We continued on towards the more desolate outskirts and finally Tomás slowed down, honking his horn indicating we were there. I stopped the car and peered ahead. The house was hidden behind sickly trees that were attempting against the odds of a cold spring to burst into life.

Tomás was already standing outside his car. He opened my door and together we began walking down the silent track towards the house. A feeling of unease passed through me and I turned, glanced around, seeing only a thin stray dog.

We opened a dilapidated gate, although the farmhouse that appeared in front of us was newly whitewashed and stood as a jewel in its overgrown surroundings.

A chair-swing sat at the front of the house and a girl lay lengthways across it, her eyes closed. She was wearing a short, billowy red dress, her stomach swollen. Tomás turned to me and mouthed, *shush*. He crept up behind the pregnant girl and placed his hand on her forehead.

She opened her eyes. 'Tomás!'

'Cristina, my love. Bit cool for sunbathing?'

She sat up, grinned at Tomás and then looked towards me. '*Hola, señora.* You must be Isabella Adame?'

A mild smell of chocolate blew across the veranda and I noticed an open box by her seat. L'Atelier du Chocolat. The famous Bayonne chocolate company. She pulled Tomás next to her, while at the same time pushing the ornate box further beneath the seat with her foot.

'I am, and you are . . .?'

Tomás interrupted. 'This is the mother of my child, and my very-soon-to-be wife, Cristina.' He took a breath. 'Cristina is also Rafael's niece.'

Cristina plonked a kiss on his cheek. 'I hear the demonstration did not go well last night?' she asked Tomás in a subdued tone.

'No, it didn't.'

'Congratulations are in order by the looks of things?' I said to Cristina.

'It's not really *congratulations*.' She giggled self-consciously. 'Tomás and I should have married first.'

'The world is changing. It's fine,' I said. Cristina was around eighteen. Same age as Tomás. What was she doing here? It wasn't a place where a young and pregnant girl should be. 'Are you living here?' I asked her.

She glanced at Tomás, her forehead creased in sudden anxiety, and it was he who replied. 'At the moment, yes. Until we marry.'

I was about to ask more – always the journalist – when the door, which had been slightly ajar, opened. The man who stood in front of me looked very like Cristina: high forehead and dark brown hair, as opposed to Tomás's jet-black mane. He had the same shaped nose as Cristina, wide at the nostril with a narrow bridge. Deep frown-lines on his forehead hinted at the future ones on his niece's. He looked more like her father than her uncle.

Rafael Daguerre was six foot, at least. Some would say skinny, but I thought more sinewy and muscular. Lean. Faint pockmarks marred his complexion and a huge horizontal scar ran across his forehead. I guessed that normally you wouldn't be able to see the blemish, as his hair would cover it. However, he'd just come out of the shower and his wet, thick chestnut hair was slicked back.

I opened my mouth to speak and for the first time in my life I was unable to find the words.

3

'Cristina lives here,' Rafael Daguerre said, drying his face with a crusty blue towel, 'because Tomás's mother would be given a hard time by her neighbours if she lived with them at the moment.'

At last I found my voice, determined to find it. During my career I'd come across numerous men as arrogant as the one standing in front of me. He was no different to any of them, and almost a cliché. '*Señor*, perhaps you should be encouraging Cristina to go and live with her own parents?'

The muscles in his face tensed but then in only a moment and unexpectedly, his expression softened. 'Cristina is unable to live with her own parents because they are both dead.'

'Ah, then I apologise. But still, I believe that Cristina should not be living here . . . and I'm sorry if you do not like my opinion.'

'I respect your opinion.'

I tried to pinpoint derision in his tone but there was none. He hid it well. 'That's good to know.'

Finally, a smile slipped onto his symmetrical features. 'Rafael Daguerre. Welcome, Isabella Adame.'

I held out my hand. He didn't take it, instead clasping me gently by my elbow and guiding me nearer to him. It took me a few moments to pull away. I convinced myself his familiarity had taken me by surprise, and this was the reason for my delayed reaction. No man in Spain would treat a woman who they'd just met that way – no man a woman could trust anyway.

'What happened to Cristina's parents?' I asked, fingering the top button of my blouse, and then my locket.

'Cristina's mother, my sister, died six months ago. My brother-in-law, Cristina's father, was taken by the Civil Guard a year ago.'

'I see. But, *señor*, this is an isolated house. You are an activist. All information can be bought. The girl isn't safe here and you know it.' I remembered the earlier feeling of unease.

His eyes lit. 'A woman with spirit.' He glanced at my ringless hands and heat rose in my face. 'I appreciate your concern for Cristina,' he carried on. 'And Tomás tells me you've been no problem to work with these last weeks . . . in fact the opposite. I'm familiar with your editor and his publication, *Le Canard Enchaîné*. He is fair. Will you write a balanced article?'

'That's what I do, *señor*.'

'And you do it well. You are sympathetic to Basque independence. But, unlike your mother . . .' His voice trailed off and so did his eye contact. Still looking downward, he said quietly, 'You aren't extreme.'

Daguerre and I were still standing in the doorway, Tomás and Cristina sitting nearby on the veranda. 'Tomás told me that your uncle knew my mother?'

'During the civil war, yes, he did. Before Sofia disappeared.'

Turning, I threw a questioning look towards Tomás, destabilised with Daguerre's use of my mother's first name.

'It's why I wanted you to come, Isabella,' Tomás said, his voice low. 'Why Rafael wanted you to come.' I caught Tomás's slight, almost imperceptible questioning shrug directed at Rafael. The older man's features were unreadable.

I inclined my head to Tomás, but said to Daguerre, 'No, I'm not extreme, *señor*.' Questions about my mother would come later.

'Leave Tomás and Cristina outside. Come in, and sit,' Daguerre replied, leading me into the house.

Once inside, he continued. 'It's going to take years for the government to clean out Franco's men. I'm sure you're aware that already the government is disposing of civilian Basque nationalists and using mercenaries from abroad to do their dirty work for them, and so keeping their own hands clean.'

'This is part of what I'm investigating.'

Daguerre pulled on a wiry brown wool jumper. 'The government intends a complete amnesty regarding Franco and his war crimes.' This was something of which I was aware. 'Bodies are being found all over the country.' He dragged out a chair, moved to take my elbow again, decided against it, indicating instead with an extended arm that I should sit down, all the time watching me.

'*Señor* Daguerre, it would be good if you were able to give me more information about this. Nothing will be published in a Spanish newspaper, but *Le Canard Enchaîné* and France, is a different matter.'

'I can give you much.'

'Excellent.' I lifted my arm, found a tendril of hair and twisted it around my finger with too much vigour. 'And your uncle. Is it possible for me to meet him?'

'Of course. I will take you to meet Miguel later this afternoon. He lives further into the valley,' he said, moving nearer. 'He would very much like to talk with you, Isabella.

And I'll take Cristina to Miguel's tomorrow too. You are right, *querida*, she will be safer somewhere else.'

Querida was an affectionate and personal term, and I flinched with its use. So arrogant, so rude, so obstinately self-assured. Daguerre held every character trait I'd assigned to him, and before we'd even met.

'Please make yourself at home,' he continued. 'Bathroom is over there if you want to freshen up.' He pointed to the back of the house. 'I'll leave you in peace.' He turned and made his way outside.

Despite the crisp spring temperature I was too hot and the grime of the previous night still clung to me, the smell of my perfume long gone. In the bathroom I began washing away the dirt of the past forty-eight hours. I splashed water on my face and used the jasmine soap, looked in the mirror, despising myself as I wished I hadn't left my make-up in the car.

When finally I made my way outside the front porch was empty. I smelt cigar smoke and followed its path. The three of them were sitting at a small table, its wood silvered by the elements. Cristina ate from a plate of cooked vegetables, *menestra*, whilst Tomás and Daguerre sipped anise. It was Daguerre who smoked.

'Terrible habit,' I said.

He stubbed it out. 'Then, Isabella, I will stop.' The cigar glowed in the bright red ceramic ashtray.

Tomás laughed and Cristina nudged him.

Daguerre got up, saying to Tomás, 'I'm taking Isabella to Miguel's. We'll probably be gone all afternoon. Remember where the guns are kept.' He flicked a glance towards Cristina. 'Get your things together, *niña*, ready for tomorrow when I'll take you to Miguel's. Perhaps stay there until the baby is ready to be born.'

'It's safe here, isn't it?' Cristina asked, her pretty forehead creased into a frown.

Tomás placed a protective arm around her. 'What have you heard, Rafael?'

'Things I'd rather not hear.' Daguerre sighed with weariness. 'We know what we are dealing with concerning the Civil Guard, but the foreign mercenaries are a different matter. And, more efficient than the pot-bellied Guard.'

'I didn't see any pot-bellied guards last night,' Tomás said, unsmiling.

'But, Tomás, did you see any foreign mercenaries?'

Tomás didn't reply.

'They know how to remain unseen.' Daguerre raked his hand through now dry hair. 'We'll take Cristina to Miguel's tomorrow.'

'Is there something you're not telling me?' Tomás asked.

'Yes, is there, Rafael?' I echoed.

Rafael looked straight at me and ignored Tomás. 'I like you calling me Rafael.'

4

Daguerre drove an ancient truck that looked as if it might have predated the civil war, even Franco himself. He wiped the old leather with a rag that was dirtier than the seat, and we set off. Quickly, the lack of suspension as well as the smell of petrol fumes threatened my usually iron constitution.

'Thank you for doing this,' I said, with not a little of a begrudging tone in my voice, and I wound down the window a crack. 'Although I'm not sure why you are.'

He turned his head. 'Does there always have to be a reason?' The corners of his lips lifted into an amused semi-smile. 'Sometimes we do things because, *eskubidea sentitzen dute*.'

'I'm sorry but my Euskardi is almost non-existent.'

'Sometimes things just feel right.' He rotated his head back, his line of vision secured on the road. 'And I trust you.'

I took in his profile, the clean-cut lines of his cheekbones, the superiority of his expression. 'Is it wise to trust someone you do not know?'

'Tomás trusts you, and I trust Tomás. It's enough for me.'

I only nodded in response, because I had no reply. A man like Daguerre would not trust so easily. He was either lying, stupid, or knew a lot more than I could ever guess.

By the end of the day I hoped to know which explanation was true.

'When Miguel realised who Tomás was working with, he asked Tomás to bring you here,' Daguerre carried on. 'Your mother is somewhat of a legend in this region . . . so Miguel has told me.' He turned again. 'Miguel doesn't talk of the civil war, but he's keen to see you, Isabella.'

I didn't want to beg information although, despite my initial feelings towards this man, and with reluctance, I admitted there was something indefinable about Rafael Daguerre which did put me at my ease. How could that be? 'I know very little about my mother, especially her later life.'

'What do you know about Sofia, about your family . . .?'

How much to tell him? What did I have to lose? I wanted to find out what his uncle could tell me about my mother. I was desperate to know.

'In early 1937 Sofia left Barcelona to pick up Calida and Aurelio, her "adopted parents" and the couple who were to later bring me up. She collected them from the Basque region to take them to a more stable area of Spain for the duration of the civil war. On her return, she met my father, a French brigader. It was a whirlwind romance, so Calida tells me. And short-lived – he died at the Battle of Brunete the summer of 1937.'

I stopped talking and my eyes rested on the passing scenery, watching the hills rise and fall along the hazy horizon. I was enjoying the rush of wind pushing through the open window and caressing the skin on my face. 'When my mother disappeared, Calida and Aurelio took me to France. My grandfather died during the civil war and so it was they who brought me up, as they'd practically brought up Sofia.'

I was revealing far too much; I was there to interview Daguerre, not the other way around. The caution I always had securely in place and which had seen me through twenty years in the field was evaporating. But I carried on regardless. 'Calida told me that my grandfather and mother didn't see eye to eye, and understandably, seeing as he was a Nationalist and Sofia a Republican.' I paused, thinking of my next words. 'Although Calida hasn't told me as much as I'd like.'

Calida and Aurelio Parrello-Rossello fled civil war Spain in 1937 with me, a newborn baby, and after the disappearance of my mother. It was deeply ironic that after leaving one oppressive regime, a few years later they found themselves in the midst of another in Occupied France. I hadn't seen Calida for nearly a year and, galvanised by a letter I'd received from her the day before I'd left for Bilbao, my plan was to visit France as soon as I'd finished this assignment. In her letter Calida told me there was something of *urgency* she wished to discuss. I missed my adopted mother, even now, even after so many years of living in Spain. A week in Marseille with the indomitable Calida was a welcome thought.

Daguerre replied, 'I think that many who lived through the civil war do not talk about it very much, if at all. Perhaps Calida is one of those people.'

'Maybe.' I pulled out a compact mirror from my bag and checked my face.

'You look very beautiful. Stop worrying.'

'Please stop being so familiar with me, *señor*.'

'Rafael. Call me Rafael . . . please?'

As well as the mirror, I'd also retrieved my notebook. 'I take it you have a job . . . Rafael?' I needed him on my side.

'I mine red haematite iron ore.' I saw his huge grin in profile. 'But not at the moment.'

Whatever Daguerre was he possessed a sense of humour and I was grateful for that, although often the most engaging and charming people could be the most dangerous.

'Perhaps, then, you can tell me about Vitoria?' His take on the recent unrest in the mining town would be something I could easily link with the article I'd been commissioned to write.

'I'm sure you already know what happened in Vitoria.'

'You tell me.'

'The strikers, all miners, took refuge from the Civil Guard in Vitoria's church. After being forced out of the building with tear gas, and on the church's steps, five of the men were shot in cold blood. So you see, our first non-Franco government shows itself to be as contemptuous of democratic principles as Franco himself. Franco is dead but nothing has changed.'

'But your organisation is causing havoc. It is illegal.'

'I disagree with the path it's taken.'

'Then leave. By being associated you are guilty.'

'I was there at its emergence and, perhaps,' he smiled sadly now, 'if I stay, I can do something from within.'

The clouds above finally burst open and unrelenting rain poured down.

'It is 1976.' He clicked on the windscreen wipers. 'Franco's been dead less than a year, but it's obvious the central Spanish government will continue to ignore the Basques. We've waited and patience is thin. The window of opportunity is now.'

I sighed. 'It's Lucifer's dance. Not yours.'

'For an experienced journalist, you're naïve.'

'Not naïve. Worried. Worried for Tomás, Cristina, other young people who can have no real understanding as to what they're getting involved in.'

'The youth see a future they want.' He stared at me and veered from the road. 'See, when concentration is taken, we fail.'

'Cristina's your niece. She's having a baby.'

He thrust his foot down on the accelerator and the truck swerved on the new wetness. 'Revolution comes from the young.' His eyes didn't leave the road. 'Your mother had the passion and the guts to do what she thought was right. She was nineteen when she fought with the Republicans.'

I flung my arms out into a gesture of helplessness. 'Exactly. Too young. Have you ever taken another's life?'

'No. And do not intend to. I'm not a main player in the organisation, Isabella. I am not the leader.' My editor had been right. 'Our organisation fragmented into two distinct parts a year ago. I sit with the liberals. The man who's leading is a radical.'

'His name?'

'This, I cannot tell you. But, suffice to say, we do not these days see eye to eye.'

'So, you oppose him?'

'Not publicly. But there are problems. I have known him . . . a very long time.'

'Does Tomás know about him?'

'Tomás knows what I want him to know. But no one, apart from a handful of others and me, are aware this man is vying for the top position. And he's achieving it.' He touched his scar. 'I have no wish anymore to be part of the movement.'

I wasn't sure if I believed him although with reluctance I was finding myself wanting to. 'Then what do you plan to do?'

Again, he fingered the discoloured blemish. 'I'm in touch with an official within the National Assembly in Madrid. I have information he wants.'

'Which official?'

Silence.

'I'd like to know,' I pushed.

The road we travelled was deserted but Rafael still checked the rear-view mirror before pulling up onto a narrow track. He switched off the engine and turned to me. 'The judge, Bernardo García.'

I'd met Bernardo García once, very briefly. If Daguerre was telling the truth, and I wasn't convinced he was, then he really was serious about leaving the organisation. 'I see.'

He inclined his head, flicked on the ignition and in silence we continued to drive upwards, heading to the next valley, to Daguerre's uncle.

My focus was now on my mother and not my job.

5

Miguel's abode was a log cabin and with a small out-building standing nearby, both nestling unobtrusively in the jade-coloured valley. It had been constructed very near to one of the area's many streams and the man-made wooden building blended with the natural landscape in the way only something aged is able to do. The solitary visible sign of its occupancy was dark smoke swirling upwards from a small chimney.

Daguerre pulled up and jumped from the truck, quickly making his way around the vehicle. He opened my door and offered his hand.

'I can manage, thank you.'

'I'm sure you can.'

Straightening up I caught his eye, irritated at the grin that was slowly unfurling on his features. I turned away, looking instead at the surrounding lush but isolated land-scape. 'Does Miguel have a car, transport?'

'No car.'

'How can he live here, alone?' The silence surrounding us was white.

'Miguel gets visitors, Tomás and Cristina. But this is the way he likes it. Alone. He built this place just after the end of World War Two. Lived here ever since.'

'A hermit?'

He nodded. I suspected Rafael Daguerre himself wasn't

naturally sociable, but his expression had relaxed markedly as we'd neared our remote destination, and Miguel.

On cue, a man appeared in the doorway. As his home blended with its surroundings, the man seemed to merge with his house. The door opened wider and the smell of freshly baked bread hit my nostrils, fusing with the aroma of petrol from the truck.

I studied the man who had known my mother.

I'd expected someone as tall as Rafael Daguerre. Miguel was not tall, five-five at the most. His head was bald, his face creviced, although the smile he gave was as youthful as a child's.

'*Sobrino*,' Miguel said, and then smiled widely at me. 'You've come with a beauty.' His eyes squinted in the fading sun. 'Isabella? Sofia's daughter?'

'Yes.' I held out my hand. Miguel avoided it, and with strength belying his stature he lifted me from the ground. Normally this familiar gesture would have thrown my reticent nature but knowing Miguel had known my mother made me less cautious. Warmth pleated through me because immediately, I liked Miguel.

'You are Sofia,' Miguel said. 'As God sits in Heaven. It is as if she's come back. Come in, both of you, I have anise and stew, freshly baked bread.' He looked towards the truck. 'Tomás and Cristina not with you?'

'Back at the house,' Daguerre replied. 'I'm going to bring Cristina over here tomorrow. Is that okay?'

'More than okay. Make sure you bring supplies, though. Since she's been pregnant I can't keep up. She's developed an appetite for *menestra* as well as chocolate. Can't understand anyone wanting only vegetables.' His small black eyes sparkled. 'I ate enough vegetables throughout the war to never want to set eyes on them again.' The eyes settled on me. 'Come through, Isabella.'

As Miguel's strength belied his build, the inside of his home misrepresented its exterior. Inside was warm, perhaps a little too warm. Huge logs blazed in the hearth, the orange flames reminding me of the night before but, instead of the smell of burning rubber, I inhaled the pleasant aroma of seasoned, smouldering wood.

Miguel's kitchen area was a small ceramic sink, and underneath a cupboard with curtains hiding its contents. A crude cooker perched on a round table in the far corner, while a tiny refrigerator sat on another table. Above the sink, the window was adorned with pretty azure-blue curtains, matching those hiding the cupboard's contents.

It was clearly a working space, with pots holding herbs, while garlic, hams and chorizo hung from the ceiling. Two red ceramic bowls sat on the table filled with black pepper and salt, and I guessed that Miguel cooked well. The bowls were identical to the ashtray Daguerre had used to stub out his cigar earlier and I sensed the brazen red dishes held part of Miguel's story. Inside his home a tinge of something that I found difficult to identify or, more honestly, difficult to admit to, folded over me. I had only Calida. For years it had been just the two of us.

'Get the anise and brandy out then, old man.' Daguerre watched me as he spoke to Miguel.

'For you?' Miguel asked me.

'Why not? Small though.' I felt my lips lifting into a smile.

'Your mother liked brandy,' Miguel said.

'Did she?' My heart beat a little faster inside my chest. So much I wanted to know.

He nodded. 'I'm guessing Calida and Aurelio have told you all about her?'

Rafael interrupted. 'Brandy first. Then let's sit and talk.'

I drank the large measure in one gulp and as Rafael and I sat in silence on the small sofa adjacent to the log fire, Miguel became industrious in the kitchen. He returned with a plate of cut chorizo and pickle, and then went to sit on a stool opposite the sofa, placing the plate on the small table next to him. Daguerre watched me with an amused expression as I pushed the food in my mouth. I was starving.

They waited for me to finish before Miguel began, his own plate remaining untouched. 'Tomás has told me about your career, Isabella. And that you are here investigating the Civil Guard. How long have you been living in Barcelona?' Finally, he scooped up a spoonful of the delicious pickle and popped it into his mouth. 'When did you leave France? Are Calida and Aurelio still alive?'

'Too many questions, Uncle. One at a time,' Rafael said.

'It's fine.' I turned to Miguel. 'The Nazis, together with the Vichy Gendarmerie, dynamited and burnt down our French home in 1943 during the Marseille roundup. I was five. Aurelio was taken to the internment camp at Compiègne. We never saw him again. Calida is still alive, still lives in France. She's more French than Spanish these days.' This last sentence brought a grin to Miguel's face.

I carried on. 'I left France in 1956 when I was eighteen to return to Franco's Spain, and against Calida's better judgement.'

'I am very sorry to hear what happened to Aurelio, niña.' Miguel glanced at Rafael with what I thought was an anxious expression. 'Does Calida mention anyone else from the civil war days?'

'In what sense?'

'Nada—' He wavered for a fraction of a second. 'Calida and Aurelio loved Sofia like a daughter.' He chuckled. 'You're like your mother. A rebel, returning to Spain.'

'I suppose I gravitated to Barcelona because that was where my mother lived before she disappeared.' I paused for a moment, unsure how far to prod. 'And where she probably met my father?' Miguel's head dipped, his eyes fixed on the near-threadbare Catalan rug. 'Did you know my father too, Miguel?'

Rafael pushed the chair he'd been sitting on backwards, its legs scraping hard on the stone floor, and stood. 'My uncle's memories of the civil war can be sketchy, Isabella.'

Miguel lifted his head but he did not look at me, his gaze fastened on Rafael.

'Did you know my father, before he died at Brunete—'

'Shush!' Rafael hissed. 'I hear something.' He glanced at Miguel. 'You expecting anyone?'

'No.'

Rafael moved quickly towards the kitchen window and pulled back the pretty curtain. He turned and walked to the door. 'It's Cristina and Tomás.' As he opened it a flow of fresh damp air entered the room and Rafael Daguerre crossed his chest.

Miguel and I had both made our way to the door too.

A pale Cristina and an even paler Tomás fell from the car. At the sight of a distraught Tomás and a distressed Cristina, the disappointment I'd experienced with Miguel's reluctance to talk about my French father dissolved in an instant. Perhaps Miguel hadn't known my father; perhaps my mother's affair with him had been brief and secret, and that was why Calida had so little information about him.

'What's happened?' Rafael rasped.

I'd spent the last two weeks with Tomás and his cavalier humour, and I saw immediately that whatever had happened was serious.

6

Once safely inside, Tomás began recounting the unfurling of events which had occurred soon after Rafael and I had left Balmaseda.

'As Cristina craves *menestra*,' he started but his breaths were rapid, his voice almost inaudible, 'she also lusts for the coolness of water on her belly, so I took her to the stream to bathe. She became too cold and we decided to return home. I knew something was amiss straightaway. I told Cristina to stay where she was, and I made my way around to the back of the house. I saw a man jumping over the wire fence, but made the decision to go back to Cristina and not go after him.'

Cristina hunched by the fire on Miguel's stool while Tomás spoke. The last hour had seen the temperature drop by more than a few degrees and the air had taken on the ominous smell of the oncoming deluge of rain.

'Did you see him?' Rafael asked Tomás.

'Not from the front. He must have had a motorbike nearby, I heard it. I'm sorry, Rafael, I didn't want to leave Cristina—'

'I didn't want you to leave Cristina either. You did well, Tomás. But it's important to tell me anything you saw that might in the future enable you, or me, to recognise him.'

'He had a bald head, I noticed the last of the sun reflecting off it.'

'And a motorbike?' Rafael asked.

'A fucking loud one.' Tomás mouthed an apology to me.

'And he'd been inside the house?' Rafael carried on.

'Definitely. I'd guess he was finishing up when we got back.' He threw a look at Cristina. 'Cristina was coughing loudly. He must have been downstairs, in your study, and heard her.'

Rafael paced the room and Cristina moved onto the sofa, sitting next to me. 'Was anything missing?' Rafael said.

'It's a bit of a mess but the guns were still there. I don't know if anything else is missing. You know who he is, don't you?'

Rafael shook his head and turned to Miguel. 'Uncle, it might be an idea if we all stayed here tonight. Is that okay with you?'

'Of course,' Miguel replied.

'I'll go back and collect some things.' Rafael was already getting ready to leave.

'You *do* know who he is, don't you?' Cristina's voice a whisper.

Rafael didn't answer.

'Shall I come with you?' I said, attempting to deflect the atmosphere.

'No, but thanks for the offer. I'll pick up your bag while I'm there, Isabella.'

'Bring back your camping stuff too, Rafael,' Miguel said. 'Tomás, Cristina and you can sleep in here. I'll sleep outside. Isabella can have my room.'

I interrupted. 'Please, you don't have to give me your bed, Miguel.'

A smile hovered on Rafael's lips. 'I'll bring the sleeping bags. Isabella and I will sleep outside . . . underneath the stars.' His eyes shone like the constellations of which he spoke.

'Whatever you two wish,' Miguel replied. I was unable to read his expression.

'I don't have a problem where I sleep.' I would not allow Rafael Daguerre to bait me.

Rafael was already heading towards the door and moments later I heard his truck come to life outside.

Cristina had fallen asleep on my shoulder. I viewed her swelling stomach and asked Tomás, 'When's Cristina due?'

'July,' he replied.

I stroked her forehead and she stirred. 'Some time yet then.'

Watching Cristina wake encouraged my own tiredness to wash over me. I yawned, trying to shake it off.

Disappearing to his kitchen space, Miguel made more food, and while we waited for Rafael's return Cristina told me about her parents. Her mother had died of cancer. The body of her father had been found just under a year ago, in a river outside Valencia, weighted down, which she said, had hastened her mother's demise.

'Who was responsible?' I asked.

Miguel had finished and returned to sit with us. He placed plates of food on the small table. It was Miguel who answered. 'We have no evidence, only hearsay, but it was someone working from within the Spanish government.'

With adroitness that I admired Miguel skilfully ended that conversation and moved on to more of Sofia's story. Cristina and Tomás were entranced and listened as intently as me as Miguel filled in the wedge of her life at the dawn of the civil war, starting with a trip she took to Bilbao in early 1937, and one on which Miguel had accompanied her. No mention, though, of a French brigader, a man with no name and who had died at Brunete before I was born. But because I was grateful to hear anything about my mother, I didn't pursue more questions about my father. I would broach this subject again with Miguel when the time was right. If I'd learnt nothing in twenty years as a journalist, it was not to push a source – not on a first meeting. Time, I was confident, would eventually do my job for me.

7

Rafael returned to his uncle's home and reported the house in Balmaseda was okay, but when Tomás asked him if anything was missing from his study Rafael only grunted. I suspected that by then Tomás just wanted to sleep. Cristina had already gone to bed in Miguel's room and Tomás joined her soon after Rafael's return.

Miguel was busily making his bed on the worn sofa. 'There's enough room in here for you both to sleep inside.' He pointed to the floor. 'I have plenty of cushions stashed away.'

'You snore too loudly, old man,' Rafael said. 'Anyway, it's a beautiful night to slumber under the stars, do you not think, Isabella?'

His baiting tone from earlier had disappeared or was I was only imagining it? I was too tired to think coherently anyway. 'I do. Did you bring sleeping bags?'

'I did.'

Miguel guffawed from the depths of his sofa.

'Well, let's find a spot, I'm exhausted,' I said.

By the time I'd brushed my teeth, changed into pyjamas and pulled on a jumper, Rafael had already made a camp underneath an oak tree not far from the house and was halfway through making a fire.

'An outdoor man, I see?'

'Love it. And you?'

'Generally only through necessity.' I shivered. 'But I don't mind.'

'The fire will build soon. Come, sit.' He threw the sleeping bag towards me. 'You can sleep inside if you wish, although I'd advise against it. Miguel really does snore like a steam train.'

I laughed. 'It's the Guernikako tree, isn't it?' I pointed to the living monolith.

'Yes, the Freedom Tree. The symbol for Basque culture and independence.'

'Was anything missing from your study?' I wrapped the sleeping bag tighter around my body. 'You know who the man was, don't you, who broke in?'

He poked at the baby flames of the fire and quickly they grew in intensity. 'See, it doesn't take much to begin a fire. In answer to both questions, yes . . . But the less Tomás knows, the safer he and Cristina will be.'

'Anything you tell me stays between us. You say you trust me, then tell me.' I paused. 'I can help. My article, my work, my connections . . . I can influence.'

'I believe you can. The man who came to the house is nothing to do with the Civil Guard or the mercenaries, or the government. He is on "our side". He works with the man who is gaining influence within the separatist movement – the man I do not agree with.'

'What was he looking for?'

'Information they want.'

'And that is?'

He shook his head as he poked at the fire with ferocity. 'It's better I know.'

He sighed. 'The itinerary of a very influential person, the chief of police of Guipúzcoa, who has a public engagement soon. It's been kept quiet – the details and the exact date.

36

But I know what my "comrade" is planning, and is why I've tried to keep the intelligence from him.'

Guipúzcoa's chief of police: his name was always whispered with horror, although after Franco's demise the political chatter was becoming louder about the man who'd terrorised the region for years. A coward and a professed Catholic. A man who undoubtedly visited the confessional regularly, begging his God's forgiveness for crimes he continued to commit, murders he carried out with appalling enjoyment. He encapsulated Franco's dictatorship. A dictatorship which had destroyed its country, and its people.

'And did they find the itinerary?'

'Yes. It's gone.' He smiled grimly. 'I didn't hide it. I didn't think he would go this far. If anonymously I alert the authorities, I risk putting other liberal activists in danger. And . . . the government might not even act on the information I give them.'

'Are you going to give me a name of the man in your organisation . . . your old friend, I'm guessing?'

'He is no friend of mine now, and no, I will not give you his name.'

'I don't intend to use it.'

'You don't need to know, and better if you don't. You're already in some danger. They will know you're here. They probably followed you and Tomás from Bilbao.'

'They didn't know about your house in Balmaseda?'

He shrugged. 'They do now.' He pointed at Miguel's home. 'Cristina will stay here, with Tomás for now.'

I'd slid downwards, propping myself up on an elbow. 'Has Miguel ever mentioned my father to you, Rafael? Or anything about the affair between my mother and a French brigader?' I swept away a tendril of hair from my cheek. 'Calida told me he died fighting in the civil war . . . but what if he didn't, what if he's still alive? I've never been able to find anything out about him, and I've spent a lot of time trying to.'

'Miguel hasn't spoken about your father . . . But why would he to me? There is no reason.'

I squeezed my eyes shut for seconds and then opened them. 'My mother's body was never found. It sounds ridiculous but . . . but . . . what if somehow, and somewhere, both of my parents are still alive?'

'Shush, allow your mind to rest.'

'What if neither of them wanted to be found by me?' I pushed on.

'Come, let's move to nearer the stream,' he said. 'I like to hear the water as I sleep.'

Rafael didn't know anything about my mother and father; how could he? It was Miguel who I needed to question further.

I took his proffered hand and he pulled me up. Efficiently, he gathered our things and I allowed him to take over and, in a moment of lucid clarity, admitted to myself that this was the first time in my life, since leaving Calida and France at eighteen, I'd let anyone do so.

Near to the stream we stopped. Rafael lay out his sleeping bag and indicated I did the same. I placed mine a good few metres away from his and glanced at him. He said nothing, and I moved it away a little further.

We both lay down and zipped up our respective sleeping bags, the space between us was more than adequate. Still no words passed between us.

Rafael's eyes closed quickly giving me the opportunity to study the man already gently snoring next to me. A tentative smile enveloped his resting features and I acknowledged the strangeness of the last forty-eight hours.

Before I began to drift into my own sleep I heard Rafael speak from the depths of his.

Scilla.

The name of the bluebell flower my eyes resembled, and those of my mother, and I came to my intuitive decision about Rafael Daguerre.

He did not lie, he was not stupid, and he did know a lot more than I'd originally thought.

8

Drops of water woke me. I'd forgotten about the Basque rain and early-morning rasping wind. I shivered inside the sleeping bag, although despite the cold I'd slept better than I'd done for months, if not years. Still not fully awake I shuffled closer to Rafael's sleeping form, my index finger hovering over his scar, but stopped myself, quickly shoving my hand back inside the cover.

He opened one eye and grinned. 'It feels too early.' He grinned more, if that were possible. Then his expression became serious. 'Beautiful eyes.' His words were soft, his tone subdued and hating that it did, the compliment brought heat to my cold face.

'Like my mother's.'

'Isabella.' He turned sideways. 'Tell me what you know of your grandfather.'

'Severino Herrera? He was a colonel in Franco's army. He was estranged from my mother. Sofia and my grandfather were on different sides of the fence in the civil war.'

'And you know your grandmother was originally from the Basque region? That was where she and Herrera lived until the late 1920s. Where your mother, Sofia, was born.' He hesitated for a moment. 'You know of your grandfather's . . . instability?'

'I'm aware my grandparents originally came from this region, yes, but Calida has never mentioned "instability" regarding my grandfather. Have the years embellished your story?' I lay sideways now too, mirroring Rafael's posture.

'The story needs no embellishment. Unfortunately.' Rafael flipped over and lay on his back, staring at the lead-coloured sky above. 'Severino Herrera didn't die at the end of the war, Isabella.'

'That's not true,' I said quietly. 'He was killed in early 1938. It is recorded, I found the records.'

'The records are falsified,' Rafael said. 'Like many of Franco's officers after the civil war, many fled for South America and Cuba, other places in the world too. And they had enough influence to falsify the records. Severino Herrera was one of those men. Even though Franco prophesised victory before the end of the civil war, some, like your grandfather, knew that eventually the world would examine the atrocities in Spain during that period. He knew eventually that he, and others like him, would be hunted. Franco himself, as he courted European trading agreements during the 50s and 60s, paid lip service to hunting out these renegade soldiers. But he had to pay more than lip service, sending a few token ones to prison to appease the European democracies with whom he wanted to do international business.'

I thought back to the barren conversations I'd had with Calida; she'd talked little about my mother and had said next to nothing about my grandfather, and the same concerning my French father.

I'd believed all of my immediate family were dead.

Rafael carried on. 'Are you all right, *querida*?'

'I'd prefer if you didn't use that word.'

'I have no wish to offend you, Isabella.'

The truth was – he was not offending me, but I had to draw a line. Somewhere there had to be a line. I was losing control of both my emotions and the world I'd carefully built around myself.

'You don't know if my grandfather is still alive. If he was . . . if he was, then . . .' *Then my grandfather would have found me.*

'Your grandfather is still alive, *quer* . . .'

'There are too many things I do not know about my family. My mother, my father—'

'And it's time that you find out . . . I'm sorry—'

I was about to answer, to ask *why* he was sorry, when I looked up to see Miguel staring down at us.

'The rain will turn into a downpour very soon,' Miguel said. 'I have eggs and bread for breakfast. You two should come inside.' Miguel wore an apron and held a wooden spatula in his hand.

'You like cooking, don't you?' I said, smiling up at him.

'I do.' He crouched down. 'I learnt a lot about cooking from Sofia, as did . . .'

'Who, Miguel? My father?'

'All of us staying in the house in Barcelona.' He was smiling but I saw a hint of sadness. Or was it guilt? I couldn't be sure but, as much as I sensed that Miguel was holding something back, it was impossible for me to be angry with him. I liked him too much.

He carried on. 'Sofia taught me to cook, I taught her how to fire ceramics.'

'Fire ceramics?' I asked, puzzled.

'My pottery.'

I remembered the red dishes and the old out-building next to the house that I'd spotted when Rafael and I first arrived. 'You taught my mother to make ceramics?'

'I tried. She didn't have, how would I say, the skill.' He laughed. 'She made a few things.' He glanced at Rafael.

42

'Rafael has one of Sofia's efforts.' I thought of the red ashtray at Rafael's house. The smile slipped away from Miguel's face. 'Did you two talk last night?'

Rafael sat up and I noticed the night's growth on his chin. I paid attention to his features and the hairs on my arm prickled gently underneath the sleeping bag's fabric.

'There's time yet to talk, Uncle.'

Miguel lifted his shoulders imperceptibly. 'Do you like to cook, Isabella?'

'Not really.' That wasn't strictly true. I did like to cook when I had someone to cook for, and to eat with. But that was a rare scenario for me and only happened when I invited my best friend Ignacio, who lived in the same apartment building as me, to dinner. My family was small, and my circle of friends even smaller. If I had time to think about the deeper fabric of my life there was too much which was lacking, as Calida too often pointed out. So difficult to accept a truth from someone you love, in fact harder than taking on a truth from someone who means nothing to you.

'What do you do,' Rafael said. 'In your spare time, apart from gallop around the world looking for stories?'

'I dance. The flamenco.' When was the last time I danced? Too long ago. And as I contemplated Rafael's enquiring expression, the contours of his face, the small hollows directly beneath each cheekbone, I tried to remember the last time. I could not retrieve the memory and in that moment I accepted something within the monotone mosaic of my life had to change.

'I can see that,' he said, his gaze searching my face.

'Not well, though.'

'I *can't* see that.'

His comment pleased me more than it should, and again I reminded myself who he was, what category

43

of man he was. Rafael Daguerre was not the person I thought he'd be.

'Inside now, before it pours,' Miguel instructed, cutting into my thoughts.

'Are Cristina and Tomás awake?' Rafael asked.

'Unbelievably, yes. Both out before dawn, going for a walk. Cristina's finding it hard to sleep.'

I thought about the young couple; Cristina waking too early, probably uncomfortable, undoubtedly agitated after the house break-in, and wanting to get up and go out for a walk to clear her head. Tomás rising with her, reluctantly being pulled from his own sleep but not complaining. Two people so in love, with each other, and the world. A flash of consummate grief of what I didn't have consumed me.

Miguel straightened up into standing. 'Before they left, Cristina mentioned an idea she's had. A good one. Being pregnant suits her.' He pointed his spatula towards the house. 'Come in soon.'

9

Rafael and I returned to the house and as I huddled near to the fire, which Miguel must have got up very early to get going, Rafael made his way to the shower.

Miguel worked in his little kitchen, appearing much more relaxed than the evening before. I pulled the sleeves of my jumper over my hands because despite the warming air of the house, the chill cut into my bones. I joined Miguel and wedged my bottom on the strip of table that housed his oven. He stopped chopping Cristina's vegetables, turned and smiled.

'*Menestra* for you, Isabella?'

'Not for me, no. Thank you . . . Miguel, I'd really like to know more about my father. Anything about him . . . if you know anything?'

With vigour he carried on chopping, lacerating the carrots. I pushed on. 'It's been hard for me, not having known either of my parents.'

Finally, he turned; the irises of his obsidian eyes darker in the morning light. 'What has Calida told you exactly?'

'He was French and killed at the Battle of Brunete in the summer of 1937. Calida never gave me a name. She said my mother never told her.'

He tipped the vegetables into a frying pan and the sound of hot fat sizzling filled the space. He picked up the spatula and began stirring. From the periphery of my vision I saw Rafael go sit in the spot near the fire that I'd vacated, wet hair slicked back, the scar on his forehead vermillion red. I placed my hand on Miguel's arm. 'Did you meet him, Miguel?'

'I did.'

The breath I'd been holding suddenly escaped my throat in a long heave of relief.

'They met in Barcelona?' I asked. Rafael was by then standing in the open wooden archway that delineated the beginning of the kitchen space.

'They did, Isabella . . . that is where Sofia met Jack,' Miguel replied quietly.

'Perhaps you mean *Jacques*?'

'No, *niña*. Jack.' Miguel shot a glance towards Rafael. 'Jack didn't die at Brunete.' He patted my hand. 'And Jack Hayes was as English as they came. He was not French.' Miguel found my eyes. '*Dios mío*, that Calida said he was French . . . why . . .'

Yes, why? But a reply jammed in my throat and I shook my head and knew Miguel told the truth.

'In the spring of 1937, *niña*, Jack took Sofia and . . .' His sentence slid away, but then he carried on. 'Away from Barcelona, to Sabadell to stay with Calida and Aurelio, the place Sofia had taken them earlier in the year so they would be safe.' His expression faded into a past I felt he had no wish to remember. 'Just before Jack and Sofia left Barcelona for Sabadell, Sofia told me she was pregnant, although she hadn't told Jack. I thought Sofia would tell him when they got to Sabadell, but—'

'Pregnant with me?' I whispered.

'Yes, *niña*, with you.'

'Jack Hayes.' I heard the flatness of my voice as I said the name.

46

A name which had never crossed Calida's lips.

I glanced at Rafael, pleading for some direction. His head jarred fractionally.

'Jack Hayes *is* your father,' Miguel said.

The kitchen suddenly became stifling and pushing past Rafael I made my way outside onto the wooden veranda. Despite the heavy cloud cover the morning light was growing brighter but the quietness, which hung like a physical entity around Miguel's abode, hit me as hard as the rumble of noise when I opened the balcony doors of my Barcelona flat. Silence and noise, opposites so far away from each other and yet joined in their extremes.

I lowered myself down and sat on the step, embarrassment seeping into the sinew of my body – I had allowed my lifelong guard to slip. And why? I slumped forward and shivered, feeling the dabs of rain pricking my cold skin. Because I wanted to know, wanted to know about my parents. I peered up at the sky, at the sun that was desperately trying to find its way in, producing the effect of a dark outline on the edge of each cloud; like a tracing, although the inside shimmered with the tantalising youth of a new day.

How could I have spent my whole life *not* knowing that I had an English father who'd *not* died at Brunete? Was I like the majority of Spain, insofar as I'd been remiss in not investigating what had *really* happened, even regarding my own parentage, about my own mother and father? My grandfather too.

'Come back in, Isabella.' Miguel had appeared. He took a gentle hold of my elbow and led me into the warmth. 'I am sorry.'

Shaking my head, I sat down on Miguel's stool. Rafael had moved away from the kitchen area and was standing

47

with his back to the fire. He'd watched every step I'd taken from the door.

'I looked forward to telling you about your mother,' Miguel said. 'I didn't think I'd be telling you things you didn't know. I had thought that Calida would have told you about Jack. I'd thought Jack would have found you.'

I stared into the flames of the fire, a spark of memory striking me, and I travelled back into the past and to my early childhood.

It was near to my ninth birthday, October time. I remembered because the blackberries were nearly at the end of their season, my favourite fruit. Calida was opening letters whilst I sat on the porch, a big bowl of blackberries in front of me. I was popping them like sweets in between making a bracelet with beads that Madame Couchon had given to me. I watched in boredom as Calida threw each letter to one side, until she came to the last one, and then my malaise dissipated quickly. She spent a long time looking at the front of that envelope. Her interest piqued mine and before she shoved it into her apron pocket I'd already noticed the unusual stamp.

'Who's that from? Not a French person?' I'd said. Even at eight I recognised the stamp as being English.

Calida did not retrieve the letter from her pocket. She patted me on the head instead. 'Finish the bracelet you're making.' Our neighbour, Madam Couchon, was visiting that afternoon, but was inside making new curtains. 'I need to go and speak to Madame Couchon,' Calida said and bustled back inside.

I waited a few moments and then walked around the house, and listened through the back window, but only hearing the end of their clipped conversation.

Calida: 'He'll arrive tomorrow, the letter took its time getting here. You take Isabella into town for the day.'

And then Madame Couchon's reply. 'It's better this way, Calida.'

I did everything possible to feign an illness so I couldn't go into town, wanting to know why Calida didn't want me at home that day. I knew it was something to do with the letter, someone who she was expecting to visit, something related to a past before I'd been born, somehow I'd sensed this. But, Madame Couchon took me into town and when we returned Calida was drinking wine at the kitchen table. A sight I never saw, and the reason the incident, the memory, was so real and retrievable. No more was said.

Could it be that Jack had come that day? Why had Calida lied to me? And for so long?

'I spent a lot of time trying to find information about my supposed French father. Information I could never find. And now I know why. Because my father wasn't French, and he didn't die at Brunete as Calida had always told me.' I paused. 'Could my father still be alive?'

'How old would he be now?' Miguel glanced at me as if I would know. 'Jack was in his mid-twenties when he first came to Spain.' For the first time in half an hour Miguel's smile returned. 'I'm alive, so Jack could well be too.'

Rafael said in a whisper, 'If he's still alive, Isabella, he will be easy to find.'

'Yes, he will be, I'm sure. *If* he's still alive.' The petulant tone of my voice hung in the air.

'He will be still alive,' Rafael replied quietly.

Miguel nodded in affirmation.

'You two seem confident.'

'Be positive,' Rafael said.

'I'm here to work, not find out about my family.' I took a breath. I needed to take control.

'Perhaps not intentionally, *querida*,' Rafael said, 'but life has a strange way of leading us where we need to be.'

I was just about to reply when a gush of cool air entered the room. Cristina and Tomás had returned.

'Rafael!' Tomás's voice boomed. 'Has Miguel told you that Cristina has a really good idea concerning Isabella?'

'Yes, Tomás, he has,' Rafael said. 'And please don't shout. I have a headache.'

The thought of Rafael Daguerre with a headache did make me laugh.

'It's good to see your laughter,' Rafael said.

10

'Could I have another egg?' I asked Miguel.

'And a little more *menestra*, Uncle?' Cristina said, giggling.

'My God, you women will eat me out of my home.' Miguel cracked another egg.

Rafael had decided on skipping breakfast and instead was outside fixing the ominous smell of petrol that was emanating from his truck.

As we ate Miguel's hearty meal I discovered a little more about my mother, and more too about a man I'd only just found out was my father, although silently questioning why Miguel had been so hesitant to tell me about Jack Hayes the day before.

It had been soon after my mother and Miguel's return to Barcelona from the Basque region, Miguel told me, and where they had been on a reconnaissance trip for the Republicans in March 1937, when Sofia met Jack Hayes. Jack had just made his way from England to join the International Brigades and fight for the Republicans against Francisco Franco and the Nationalists. My father *had* been a brigader, as Calida had told me, although English, not French.

My mother met Jack Hayes only a little over nine months before my birth. When Miguel described the burgeoning love affair between my parents, it was then that the tears threatened.

'Do you know where in England Jack came from?' I asked, swallowing them back into my throat.

'Jack was from the middle of the country, Nottinghamshire?' He struggled with the pronunciation. 'He was a miner – a coal miner.'

'Like Rafael,' I said quietly.

'Like Rafael, yes.' The old man's eyes glistened.

I was sitting next to Tomás on the sofa. He punched me gently on the arm. 'Said you'd love Rafael when you met him, didn't I?'

'I hardly know him, Tomás.'

'Instability and unrest has that effect on relationships. Speeds them up,' Miguel said. 'That's what happened with your mother and Jack.'

Heat rose in my neck. 'I came here to find out more about the illegal organisation in which Rafael is involved. I didn't come looking for a husband, Miguel.' I paused and pulled my hair up onto the top of my head, jabbed the wooden hairpin viciously into the hastily constructed bun. To my annoyance both Miguel and Tomás chuckled in unison. What was it about this family? *It was that they were a family.*

Miguel's laughter disappeared and he looked at me. 'Calida will have had good reason for not telling you about Jack, Isabella.'

'Perhaps.' I stood, paced the room, walked towards the door, opened it, and lingered. The air was gathering heat, the early morning dew quickly evaporating. Questions flooded my mind. Was it Jack who had visited Calida after the war? Did he try and find my mother after she disappeared? And, if they had been lovers, in love, how and why did she disappear? Why had he not been there for her? So much I didn't know. And so much more I felt that Miguel could tell me. *Patience, Isabella.*

Cristina joined me on the veranda. 'If your father *is* still alive, the sooner you find him, the longer you will have with him.' Her voice was soft, like liquid velvet.

'If Jack Hayes is still alive, maybe he won't want me to find him.'

But strange and comforting warmth was fusing through me, and I wasn't entirely sure if it was due to the tantalising possibility of finding my father, or connected with the arrogant and unfathomable man I'd just met.

II

Cristina left me sitting outside with my thoughts. Ten minutes later Rafael parked up in front of the house. He must have taken the truck for a short drive to see if his repair had been successful. The aroma of petrol was strong; he'd failed.

He jumped from the driver's seat like a man half his age. With the right training Rafael Daguerre would make a good flamenco partner and I found myself thinking about him in a way I hadn't thought about a man in many years. It was as if a part of my brain had switched off, whilst another part had flipped on.

'Having some quiet time?' he asked, walking towards me. 'You look sad, what's happened in between me leaving to fix my truck that isn't fixed, and now?'

'That I have a father who I had no idea existed. For years I believed my father was a French brigader. I could find out nothing about him, and now I know why. Because he didn't exist.' I scraped the clay soil with the heel of my foot.

'Well, it's good Miguel's told you.' He lowered himself down next to me. 'And it's good he's opening up to you.'

The mid-morning sun was rising higher, the earlier clouds had cleared, the unique smell of oncoming rain had disappeared. I looked over Rafael's shoulder at the jacaranda tree which sat on the periphery of Miguel's campo;

its intense and vivid violet bloom bowing in majesty with the wind, as if in recognition of the seismic emotional shifts occurring inside of me.

'Did you already know?' I asked.

'No, I did not know about Jack. Of course I didn't.' His hand moved to his forehead and he rubbed his scar. 'Are you all right?'

'Calida lied to me.'

'She will have had good reason for not telling you about Jack. She loves you. She has been a mother to you.'

She will have had good reason for not telling you – the exact same expression Miguel had used and a shard of suspicion speared through me. But they were related, close, family. Had I not picked up some of Calida's expressions over the years? Even now I still used many of them. As rapidly as the suspicion had descended, it dissolved, and something shifted within me as this man I did not know spoke of a woman he did not know with such empathy. A woman I'd loved my entire life.

'My mother could be alive too, Rafael, somewhere, do you think? Stranger things have happened in our strange country?'

'Anything is possible,' he said, and then, almost in unison, our line of vision moved towards the Freedom Tree where we'd made the fire the night before. Rafael jumped up. 'Come, time to find out about Cristina's idea.'

I nodded, got up too and followed him.

Inside, Miguel was clearing up the breakfast debris, whilst Cristina lay on her back near the fire, her head propped up by one of Miguel's multi-coloured cushions. Tomás sat at her feet massaging them. I watched as Rafael ruffled the top of Tomás's head and it hit me again – the sense of family that pervaded this household.

'Miguel said you had an idea, Cristina?' Rafael said.

She rubbed her stomach, lifted her head and glanced at me. 'I think you should take Isabella to see Dominica Zubiri.'

'It is a good idea,' Rafael replied.

'Who is Dominica Zubiri?' I asked, lowering myself to the floor to sit next to Cristina.

It was Rafael who answered. 'A woman whose six-year-old daughter, while playing by the river, about two months ago now, found something.'

'But what does this have to do with my mother?'

Cristina hauled herself into sitting, leant her back up against the sofa. 'The little girl found bones . . . of a woman.' Tears sprung to her eyes. 'And the woman's unborn baby.' Cristina held the small dome of her stomach. 'The little girl was playing happily by herself when she found the glint of grey. She thought she'd found something precious, a silver treasure, as children do? She dug into the mud, but it was not a precious metal. Children know when something is not quite right, don't you think?' I nodded, although I knew little about children. 'She covered the bone with the river's mud and then ran to tell her mother, Dominica.' Cristina stopped.

'What had happened?' I asked.

'Dominica Zubiri's aunt, her mother's younger sister, disappeared in late 1938, during the civil war. She was seven months pregnant. Her body was never found.'

'You're telling me the girl found the bones of her great-aunt, from the civil war?'

'That's what we're telling you,' Rafael said as he paced the floor. 'Dominica's home is only a half-an-hour drive. Let her tell you the story.'

'Similar stories are emerging all over Spain,' I said. 'I've been investigating, but I'm finding it difficult to locate the truth.' And this was true; I was finding it very difficult. The new government had no wish for clarity on this subject.

Rafael rubbed his forehead. Already I knew this was a sign that he was thinking. 'It's important you meet Dominica, Isabella, but I know she's away visiting her sister. She'll be back on Friday.'

It was only Monday. I couldn't stay at Miguel's that long, I needed to return to Barcelona, write my article. See Calida; this last thought filled me with dread. Good at confrontation in my professional life, not so good in the personal arena, and I couldn't possibly impose on Miguel for such a long period.

'It will be good for you stay,' he carried on, as if reading my thoughts. 'You will be able to find out more from Miguel about your mother . . . and do more research on my organisation . . . and me, for your article. It's a win-win, *querida*.'

My professional job brain clicked on, the carrot dangled like a delicious treat, and his use of *querida* I let go.

'I have a lot more to share,' he finished, tipping back the mug of coffee he was holding. 'Stay until Friday.'

12

I stayed, and as the week wore on I did discover more about Sofia and Jack, as well as Rafael and the organisation that he'd helped form but was now, I learnt, desperate to leave. Rafael and I slept outside every night, and each night I ensured the distance between our sleeping bags became larger and larger. It crossed my mind to sleep in the house, but the truth was I was enjoying the nights underneath the stars. And it was during that time, when the air was still, the birds quiet, and only the noise of the rolling stream could be heard, when I learnt the most about Rafael and the 'cause' which had taken up all of his adult life. My editor in Paris would be delighted, as would my bank manager.

The five of us fell into an easy routine and I really loved getting to know Cristina. It did seem that as soon as I'd agreed to stay, Rafael became less familiar with me, more measured and conservative; although incongruously, like butter warming slowly on a spring day, his manner softened too. Was he trying to please me, make me feel comfortable? Or did he regret asking me to stay, was he bored, or worse, was he indifferent? Whatever the reason, he was not the Rafael I'd met on that first day and this brought a sharp feeling of dejection.

It was Friday and the previous night's rain had poured down, so much so that Rafael and I had had to admit defeat, making our camp on Miguel's lounge floor. The deluge had turned the damp soil of our outside beds into glossy mud.

Just before midday, Cristina, Rafael and I made our way towards another valley. And another sadness.

I guessed Señora Dominica Zubiri to be in her late thirties, a similar age to me. A robust woman but with an expression of worry that was etched so solidly into her features it had become part of her appearance and, although it took away a prettiness that beckoned, it left behind a beauty which belonged.

Despite her obvious unease she welcomed us wholeheartedly. It was clear she knew Rafael well and as they easily embraced, unsolicited envy darted through me.

'It's good to see you, Rafael.' She glanced across at Cristina. 'You're showing your pregnancy well now, *niña*.'

Cristina placed her hand over her stomach and smiled.

'When is your husband due back, next week I remember you saying?' Rafael asked Dominica.

'Yes, next week. His teachers' conference was in Barcelona but he's gone to Madrid . . . for other things. A dinner, in fact, in celebration of our deceased Caudillo.'

'Still hanging onto the past, and all things *Franco*? Rafael asked.

'The world will change – hopefully – but unfortunately my husband never will.'

'I would not have brought Isabella if he had been here,' Rafael said.

'I know, *amigo*. But why are you here?' Dominica looked across at me and tried to smile. 'I apologise, *señora*. It is always good to see Rafael and his friends.'

She took hold of Rafael's hand, an intimate gesture, and one that would not have occurred if Señora Zubiri's husband had been present. I was beginning to suspect that the woman we'd come to visit was perhaps an old girlfriend of Rafael's, and the reason why he would not have visited if Señor Zubiri had indeed been home.

'Isabella is a journalist and is interested to know what might have happened to your aunt during the civil war.'

Dominica turned to me. 'I would rather my daughter, Miren, isn't involved in our conversation. When her father returns it is better if she does not have to lie to him. But I can talk, as my daughter is at her friend's today.'

'This is kind of you, *señora*,' I said.

'Come, let us walk to the river.'

By the time we approached the riverbank, the rain had stopped and a thick line of dark blue had appeared in the sky above. Dominica led us to a formation of slimy rocks half submerged in the water, the algae-greenness glinting like Indian emeralds in the light.

'My daughter, found my aunt here.' She pointed to the rocks. 'The river had receded a little then, the water having washed away the wet earth that had covered her body for the last forty years.'

'Señora Zubiri, how did you know it was the body of your aunt?' I said.

She pushed her hand into the pocket of her jacket and pulled out a gold ring. 'This was her wedding ring. My mother recognised it.'

It was an unusual ring, light grooves etched into the surface; a unique design.

'My mother remembers her younger sister coming down to the river back in 1938, looking for flowers. We were on the wrong side of the line. A group of Nationalist soldiers had left the main town and were roaming the countryside, looking for a diversion. They found it in my aunt. She was never seen again. When my uncle, my aunt's husband, confronted the officer in charge of the soldiers, the officer shot my uncle. The soldiers didn't tell my mother where they had buried the body of her sister.' Dominica Zubiri's face was waxen; she rubbed at calloused fingers. 'My mother searched and searched, but nothing. It's a dark irony that it was her great-niece, who shares her name, who finally found her remains. My daughter, Miren.'

I moved closer to Dominica. 'What happened when Miren told you?'

'I told my husband, and then my mother told him what had happened with the Nationalist soldiers, with her brother-in-law. He didn't believe her, and chose not to believe me.' Her hands squeezed so tightly I saw the deathly white of her knuckles. 'My husband *señora*, is a Francoist, attended the generalissimo's funeral. A member of the right wing, the *Falange*, he . . . was a soldier in the civil war, a Nationalist.'

I felt my forehead furrow in question. Dominica carried on. 'He is a lot older than me, Señora Adame.' Her husband must be at least in his mid-fifties, perhaps older. 'He scolded Miren, told her never to play by the river again.' She looked across at Rafael. 'Such old-fashioned values. He is of the old-school.'

Rafael gently interrupted, saying to me, 'I have never met Señora Zubiri's husband . . . it is not a good idea.'

I couldn't help but question; had there been a relationship between Dominica Zubiri and Rafael, and if there had, was it still going on? An unwanted spike of envy thrust through me towards this woman who innately I liked very much.

'What happened to your aunt's remains?' I threw a look towards Rafael and Cristina. Rafael gestured towards Dominica to continue.

'My husband went to the local priest, who was himself a Franco supporter. The priest then went to see the mayor. The mayor told my husband it was not Franco's men who had murdered my aunt.'

'Was she murdered? I mean, is there evidence?' I asked gently.

'You are a journalist, *señora*, and it is good you want evidence. The remains of my aunt's skull had a hole in its side. Made by a bullet. She was murdered, and probably raped by the soldiers. The mayor, and the priest denied all of this. They took the remains and buried them in a shielded grave next to the main cemetery, out of the way, where it would not receive any unwanted interest. They demanded we did not make a fuss and kept quiet. With Franco dead, the new Spanish government does not want Spain's civil war in the global eye. They want trade, they want tourists. They don't want the remains of a murdered woman and her unborn child in the world media.'

She inclined her head towards Rafael. 'But as Rafael is aware, doing as the mayor and the priest says isn't a problem for my husband. As he agrees with them. *Bury the war*, he says. And soon, *señora*, the war, and everyone who died for that cause, will be forgotten. The proposed amnesty *will* happen. How do I explain this to my mother?'

My heart was a gnarled vine inside my chest, because it was my own mother of whom I thought. Had my mother's fate been similar to that of Señora Zubiri's aunt? I could not bear to think so, and instead grasped at perhaps the more heartbreaking scenario: Sofia was still alive, but like my English father she had never tried to find me.

There was no acute grief in losing Sofia, as she had always been unknown to me. Calida rarely mentioned my mother and so, Sofia remained not entirely real inside my mind, only an image inside a locket. The last few days had changed this perception, because through Miguel, Sofia was becoming more substantial and for an inexplicable reason, meeting Dominica and finding out about her aunt only expanded this feeling. I understood why Cristina, Rafael and Miguel had wanted me to meet this woman, come to this place with calm water and a muddy bank.

It was time to find the truth surrounding my past, to find my mother, or her body. There was so much Calida had never told me, and about my grandfather too. I'd always believed Sofia was dead, but now I was less certain. Calida could have lied about that too and at this thought a freezing wave of horror rippled down my spine.

I also needed to discover if Jack, my father, was still alive. And if he were? Then I needed to know why he'd never sought out his daughter. Perhaps Miguel was not telling me the truth. Perhaps. But I would remain open, and not only because I didn't believe Miguel would lie – and why would he – but because residing within me was a deep perception that Jack was still alive.

And if he were, then my mother could be too.

13

Mansfield, Nottinghamshire, England

Jack

MARCH 1937

Jack's shift was about over. A droplet of sweat slithered into his eye, blurring his vision in the carbon-black darkness. He couldn't wait to get up to the top, clean up, and have a pint of brown ale. Talk in the pub would either be about the abdicated King who'd just been given the title of Duke of Windsor, or how in Spain the communist party was trying to oust POUM – the *Spanish Workers' Party of Marxist Unification* – and get rid of the International Brigades too; what a disaster that'd be. He'd promised Alice he'd pop in after the pub, and before he made his way to the monthly Independent Labour Party meeting later. She was missing Joe.

His bloody brother Joe.

God knows what had possessed him to bugger off to Spain. Jack was the more politically oriented brother, the one who wanted to join POUM and go fight Franco and the fascists. It was Jack who'd joined the ILA first too. Eighteen months separated the two brothers and although Joe was the oldest, he was by far the less mature of the two, not thinking for a moment about the effect of him buggering off to Spain would have on their mum, or Alice. Or perhaps he had, and gone anyway. Selfish bastard.

Jack made his way along the pit-face, eventually arriving at the shaft.

'Too late, mate,' the foreman said. 'The others have already gone up in cage, and new shift's started.'

Four men were already turning the coal. 'I'm not that late, am I?' Jack peered at the cage which was full of the black gold.

'One of the men were poorly, wanted to get 'im t'top, so I sent the others too. And then there were next shift waiting to come down. Has a knock-on effect, as y'know.'

He'd be stuck there for hours.

The foreman shrugged. 'I'm sorry, mate, I'll make sure your wages are topped up proper.' He paused. 'I've heard some news . . . so . . . some extra money might be comin' in handy.'

'Get t'point, man,' Jack barked.

'Jimmy Windall, as usual, were full of gossip at the start of 'is shift. Like a bleedin' woman, he is.'

'What this time?'

'Word's out that Alice's ma and da 'ave kicked 'er out.'

Alice's God-fearing parents. Bloody flaky couple. There'd be only one reason for them turfing her out. 'Get it out, man.'

'She's got a cake in 'er belly, and wi' Joe off in commie Spain, there's not gonna be any weddin', is there?'

'How does Jimmy know all this?' God knows why he asked. Jimmy Windall's wife knew things about people before the people themselves did.

'Your ma called doctor for Alice. Alice's in a right state.'

'Shit.' Jack looked sideways at the cage that brimmed with coal. They'd been fast loading it today, been fast doing everything today. His mum would be in a state too.

Now he knew why Joe had pissed off to Spain.

The bull-chains began to rattle, the coal ready to see the first light of day in its long history. Jack glanced at the cage that was about to begin its journey upwards, holding its treasure. He jumped onto its side, clawing to grip the cage's iron bars, and watched as the foreman looked on in sheer surprise. A laugh rumbled in the depths of Jack's belly.

'Jack, what the fuck ya doin'?' he shouted upwards, the bull-chains now fully greased and working perfectly.

Movement up the shaft, with the coal, was always much quicker than when holding its human guests. Jack clung on. *What was he doing?* It was a mad moment; it was the thought of poor Alice, as well as his anxious mum. The thought of the whole town knowing and whispering. Jack really hated that. The whispering. He needed to get to the top.

The pit-top gaffer was waiting for the coal in the fading sunlight. As Jack jumped off the cage, sweaty and pale underneath the thick coal dust, it took a few moments for the gaffer to clock what he'd done.

'Fuck me, Jack, 'ave yer gone mad?'

Jack said nothing and handed the jaw-hanging onsetter, who was standing behind the gaffer, his shift payment slip.

The onsetter snatched it. 'I have a feelin' wages'll be a problem this week for yer.'

Shrugging, Jack was already bracing himself to go straight to the pit-manager's office. 'You're a wanker,' the onsetter continued. 'Think you're different 'cos you don't talk like the rest of us, Jack Hayes, well, you're no different. Manager'll sack you, no matter how much coal you've 'acked out for 'im. No one's indiscrupable.'

'Indispensible,' Jack shouted back, already pacing towards the office that was situated well behind the stock-heads.

★

The pit manager, George Wrigley, was a short muscular man and one of the few older men at the pit who remained unmarried. George had the patience of a vicar and the fortitude of Sisyphus, and these qualities, Jack was certain, came from him not having a wife or kids.

As Jack knocked on the door one of the young lads pushed past him. News travelled as fast at the pit-top as it did down in the shaft, and as it did in the claustrophobic town in which he lived.

George was standing behind an untidy desk. 'I'm not going to be able to let you get away with this. I can't be seen to be 'aving favourites.'

'New lad's a fast runner.'

'I know why you did it. You could've waited, Jack.'

'They took up the cage without me, I'm knackered.'

'Jack, sit down. I have some more news for you.'

'You know about Alice?'

'Course I do, everyone knows. She's well liked here.'

Alice was a secretary on the pit-top. Hard working and as bright as a button. Jack hoped they'd let her keep her job. He could have fucking strangled Joe – there and then – if he'd been there. Which he wasn't, and why Jack was there. Inside the pit-manager's office.

George carried on. 'Lots of news today. Look, I think we both know that Alice is most likely pregnant, but there's something else—'

'With all due respect, Mr Wrigley, can you just tell me?' What news could top what he'd already heard?

'Joe's been reported missing in Spain.' George shuffled a piece of paper. 'Seems he was fighting at the Jarama River offensive, and went missing.' He looked at Jack hard. 'Not dead, but missing.'

'Missing?' Jack couldn't help but notice his own

uncomfortable repetitions. 'How did you know before me mum?'

'I didn't. Alice's been in, to tell me.'

'My God, never rains, eh?'

'No, it doesn't.' George sighed heavily. 'But this doesn't change how I've to deal with what you've done today.'

'I work hard.'

'I know, but no one's—'

'Indispensable?'

'No. I'm sorry. Look, give it a month or two and I'll be able to reinstate you. People's memories are short. But you're an active union man, I 'ave to make an example, and don't start spouting union stuff to me. What you did today is a sackable offence and you know it.'

'It's fine. I've already decided.'

'Decided what? To lose your job?'

'No, I'm going to Spain. Going to find Joe. Send him home to marry Alice. But I might stay in Spain.' Jack took a breath. 'And fight. It's me who wanted to go.'

'Right, then.'

'I mean it.'

'I know you do.' George stood. 'Look, I've a brother-in-law in the merchant navy, with connections. He'll be able to arrange a passage to France. I'm sure you know what to do concerning getting papers and everything in Paris.' He sat down again. 'I'll pull all the strings I can, and you'll have a job waiting for you when you get back. You're a good miner. I'll sort out this mess.'

'I appreciate that, sir.'

'I know you do.' George Wrigley shuffled a few more papers.

'I plan to leave as soon as possible.'

'Do you have enough money?'

As well as being patient, George was also kind and generous to his men. Something else a family'd knock out of him. 'Thanks, but yes I do, it'll probably leave Mum short though, especially as she'll be looking after Alice.'

'I hear her parents don't give anything away.'

'No, sir, I believe they don't.'

'Well.' George cleared his throat and rearranged yet more papers. 'We have a small fund, I'll make sure that Magdalena and Alice don't go without while you're gone.'

'That's good of you, Mr Wrigley.' Probably George's *personal* fund. Jack owed him.

'And I'll make sure your pay is honoured for this week, including today's. Brother-in-law's ship leaves Saturday night.' Wrigley foraged around the mountain of papers on his desk. 'You'll have to travel rough, but you'll be all right, lad. Strong as an ox, you are.'

Jack shook George's hand. 'Thanks.' There was nothing else to say.

'When you find your brother, tell him there'll be no job here. He's over-stepped the line this time. Alice is well liked.'

Grunting, Jack turned and left. He'd already decided to give the pub a miss. Quickly, he walked past the ugly surroundings of the pit top.

Fucking Joe.

It was a lovely evening, if you could ignore the stock-heads and the mountains of rubble. If he could do that, Jack could've been somewhere beautiful. The sky was a stunning dappled red; the next day promised to be a corker. Tomorrow he'd planned to take Alice into Derbyshire for a picnic to help take her mind off Joe.

Jack struggled to understand how he felt about Alice, but recognised that if she hadn't been Joe's fiancée, he

69

might have fallen for her himself. Maybe he had. But she belonged to his brother. One day Jack would find someone to love, maybe someone a bit like Alice. He hoped so, because he could talk to her; tell her things he couldn't tell anyone else. She was the one he showed his writing to. Did that equate to love?

He reached the gate and saw a huddled form sitting on the ground. Alice sat with her knees folded up tightly into her chest, her shoulders jerking upwards. She lifted her head and he registered her red face in the evening half-light. Saying nothing, he went to sit next to her. She reached for his hand and no words were needed. Alice and Jack had been together on their first day of primary school. They'd shared packed lunches, had anxiously laughed together at their teacher, who they'd both decided on their first day looked too much like a man; although they'd both decided too on the day they'd left school that she was the best teacher in the world. To Alice – because the teacher seemed to instinctively understand her sad and empty home life; for Jack – because she encouraged his love of reading and ultimately his passion for writing words.

'Don't you worry,' he said quietly. 'I'll go to Spain. Find Joe and send him back. You'll marry him.'

'My parents'll have nothing to do with me. They're probably hoping that God will take away their shame and strike me down. And you know, Jack, I wouldn't mind. I wish I were dead. I'm so stupid.'

'Aw, don't say that. Look, I mean it. I'll find him. You know me, always do as I say I'm going to do.'

'You can't just go to Spain. What about your job? Your mum? Both sons in some godforsaken country.'

'I want to go. You know that. Put it off because Joe pissed off there.' He glanced at her and shrugged apologetically.

'Sorry, I shouldn't swear, been with the lads on a long shift.' He stood and offered his hand, pulling her up too. 'Did Joe know?'

Her cheeks coloured. 'I told him I could be, the next thing I know, he's gone to Spain. He kept going on about the fascists, Hitler, Mussolini, all this stuff I don't know anything about. Why? Why did he have to go? He's so easily led – God knows why he went. But I do know why, I suppose.'

She seemed calmer.

'I know Joe can be selfish, but I'm sure he didn't know you were pregnant. You know Joe, doesn't see anything straight in front of him.' He touched her hand. 'He didn't know . . . 'bout the baby, I mean.'

When Alice looked up, he knew she believed what he'd said.

Jack wished he could've believed what he'd said too.

The next day Jack did some digging around at the local ILA office and managed to talk to a few men who'd recently returned from Spain, eventually finding out that Joe really had disappeared. Two days into the Jarama offensive and Joe, a soldier in the 15th International Brigade Battalion, had disappeared. No body; Joe had just gone.

Knowing his brother could look after himself Jack held out hope, because both of them were more than able to take care of themselves; the two brothers had joined the Territorial Army in their mid-teens and both were capable of handling a gun. With the luck of the devil, which Joe seemed to possess, he *would* still be alive and Jack truly believed he'd find him.

He didn't think about the vastness of Spain; didn't allow himself to.

Joe wasn't dead. Jack *would* bring him home for Alice.

Alice was sitting with his mum at the kitchen table when he got home, drinking tea and both pretending to eat tongue sandwiches.

'Have you managed to find anything out, about Joe?' Alice asked. With the news of her pregnancy, and Joe, her vibrancy had been tarnished, her perkiness bleached away.

'Not very much,' Jack replied, catching his mum looking at him, her eyes bright and alert. She shook her head and took hold of Alice's hand. 'Not much at all,' he finished.

14

After wiping his mouth, Jack peered at the charcoal-coloured sea swirling around the sides of the ship. The pungent smell of his own puke hit him hard with the easterly wind. His stomach heaved again.

He made his way back down into the bowels of the ship, more to get out of the relentless sea wind than a desire to go back inside. As George Wrigley had said, there were no luxuries on this crossing.

Managing to find a corner where no one would disturb him, Jack pulled out his notebook and began jotting down words that described the pull he was feeling, the whirlpool of anticipation lashing at his insides. New words he didn't even know he knew the meaning of fell onto the page.

'You green?'

Jack jumped slightly and looked up. 'Green?'

'New? Joining up to the Brigades?'

'What's it to you?' Jack replied. The bloke in front of him held out his hand.

'Michael Donavan.'

Michael Donavan was youthful looking. Strawberry-coloured hair, which stuck out at odd angles from underneath his grey woollen hat that seemed too small for his head. His face was narrow, with a slight and neat chin. He looked drawn, as if he'd lost too much weight, too quickly.

'Jack Hayes.'

'You like writing?' Donavan asked, looking at the notebook, his voice raspy.

Jack pushed it back inside his bag. 'I plan to join up, yes. But I'm also going to Spain to look for my brother. He's been reported missing at Jarama.'

'Hayes, you say?'

Jack nodded.

Donavan inclined his head in a sage-like fashion. 'I was at Jarama.'

'You were?'

'Injured, minor compared to some of the men. I've been in Ireland for a few weeks recovering.' He averted his eyes away and stared at the grubby floor. 'My mother died. I've been back home to her funeral.' He made eye contact again. 'Back now though. They need every man they can find.' Donavan lit a cigarette. 'It's an ugly war.' He took a long puff and blew the smoke up towards the low ceiling. 'In more ways than one. Joe Hayes your brother?'

'He is. You heard of him?'

'I fought alongside Joe, met up with him in Barcelona.' He peered through the blue smoke. 'Your brother probably saved my life at Jarama, and a few others too.'

Christ, Michael Donavan knew Joe. The world didn't seem to get any bigger, even when you were off two thousand miles towards Spain. Jack wanted to offer condolences for his mother but thought better of it.

'When did you go to Spain?' Jack asked instead.

'Beginning of August '36. One of the first wave of volunteers to join the Spanish militia, POUM, to fight Franco.'

Donavan was very different to Jack, different class altogether. Jack knew this from his speech and, to a certain extent, the Irishman's self-assurance. Many intellectuals had made their way over to Spain, and he suspected Donavan might have been amongst this elite group. By the time Jack had given serious thought about going, and when Joe *did* go, more ordinary working-class men had caught the *Bolshie fever*, as the papers called it. Although Joe was no intellectual, no Bolshevik either.

'Do you know what happened to him?' Jack tried to envisage Joe as a hero. It was difficult.

'I don't.'

'Do you think he's dead?'

'No.' He ground the cigarette into the floor. 'Joe saved my life, but word went round that he's gone over to Franco's lot.' He looked at the mushed-up fag end. 'It happens.'

'Bloody hell.' Typical Joe.

Donavan made his way to the door, lighting another cigarette, pulling the grey hat over his ears. 'I'm making my way to Barcelona. You might want to come with me. There's someone there you should meet. She knows everything . . . and she knows Joe.'

'Who?'

'Her name's Sofia.'

Jack was more than relieved when his feet touched the hard soil of Brest. His belly, although achingly empty still felt as if there was a bloke inside, squeezing hard, and he wondered if he'd ever stop puking. He inhaled deeply. France even smelt different to England. Fresh and balmy. The air clear, precise.

'So, what now?' he asked Donavan.

'I've got us a lift to the train station.' He pointed to a lorry at the far end of the dock. 'First, a quick stop in Paris, check into HQ, but then onto Figueres in northern Spain, the staging post for people like you, who've just crossed, but then onward, to Barcelona.'

Jack would be sticking with Michael Donavan. Barcelona was the place to start looking for Joe; although that wasn't the only reason he'd stay with him. Jack liked Donavan. And there was the woman Donavan wanted him to meet. *Sofia.*

'Will anyone in Paris be able to give me any information?' Jack asked.

'You mean about Joe?'

'Course I mean about Joe.'

Donavan lit another cigarette, enjoying his own obtuseness. The cigarette hung limply from the edge of his mouth; he cracked his fingers. 'Wasn't everything that he seemed, your brother. Popular though.' Donavan glanced sideways at him. 'With women, and men. Sofia's the one who might be able to tell you more about what was going on inside Joe's complicated head.'

'You telling me Joe was having a relationship with a Spanish girl?'

'Christ, you sound like my grandmother. Why so surprised? There's a lot of fighting going on in Spain.' Jack thought Donavan's grin would fall off his face. 'As well as a lot of fucking. A relationship? With Joe? I don't think so.' He smiled. 'All Sofia's interested in is *the cause.* Sofia's ardent. When I first arrived in Spain, as I said, I joined the Brigades to fight against Franco. Then I met Camillo Berneri. He took me under his wing. Fascinating bloke, from Italy originally, until Mussolini threw him out. Anyway, that's how I know Sofia. At Berneri's house, we both stay there. Sofia's his biggest supporter. She's extreme, like Berneri. Another bloke staying there too who you'll like. Miguel. A good man. You'll be fine with us, Jack.'

Donavan went on to talk more about Sofia Adame and Jack listened intently.

'Sofia's the daughter of a Nationalist colonel and her godfather's General Emilio Mola.' Donavan clocked the blank look on Jack's face. 'Mola's one of the most powerful of Franco's generals, aside from Franco himself. He's half decent for a Nationalist, compared to Severino Adame Herrera anyway – that's Sofia's father – who's completely mad, and a sadistic bastard too. Not a very nice piece of work.'

'And this girl, a daughter of a Nationalist. She's against Franco?'

'Sofia's a Republican through and through.' He tugged at his hat. 'Wait until you meet her. No man meets Sofia and doesn't fall a little in love with her.' Donavan's green eyes shone in Brest's high afternoon sun. 'Perhaps, only me.'

15

A week later, Michael Donavan and Jack arrived at Barcelona's Estació de França railway station. Barcelona caught Jack's imagination and captured his heart – because the city itself had a heart. Beating and pulsing. It was a feeling he wanted to scoop up and put in a box. The streets teemed with life. The dullness of the town he'd grown up in was in powerful contrast to a city, which although in turmoil, still revealed its inner life on every street corner and café they passed. Jack gulped in the strong odours of garlic, black pepper, of strong coffee mixed with cinnamon.

As they moved through a street that opened up to a large square, a plaza, Donavan talked, explaining how the working classes had taken the city, collectivised everything, and that this collectivisation had spread outwards into the local rural communities and farms.

'In this new Barcelona everyone's equal. True socialism, Jack. But it's already changing. The equality amongst the people which existed just six months ago is eroding fast. The Republican government are controlling the working classes in just the same way as they did before the civil war.'

Jack peered upwards, craning his neck at the Republican flags as they rippled in the Barcelona wind, hanging from every public building like watery fabric waves, and giving the city an incongruous festive feel. He wanted to be part of what he saw, something so different from the life he'd just slipped away from, and a life that already seemed far away. Over the past year he'd spoken with men at the ILA meetings who'd been here and seen all of this from the beginning, and now he understood why so many wanted to return.

'So where we heading?' he asked Donavan.

'Home. Not that far, Barcelona's not big.'

Barcelona seemed very big to him and he acknowledged how small was his world.

To Jack, Barcelona was huge.

'Come on,' Jack said, pulling at Donavan's arm. He pushed a finger into the insubstantial fabric of Donavan's jacket and came to bone easily. 'I'd like to meet this woman, Sofia.'

'Can't wait to introduce you! Not sure if she's back in Barcelona, though. She was in the north, Bilbao, when I left for Ireland.'

Jack noticed a boy running behind them and, slowing, he allowed him to catch up. Dark brown skin, and dressed more raggedly than other children he'd seen.

'He'll be wanting money,' Donavan said. 'Don't stop unless you're prepared to give him some. There's not a lot of begging going on, but the gypsies of the city are constant offenders, although you can hardly blame them. They sit in no man's land in all of this. Hated by the fascists,' he wavered, 'and by the Republicans too.'

The boy was now standing next to Jack. There'd been little wind but now a strong gust whipped up; the smell of the boy was strong. Mature sweat and even more mature piss.

The boy pulled out a green thing from his pocket, and held it up. '*Quieres*? It looked unfamiliar but edible. '*Para comer?*' the boy carried on, looking at Jack as if he were stupid.

'*Sí. Veinte centimos?*' Jack said.

'Offer him ten centimes not twenty,' Donavan said. 'You've decent Spanish, Jack.'

'Thanks, those lessons paid off.' Jack pulled out a ten coin and gave it to the boy, who then handed him the green food, bruised and squashed from being in his pocket. Jack was grateful it came naturally wrapped.

The boy sauntered off, satisfied, although his smell lingered a moment or two longer. Jack studied the fruit; he was sure it was some sort of fruit.

'It's an avocado pear,' Donavan said, a grin covering his face.

'Quite fancy something sweet.'

Donavan handed him a penknife. 'Peel and eat. '

Jack did as he was told and a moment later was spitting it over the beautiful stones of Barcelona's famous Las Ramblas. 'Fucking hell.'

Donavan doubled up with laughter. 'Soon the avocado pear will taste like a little bit of heaven. You've only just arrived.'

They were well inside the heart of the city, near to the Plaza de Catalunya in the Barrio Goticó district and then heading eastwards to Berneri's house.

'You look knackered, mate,' Donavan said.

'Don't know what I would've done if I hadn't met you.'

'You'd have been fine. The Catalans would have looked after you. Here, no matter what your political beliefs, even just out of a sense of good manners, you would have been looked after. It's a great country, a sad one now, but still a great one.'

Jack was tired physically, and mentally weary too. When he'd first set off on this journey, Jack had been filling the role that had been his for much of his life – the person who got Joe out of the proverbial shit. But his journey was turning into something more. He'd do everything he could to find Joe, but would be joining the fight against General Franco too.

16

Donavan's pace had slowed considerably and it was only then that Jack noticed his limp. 'You need to sit down a bit? Jack asked.

'Nah, I'll be fine. Shrapnel in the leg. They got it out but it bothers me when I'm tired for some reason. I hate having a fucking limp. Makes me feel like an old man.'

Donavan was younger than Jack by two years, aged twenty-two, and as much as Jack tried to imagine Donavan with a rifle, in a war, he couldn't quite manage it. The image obstinately absent.

Night was falling on a quietened Barcelona and despite Donavan's snail's pace they finally reached their destination; an ancient building with beautiful curved iron railings outside each of its front windows. Well kept, although the insidious beginning of neglect was too apparent.

'Your new home.' Donavan indicated the building with both arms. 'Camillo Berneri's house.' Donavan had perked up on the last leg of the journey.

Jack's own legs were weary. He was cold, hungry, and desperate to get inside, craving a pint of brown ale too, and beginning to question if he could really find Joe. In England Jack was considered strong, resourceful, too clever by half, some said. Here, in this colourful and chaotic country he felt as if he were nothing. But he had to find Joe and encourage him to return to Alice. Then he'd help the Republican cause.

He could drive a lorry, a truck. He could use a rifle, and smiled inwardly; he even had his own gun.

He heard the faint sound of heels on the cobbled pavement and peered in the direction of the faultless rhythm.

And then Jack saw her. The Spanish girl.

He forgot the brown ale, the unshaven face, the extreme tiredness. He forgot about Joe, Alice, and the war. Donavan became invisible.

A tall, raven-haired woman was walking towards them. Jack couldn't make out her features in the darkness of the Spanish night but watched her elegant strides, her hair dance in unison with those purposeful steps, inhaled the exotic perfume surrounding her.

He was entranced.

As she came closer, he noticed her tanned hands holding bright red fabric draped around a long slender neck. All day he'd watched people who wore uniform grey, black, and shades of brown, and now. This. With every one of her steps, purple trouser fabric flicked out from beneath a rich blue coat. Jack took in every detail, because he knew, before she had spoken, this was the woman he'd love.

When finally she was close enough for him to touch her he realised he'd forgotten to breathe.

She squinted at Donavan. Still, she hadn't said a word; and Jack saw her properly. His heart suddenly grew much bigger, the inside of his chest so full. Her eyes violet, and a surprise with such black hair, reminding him of the blanket of bluebells which covered the fields near his home in late spring, although he conceded the shade was probably darker due to the moonless night. Lightly slanted and almond in shape. Her lips full and red. Her face too thin to be considered classically beautiful. Her nose long and straight.

He looked closer; her skin perfect.

Sofia was perfect.

'Is that you, Michael Donavan?' She spoke in Spanish.

'My God, Sofia, you're back,' Donavan replied.

As Donavan spoke, a clear sound of bells bounced through the night air. Twelve chimes. It was later than Jack had thought, although every trace of fatigue had evaporated.

'We've been back for two weeks,' Sofia replied. 'Miguel is inside, he'll be glad to see you, Michael, as I am. Are you recovered?' She wavered. 'And your family, all is well as it can be? I am so sorry to hear about your mother.' Her Spanish was rapid and Jack was finding it hard to keep up.

'Darling Sofia, can you speak in English?' Donavan said. 'It's so much better than my Spanish.' He grinned, almost comically. 'My father is fine, being looked after by my three sisters.' He touched her elbow. 'And you? Did you manage to bring back Calida and Aurelio?'

'They are safe. But your father, that is good. A close family. But, Michael, you are no better than your British counterparts who can't be bothered to learn our language.' She'd spoken in English. She turned to Jack and Sofia Adame raised an eyebrow. The most beautiful facial expression Jack had ever seen. 'Who is your friend, Michael?'

'*Mi nombre es Jack Hayes. Encantado de conocerle. Mucho gusto.*' To his own ear his Spanish sounded stilted. He studied the woman in front of him. Sofia was at ease with herself, relaxed. Liberated. The formality of his greeting sounded wrong, even in Spanish.

'Jack . . . Hayes?' she said in English, stepping closer; he smelt her perfume. 'Are you Joe's brother?'

Jack nodded.

'Ah, Joe.' She studied him. 'You don't look like him, Jack Hayes.' She smiled. 'You look better.' A pause. 'And, you try to speak Spanish. *Bravo*.'

The warmth rose in his neck. Donavan laughed, the sound ricocheting through the quiet street.

'Are you here to fight?' Sofia continued.

'I'm here to do what I can. And to find Joe, to tell him to go back home.'

'Find Joe. Yes. We need to find Joe. But, I don't think he will do as you ask. He won't go home.' She swept the hair away from her face and he saw her features more clearly. 'Is there a reason why you want Joe to go home?'

'Family reasons. '

She hugged herself. 'It's cold. Let's go inside. You both look as if you need food and a bed. There's a few others in the house at the moment, and Miguel, me. Plenty of room.'

'Berneri isn't here?' Donavan asked.

'No, he's away, but we expect him back soon, in the next week I hope.' Sofia led the way towards the door, opened it and allowed Donavan, and then Jack, to pass.

The house smelt musty and of what he knew now was garlic and pepper, yet as soon as he set foot in the hallway it felt the right place to be. Sofia took off her coat and flung it on an old, gnarled chair. The belt that gripped tightly around her middle emphasised a tiny waist, and not so tiny breasts. Seeping warmth settled on his cheeks. What the hell was wrong with him? Jack tried to calculate her age. Anything between eighteen and twenty-five but his intuition told him that despite her blatant self-assurance she was nearer to eighteen. Something fluttered deep in his groin. He took off his own coat and placed it on top of Sofia's.

Sofia glanced at him, and then at the two coats laying together. 'I think you'll be fine here, Jack.'

There were so many questions he wanted to ask and those questions should have been about Joe, about what had happened before he'd left for Jarama, the sort of man Sofia thought he was; was this Joe a different man to the one he'd grown up with?

Jack had no desire to talk about Joe.

'Jack will be fine here, Sofia. That's for sure.' Donavan said, opening the nearest door, and pushing it open fully with his foot. 'Ah, a fire. Miguel is around. The only one to bother with a fire. Where is the diminutive man?'

'Probably outside cutting wood, or in the outbuilding with his pottery. He couldn't wait to get back to his *horno*,' Sofia said.

'*Horno*?' Jack asked.

'A kiln,' Donavan explained. 'Miguel's hobby. Pottery.'

Sofia and Jack followed Donavan into the room. A large mahogany table sat in front of the window that overlooked the street. Jack counted twelve chairs, all in various positions, some tucked under the table, some jutting out. It was a table that was used, and he guessed not only for eating at, but as a meeting point. Berneri's house was a gatherer of people. Two old and worn sofas sat at the other end of the room. A fire blazed in the centre of the back wall. Next to the fire, on each side, were paintings of people dressed in what looked like rags and from the previous century, a few photographs and one tarnished gold crucifix.

Donavan flopped onto a sofa, while Sofia sat on a chair near the window. And then a gust of cool air entered the room and Donavan shot back up.

Jack assumed the man standing in front of them was Miguel. He was a slight man and wore a navy jumper tucked into baggy trousers, a thick brown belt holding all the clothes in place. Miguel had a more European complexion, pale, and this accentuated the darkness of his hair, a boot-polish black. His face round, with small black eyes. He held too many cut logs, and when he saw Donavan he dropped them all, one landing on his foot.

'*Mierda!*' he mouthed.

Despite Miguel standing on one leg and nursing his foot, Donavan managed to hug him. '*Es bueno verte.*'

'You too,' Miguel said, smiling. He'd placed his foot back onto the floor and turned his head to Jack, shrugging his narrow shoulders in question.

'Met Jack here, on the ship coming over,' Donavan explained. 'He can drive a lorry. I recruited him.' He laughed loudly. 'Well, Haldane recruited him in Paris. He has his papers.'

'Come, your room is still here. I cleaned it. Must have known,' Miguel said, leading Donavan away. Looking over his shoulder at Jack he carried on, 'Could you make sure the fire is out before you go to bed? There's a room ready next to Michael's. Sofia will show you. I'm off to bed too.'

And that's how Jack found himself alone with Sofia for the first time: in a hot room that smelt of burning logs, which mixed perfectly with her perfume. A smell Jack would never forget.

She dropped onto the sofa and kicked off her boots, reclining into its softness.

'Are you not tired, Jack Hayes?'

'I was, but not now.'

She patted the sofa. 'Sit.' He did. She turned, facing him. 'Tell me why you want to take Joe home.'

'I need to find him first, he might be—'

'He's not dead. But you do not answer my question.'

'I'd rather not talk about Joe and why he should return to England.' He wanted to tell Sofia everything. Now. Here.

And he wanted to know what had happened between his brother and her. He couldn't imagine Sofia with Joe. Or didn't want to.

'But I would like to know.'

'Do you like Joe?' He heard the absolute stupidity of the question.

She slid onto the floor, rested her back against the sofa, pushing her legs outwards, stretching them like a colt. Slowly, she rolled up the sleeves of her sapphire-coloured shirt. 'Like him? He is different to the Spanish men, but then, so are all the foreigners coming to our country. Joe is fun. Not serious, or so he would like everyone to believe. He's a man who doesn't know who he is, or would rather not look in the mirror.'

'What do you mean?'

'I don't think you know your brother very well.'

'No, it's you who doesn't know him.'

'Then tell me, tell me why it is so urgent he returns to England? I take it you do not plan to return so hastily?'

'Joe has a girlfriend in England. Her name is Alice. She's pregnant. Her parents have kicked her out.' Jack wasn't sure if she understood this phrase. 'Made her leave the family home. She's staying with our mother. I need to take Joe home, so as he can marry her.'

'And what if Joe doesn't want to marry Alice?'

Jack studied his feet and didn't answer.

'What will happen?' she prodded.

'Then I'll look after her. '

Sofia stood. 'You are very different from your brother. Will you marry Alice?'

'I care for her. I'll look after her. Not much of a life for an unmarried mother where I come from.'

'It is the same here, in Spain. I feel for Alice.'

'She doesn't need your sympathy, Sofia, she needs Joe to marry her.'

She seemed to crumple. 'I'm sorry, I didn't mean to be—'

'No, I'm sorry. It's not your fault. Donavan says you and Joe were friends?'

'He allowed me to be a person I've never been allowed to be.'

'And who's that person?'

'A normal girl, who wants to get dressed up and go out.'

'Sounds like Joe, I have to say. I think he's probably the best-dressed man in our town, and I'd guess, in Spain too. Joe likes a party, that he does.' He scrutinised her reaction. Was she having a relationship with his brother? It sounded as if they were yet . . . he couldn't believe it. Joe had Alice and Sofia, he was sure, would not be attracted to Joe. He was sure.

'Joe is *mezclado*.'

'I don't think I'd ever call my brother mixed up.'

'You don't know him,' she said.

'Oh, I do know him.'

She lifted her shoulders in a question. 'I am sorry about Alice. And there is nothing between Joe and me. We are only friends. And Jack, for what it is worth, I do not think he is dead. Call it the Catalan sixth sense.' She searched Jack's eyes, her own bright, and a colour he thought he'd never see again. 'Because you love him, or because of Alice?'

The warmth that was building so quickly towards a stranger, he found both intoxicating and perplexing. He finally replied. 'Both.'

She sat down again next to him. 'This is good. That you love your brother. Family relationships are important.'

Jack remembered what Donavan had told him about Sofia's father. 'Do you have brothers, sisters?'

'No. Which is probably a good thing, considering my father.'

'Donavan has told me about Herrera.'

'Has he? It's no secret that half of Barcelona would like me dead for being Severino Herrera's daughter.'

The thought of Sofia dying brought a feeling of dread. 'That's not what Donavan says.'

'Half of Barcelona, Jack, not all.' Her violet eyes shimmered in the fading roar of the fire. 'The other half love me.'

Jack saw why.

She carried on. 'So your plan?'

'I don't really have one.'

'You drive?'

'I do.'

'I have become involved with the British Red Cross. We need drivers, and drivers who can fight too, if needed.'

'I'd do that.' Jack took off his shoes, pushed them away. 'You're passionate about your cause.'

'I joined POUM at the beginning of the conflict, I'm a supporter of the Second Republic, I hate what Franco has done – rebelling against his own government, killing his own people.'

'And where does Camillo Berneri fit into all this?'

'Camillo's beliefs are a little more extreme than ours, POUM's, but Camillo Berneri is my friend, he is a natural leader, and this is his house.' She walked towards the window and looked to the outside. 'We all live here for nothing, give what we can, in whatever way we can. But back to my question, Jack. The Red Cross?'

'I'll do anything to help.' He glanced at her. 'I really will.'

'And I think you will. We'll talk tomorrow. Come, Jack Hayes, I'll show you your room.'

Sofia pushed open the door of the bedroom, which smelt even fustier than the dining room downstairs. She jumped on the bed. He couldn't help but smile. She spoke with wisdom but her movements were those of a girl.

'The most uncomfortable bed in the house but you'll cope,' she said. He waited for her to move, a bit embarrassed about her sitting on the bed. Finally, she sprang upward and punched his chest as she walked by. 'Don't look so shocked.'

'I'm not shocked.'

'Yes, you are, Jack.' She sauntered from the room, head held high, slim hips swaying.

Sofia was like no woman he'd come across before but his thoughts moved to Alice and the baby growing inside her, and then to Joe.

He lay on the bed staring at a grey ceiling, counting the numerous damp patches, finding patterns in the black mould which collected in the ceiling's corners, attempting to push Joe from his head, allowing his thoughts instead to settle on the image of the woman he'd just met.

Jack fell asleep thinking about her and the next morning woke up with the same picture in his mind. Violet eyes, rich inky hair, and vivid-coloured clothes.

The Spanish girl, Sofia Adame.

17

Civil war simmered but the first few weeks that Jack spent in Camillo Berneri's stone house were relatively peaceful. They existed in what seemed like an airtight vacuum, their lives paused in a cut of time, and where everything happened in the kitchen, its walls covered in brightly coloured ceramic tiles, or in the old dining room, the rectangular oak table dominating. Miguel's bowls lay around everywhere.

In those first weeks Jack listened, learning as much as he could about both Spain, and Sofia. She was keen to tell Donavan about the political events unfolding in the Basque country; the place she and Miguel had recently returned from the night he'd met her.

'The Basque people are split,' she said. 'Do they trust the Republicans and believe they will be given independence from Madrid with a Republican victory, or would they be better off with Franco and a Nationalist victory? There's no question. The people have to trust the Republicans.' She sighed heavily. 'But I'm more worried about Calida and Aurelio.'

'You brought them back, though, to Catalonia?' Donavan asked. 'That was the reason you travelled to the Basque region with Miguel?'

'We've brought them back for their safety, yes. They are in danger, and from my own father. He blames them for who, and what I am,' Sofia said quietly.

'Where have you taken them?' Donavan asked.

'Somewhere safe, *mi amigo*.'

'And the other business? You saw Emilio Mola?'

'Yes. I saw my godfather.'

Sofia flicked back her hair and began chopping onions, expertly ending the conversation. Silence descended on the kitchen and all three disappeared into their own thoughts, Jack's though, predominantly directed towards the new people he'd met. Donavan and Sofia in particular.

He glanced at Donavan, who was perched on an old rattan chair at the far end of the kitchen, smoking, his gaze fixed on the small window that overlooked the walled overgrown garden at the back of the house. He didn't look well, his health wasn't as good as it could have been. It was as if he'd used the last slice of his vitality getting back to Spain and, as so often happened, as he'd relaxed came a leaking of his energy.

Donavan spent a lot of time at La Cocina, the local café, while Jack found himself spending most of his time with Sofia, although he was getting to know the others who were staying in Berneri's house too, including a girl only a little younger than Sofia. Sofia had met her during her work with the *Mujeres Libres*, an organisation set up to help the women of Spain. Sofia had befriended the orphan, both parents having died in the conflict, and brought her to the house. The girl was an accomplished seamstress, and this was her contribution to the *Mujeres Libres*.

Sofia had flung herself back into the war effort soon after her return to Barcelona, but she was determined to return to the Basque country at the earliest opportunity to help the British Red Cross – the organisation she'd mentioned on the first night they'd met.

Jack was still leaning against the kitchen table, pretending not to watch Sofia as she continued to chop and prepare, but he was watching. How could he not? Her entire presence was like a magnet, and he tried not to think of her with Joe.

'Where are you, Jack?' She broke into his musings and finally stopped her busyness. She put down her knife and stepped closer to him, rested a delicate hand on his arm and a sliver of electricity funnelled through him.

'I was thinking of you.'

She smiled and her violet eyes lit like bluebell flowers in the moonlight. 'I like that you are thinking of me when I'm standing only a few paces away from you.'

Something small, yet at the same time quietly volcanic, was happening between the two of them.

Donavan coughed and flicked his cigarette through the open window. 'Think I'll go and get some air.'

'Michael,' Sofia said. 'How are your enquiries going regarding Joe?'

He was standing by the door, ready to escape. 'Not coming up with much.'

'I think, Michael,' Sofia carried on, 'you should give yourself time to recover your strength before you go all out looking for Joe.' She picked up a peeled carrot and took a bite. 'And before you and Jack make your way south to Albacete too. You need to rest.'

He and Donavan had already decided between them that they were giving themselves a few weeks to find Joe, and if they couldn't locate his brother in those weeks, they'd admit failure and make their way to the International Brigades headquarters in Albacete.

'Might be a good idea,' Donavan said, taking them both in. 'But what's Jack going to be doing while he waits?'

'Come with me to the north, help with the Red Cross?' she said, directing it as a question to Jack.

Before Jack could reply, Donavan said, his green eyes shimmering in the afternoon light, 'I don't think you need to ask him, Sofia.'

Just over two weeks after arriving in Barcelona from the Basque region, Jack set off there again, but this time with Sofia. It was during the train journey to Bilbao when he learnt more about this woman who had so quickly captured his heart.

Sofia was the goddaughter of General Emilio Mola, and Mola had been a close family friend of Sofia's mother, Hilgardi. After Hilgardi's death when Sofia was three, it was Mola who'd steered the course of her early upbringing.

'Perhaps Mola knew back then,' she said, 'where the mind of my father lay. In a gutter. And that's why Emilio sent me to live with Calida and Aurelio.'

Severino Adame Herrera had managed to maintain his career because of his ties to Mola. Mola wasn't as fond of his goddaughter's father as he had been of her mother, Hilgardi. Sofia's main priority on her earlier visit to Bilbao had been to bring her 'adoptive' parents back to Catalonia, making sure they were safe from Herrera, taking them away from the place where he could easily find them, but she'd also met with Emilio Mola too.

Sofia fidgeted on the hard seat of the train and continued, 'When I was old enough, I understood why Emilio had made that decision, when I realised what my fath . . . Herrera . . . what he's capable of.' Her narrow face darkened.

'You lived with Calida and Aurelio?' Jack asked.

'Yes, in Bilbao. They were like a mother and father to me.'

'What did your father have to say about that?'

'Nothing. It suited him. As long as I was out of the way, and that I didn't create any scandals.'

'And did you?'

Sofia's serious face broke into a grin. 'A very big one when I joined the Republicans. I haven't seen Herrera since early 1936. In Bilbao, Emilio warned me that Herrera knew where Calida and Aurelio were located. I wanted them to cross the border into France, but they won't leave Spain.'

'Will Herrera try to find you?'

'I'm protected from my father by Emilio Mola. If anything happens to him, that's when I'll be in danger.'

She stood, stretched out her long legs, disrupting the sleep of the old lady who sat next to her. The smell of Sofia's perfume lingered. How did a smell become a memory?

'And Emilio Mola, how does he feel about you being with the Republicans?'

'Publicly, he's washed his hands of me. I make his position tenuous. But he's told me pertinent things. However, I'm certain Emilio is taking care of his own back.' She shuffled on the seat. 'I'm glad you could come with me, Jack.'

The train meandered northwards; Sofia fell asleep with her head resting on Jack's shoulder and he smiled listening to her dainty snores drifting upwards. After an hour she lifted her head, groggy with rest and as if it was the most natural thing, her lips found his. He held her chin lightly, and kissed her.

The old lady sitting next to Sofia clapped and grinned a semi-toothless smile. '¡Otra vez!' Again!

At the stop before Bilbao, the old woman gave Sofia a lucky flower. '*Flor de la suerte.*' Sofia took it and tried to give the woman a few pesetas. The woman shook her head and shuffled towards the open door of the train.

'It's a Spanish bluebell, my favourite,' Sofia said. She handed it to him. 'Keep it safe.'

Jack took it and pulled his bag from underneath the seat, retrieved his notebook and set the flower in between two back pages, gently flattening it. He closed the notebook, pushing it underneath his bottom.

Sofia laughed. 'What *are* you doing?'

'Pressing it.'

'Jack, I like you.'

'Do you?'

'I do.' She snuggled down and when she next woke they were less than an hour away from their destination.

18

Jack and Sofia arrived in Bilbao on the 25th April. It had been arranged that Sofia would be an extra pair of hands at the main hospital in the city. The seriously injured soldiers were being moved to the better-equipped hospital in the centre of Bilbao. Sofia's role would be administrative. She'd be good at that; she was a born organiser and leader. And Jack would drive a lorry, a truck, an ambulance, whatever was available; it didn't matter as long as it moved.

'Dr Fuente is picking us up. I telegrammed him before we left.'

As promised, Dr Fuente was waiting outside the station. A tall man with a mop of grey hair, wearing a crumpled suit and a red bow tie. Fuente strode towards them with long and confident steps.

'*Sofia! Me alegro de volver a verle. ¿Cómo está?*' After his greeting, Fuente gathered her under his left arm and took Jack in quickly with his small, thoughtful eyes.

'*Este es Jack Hayes, preferiría que hablemos ingles?*' To Jack, Sofia said, 'Would you prefer we spoke in English?'

'I'm having a bit of trouble. My teacher in England taught Andalusian Spanish, so it's hard for me to keep up,' he explained.

'Ah, good thing we do not speak in Euskardi then, Señor Hayes,' Dr Fuente said with a smile.

Fuente's English was perfect.

'Dr Fuente studied medicine in England, London,' Sofia said. 'That's right, *señor*?'

'The Royal London Hospital. I adore England, but it seems your prime minister, Señor Hayes, is wringing Spain dry.'

Dr Fuente didn't wait for Jack's reply and pointed jovially towards his car.

The next morning, Jack was woken by gentle tapping on the door. He opened it to a pretty girl, around sixteen. Large chocolate eyes stared at him. She had a devil of a smile.

'Mama said to tell you there is breakfast downstairs,' she said, caressing her own neck.

'Thanks, I won't be long—'

'Paloma.'

'Your English is very good . . . Paloma. Please tell Señora Fuente I'll be ten minutes.'

'Sofia is already downstairs.' With this information Paloma's face fell. 'She's only a few years older than me.'

'Yes . . .' Jack searched her face and then watched as she placed a small hand on her hip.

'See you downstairs,' she said, her long lower eyelashes sweeping the top of her cheek.

Jack pushed the door closed and sat on the bed, his mind with Sofia. She'd stayed at the hospital the night before. The thought of her sent a jolt through his body and a hunting contentment through his mind.

The Fuentes' dining room was formal. Jack tugged at the waistband of his trousers and made his way straight towards Sofia, who was already sitting at the table. Paloma was nowhere to be seen. Señora Fuente, a striking woman with dark blonde hair coiled into a loose bun at the nape of her neck, sat at the table's head.

'*Has dormido bien? Señor Hayes?*' she asked.

'Yes, I slept really well, and I'd like to say how good it is of you to have me staying with you,' he replied in Spanish.

'The pleasure is ours, Jack,' Dr Fuente said. 'My wife doesn't speak English, so thank you for speaking in Spanish.' He smiled conservatively. 'But to business. Your driving skills will be much appreciated. There are still a lot of wounded who need to be brought to the main hospital here. That will be your job. And Sofia can do what she does best – organise, liaise and,' he tittered slightly, 'drum up funds and support.'

'Where will I be going? Will I have a guide?' Jack asked in English.

'Guernica first. A reconnaissance trip to begin with, and Sofia will go with you. A few days there, orientate yourself, then bring Sofia back to Bilbao so she can start working in the hospital here. How does that sound?'

'Sounds perfect, Dr Fuente,' Sofia said, rubbing Jack's lower leg with her foot underneath the table.

'I would like my daughter, Paloma, to go with you both. I think she would benefit from seeing more, doing more,' Dr Fuente said.

Jack thought about his quick introduction to Paloma upstairs, and sighed. He'd wanted to be alone with Sofia on the journey.

Fuente continued. 'Things are moving quickly in the north. Hitler's Condor Legion is being mobilised, and intelligence informs us they will be ready to begin aerial bombardment within a month. The Nationalists are blockading the ports. Supplies for everything, including much-needed medical supplies, have dried up.'

'Isn't it too dangerous for your daughter to come with us?'

'It's not a problem, is it?' Fuente said.

'No, of course not,' Sofia interrupted. 'She'll be safe with us.'

'Good. You all leave today,' Dr Fuente finished.

The truck had been converted into an ambulance, back seats ripped out and replaced by wooden boards, with six boxes of medical supplies pushed towards the back end.

Jack drove, Sofia sitting next to him, and Paloma next to Sofia. Initially, Paloma had got in first and plonked herself alongside Jack. Sofia though, was having none of it.

Jack predicted a small war.

Sofia remained quiet for most of the journey, only making sure Jack drove in the right direction. Paloma chatted, a lot, and Jack rapidly came to the conclusion that Sofia's quietness was due to Paloma's loudness.

It was around 2.30pm when they approached Guernica from the east, and on the only road feeding into the town. There was no military presence there, but many of the casualties from the frontline had been moved to Guernica. It was Jack's job to take as many of them back as was possible. Fuente had given him clear instructions on the type of patient he should return to Bilbao. Jack had pointed out that he'd bring back whoever he wanted, and hopefully all of them. Fuente's smile had been both wry and sad. 'There will be too many. Concentrate on those who have the best chance of pulling through, I'll give you a list of what you should be looking for. If the infection has taken a mortal hold, then leave them in the care of the nurses at the medical facility . . . and the priests.' Jack had looked at him in question, and Fuente had answered, 'The priests will be more beneficial than a surgeon.'

'I think we should stop off for something to eat,' Paloma said, interrupting Jack's thoughts.

'You should have eaten the breakfast your mama had prepared for you,' Sofia scolded gently.

Paloma snorted, and Jack let out a laugh. Sofia gave him a look that he could've only imagined a wife of twenty years would have given. He stroked Sofia's knee. Paloma glanced down at his hand and huffed.

They drove into the town, the sun was bright, the sky cloudless. The streets bustling with people. It was market day in Guernica.

'I'm really hungry,' Paloma whined.

'Let's get something to eat,' Jack said as he drove past Guernica's church.

Sofia looked towards the grand building. 'I'd like to go inside later.'

Jack inclined his head and Paloma huffed yet again.

They found a café in the town's square where Paloma ate tapas, Jack drank a coffee and Sofia sipped water. The town was packed. Hundreds of farmers bringing the fruits of their labours, their crops, to the main square. Business was brisk, not one foot of the square was empty of bodies.

'So,' Sofia said, 'shall we get to work? See what the facilities are like, and offload the supplies?'

Fuente had given them plenty of his coveted medical supplies, with strict instructions to give them only to the main nurse, an English lady, Penny Gibson, who'd been in the region since early March. 'Experienced,' Fuente had said, 'and sensible.'

'No, let's go inside the church first,' Jack replied, wanting to please Sofia. There was no rush.

Paloma's pretty eyes rolled. 'Do we *have* to?'

Jack was beginning to wonder if Fuente had sent Paloma off with them to get her from underneath her mother's feet. 'Yes, we do.' He took Sofia by the elbow. Paloma didn't move.

'Come on,' Sofia said, strictness in her tone and which did make him laugh. There weren't that many years between the two women.

'Listen! I hear something. In the distance,' Paloma said, the whiny tone gone.

A low-grade rumble; she was right. Jack peered into the distance at green hills.

A perfect day. And a clear day to see the approaching planes.

'My God,' Sofia whispered. 'Planes. Are they ours?' She strained her eyes. 'They're not. German planes.'

'This soon?' Jack said.

'Earlier than we'd anticipated, but there is no reason to attack Guernica,' Sofia replied. 'Emilio Mola promised me this wouldn't happen.'

Paloma began to cry. She got up from her seat. 'The town is being used as a Republican communications centre, Sofia. Surely you knew this? It's why the town's being targeted.' She crossed her chest. 'My God, I'm going to the church.'

Paloma, Jack realised in a slice of a second, knew more than he, or Isabella, had given her credit for. Perhaps this was why her father had wanted her to come, because she had knowledge of the area, and they did not, including Sofia.

Sofia caught Jack's eye, and then looked up at the skyline; the planes were becoming larger as they got closer. 'Yes, you go into the church, *niña*,' she said to Paloma.

'You two also?' Paloma replied, fear lacing through her words.

Sofia looked at Jack; he stared back and lifted his shoulders.

Paloma had pulled herself together quickly. 'We'll be safer in the church. They'll probably target the main road coming into the town so as to cut it off.' She began to move. '*Con rapidez!*'

The planes above buzzed, people ran from the café, spilled out from the church, people who had been busy at the market began to scatter like insects being dislodged. Horror, fear and chaos descended in seconds. Some of the men ran away from the church, probably to find their family and warn them. Everything happened too fast.

Sofia spoke. 'You go to the church, Paloma. Jack and I will make our way to the medical unit.'

Paloma's features contorted in terror. 'You think they will bomb the town? Even Franco will not bomb his own people. It's the roads they're after.'

Sofia threw Jack an anxious glance. If Paloma were right, the Germans would be targeting the town itself. But they had no time to move away from the centre. Jack squinted towards the truck he'd parked on the town's outskirts.

Sofia shook her head. 'Go now, Paloma, to the church.'

The young woman hesitated, the paralysis of delayed shock taking hold.

'Now!' Sofia shouted. 'We'll come back for you.'

Paloma's petite body began to move.

A tall, well-built man clasped his arm around Paloma's shoulders. Jack clocked the yellow scarf wrapped around his neck. 'I will take her to the church. She'll be safe with me,' the man said, and they hurried away.

The planes were so near now that Jack saw the motifs on the side. Swastikas. They flew in close, although there was still time for them to pull around. They would turn soon, surely, back to from where they had come, but he knew that wasn't going to happen. In that moment a loud and crushing bang rang out into the spring air. Jack looked towards the carnage of the road which the bomb had obliterated, thick dust and debris blanketing out the April rays.

Jack pulled at Sofia, 'Come on!'

They began running down the road towards the medical centre, which was a fair distance from both the café and the church. By then, and at the same time, they both realised the planes had no intention of turning back; they were heading straight towards the centre of the town, the square, and the church.

'Fuck. They're bombing the town,' Jack mouthed.

Sofia looked at him, 'No . . . no . . . Emilio Mola said this was not the plan.'

'Fuck what Mola said.' Jack grabbed her arm, unsure what to do. It was too late to retrieve Paloma from the church.

Too late.

One plane split away from the others, flying low in the direction of the church. Sofia ran towards the old building. Jack sprinted and caught her. 'Too late.' He pulled her back and then practically carried her, running up the street with the horrendous sound of buildings crashing and falling ricocheting through his ears. Finding a house with a large porch, Jack put her down roughly, pushing her into the doorway as a veil of dust travelled up the road like a sandy oncoming wave. They could see nothing.

'Oh my God, my God. Paloma,' Sofia gasped.

The dust and debris settled a bit and that's when Jack saw.

The church half decimated; people poured out from the holes which had been blown into its sides.

'Come on, we'll find her.' But then a second plane appeared as if from nowhere, unloading death fare from its underbelly, and again targeting the church. Jack pulled Sofia down and lay on top of her, holding her writhing body so she couldn't move. He looked upwards and listened to the mixture of screams and moans. The planes hummed and buzzed, flying low. They hadn't yet finished. Surely they wouldn't come back to bomb the church again.

He knew this because there was so little of the church left to bomb.

Jack pulled Sofia up, hearing and seeing the plane returning, flying so low he felt he could reach out and touch it. Something dropped from the metal monstrosity, something small, like a grenade, landing in the middle of the church's debris. And then in only moments, the remains of what had once been a place of worship, a haven, sprung into wild, uncontained flames.

Sofia looked up at Jack, tears like rivulets of water on cracked glassy cheeks mingled with her blood. If he'd had time to cry, he would have done so too. There'd been no need for Paloma to come with them. Dr Fuente only sending her along to shift a teenage attitude. His eyes fell onto the annihilated church and took in the flames and the chaos.

'You stay,' he said to Sofia.

'Go and look for her . . . *Dios mío*, Dr Fuente . . . *Dios mío*, Señora Fuente . . .' Sofia sat back down on the ground and huddled into a ball. The flames from the church were strong and made the surrounding air warm. Speaking to the ground, she said, 'Look for her, Jack.'

He ran around what had been the back end of the church where the fire had not yet taken hold. It was then he saw the bright yellow scarf of the man who had taken it upon himself to be Paloma's guard. Attached to the scarf was the lifeless body of the man. Jack moved nearer and knelt down, pulling away at the rubble, and at a strangely intact gargoyle which had sat at the western side of the church – he'd noticed it as they'd driven by earlier. It was then Jack saw Paloma's tiny hand, recognising the fragile silver bracelet hanging around her wrist. He felt for her pulse. Glancing upwards, he heard the terrible moans of pain, cries of horror and disbelief. And for a moment he was unable to move. Frozen in a pause of time, but the threatened movement of unstable masonry shoved him into action. And then strong hands on his shoulders, pulling him away. The last thing Jack remembered was the satanic smile of the gargoyle, the limp hand of a young girl who shouldn't have been there. The brilliance of the yellow scarf.

19

Jack woke to the sound of frantic noise, and a nurse who told him her name was Penny, doing something to his face. And then he turned his head and realised who held his hand. Sofia. Her face still dirty but the tears had gone.

'You'll be all right, Jack. Penny says you'll be fine,' Sofia whispered.

'Paloma?' But Jack knew the answer. He remembered, and Sofia's face told him.

'The kind man too,' she said, her voice fragmented.

'The planes?'

'Gone for now, but they'll be back. Fucking Mussolini. Italian as well as German planes. Camillo said this would happen. But Emilio Mola promised . . . and I had hoped—'

Jack tried to move but everything hurt.

Penny interrupted. 'You'll feel rough for a few days, but nothing broken.' She glanced at Sofia. 'I have to get on, so much to do.'

'Thank you, Penny. I'll look after him.' Sofia stroked his hand. 'We have to return to Bilbao, Jack. Take Paloma home.'

'The Fuentes—' he croaked.

'I know.'

'The church—'

'Franco will do anything. He has no heart. He is a bastard.'

Jack attempted a nod and tried to move.

'You need a few hours' rest,' she said.

'No time. I think we can fit six injured into the truck, as well as Paloma's body. Ask Penny, the doctor, whoever, who will benefit the most from treatment in Bilbao.'

'How am I going to tell Dr Fuente, Jack?' she said, her voice a whisper.

He shook his head.

He didn't know how.

They left late in the evening, arriving back in Bilbao as the sun was about to rise. Paloma's body, and five others who were injured – civilians from the bombing the day before – four women and one man, in the back of the truck. Jack had promised Penny he'd return for others.

Dr Fuente peered into the front of the truck. Jack switched off the engine and told Sofia to stay. Quickly, he got out and put his arm around the doctor's shoulders, taking him inside.

It was Jack who told Fuente what had happened to his daughter.

'I had a strange feeling last night,' he said. 'So strange that I didn't come home from the hospital, somehow I could not face seeing my wife.'

Dr Fuente had insisted on Paloma going with them to Guernica, but how was he to know? How were any of them to know? Jack's heart ruptured for this man, and his wife.

Alone, Dr Fuente refused Jack's help, and retrieving his daughter's body from the truck, he took her inside the hospital and cleaned her.

Paloma was lying in the hospital's chapel of rest when Señora Fuente saw her daughter again. Jack heard her animal-like wails of despair from too far away.

A few hours later Dr Fuente was back in his theatre operating on the living patients they'd brought back from Guernica.

It was agreed Sofia would stay only for a week to set up the administration for Dr Fuente, and then return to Barcelona. Jack told the Fuentes he'd stay for two weeks, and ferry the injured at Guernica back to Bilbao.

In between trips he continued to stay at the Fuente household; they'd both insisted, and before she returned to Barcelona Sofia stayed there too in the room next to Jack's. It was amidst the horror and the grief which pervaded the house when Jack saw the real Sofia.

Neither of them could forgive themselves for what had happened to Paloma, but more so Sofia because she blamed herself because of her connection to Emilio Mola. Without doubt, Mola would have been involved in the planning of the air strikes on Guernica. Sofia held herself completely responsible for Paloma's death, as well as the hundreds of other civilians.

In the Fuentes' home Jack and Sofia did not share a bed but they talked into the night, about the war, her family, and a little about his. Jack held her, he got to know her. What had happened in Guernica could have become a barrier. But it did not, and in the end made them closer.

20

Jack returned to Barcelona a week after Sofia. It was Michael Donavan who met him at the station; Jack saw his mop of strawberry hair poking out from the grey hat as soon as he stepped off the train.

'How are you?' Donavan took the heavy bag from Jack's shoulder, a cigarette hanging from his mouth. He coughed. 'Sofia's at home waiting. Camillo turned up last night.'

'He's back? I've been looking forward to meeting him.' Jack heard the monotone of his own voice.

Donavan nodded. 'I'm so sorry. Miguel knew the Fuentes well. It was Paloma who took care of Miguel's young nephew while they were in Bilbao.'

'Nephew?'

'You haven't met him yet, came while you've been away. Miguel has taken him in for a while to help out his sister. Quiet boy. Miguel's sister wasn't coping, her husband's fighting in the south, so she sent him to Barcelona.'

Jack nodded absent-mindedly. He was thinking of the mischievous Paloma, the unguarded lust for adventure in her eyes; the devastating grief in her parents'. Sadness overcame him again. The couple would never forgive themselves. He'd seen it in every move they'd made over the past weeks. At Paloma's funeral he'd thought Señora Fuente would climb in the hole with her daughter's coffin. She did not. Instead she climbed into an emotional crevice and Jack questioned if she'd ever return. Jack returned though, to the now. 'Paloma looked after him?'

'Yes, Paloma was given the job, but she liked doing it. She liked him, Miguel's nephew.' Donavan smiled. 'He's a good lad.'

'How old?'

'Around seven.'

Jack could well imagine Miguel taking on the father-figure role. 'How's Sofia?'

'She's okay. Flung herself back into everything here.' Donavan slowed in his walking, threw the cigarette he'd been smoking on the damp street and took another from the packet that was wedged in his outside pocket. 'I have some news.'

'Good, I hope.' Jack strode forward, distracted.

'About Joe.'

He stopped. 'Joe?'

'Yes, Joe. Your brother, remember?'

'Go on.' Joe had been a long way from Jack's mind the last weeks and a tinge of guilt overtook him.

'He's alive.'

'You've seen him?'

'No, but I hear he's staying in a village outside Barcelona. Only found out this morning. The news is all over the cafés. Joe made as many friends as he did enemies. Some are delighted, others suspicious. What do you think?'

'Haven't had time to think. Why suspicious?'

'People sit in two camps where Joe Hayes is concerned. Some think he may well have come back as a Nationalist spy.'

Jack spluttered. 'Come on!'

'It happens.'

'Sofia doesn't believe Joe could do something like that,' Jack said, pulling up his trousers; he was losing weight fast. 'Joe just turned up?'

'News travels fast. It's good news though, isn't it?'

'Course it is.' Donavan's gaze made him feel faintly uncomfortable.

'Although my feeling is,' Donavan continued, 'Joe's not going to be too happy at returning to England. By all accounts, he's regaling everyone with stories of how he was captured by the Nationalists and then managed to escape. He's enjoying the attention.'

'The hero, eh?'

'I know. I owe Joe my life but something isn't right. You don't get away from Franco's army. What if he did do a deal?'

Maybe Joe had made some sort of agreement, it was something Joe might do. But Jack believed Joe had made no deal, although he'd no idea what Joe planned on doing, and a sickness rose in his belly with the knowledge that Joe had no intention of returning to England. What would *he* do? How could he be with Sofia, and look after Alice, and the baby?

'I know what you're saying,' Jack replied, 'but I don't think even Joe's capable of that. Does Sofia know?'

'Not yet. Joe's going to be pissed off, though.'

They walked in silence back to Berneri's house. Livid probably, thought Jack, about Sofia and him.

Sofia was standing by the dining room window when the two men returned. Through the glass Jack saw the paleness of her face, its luminosity urging him forward and she was at the door and in his arms before he knew it.

She took his hand. 'How are Dr and Señora Fuente?'

He didn't lie and say they were bearing up because they weren't. What had happened at Guernica was not war, it was murder. The old market town, the symbolic centre of Basque government, had been bombed and was the truest sign yet that Franco was in Hitler's pocket. The

113

consequences of Guernica were colossal, bigger than anyone could have predicted. Within months of the atrocity, the response from the outside world would become inseparable from the response to Spain's civil war itself. The West were unable to turn a blind eye for much longer to the chaos in Spain, although they tried, taking as fact the media rhetoric of Franco's government – that it wasn't the Nationalists who'd caused the carnage on that Monday market day in the ancient town, but the Basques themselves who'd burnt their own town to the ground.

Jack finally answered. 'Not good.'

Donavan coughed.

'You should see a doctor, Michael,' Sofia said softly.

'I'm seeing no doctor.' Donavan peered towards the dining room. 'Camillo here?'

Sofia tipped her head towards the door and the three of them walked through.

Camillo Berneri was sitting in a dining chair by the window. He was a small man, with a high, prominent forehead and receding hairline. His face was as petite as his frame, with a triangular chin that ended in a slight point. He was sipping a glass of water.

'This is Jack Hayes, Camillo,' Donavan said in English.

'Jack Hayes.' His accent was heavy but his English adequate. 'Here to find your brother – Joe. And you, Jack,' he moved his head towards Sofia, as if including her in the question, 'what are you?'

'He's with us, Camillo,' Sofia said.

'With us, Sofia? Or with you?'

'With all of us.' She flashed Camillo an impatient look and that was the first time Jack saw Camillo Berneri's wry smile. Sofia lifted her head and a faint flush of pink appeared on her cheeks.

114

Jack looked directly at the Italian. 'I came to find Joe and persuade him to go home.'

'You've spent the last few weeks *not* looking for Joe. Sofia has told me everything. Your honour is unquestionable. Guernica is both a tragedy and a horror. But it is good you saw first-hand what happened.' He lowered his gaze. 'I am very sad to hear about Paloma Fuentes. Very. And Donavan likes you. As does Sofia. And so, I will too. But there are more important things to worry about at this time. Events are escalating.'

He paused for effect. His eyes swept over the room. 'Guernica is only the beginning. Franco's propaganda is obscene, but the British and French governments will believe it, as it suits them to do so.'

'With all respect, sir, the ordinary English people have no idea what's going on here in Spain,' Jack said.

'They *don't* want to know.'

Donavan intervened. 'Stop giving Jack a hard time, Camillo. He's *with* us.'

Camillo Berneri slumped back into the chair. 'You probably are, Jack.' He glanced at Sofia with fondness, pointing a slender finger. 'Take care of her and I can forgive you, and your brother, almost anything.'

Sofia sat down on the floor at Camillo's feet. 'Stop worrying.' He patted her head with fondness and she reached up to kiss him lightly on the cheek. 'You are such a dramatist!'

Donavan coughed. 'I've some news. Joe's alive. He's staying at a farm on the outskirts of Barcelona.'

Sofia jumped up. 'Ah, Michael! But why hasn't he come back here?'

'I had my doubts about Joe,' Camillo said, giving Sofia a slight shrug of his narrow shoulders.

'Camillo's a little paranoid,' Sofia said to Jack. 'About Joe.'

In Camillo's position Jack didn't think he'd have trusted Joe either. But Sofia had trusted him, as had Miguel.

'There's no reason to believe Joe made any deal,' Sofia continued. 'We should allow him at least to explain himself.'

'Joe is the least of my problems,' Camillo said. 'We need to plan. Gather around.'

As Camillo talked, Jack listened. The Spanish conflict became at once more understandable, and more complicated. At the end of Camillo's speech and thinking about Joe, Jack accepted the relationship with his brother reflected much of what was happening within the civil war, and within the Spanish families involved; one brother fighting for Franco, the other, for the Republicans. Relationships between blood relatives were as fragmented as Jack's with Joe.

After the meeting Jack made his way upstairs to change the clothes he'd been wearing for two days. He opened the door of the room that Sofia had shown him on that first night to find it tidy and clean. He'd left one change of clothes in the musty-smelling wardrobe but on opening it, saw they'd disappeared. Had Miguel used them? There did seem to be a problem with holding on to clothes in the house – only Sofia had more than two outfits.

Throwing his stuff onto the bed, he opened his bag and then heard a rustle.

'Looking for these?' Sofia said. The clothes from the wardrobe hung over her arm.

'They didn't need washing,' he said with a smile.

'I know.' She grinned. 'I haven't washed them. I'm not your mother, Jack. I've moved you into my room. Together with your clothes.' The grin slid from her face. 'Although I'd rather you weren't wearing any at the moment.'

That's what Jack loved about her. The honesty, the freedom she oozed. Nothing had happened between Sofia and Joe, he knew that. And if Sofia were sticking up for Joe, then the rumours about him *must* be wrong; this was a war and the fear, the uncertainty, made everyone question everything.

She pulled him towards her room and they heard noise downstairs but didn't care. Jack took his clothes, which hung over her arm, and threw them on the floor. Picking her up, he laid her gently on the bed.

That night, they were not draped in the pain of Guernica, and he would have been lying to himself if he'd said he hadn't given any thought to Sofia's past, and the loves of that past. but Jack felt, and felt it intrinsically, that Sofia and Joe's relationship had been no more than flirtatiously platonic.

And this feeling was consolidated when Jack discovered he was Sofia's first love; something he knew long before he felt her body's warmth enclosing him.

21

The next day was the first of Jack's life that he woke up next to Sofia. She rolled over and moulded herself to his body, although as he stroked her forehead he found himself worrying about someone knowing they'd shared the same room, the same bed. Sofia had no care for such things and Jack loved that.

On hearing a heavy knock on the door, Sofia turned over. 'Come in,' she said, and as Donavan poked his head into the room Jack covered her breasts. She kicked him under the covers. 'Michael doesn't mind naked women.'

'I'm sure he doesn't.'

'Ah, there you are.' Donavan looked at them. 'You two staying tucked up all day?'

Jack swung his legs from the bed, pulling on the trousers that lay on the floor from the night before, and then sat on the edge of the bed. Donavan walked to the open window and lit a cigarette. Sofia, and with no embarrassment at all, put on a worn-looking, multi-coloured silk dressing gown, all vibrant reds, daffodil yellows, and bluebell blues. Donavan didn't flick an eyelid. Sofia joined Donavan at the window, took the cigarette from his hand, puffed and coughed.

Donavan carried on. 'So what's the plan for today?'

'It's time to take Jack to meet Kitty Markham.' Sofia handed the cigarette back to Donavan.

'Ah, the delectable Kitty,' Donavan replied.

'You'll like her, Jack,' Sofia said.

'I'm sure I will.'

'And you, Michael, what are your plans?' Sofia asked, sitting back down on the bed.

'Out to find two things today. Some decent food.' He smiled at her. 'Thought we could cook a special dinner for Camillo this evening. Miguel's volunteered.'

'And the second?' Sofia probed.

'Find out where the bloody hell Joe is. And bring him back before we leave for Albacete.'

'That should be my job,' Jack intervened.

'I know my way around. Leave this one with me.' Donavan walked towards the door and pushed it open. 'You go and meet Kitty. That'll be an education in itself, trust me.'

A skinny boy waited outside. 'Come in.' Gently, Donavan guided him into the bedroom.

Sofia immediately enveloped the boy. 'Has Miguel been keeping you busy?' she said to him in Spanish.

The boy nodded. '*Sí. ¿hoy voy con Donavan?*'

'He wants to come with me, is that what he said?' Donavan asked.

'Yes,' Sofia said. 'Look after him, and not too many bars, please.'

The boy's face cracked open in a wide grin and Jack suspected he understood more than Donavan gave him credit for.

Only Miguel remained at the house, and he was busy in the out-building that held his kiln and guitar. Either Miguel was cooking, making pots or strumming his guitar.

Jack stayed in the kitchen with Sofia, who was sitting cross-legged on the floor. She pulled her colourful oversized trousers upwards above sand-brown knees and something primal jerked inside him. 'So tell me more about Kitty,' he asked.

'She's a journalist. I met her at the beginning of the war, while I was working at the Catalan Generalitat. She's the sort of woman I'd wish to be like. I admire her.'

'Why do you want me to meet her? Although I can't wait to.' Jack had read many of Kitty Markham's articles. She was a popular columnist amongst the lads at the local ILA office, despite being a woman, and American.

'She knows Joe. She's more astute than me.'

Jack laughed. 'You have some nous, Sofia, I'd say.'

She screwed up her forehead.

'You know what you're doing,' he explained.

'I want you to meet her. She's my best friend. She's clever, writes articles for a New York newspaper. She has articles published in your English *Manchester Guardian* newspaper too. She knows everything, everyone.'

'I know about her articles, but Donavan tells me it's you who knows everything,' he said, trying to keep a straight face.

'I try to know everything, but I don't, and sometimes you know, I'm . . . *demasiado cerca*, too close. But it's dynamic women like Kitty who've helped me understand more about the politics of my own country.' She rubbed his shin with her foot.

'I was only joking. I look forward to meeting Kitty Markham.'

'She doesn't live far from here. She has a very nice apartment.'

'A real communist, eh?'

'Don't be sarcastic. She has a very influential lover.'

'And who is that?'

'The Spanish prime minister's nephew.'

'Ah, of course.'

She poked him in the ribs.

Kitty Markham was the most flamboyant of communists.

Kitty's, or more truthfully her lover's, apartment, was situated in San Jaume square, which Sofia pointed out was the political centre of Barcelona. As with many of the buildings around the area, the prime minister's nephew's apartment was suffering from the result of the huge pigeon population. It was covered in their shit.

Sofia pushed the main door open and together they walked up a flight of stairs. They approached an apartment door and Sofia opened it.

'Don't people knock in Spain?' he said.

'I don't knock with Kitty.' She was already striding through the enormous and grand hallway. Jack had never seen such opulence.

'Kitty! You home? Someone I'd like you to meet.' Her voice bounced back from the walls and tall ceilings.

Jack heard a movement somewhere within the depths of the cavernous space.

Like a young child, Sofia flounced from room to room.

Finally a door opened and a woman appeared. 'Sofia! I didn't know you were back. Been a little worried about you. I was just about to break my own rule and ask Federico to do some asking around for me.'

Kitty Markham's thick blonde hair surrounded a pale, almost alabaster-like complexion. A wide forehead, a slim but slightly uneven shaped nose. Small blue eyes. Taken on their own none of these features were particularly pretty, but put together she became a very handsome woman. Jack couldn't put an age to Kitty Markham.

Sofia ran towards her, almost jumping into her arms. Kitty held her tight.

'And who's this?' Gently, Kitty pushed Sofia away and peered at Jack. 'Ah, at last, I see the flower has opened?'

'Kitty, this is Jack.'

Kitty pulled a wrap around a curvy body. Large breasts were prominent under the silk fabric. 'I approve.'

'Kitty!' Sofia said.

'How did you two meet?' Kitty asked.

'Michael found him on a ship coming from England and brought him to Camillo's.'

'How is the demented Donavan?' Kitty's face became solemn. 'Is he recovered?'

'He's well,' Sofia said.

'Excellent.' Kitty lifted her chin.

'Kitty, Jack is Joe's brother. Jack came to Spain to find him.'

'Then I don't approve.' She turned to Jack. 'You're different from your brother.'

'I like to think so,' he replied.

The three of them moved to the kitchen where coffee was brewing on the stove; the smell bitter and strong.

Kitty continued. 'I tried to tell you, Sofia, about Joe Hayes. I've been around for too long not to know his type.'

'What *type* of man *is* my brother?' Jack asked, leaning against the wall.

'Disgruntled. Lost. Confused. A loose cannon. The potential to become dangerous.' Her American accent became more pronounced. 'I'm a New Yorker. A journalist. I know a decaying apple when I see one. Federico's been ferreting around for me, regarding Joe's disappearance. He's found out very little, only stories of betrayal on both sides.' She directed her words to both Sofia and Jack. 'It might be time to leave Barcelona, Sofia. Maybe with Jack?'

'Joe's back. He's in Barcelona,' Sofia said. 'And . . . I'm not leaving the city.'

'Ah, I see. No matter. I think it is time for you to leave. Federico is as worried about you as I am.' She placed her hands on her hips. 'I knew Joe would turn up. Like a bad penny.'

'Kitty, stop it. You never did like him.' Sofia mirrored Kitty's posture, her hands grabbing at her hips too. 'I'm not going anywhere. And Jack and I have only just met, Kitty.'

'So? I met Federico on the Saturday, I was living here on the Sunday.'

'I'm not like you, Kits.'

'Thank God, eh?' Her laugh was loud, infectious and a bit dirty. Her hand moved to Jack's hip and dropped downward, touched the lower part of his inner thigh. She rubbed it fondly, as a mother would fondle the head of an errant child. Jack could never work out how she managed to do that with no sexual innuendo whatsoever. He liked Kitty Markham.

Sofia rolled her eyes with affection at her outrageous friend, but her expression quickly became serious. 'Things aren't good, are they?'

'Are you referring to the mess of the Russians interfering with Republican ideals, or Joe?' Each hand was now wedged on her rounded hips.

'The Russian problem. I'm not sure about Joe yet,' Sofia replied.

'I've met too many *Joes* in my life. But concerning this bloody war, Federico tells me the prime minister is, if only in private, worried. The Russian communists are tightening their grip on Republican interests. Despite the protection I might have enjoyed by sleeping with the prime minister's nephew, it is ending. I'm on the top of Franco's list of *undesirable* journalists.' She laughed, 'And of course, I'm a woman. And American.'

Sofia's expression darkened. 'Maybe it's you who should be leaving, Kitty?'

'Maybe.' Kitty said to Jack, 'Where you staying?'

'With Donavan and Sofia,' he replied.

'Thought so.' Kitty's eyes sparkled in the noonday sun that was making its way through a large, cracked window.

Sofia kicked her friend lightly on the ankle.

Jack was glad he'd met Kitty because he felt by meeting someone close to Sofia he came a bit nearer to really understanding her, and Kitty was one of those characters who you could never forget; someone who got under the skin. Someone you'd do things for. She inspired and shocked, although Jack did wonder why Sofia had taken him to see Kitty. It took him a while to realise he'd been vetted.

However, as they made their way through Barcelona's streets Jack's mind turned to Joe.

It was time to see him.

When they returned, Donavan and the boy were back too, and with enough chorizo to feed everyone. Donavan mumbled that he'd circled the city twice looking for it. Miguel whisked his nephew off, along with the food, and disappeared into the kitchen to prepare dinner.

'But *have* you found Joe?' Sofia asked Donavan.

'Harder to find than the food.' Donavan smiled wanly. 'What do you think of Kitty?' he asked.

'I find her wonderful,' Jack replied.

Donavan nodded in affirmation but was obviously distracted. 'I've been into Catalunya Square. There's unrest in the city since the reshuffle within the Catalan government. The post of "Minister of Justice" has been given to a Spanish communist.'

'That's good, though?' Jack asked.

'Should be, but he's in the back pocket of the Russians.'

'That is *not* good,' Sofia interrupted.

Donavan shook his head. 'There's talk of cancelling the May Day parades.' He rummaged in his pocket and pulled out an empty packet of cigarettes; he threw it on the floor, crushing it with his foot. 'Talk they will disband the International Brigades too.'

Donavan was clearly dying for a cigarette. Jack opened a drawer where he was sure he'd seen a spare packet. It was still there. Jack handed one to him, Donavan lit it.

'Any news about Joe?'

'I've met up with him,' Donavan said, glancing at Sofia first.

Sofia rose, picked up the cigarette packet, took one out. 'And?'

'Full of it,' Donavan replied.

She flicked her head back. 'Where did he go, and more importantly, how did he get back – if the Nationalists captured him?'

'You don't know if that's what happened,' Jack said quietly.

'It *did* happen. He was captured, Jack,' Donavan explained.

'Did he make a deal with the Nationalists, Michael, do you think?' Sofia asked.

'A Nationalist soldier who was guarding Joe – his grandmother was English – so it seems Joe used his charm and *Englishness*, and the soldier turned a blind eye when Joe escaped – that's Joe's story.'

'*Que son tan credulous.*' Both men both looked at her. 'You're so gullible,' Sofia repeated. 'There's absolutely no way they would let him go. You know that, Michael.'

'I'm not so sure,' Jack said.

'There's a side to your brother you can't understand.' She stroked his hand. 'You're two different creatures, *muy differente*,' she repeated in Spanish.

Donavan intervened. 'You're being harsh, Sofia. Joe's story does seem implausible, but you have to hand it to him, he could pull it off. Has the luck of the Irish. Joe wants to meet up with you,' he finished.

'Have you told him about Jack?' Sofia asked.

'Not yet. He doesn't know Jack's in Spain.'

'Michael, you'll take me to him. Let me meet him first, alone. I need to explain to Joe, about you,' Sofia said, looking at Jack.

'I'm coming with you,' Jack said.

'For the love of Mary, we'll all go,' Donavan said. 'He's staying in Sants. We'll get a lift there.'

PART TWO

22

Near Balmaseda

Isabella

May 1976

On the return journey from Dominica Zubiri's home a pregnant Cristina, although still obviously affected by the tragedy of Dominica's story, was effervescent . I'd known Cristina for such a short time but length of time did not always equate to depth of understanding. I admired her for having no guilt becoming pregnant before marriage. To me, it signalled her strength of character. I'd met many Catholic Spanish girls in the same position but who did not share Cristina's enlightened disposition, or probably more truthfully, the compassionate awareness of those close to her. Occasionally parents stood by their pregnant daughters, but often did not.

I'd researched reports related to the megalomaniacal Franco and which were emerging simultaneously alongside the whispers regarding his war crimes. His dictatorship had taken a swift iron grip on Spain, interfering with every aspect of life, from the banning of the Euskardi language in the Basque region to reducing the number of 'bastards' being born in Franco's 'perfect' Spain. The dictator had hoped to alleviate the problem of illegitimacy by sending the pregnant girls to a convent for the birth; the baby was then adopted by upper-class Franco supporters. In most cases this was done without the consent of the mother, and often, without the consent of the grandparents either.

There were no official written records of the adoptions and so the biological mothers had no way of tracing their babies. It was a scandal that had been covered up by Franco and the Church. When I'd first investigated I discovered that many of the adopted children suffered with various hereditary medical conditions. The adopted parents, who were not monsters, had then come clean about the adoptions, hoping that by finding the biological parents they would then be able to help their ill children.

Still now, the story wasn't common knowledge and simmered in the background of post-Franco Spain. As I watched Cristina humming happily I knew I'd revisit the story again, because I wanted to ensure girls who weren't as fortunate as Cristina would always have a choice. I liked to think that was why I felt Cristina's lightness inside the car – because she felt exceptionally safe with her situation.

Rafael though had clung on to a gloomier mood, and I wondered if it was unconnected to recent events, or the murder of Dominica Zubiri's aunt, but linked instead to seeing Dominica Zubiri. I'd seen the light that shone in her eyes when she talked to Rafael. It was radiant. I'd seen too, the reciprocating warmth and gentleness in Rafael's expression when he spoke to Dominica.

The journey back to Miguel's was turning out to be tortuous, last night's rain causing small localised floods of the narrow valley road. Cristina's chatter had died down and Rafael's silence and broody reflection, together with the easiness between him and Dominica Zubiri were like iron nails wedged into the sole of my foot.

'You and Dominica seem close,' I said, although staring ahead onto the road and not at Rafael.

He didn't answer immediately but his knuckles whitened as his grip on the steering wheel tightened. 'I have known Dominica since childhood. She married a man I recommended she did not marry.'

'But she *chose* to marry him,' I replied. 'Did you want to marry Dominica?' I heard Cristina's supressed gasp in the back seat of the Citroën.

'I offered to marry Dominica when she told me she was pregnant.'

'With your child?' The ribs inside my chest rattled with the rapid beating of my heart.

'No, Isabella. Gorane Zubiri's child.'

'Her husband? I don't understand.'

'You should not make assumptions. Things are often not how your perception reveals them to you.'

Air rushed into the car as Cristina wound down her window.

'Tell me, Rafael,' I said.

'Do you need to know?' He turned to me.

'I do.'

His eyes travelled back to the road. 'Gorane Zubiri all but raped Dominica, and then when he discovered she was pregnant, and suffering it would seem a belated guilt, he offered marriage. I told her she did not have to marry him and I would marry her. She turned down my offer because she did not turn down her responsibilities to her child. And, she would not take my charity.'

'Do you love her?' I'd said it. I could not believe I was saying it.

'Like a sister.'

'I'm sorry.'

He did not turn again, his line of vision resolutely fixed on the road. 'I am sorry too, Isabella. For all of the mistakes I have made . . . since being very young. I wanted to help Dominica.' He paused and the car slowed. 'I wanted to do the right thing.'

Silence fell within the confined space of the car, although it was a serene quietness.

When we neared Miguel's it was Cristina who broke it. She began to sing.

I loved Cristina already.

I went to freshen up and time in the bathroom gave me the freedom to consider what Rafael had told me. I would not ask more. I knew enough, and guilt filtered through me about Dominica Zubiri. Cristina had told me, out of Rafael's earshot, that Dominica had been only sixteen when she fell pregnant. Dominica was younger than I'd thought, the weariness of her life having added the years. *There was conjecture*, Cristina had said, *about Dominica's stance on Gorane Zubiri's assault. But only sixteen*, Cristina had whispered. *Just a child.*

All my clothes were so grimy and needed washing. In silence Rafael had given me one of his old shirts to wear; an olive branch, I think. He had smiled as he'd handed it to me.

On putting it on, it was as long as a dress, its hem sitting an inch below my knees, but I liked the colour, a vibrant blue, and which I knew matched near perfectly the colour of my eyes. Had Rafael chosen it because of that fact, I asked myself as I viewed my reflection in the bathroom's tiny mirror. Was it too short? I yanked it down again before leaving the room.

I went to sit next to Cristina on the sofa and inside Miguel's warm home a silent and unspoken agreement settled, that none of us would speak of anything which might make us sad. Even Rafael had relaxed, his earlier solemnity dissipated. Perhaps Tomás and Cristina wanted to evade thinking about the world into which their child would be born; Rafael wanting to allow his conflict surrounding Dominica to fade, perhaps contemplating of how he was going to approach the problem of the chief of police of Guipúzcoa and the missing itinerary. Miguel trying not to think about something that had happened many years before, but which still bothered him.

And me. I wanted to think about a father who, up until the last week, I hadn't known existed, and perhaps a father who would want to know *I* existed. A father who could tell me about my mother. This was what brought a lightness to me.

Miguel and Tomás had been busy while we'd been with Dominica. We had returned to a feast.

'I'm teaching Tomás to cook,' Miguel said, his face a chilli red. 'I want him to be a modern husband.'

'I don't want a modern husband, Miguel,' Cristina replied. 'And, I don't want food poisoning.'

Tomás pushed Miguel from the kitchen area, a strong smell of fish following him.

'What are we eating?' I said.

'Cod,' Miguel said.

'Surely you don't find cod in the river?' I said.

'*Chica de ciudad*! *Baccalau*, it's salted. It doesn't need to be fresh. You really are a city-girl.' He tapped my knee. 'Sofia taught your father this recipe.' Going back in time inside his head a smile appeared on his face. 'But then, during the civil war, she didn't use cod, couldn't get hold of it.'

'What did she use?' I asked.

'Beans, chickpeas, always beans or chickpeas with every-thing. Occasionally rabbit. Sofia was good on the black market. She could find rabbit when no one else could. A legend.'

I was desperate to ask more, but thought about the easiness of the atmosphere and didn't want Miguel to feel he had to talk about my mother.

'Go get your guitar, Miguel,' Rafael said as if sensing my thoughts.

Miguel disappeared into his bedroom, returning with a battered-looking instrument. 'After supper, I will play.'

'*Bravo*!' Cristina said.

The cod tasted like nothing my taste buds had experi-enced before, the sting of bitterness, the enveloping sugges-tion of sweetness – all in one mouthful. I glanced into the kitchen space where the remnants of herb plants were scattered over the confined worktops, together with other culinary secrets. But I was no cook and wouldn't know where to start sourcing good ingredients; I was only able to find good restaurants.

The smell of food, the feeling of warmth, both emotional and physical, the effects of the anise at once dulling and exhilarating my senses made my apartment and life in Barcelona seem a long way away. It was if I was sliding around in a bubble that itself slid on the tenuous surface of life. A slide on a slide.

I looked at Rafael who reclined in his chair, his eyes closed, his thick dark lashes, which with his neck bent forwards, lay on anise-pink cheeks. For the first time since I'd met him I sensed Rafael's muscles loosen. Then his eyes opened, his features settling into an uncluttered expression and his gaze rested on me.

Cristina asked for more vegetables and I rose from my chair to get some from the pot on the stove. Miguel had been right, Cristina's craving for them was indeed gargantuan. I swayed, knowing I was halfway to becoming drunk and this did not bother me. Rafael saw the sway and lightly touched my bare thigh as I passed by him and the beautiful shock that ran through me took away a breath.

An hour later and Miguel sat and played, beginning with traditional Basque music, but as he loosened, his playing relaxed into mainstream Spanish. He then strummed the famous Eva Peron songs and Cristina sang. The music, the anise and wine, the easy company, made my body soften in the way it did whenever I thought of dancing.

Cristina stopped singing and I stood, the music too much to bear, too enticing. I'd been brought up in France, but by a Spanish woman who adored the flamenco; it had been Calida who'd taught and encouraged me to dance. By the time I was sixteen I'd travelled to Spain several times to competitions in Madrid. I'd even won a few. I could never have been the best of the best, and had no wish to be; I only loved to dance. It brought sensuality to my life that was missing in sexual relationships. I craved for love and sex to give me what dancing brought to me. They never had. I looked at Rafael. He moved to the very edge of his chair.

Sensing what my body craved Miguel increased the tempo. Earlier his guitar playing had been jovial; now it became as sensual as I silently demanded. Before I lost myself completely I glanced at Tomás and Cristina. They watched, their faces spread in anticipation.

As muscles lengthened, my body allowed the *dancers' void* to envelop me. My hips became things not belonging, my shoulders twisting slowly in the opposite direction. I lifted a leg and slowly it found its first step on the stone floor. A stamp as I swivelled, a rapid turn of my head. Hips rotating languidly to the rhythm, I allowed the music to show me the way. My head turned in a controlled snap, and I found Rafael's face. His expression soft yet expectant, pupils dilated. I made the few steps towards where he sat. And as Rafael's long blue shirt floated near to his face, he took hold of it gently and pulled. For a moment I held my position, bent forwards and ran my finger along the scar on his forehead. Forgetting about the others, forgetting everything as the smooth pulse of desire that had been building from the moment I had set eyes on him raged through my waiting body. I pulled at his fingers, freeing my blouse and giving the music permission to take me across the small space of the room.

Miguel worked the magic of the acoustic guitar. Gradually the beat and tempo increased and I danced. Feeling droplets of sweat run like tears down my chest, the music took me away, removing me from where I was, away from each person in the room. Apart from Rafael. The sound held my hand, taking me to a place where all seemed perfect and I knew it was a place where Rafael waited.

And that was always when I was solidly inside the void, near to the end, when nothing existed only the thumping beat, the raw energy, the infinity of music. Lorca called it the duende; he described it as something that surged upwards, climbing through you. The dance was never only the technical ability of the dancer; the dance relied heavily on the dancer's spontaneous creativity too.

The Dance was a magical spirit that possessed you.

Miguel's guitar eased its rampage of depletion, and the dance, as it always did, came to an end. My eyes had been closed and when finally I opened them, I moved a finger to my cheek and as I felt the warm sweat between my breasts cooling, I felt the hotness of tears. Feeling as if there wasn't enough oxygen inside my body or the room. I looked around the small space. Tomás and Cristina were not where I'd left them ten minutes before. I glanced at Miguel, and he nodded towards his bedroom. They'd left before I had finished. Flamenco music had that effect on lovers.

Miguel rose. 'It's been a long day, for me anyway.' He took my scorching hand and placed it on his lips. 'That was quite beautiful, Isabella. And accomplished.' He smiled. 'Not bad for a girl brought up in France.'

'And you, a dark horse, such great guitar playing. You do know that the dancer is only as good as the music?'

'Some things I do well, *niña*.' He yawned and placed the guitar on the floor, then walked towards the door and opened it, a glint of humour in his eyes. 'The weather has cleared, the stars are bright tonight, like Isabella's dancing. A perfect evening to sleep outside, my friends.' He turned and made his way to the bathroom.

Rafael hadn't spoken. I looked at him as he rose from his chair, still not speaking. Moving towards me he put his arm around my shoulder; I was acutely aware of the cold dampness of my shirt, the faint odour of dancing sweat.

He pulled me closer and took a breath. 'You smell like life, Isabella. Real life. A life I want to be a part of. Of which I've always been a part.'

His sentence I didn't understand and I wanted to ask him what he meant, but then he found my lips and I felt his strength as he pulled me into the hardness of his body. The void devoured me again.

Rafael gathered our sleeping bags and blankets and together we stumbled outside towards the Freedom Tree. And not feeling the bitter cold, the sharpness of the wind, Rafael unbuttoned the shirt that had been my flamenco dress. It hung open as he pressed my bare stomach into the wiry jumper he wore. I pulled away, tugged the coarse fabric upwards, and he swept me into his arms as if I were a china doll. He laid me down beneath the tree and slipped off the shirt, covered my body, which should have been cold but was not. I looked up to him, thinking of the moment, only a week before, when I'd first seen him. I had thought what I'd felt was pure desire, but as he took off his trousers and slipped underneath the blanket with me, scraped the hair from my face and looked into my eyes, I knew this was untrue. Could you fall in love so quickly, so easily? As his face moved towards my neck, and lower, as I felt ripples of need flow through me like undulating waves, I knew you could. He kissed me. Stroked me, sent electric currents over every inch of my skin but I couldn't wait. I pushed his palm down hard towards me, impatient. He caught his breath and like the imperceptible turn in the dance, he was consumed. I held his face in cool hands as he sank deeper and as the surge of ecstasy filled every part of me I found an end that surpassed any dance, and any end. My hands gripped and clawed on skin like hot stone and I sensed a release stronger than my own and knowing this, my own rolled through me.

The canopy above us was a desert sky and a long time after loving him, in between him playfully licking my earlobe, Rafael pointed out the vibrant constellations. It made me laugh, our post-lovemaking astronomy lesson. And that was the thing about Rafael; a man with love, with purpose, an underlying sadness that mirrored my own, but he could make me laugh.

For the remainder of my life I would remember that night as the night I became truly conscious, truly aware. Truly myself.

23

Five days had passed and it felt like five months. Since the dance Rafael and I had been inseparable. It was happening too quickly and yet not quickly enough. I trusted Rafael immediately and unconditionally. I admitted I lusted for him, desired him and had done so from first setting eyes on the nephew of the man who had known my mother, but there was much more to the diaphanous connection between us.

The previous day Rafael and Tomás had returned to the house in Balmaseda and brought everything Cristina would need to stay at Miguel's. Rafael was sharing very little with Tomás, who baulked against being kept in the dark, becoming petulant for a few hours, although, being Tomás, he couldn't keep it up for long. Only Miguel and I knew of Rafael's plan – to travel to Irun and meet with the man who'd ordered the ransack of his home, and who sought to take full control of an organisation which together he and Rafael had both nurtured from the beginning; but an organisation from which Rafael now wished to disassociate himself.

It wasn't yet nine, and the morning was cool and damp. Cristina and Tomás had left earlier with Miguel to hunt for rabbits. Miguel had decided to cook rabbit stew, intending to show me how Sofia had made her famous gravy. Everything Miguel recounted about my mother was benign and uncontroversial, and I think he did this on purpose, drawing a real picture of my mother for me. Whenever over the last few days I'd asked questions about Sofia's early life Miguel always seemed to find a diversion.

Rafael and I were sitting on Miguel's sofa, and knowing Miguel was unable, or unwilling, to tell me about Sofia, I decided to question Rafael more deeply about the movement he'd been so heavily involved with, and for so many years.

'You must have been aware where it all might go?' I asked.

'You never know how your newborn will turn out to be, *querida*.' He smiled with satisfaction at his metaphor. 'No, I never thought it would go in the direction it has. Violence was never part of the agenda . . . at least I'd thought. But it seems it was only me and a few others who envisaged a peaceful independence from Madrid.'

I moved and sat on the floor at his feet, my hand rubbing the compact muscle of his calf. 'Tell me more about your life.'

He loosened the top button of his shirt. 'My mother had been unwell before the civil war, but she worsened, and by then my father had been killed during Franco's annihilation of Granada. In early 1937, Miguel took his sister – my mother – to a nursing home in Irun. I was around seven and Miguel sent me to live with a family he trusted to look after me, as he wasn't able to during the war.'

His chronic grief was worn hard onto his features, a part of him, like the scar on his forehead. I wondered which gash had occurred first.

'I'm so sorry.'

'It was a long time ago. And Miguel has been like a father to me.'

140

'During the war, before she went to the nursing home, were you with your mother, or with Miguel?'

He turned his head away and fixed his eyes on the wall. 'Rafael?'

'During the war I was in Irun, with the family Miguel had left me with.'

I moved my hand and took hold of his chin, turning his face towards mine. He smiled the saddest of smiles and I could not bear it.

'You're no youth,' I said, trying to lighten his mood. 'As I'm not so young myself.'

'You are ageless, *querida*.' Now his smile was real and not sad, and that had been my aim.

'I have to admit, I do feel less old since being here.'

'I have that effect.' He grinned.

'On women?'

He moved closer, pulled me towards him and I lay my head on his lap.

'Dominica and I were never romantically involved . . . but there have been women.' He stroked my cheek. 'But no one important, until I saw you, ag—' He stopped speaking, but then carried on, 'And your first words reprimanding me, about Cristina.' Again he paused. 'I want you to be part of my life, Isabella.'

I tilted my head. 'This is all too quick but I do not care.' I closed my eyes, thinking of the questions I wanted to ask but deciding instead on humour. 'How old *are* you, Rafael?'

'Forty-six. An old man.'

'Eight years older than me. You don't look that ancient.'

'You are biased.'

'I think I am.' I flipped onto my back. Thirty-eight. Too old to have children. Calida was always reminding me.

'Tell me about the man who broke into your house.'

He moved his hand to my chest, cupped my breast. 'Isabella, the time has come that I leave the movement and break the ties with the man who was once my friend.'

'They, and he, will never let you go, Rafael. Not alive, anyway.' Just saying this, my blood turned cooler.

'Ah, *querida*, there is always a way. And I shall find it.'

I wanted him to cease his involvement but worried for the consequences. There could be no easy divorce.

A blast of cool air entered the room. Miguel, Tomás and Cristina had returned, a rabbit hanging over each of Tomás's shoulders.

'A few hours and food will be ready,' Miguel said, his face crimson from being outdoors.

As Miguel cooked, and with no cajoling needed from me, more of my mother's story unwound; the hunt for the rabbits had loosened him up. He told me about when he'd first met her in Barcelona at Camillo Berneri's house, he told me about their trip to Bilbao, he told me about her vivaciousness and beauty.

'Sofia was like you, *niña*, beautiful, on the inside and the out. It was no surprise Jack fell for her, none at all. Everyone did.' He looked up as he began skinning the second rabbit. 'And not just the men, women loved her too.' Expertly, he hacked off the rabbits' feet and I looked away.

I was aware of the bohemianism which permeated throughout Barcelona and Madrid in the years leading up to the civil war, and from what Calida had told me, my mother had been a part of that world. Hemingway had been mentioned and Sofia had stayed a weekend in Madrid with La Pasionaria. When I was growing up, Calida would sometimes shake her head when I did or said something unusual, saying I was just like my mother. I was not like my mother. She (in my head) was a free spirit in a way that I was never destined to be. I glanced at Rafael who sat in the corner of the room, deep in thought.

'My mother was popular?'

'Absolutely,' Miguel replied.

'What more is there I should know about Sofia?' I asked softly.

Miguel's demeanour changed, reminding me of Calida's manner when I asked too much about my mother. Over the last five days and knowing what she had kept from me, I was beginning to think Calida's silence on the matter of my past covered some sort of culpability.

'I was young,' Miguel said. 'Not much younger than Sofia, but less mature. I didn't really understand a lot of what was happening then. Though close to me, Sofia kept things from me. She protected me, as she tried to protect Calida, Aurelio and . . .' He glanced at Rafael.

'Protect them from the war? No one could protect them from that, not even my mother.'

'Not from the war directly.' Miguel stroked the rabbit's amputated paw. 'But from your grandfather.'

'My grandfather?'

He shook himself, made a decision. 'Your grandfather was insane, *niña*. And probably still is.'

'Tell me *something*, Miguel. *Please.*'

'Jack came to Spain in 1937, initially, to find his brother.'

'Jack has a brother?' My family grew.

Miguel nodded and at the periphery of the room Rafael's body jolted to attention.

'Yes, Joe. Joe came with the first wave of brigaders in the autumn of 1936. He went missing at the Battle of Jarama in February 1937.'

And more.

143

'Sofia and Joe had enjoyed a friendship. I knew Sofia. It was only a friendship with Joe, but then the rumours began.' He looked up. 'Then Jack turned up.'

'Was Joe found? What rumours?' I asked.

'Oh yes, Joe was found, but by then Sofia was with Jack. Joe wasn't happy about that.' He stopped talking and sat on the small stool. 'I didn't realise until a long time afterwards, how unhappy.' Miguel's voice had lowered with talk of Joe. There was more to know here and perhaps the part of the story that gave Miguel the haunted look that was never far from the surface. 'The rumours . . . how Joe had managed to escape the Nationalists, when all of his comrades had not.' In a jerky movement he stood, moving quickly as if shedding any more memories.

I stood, stepped closer to him but then felt Rafael's warm hand on my elbow as he gently pulled me back, shaking his head at Miguel.

'Let us allow Miguel to cook,' Rafael said. He took in Cristina too. 'The three of us will go out, walk along the stream. Work up an appetite for the famous stew.'

As usual it was Cristina who lightened the dulling atmosphere. 'All this talk of the past is necessary, I know, and important, but perhaps Miguel has no wish to talk about it today?'

Miguel grunted.

Cristina was right. I'd pursue Miguel about Joe later.

We began our stroll along the stream and my preoccupation with Joe ceased as Cristina suddenly stopped walking, groaned, clutched her stomach, and fell to her knees.

24

Barcelona

Jack

MAY 1ST 1937

Jack had never been scared of Joe. But as he, together
with Donavan and Sofia, left for Sants to meet his older
brother, and as he looked up into the perfect Barcelona
sky with sun flooding through low-lying clouds, a feeling
of hesitancy streamed through him. It wasn't until they
were nearly at their destination he realised the feeling
wasn't hesitancy at all, but a gnawing feeling of fear. Fear
of what Joe's reaction to Sofia and him, together, would
be. Joe'd be livid, because he'd see it as Jack treading on
his toes, interfering in his life. Joe had always hated him
doing that, and Jack admitted to himself, he did do it. And
Jack thought of Alice.

It had been five months since he'd seen his brother,
and Joe had changed. That bloody bravado attitude hadn't
altered, Jack saw that as soon as he walked into the café and
before Joe saw him, but physically Joe was different; his
clothes hung from what had once been a rounded frame.
His high and wide forehead remained the same but his
face was gaunt. He even looked shorter, and an obvious

curve had appeared in his spine. Looking across the café, Jack hardly recognised him and then fleetingly a flutter of family pride wafted through him: Joe'd gone to fight the Nationalists, had done what he'd set out to do.

His brother was sitting at a large round table in the corner surrounded by both women and men. There was something about him, an almost feminine bearing that oddly, never failed to catch the attention of the opposite sex. Although Jack noticed the men were as enthralled with his conversation as the women. He guessed Joe was telling war stories.

Joe had been engrossed in conversation until he saw Sofia. Jack wasn't sure if he'd seen him and, if he had, Joe made no acknowledgement. Indifferently, he got up and made his way towards Jack and Sofia. His eyes never left Sofia.

'Sofia, my beautiful communist.' His words as slick as oil. 'Donavan said you were back in Barcelona, safe and well. How are you, my love?' He kissed her on the cheek.

'I'm fine, Joe. How are *you*?' Sofia replied.

'Good. Alive.' He brushed at his coat with both hands, as though emphasising his presence. 'Are you happy to see me alive?' As he finished the last words, he turned his head a fraction and finally looked at Jack. 'Hello, brother. Bit of a surprise, to say the least. What brings you here?'

Donavan had been talking with friends outside, but was now inside the café and walking towards them.

Jack watched his brother, who was acting as if he were sitting in a local pub and they hadn't seen each other for a week. He heard himself grunt. Words deserted him.

'Come on, let us sit down,' Sofia said, moving towards Joe's table. She whispered something into the ear of one of the girls and within moments they all jumped up. Jack, Sofia and Donavan sat down.

'I came to find you, Joe,' Jack said. 'Mum's been worried sick. We were told you were missing, maybe dead. I came to find you and take you home.'

Joe laughed so loudly that the people surrounding them stopped talking.

'You rescuing me, like you al'ys like to do? Rescuing me from sommat I've no need to be rescued from?' Joe's eyes darted to Jack's hand holding Sofia's. His newly thinned face sucked in, vacuumed from the inside, cheeks more hollowed, if that were possible.

Joe continued quietly. 'Please, don't tell me, you two are fucking?'

Donavan banged the table hard with his hand; the drinks trembled, only just managing to stay upright. 'Joe, you stupid bastard, what the hell's wrong with you?'

'Yes.' Sofia squeezed Jack's wrist and looked at Joe. 'We are indeed *fucking*, as you so delightfully put it, Joe.'

Jack could have belted Donavan as he began to laugh uncontrollably. 'Bloody hell, Sofia, glad I don't have to take you home to Ireland.'

Her full lips lifted. 'I think the likelihood of you taking *any* woman home, Michael, is highly unlikely, don't you?'

'Touché!' Donavan replied in a genuinely sanguine tone.

She rubbed Donavan's arm.

'There was nothing between you and Sofia. Nothing,' Jack said, watching Joe.

'Is that what she's told you? Well, Jack, d'ya believe her?' his brother replied.

'I know.' Jack wanted to mention Alice. Did Joe know? Know that she was pregnant? His insides imploded. He wanted to get up, go to the cramped toilet on the other side of the café. Instead, he took a deep breath.

Sofia remained silent.

147

'What, and you think Sofia wants you?' Years of loathing crept onto Joe's features. Day upon day of collected hatred. Why did Joe feel this way about him? *Maybe it's me.*

'I'm with Sofia, and that's all there is to it,' Jack said. 'What about Alice?' *Joe bloody well knew.*

'What *about* Alice? How is she, Jack?' He laid his hand on Sofia's knee. 'Has he told you 'bout Alice? My girlfriend and Jack are very close, aren't you, Jack? Off together all the time. You show her your writing, don't you, brother? Very cosy.' Sofia flung off his hand and Joe smoothed back his lank hair. 'Maybe you're the father, Jack. What d'ya think?'

The little bastard did know. Jack catapulted from the flimsy chair; the drinks jumped on the table, and this time all of them spilt, causing a small pond to form on the veneered surface.

'You knew, didn't you? And you left her.' Jack grabbed his brother by the lapels of his jacket and pulled him bodily over the table.

Jack's punches came fast. Then after belated seconds Joe fought back, and picking up a half-full bottle, banged it against the table's edge and then deftly attempted to smash it into Jack's face, but he missed his target, catching Jack's ear. Jack felt no pain, only anger, which had been festering for longer than he could remember.

Donavan got up and tried to pull them apart. The owner of the café made his way over and roughly pushed Sofia away from the fighting, leaving Donavan to sort out the two *ingleses locos*.

Sofia hadn't said a word, and allowed the owner to take her away. Very unlike Sofia, he thought, in between the pain that was now shooting rhythmically through his ear. She was angry.

'For God's sake, will you two stop!' Donavan's voice had the desired effect.

Joe pulled at his torn jacket 'She's a whore, you should know that, Jack. Not worth it. Mad as well . . . Mad as her father. He told me—'

Before he could finish the sentence, Jack went for him again but this time with more precision, punching him hard in the face. The sound of a breaking nose snapped through the warm air of the café. By now, the other café goers had moved outside.

'Stop!' Sofia had made her way again towards the table. She faced Joe. 'What do you know about Herrera . . . my father?' She spat out the word 'father' as though it was something that'd been stuck inside her mouth for far too long. 'You've met him, haven't you?'

'No, I haven't met him. How could I? I only know what you've told me, or don't you remember? You seem to have a selective memory, Sofia,' Joe said, holding his face. He glanced angrily towards Jack. 'Bastard, you've broken my fuckin' nose.'

'You're bloody lucky I didn't break both your fucking arms,' Jack replied, his breaths fast and raspy.

Donavan grabbed hold of both Joe and Jack. 'Come on, let's get some air. You're like two bloody kids. There's a war on, if you two hadn't noticed. You should be fighting the Nationalists, not each other.' He looked at Joe. 'You need to go and get your nose sorted out, mate. And both of you, we need to put this behind us. There's more important things to be fighting about.'

Joe calmed down, put his hand on Donavan's arm and for a second Jack thought he saw something pass between the two men, but then Donavan pushed Joe away.

Jack scowled at his brother. Joe shrugged, while Jack's pulse slowed and bizarre calmness surrounded him. He looked through the window at the café goers waiting outside; the excitement of the brothers' disagreement vaporising rapidly, and already unimportant. Their squabble symbolised the real problem of the civil war; the mixed alliances, the fudgy line between fact and lies. Who *could* you trust? Jack and Joe's opposition to each other mirrored the hostility that existed all over Spain, between families that had once lived peacefully together, and friends who couldn't trust each other anymore.

Unease broke out inside him and as Jack watched Sofia, who was already storming down the street, he guessed her own was growing.

Jack still gave Joe some benefit of doubt. But he knew Sofia didn't.

25

The three of them watched Joe walk towards the east road leading away from the Sants district. After a few minutes he turned right and disappeared, still holding his nose.

Sofia flung her head high and huffed a lot because despite what had happened in the café, and to her disbelief, Donavan had arranged for Joe to come to Camillo Berneri's house in two days' time.

'You two go back to Berneri's, I'll meet you there later,' Donavan said, ignoring Sofia's stony face. He set off following the opposite direction to the one Joe had taken.

The walk back from Sants took a while and the silence between Jack and Sofia wasn't broken until they reached the house.

'I can't believe you asked him over for the meeting.' Sofia threw her bag on the ground and sat on the bottom step that led to the front door. Sitting with her knees apart and slumped forward, she stared with resolute anger at the uneven stones of the street.

Jack sat down next to her. 'I didn't. It was Donavan. Anyway, we need all of the men we can get.'

'That's not the only reason, is it? Either for you, or Michael? He's *your* brother, and Michael, well, he just feels beholden to Joe because he saved his life, and I understand that,' she turned towards him, 'but something isn't as it should be. Joe is up to something. I'm so sure.'

'You don't really think he's *spying* for the Nationalists?'

'Before, no, I didn't. But after seeing him today, the *vitriolo*, it's deep, and it's destructive. Joe *is* destructive. That's what he is. He mentioned Herrera.' She stood up. 'Let's go inside, have a drink, come on.'

The house was unusually quiet. They made their way into the kitchen and she found a bottle of brandy, poured two huge measures of the dark liquid and carried on talking.

'When I first met Joe there was something about him that attracted me. Not physically, it was his attitude, so free, passionate, and fun. He told me a lot about his life in England – that he felt trapped.' She swirled the brandy around her glass. 'He told me about you, Jack, and how all of his life he's lived underneath your *glory* as he put it.' She finished off her drink. 'And then, I met you. Will you tell me about Alice? Tell me about her, this poor woman, a woman who's able to love Joe and is carrying his baby, *dios mío*. I don't know what's more tragic, Alice loving Joe, or being left pregnant. And then, Jack, tell me about who you are to Alice. Tell me that.'

Jack was standing behind her chair and she rested her head on his stomach. 'I told Alice I'd bring Joe home to marry her,' he said quietly.

'And if he'd been dead, or if he doesn't marry her, what then? Because I don't think Joe will marry anyone.'

'I know.'

'And so, *you* will marry Alice?'

'How can I? Not now I've met you. I told her I'd look after her. Alice would never let me marry her knowing I don't love her. Alice'll understand. She's my friend.'

But as he said the words, Jack did question if Alice *would* understand and deep inside he accepted that the oldest friend he had, the person who, apart from his mum, he trusted the most, would expect him to marry her, if Joe didn't.

'She'll expect marriage. I'm a woman, and I know these things.' She turned away from him and he clocked the tilt of her chin, a hint of a flush in the nape of her neck, which he'd come to recognise as disgruntlement and anger – a sign that Sofia wasn't happy with a potential result.

He placed a hand on her arm. She flinched away. 'Sofia—'

She touched his face, traced a finger from cheekbone to his lip but she did not reply.

Two days later and in the middle of the meeting that Camillo had called, a letter arrived from England. It was Miguel's nephew who tapped Jack on the shoulder, looking shyly towards Camillo but with obvious defiance in his eyes. Jack liked the young lad.

The serious Camillo smiled tightly but with good humour at the skinny boy. 'What is it you want with Jack?' he asked in Spanish.

The lad was as a bright as a button, picking up a lot of English too, and it was in the English language he answered.

'Letter for Señor Jack Hayes.' Holding it up, he handed it to Jack, who recognised his mother's writing straightaway. He put it in his pocket.

Camillo sighed loudly. 'I can see you are impatient to read it, Jack.'

'It's from my mother.'

'Mothers are important. Take yourself away for a few moments.' He tapped the table with his middle finger.

The boy helped pull Jack from the chair, the small hand hot and sweaty. Jack grinned at him, wanted to ruffle his hair but then thought better of it. He studied Camillo instead. The Italian was easily likeable. Jack respected him, although was at the same time a bit in awe. His own education had been average but thanks to his mother he'd a greater knowledge of the world than many of the men he'd worked alongside; Jack's mind had always been ravenous for facts and thirsty for explanation.

The boy pulled at his hand again, steering him to a small room at the back of the house and then left him with the letter. Jack opened it quickly and found himself comforted by the familiar, rounded, artistic strokes of his mum's pen.

Dear Jack,

I hope this letter finds you well. Little news makes it to this part of the country, it's Mr Wrigley who seems to know more than anyone. He's being very good to us, Alice and me. I've only received one letter from you, Jack. I don't know if there are more, but I've only had one. Have you got news of your brother? If it's bad, you have to tell me, promise me you'll tell me?

I have some bad news. Alice seems to have gone downhill, mentally, I mean. I didn't want to tell you this in a letter but she tried to take her own life, and I think she meant it. But the baby is fine, thank God.

Please try and write soon. If Joe is still missing, and I can't bear to write this, but if he's dead, then you should come home. Alice said that you will take care of her, and the baby. You will, won't you? You two have always been close, and love can grow. I hope it doesn't come to that because I'm willing with every fibre of my body that Joe is alive.

I hope you are well, and looking after yourself. The bits I'm picking up on the radio about Spain don't sound good. We have heard about a bombing in the north of

the country, but news is thin. The government, I'm sure,
is trying to keep news of Spain away from the public.
Come home soon, Jack. With your brother.

With love, your mum.

He could hear her speaking; Magdalena, his mother, with her still-strong Austrian accent covered like thin honey with a Nottinghamshire twang. Alice, though. *Tried to kill herself?* That wasn't the Alice he knew. But did anyone ever know someone else that well? He thought he'd known Joe, although it had turned out he was a man Jack didn't know, and probably never had. Had the war changed his brother? He didn't know, but something had.

Jack returned to the dining room to find that Joe had turned up.

He looked directly at his brother and his misaligned nose and a twist of guilt spiralled through him thinking of their mum's love for them both. He'd never felt so torn in his whole life. He was being pushed into making the most impossible choice. Sofia or Alice. His brother or Spain. But Jack had already made his choices and the ripping of his insides that this caused would never leave him.

He and his brother managed to get through the meeting without saying one word to each other.

Jack didn't mention their mum's letter. He'd wait.

26

Sofia had arranged to meet a group of *Mujeres Libres* members at La Cocina where she was giving literacy lessons.

'There will be no real revolution unless the women can read.' She kissed Jack lightly on the cheek and glanced at Donavan. 'I'll see you both later.'

Sofia had survived without him, and well, he knew that, but thinking back to the scene with his brother in the café he questioned if Joe had mentioned Herrera? Jack was so sure he had.

Jack waited until he knew Sofia had left the house, before saying to Donavan, 'Sofia's an unusual woman.'

'She is, but there're many like her. Kitty, for example.' Donavan lit a cigarette and opened the curtains wider allowing a cascade of light to enter the room.

Jack rubbed his left ear vigorously and pulled at the collar of his shirt.

'Get it out, man,' Donavan carried on. 'What are you really trying to ask? Emotions are heightened, loyalties tested in conflict, Jack.' His grin was slitting the lower half of his face in two. 'Inner demons, hidden passions unleashed.'

'Sod off.' But Jack said it with a smile that competed with his friend's. 'Do you think Sofia felt anything for Joe?'

'They had a lot of fun together . . .'

Both of them turned as Sofia entered the room; neither had heard her return to the house. She stood as a silhouette in the doorway.

'I'm more than capable of telling you myself about Joe.' She made her way towards the two men, head held high, back as straight as a dancer.

'You're back soon.' Donavan had the good grace to redden.

Sofia leant against the wall and pulled a cigarette from her coat pocket, indicating to Donavan she needed a light. 'Leandro has closed the café for the morning. We've arranged to meet tomorrow instead.'

Donavan took a few steps towards her, lighting her cigarette. 'I think I might take a walk then.' He pulled on his hat.

'You don't have to, Michael.' She searched his face. 'You don't look well.'

'I'm fine. Need some air. I'll be back for dinner.' He looked expectantly at the basket Sofia was carrying. 'What's on the menu?'

She laughed. 'Salted cod . . . without the cod, just vegetables.'

'Interesting.'

'With my famous gravy too.'

'Bizarre mixture and I look forward to it,' Donavan said. 'I'll see if I can find something myself. I heard there's more chorizo somewhere in the city.'

Jack heard him wheeze as he made his way to the front of the house.

Sofia began her work, fast and anxious, cutting the onions into the smallest of pieces.

'I need to talk to you.' Jack leant against the table.

'There was nothing between Joe and me.' She shook some unknown condiment into the simmering liquid.

'I wasn't—'

'Everything between us . . . how can you even think about asking?' She paused for moment, her brow creasing in what he thought was uncertainty. 'You *know*.'

He took the spoon from her hand and carefully lifted her onto the thick wooden table. Her violet eyes rippled with suppressed anger but then she found his groin with her knee and rubbed it softly. 'I *do* know.'

Kissing him, her tongue pushed between his lips for only a second and then she pulled back. 'I was worried about Joe, when he left for Jarama, but I worried only as a friend. I'd thought he was harmless but now . . . I'm just not sure.' Her features set into solemnness again.

The enormity of the world was moving along at an ever-escalating pace and it didn't have time to wait for them. Jack scooped her up, carrying her upstairs, and pushing the bedroom door open with his foot he laid her on the bed, taking in the sight of her.

Watching Sofia was like listening to a perfect poem, like the feel of a cool gust of wind on the hottest of days, the relief of drinking cold water at the height of a thirst.

'I never want to leave you,' he said.

'I know.'

And for the first time in Jack's life he told a woman he loved her.

An hour later Donavan bounded into their room with only a preliminary knock. It seemed he was feeling better but stopped short when he saw them in bed.

'Come in, close the door.' Sofia pulled the heavy sheet over herself and patted the bed. 'Here.' She giggled. 'Please, don't be *tan burgués,* so bourgeois, Michael, I'm not going to eat you!'

'You might have to, the dinner's burnt.'

'*Dios mío!*' She moved to the side of the bed and stepped out.

'Sofia, what *are* you doing?' Donavan asked.

'Going to save the dinner, of course!'

'Get back in, *amiga.* I've rescued the food and I've left Camillo and the others to finish the rescue.'

She slipped back into the small nest. '*Bueno.*'

All of the inhabitants of Camillo Berneri's house were sitting in the big and dank-smelling dining room, eating Sofia's cod without cod, and special but burnt gravy.

Camillo finished chewing. 'The Republican government believes the Basques are trying to negotiate a separate peace with Franco. But I know this isn't true.' He turned to Sofia. 'Are Calida and Aurelio safe?'

'They are, Camillo.'

'It might be time for you to go to England, Sofia . . . with Jack.' Camillo said.

Jack took hold of Sofia's hand. 'We're not going anywhere.'

'Perhaps when the fighting's over Emilio Mola will *take care* of Herrera,' she said. 'But until then—' She got up and walked towards the window, pulled up the heavy curtain and stared into the deserted cobbled street. 'I am not leaving Spain.'

Camillo rose from his chair. 'I'm going to try to get some rest, and I suggest you two do the same.' His eyes twinkled. 'Proper rest, I mean.'

27

The Barcelona 'May Days'

MAY 4TH 1937

Sitting on the bed that he shared with Sofia, Jack was
finishing his latest diary entry. He stared at his notebook
and reread his words.

> *The conflict in Spain has taken another convoluted turn.*
> *The last days of April have seen fighting begin on the*
> *streets of Barcelona – the city is being engulfed in its own*
> *civil war. One Spaniard pitted against the other and*
> *Republicans fighting with each other too.*
>
> *It is truly a civil war within a civil war. Brother*
> *against brother. Friend against friend. This civil war is*
> *personalised, random and ambiguous. The dignity, hope*
> *and humility of the people is being ripped away, and*
> *from the very fabric of society itself.*

'Jack!' Donavan was shouting up the stairs. 'Put that bloody
notebook away, and come down. We're waiting for you
so we can get started.'

Jack snapped the diary closed, pushed it underneath the
bed and made his way downstairs.

Everyone was congregated in the dining room, including
Domingo Ascaso, a supporter of Camillo's radical left-wing

ideals and who'd recently returned from Madrid – although by the time Jack entered the meeting, it was an agitated Michael Donavan who was doing most of the talking.

'The Russian communists are like shit. Everywhere.' Donavan was in full flow. 'And seem to know everything. Sofia should leave, with Jack. She's a golden target for many of the suspicious Russian commies.' Donavan threw a glance towards her. 'Word's already out regarding your trip to Bilbao, Sofia.'

'Where did *you* find all this out?' she asked.

'Does it matter?'

'How did you find this out?' she repeated.

Donavan looked at the threadbare rug. 'Joe, and before you say anything, he wants to protect you.'

'*Mierda*! That's shit, and you know it. Tell me, Michael, how does Joe know?'

'Joe's good at intelligence.'

'You don't need to be good at intelligence of the opposing side if you're on the opposing side, do you?' Her face had taken on a pinkish shade.

'Come on.' Jack paced the floor while speaking. 'Whatever we think of the Russian commies, they're still on our side. They're not with Franco. They're with us, the Republicans.'

Bemusement cut into Sofia's smooth, narrow features. 'You of all people know Joe is more than capable of doing a monetary deal. I know what he will do for money. And I can assure you, the Nationalists have plenty of it to bribe a discontented,' she paused, 'and stupid Englishman.'

'She may be right,' Camillo said quietly.

'Why don't we wait and ask Joe himself?' Donavan interjected.

'And you think he's going to tell us, just like that?' Sofia shot Camillo a questioning look. 'You never trusted him.'

'I didn't. But you did, Sofia.'

Sofia lifted her chin and in that moment Jack saw her youth.

Camillo continued. 'We give Joe the benefit of the doubt.' He walked towards the empty fireplace. 'There are other things we need to discuss.' No one else said a word about Joe. 'As you're all aware we have a strong hold on the Telefonica building in the city, which is imperative for our success. The government's Civil Guard are on their way there now. They want control of it and we cannot allow them to have it.'

A murmur of support rippled around the room, which grew into loud plans. Excited chatter filled the enclosed space and within a few hours the inhabitants of the house were making their way through the city to the Telefonica.

They spent the night of the 3rd of May inside the majestic structure. At the beginning of the evening humour and goodwill rippled throughout the building, but the mood changed with the appearance of the Civil Guard.

Jack peered out from one of the Telefonica's large windows and watched the more strident members of the civilian population begin digging up the heavy stone slabs near to the building, and then using them as barricades. A terrible destruction of the building, and carried out without thought for the devastation they were bringing to the beauty of their city. He turned back and scanned the room, and took in the sight of Sofia, her rifle slung over her shoulder, sleeves peeled high above her elbows.

Towards early evening, Donavan, who'd made a reconnaissance trip outside the building, returned with Joe. There wasn't enough time to question where Donavan had found his brother, and it was now irrelevant because outside rifle shots were ringing into the darkening spring air. The Civil Guard had finally arrived.

Joe sauntered over to where Jack, Sofia and Miguel were sitting and, probably still remembering the café incident, she picked up her shoulder bag and got up, moving to the other side of the room. Miguel's features contorted in anxiety, not knowing whether to stay near or follow Sofia, his loyalties tested. Finally, he followed Sofia. Jack stayed with Joe but remained quiet.

Joe nodded towards Sofia. 'She shouldn't be here.' His words cut into the silence between them.

'Sofia can look after herself.'

'She can, she can that. Not like Alice, eh?'

If Jack found out Joe knew about Alice and her suicide attempt he'd bloody break his nose again. 'I got a letter from Mum,' Jack said without looking at him.

Joe shrugged.

'You should write to her. Selfish as ever.'

'Everything all right?' he asked.

'Bloody hell, man, are you that stupid? Of course everything's not all right. Both of her sons in Spain.'

'I didn't ask you to come.'

'You knew I wanted to come here.' Jack rubbed the side of his temple. 'You left Alice pregnant and promised her you'd go back.' He punched Joe's arm heavily. 'You never had any intention, did you?' Jack imagined his fist in his brother's face. 'Did you?'

'I did, until I got here, after Jarama things changed in my head, Jack. I know you understand. They have for you too, haven't they? Admit it.' A pause. 'I didn't know Alice was pregnant.'

'Maybe they have changed for me, but what about Alice? Don't you think about anyone but yourself, ever?'

'That's rich coming from you. Mister-fucking-perfect-but-does-everything-for- himself-really.' Joe rubbed his hands together, something manic about his movements. 'I loved Sofia, y'know.'

'No, you didn't. You only wanted her because you couldn't have her.'

'Why is it you always think you know everything, Jack? What is it with you? Everything's so black and white, good or fucking bad. Life's not like that, brother, you can't always put everyone and everythin' in a nice little box. There're shades of grey. Take this war, it's not black and white. Franco is doing what he thinks is right for his country.'

'Why the hell did you join the Brigades if that's what you think?' Jack stood and looked down on him. 'Did you make a deal with the Nationalists?'

'Why'd I do that? After risking my own life for Donavan and the others. Why would I do that?'

'Some of the others think you did.'

'I'm here now, aren't I?'

Carefully, Jack laid the rifle down and sat on his haunches. 'And what about Alice? What you gonna do about that mess?'

'I'll go back to England, and I'll marry her. Does that make you feel better?' A sneer glided across his face. 'Then you and Sofia can live happily ever after.'

'Joe, fuck . . .'

A colossal noise from outside permeated through the thick walls of the building, rocking its foundations, and after moments of inertia he and Joe found themselves surrounded by shattered glass. Jack looked across the room at Miguel, Sofia and the others, who were loading their guns, already beginning to fire through the broken window. Joe sprang into action too. Jack was still sitting on the floor, feeling a warmth on his cheek, and putting the pads of his fingers on his face, he felt sticky, warm blood. He pulled out a splinter of broken glass from his flesh and, tossing it sideways, picked up his rifle.

Joe moved with agility, firing his gun with an experience that Jack recognised didn't come from their TA exercises. Jack looked down towards the street and saw at least two civil guards go down. One of them had taken a bullet in the chest.

Joe grabbed at Jack's shirt. 'Get down, man, or you'll catch a bullet.'

Jack dipped and caught a glimpse of Sofia who was effectively loading the ammunition for the others. One of their men, a boy, no more than eighteen, took a shot directly in his chest. He lay on top of glittering glass, moaning incoherently. *Madre, Madre.*

Sofia attempted to stop the blood pumping from the boy's demolished heart but it was an impossible task. His moans became fainter and then he lay still. Sofia looked towards Jack and he saw her tears. Camillo threw himself over Sofia and shouted at Miguel to *get down*. The gunfire lasted another ten minutes, and then, quietness. Jack moved towards the opening in the window where glass had been in place just moments before the attack, and peered over the edge.

'For God's sake, Jack, get back!' Sofia shouted, alarm returning her to her own language.

'It's stopped. They're retreating,' Joe said, himself hanging out the pane-less window.

Waves of relief surged through the large room.

'Everyone, reorganise!' Camillo shouted.

Joe interrupted. 'This is the quiet before the storm.'

'Is that what it is, Joe?' Camillo said.

Joe didn't reply.

'This madness *will* stop. I'm confident,' Camillo carried on. 'We'll all go back to the house separately. Miguel and Donavan, you take the dead back. Joe, you leave alone. Sofia, you go with Domingo and Jack. Like Joe, I'll go alone. It's better we're not all together.'h

Camillo was firm with his orders; even specifying which route each should take.

'Maybe I should go with Joe,' Jack said.

'Just do what I've asked,' Camillo replied.

Jack nodded.

Joe didn't utter a word.

28

Once outside the serenity of the dawn was a contradiction to the chaos of the night before, although a chill pierced the air. Jack took off his jacket and draped it around Sofia's shoulders.

She took it off and handed it back. 'Today I'm not your lover, I'm your comrade.'

'I can give my comrade a coat, can't I?'

'I'm fine.' She dragged herself along the dismembered street, falling forward as her foot snagged a pulled-up piece of stone. Jack caught hold of her.

Domingo Ascaso was walking a few steps behind.

'Come on, you two!' he said in Spanish, catching them up. 'Jack, you have to get used to the Catalan women, you'll never find the like anywhere else in Spain, in fact, come to that, the world.' His gentle laugh was infectious. It spread to both of them. Sofia linked one arm through his, the other she slipped through Domingo's.

Barcelona's population was beginning to emerge from their barricaded shops and houses, peering around self-consciously, looking now with guilt at the destruction they'd brought as they pushed stones back into the holes from which they'd been pulled.

The three of them came to the end of the north side of Las Ramblas and turned down a small alley – the way Camillo had told them to go. Domingo had begun telling a story about his fiery older sister when they heard a loud shout, and then footsteps close behind. Jack turned and saw a group of men holding rifles.

Domingo shouted. 'Run!'

Jack pulled Sofia towards him but as he did so a rifle blast exploded into the air. In a split second he pushed her willowy frame into the nearest doorway; the bullet though, had found her shoulder. He looked towards Domingo who was reloading his gun.

Jack swore he saw the next bullet coming towards Domingo. The jovial Spaniard stopped in his tracks and seemed to freeze in time, before he spun around, looking towards Jack, and then Sofia, but then Domingo dropped like an object falling from a height, hitting the ground of the morning-damp Barcelona street hard.

Jack knew he was dead before his limp body had fallen.

'We have to get out of here,' Sofia said, holding her arm.

Jack ripped off his jacket, tearing at the sleeve and began trying to wrap it around the top of her shoulder. She shoved him away. 'No time. It's me they want.'

'If you don't tie this around your arm they'll get you anyway, do as you're told for once.'

She said nothing but was already wrapping the fabric around the top of her arm.

'I think they've gone,' Jack said.

'For now.'

He bent down and touched Domingo's lifeless body. 'We'll have to leave Domingo here. I'll come back later to collect him. I can't carry him, Sofia, and help you.'

'We must take him. Camillo will never forgive us.'

Jack picked him up, placing the body over his shoulder.

They started walking.

★

They reached the house nearly an hour later and as Jack climbed the steps he remembered the first time he'd made his way up them. A lifetime had happened in a few short months.

Before reaching the top, Donavan had already opened the door. He looked at Domingo's limp body hanging over Jack's shoulder. 'Mother of God, where's Sofia?'

As he spoke she came into sight with Jack's crimson coat sleeve tied tightly at the top of her arm.

'Quick, get inside. Are the others here?' Jack managed to gasp.

Donavan pulled Domingo's body away from Jack, placing it on the hallway's floor and then went back outside to help Sofia. Jack waited until they were safely inside and slammed the door closed.

'Poor Domingo,' Donavan said.

'Domingo wasn't the target, I was.'

'Explain, Sofia?' Donavan asked.

'This has something to do with Herrera. I'm certain.' She sat on the floor, the skin around her eyes swollen, her complexion emptied of colour.

'We'll talk about Herrera later,' Jack said. 'We have to get a doctor. Go, Michael, and be quick.'

Sofia lifted her head. 'Be careful. They knew where to find us.'

Donavan hovered by the open door. 'How did they know you'd be there, that location?'

'Because, someone told them,' Sofia replied.

The doctor had left Sofia sleeping. 'She'll be fine but needs some rest,' he said in Spanish. 'I'd get that girl out of Barcelona if I were you.'

169

Jack mumbled, '*Gracias,*' as he closed the front door, and then made his way upstairs again. He bent towards her face, checking her quiet breaths, then went back downstairs.

Gradually, the rest of the group returned to the house. Jack found Donavan in the kitchen, sitting at the table drinking brandy. An unusual sight; he was an occasional drinker.

'Better be careful with that.' Jack inclined his head towards the full goblet. 'You're not used to it.'

Donavan poured half the brandy into another glass and offered it to Jack.

'Is Camillo back yet, and Joe?' Jack asked, taking a sip.

'Neither.'

'We need to leave here, find a safer place.'

It was then they heard the front door open and hearing Camillo's voice both men let out a sigh of relief.

'Everyone in the dining room, now!' Camillo shouted. It was as unusual for Camillo to shout as it was for Donavan to drink. They made their way quickly into the dining room.

Camillo scanned the space. 'Where's Sofia, Domingo . . . Joe?'

Jack took a sideways glance at Donavan. 'Domingo was shot. He's dead, Camillo,' Jack replied.

The Italian slumped onto a chair. 'And Sofia?'

'Sofia was shot too. I'm sure we were followed.'

Camillo catapulted up. 'Where is she?'

'It's all right, she's all right, the doctor's been.' Jack tried to soothe him.

Donavan paced, chain-smoking.

Camillo sank back into the chair. 'Joe?'

'Not back yet,' Jack said.

'Someone has informed.' Camillo's expression creased into even more anxiety.

'You don't know it's Joe.' Donavan's voice as heavy as the atmosphere within the room.

'I don't. But if he's not back by the morning, we have our answer.' Camillo held his head in his hands.

It was exactly six in the evening when they heard the front door being knocked from its hinges.

'*El Italiano!*' The mob shouted as they entered the house.

Jack jumped up from the chair, although before making it half way across the kitchen, four men were already standing in the doorway. One of the mob clocked Jack's glance towards the staircase.

'We're not after the whore – not today.'

Donavan's hand was grasping firmly at Jack's shirt, holding him back.

One of the thugs smiled, speaking in broken English. 'Ah, I see, both brothers interested in the whore.'

Jack lunged towards him.

'Stop. It's only me they want.' Camillo had appeared.

The leader grabbed hold of Camillo, dragging him towards the door that hung loosely from its hinges. 'Yes, it's only Berneri we want . . . for now. And we didn't kill your friend, or hurt the whore.' He tilted his head up to the stairs. 'Though it's fine by us. You fuckers should learn to be loyal to each other. Fucking *English*, no loyalty.' He spat and the phlegm settled on Jack's leg, which hung for a second on the corduroy and then dropped onto the floor.

Jack shot a glance at Donavan, who answered the silent question with his expression. *There's nothing we can do . . .*

They watched as Camillo was dragged into the street. The biggest of the men held Berneri's arm at a distressing angle behind his back and then easily pulled it hard. A peculiar sickness permeated through Jack's body as Camillo's face turned powder white.

The men laughed and carried on dragging Camillo down the street.

Jack and Donavan watched with hopelessness until they disappeared and then Jack raced upstairs, flinging the bedroom door open and looking towards the bed where Sofia lay. She was still sleeping peacefully.

Feeling calmer he made his way back down to the kitchen. 'We have to help Camillo, Michael.'

'We can't do anything to help Camillo.' Donavan raked his hand through filthy hair. 'Joe's involved. This *is* to do with Sofia. And the person who wishes to find her *is* Herrera.'

'For Christ's sake. She's Herrera's daughter.'

'Mad people do mad things.' Donavan took a wheezy breath.

'And Joe?'

'I think he scarpered after the Telefonica.'

'But why did he even turn up there?'

'I made him, remember? I found him,' Donavan answered, fatigue scored into his voice.

'What a sodding mess.'

'We have to get Sofia out of Barcelona,' Donavan finished.

Jack heard a rustle of movement in the doorway; Miguel and his subdued nephew were standing each side of Sofia.

'I think that might be a good idea,' Sofia said with resignation.

29

Sitting in the kitchen worrying about Sofia, Jack heard a muffled cough. Miguel's nephew had a habit of padding around the house like a ghost, but the boy had a quiet self-assurance that Jack admired.

'You all right, son?' Jack asked in Spanish.

'*Sí.*' He held a letter in his hand. '*Sé que es un mal momento, pero una carta ha llegado de Inglaterra.*'

A letter from England. '*¿Para mí?* For me?' Jack asked.

Rafael nodded.

Jack took it from him, scanning the envelope. The writing wasn't his mum's beautiful strokes.

Rafael padded away.

He quickly read its content. From Alice and although short, he felt her warmth within the words. She told him that she had no wish for him to feel he had to marry her.

I could not bear that, Jack, you marrying me out of pity. Things will work out. I know Magdalena has written to you, but don't worry about me, I'm better now. I think she might have exaggerated. I like you, Jack, you're my best friend, but I have no wish to marry you.

He thought of Alice, of their childhood and the way he'd shared everything with her. But relief was pounding through him reading the last sentence and for long moments Jack did not like himself.

'From your mother?' Sofia had come into the kitchen without him hearing her.

'No. Alice. You should be resting.'

'How can I rest? Is Alice all right?'

'I'll make sure she is.'

'Perhaps you should marry her, Jack.' He looked up and found Sofia's violet eyes. Did she mean what she said? Did she love him in the way he thought she did? Or was he deluding himself?

'I can't marry Alice.' He touched the warmth of her face. 'I can help her, but I can't marry her. Not now. And, she's no wish to marry me.' He paused, his throat dry. 'Will you marry me?' He moved a thick strand of oil-black hair away from her cheek. 'I want to marry you, Sofia.'

'Oh, Jack.' A frown shadowed her forehead.

'Is that a no?'

The frown lessened and she turned, pulling a ham from the nearby hook.

'Stop it,' he said. 'Answer me. Please.'

'And Alice?'

'We'll all look after her, and the baby.'

'We're already married inside our souls, so we might as well make it official.'

Donavan opened the door to the kitchen at just the wrong moment.

'Jack and I are getting married, Michael,' Sofia said to him, looping her arm around Jack's waist.

Donavan grinned, although it slid from his gaunt face as quickly as Sofia's news caused it to appear. 'It's time we left Barcelona.'

'We go to Calida and Aurelio's,' Sofia said. 'Jack and I will marry there.'

'You have the best ideas,' Donavan said in between his coughing.

★

Still weak from her injury Sofia had gone to lie down. Jack was sitting in the dining room with Miguel and Rafael.

'Sofia will be safe in Sabadell?' he asked Miguel.

Miguel nodded and rubbed the top of Rafael's head. 'Perhaps Rafael can go with you to Sabadell? I want him out of Barcelona. He can't return to Bilbao, and he loves Sofia.'

'*Le gustaría venir*? You'd like to come with us?' Jack asked Rafael.

'Yes, Señor Jack. I will come. To take care of Sofia,' he replied in English.

They weren't doing him a favour, it was Rafael who was looking after Sofia. The boy was doing them a favour.

Jack, Donavan, Miguel and Rafael all made their way upstairs.

'I can find a truck to take us there,' Donavan said. 'My plan is this. I don't know if it was Sofia's father's men trying to kill her, or if it was nothing to do with Herrera and they really were after Domingo. But we have to think the worst about Joe. We take Sofia to Sabadell where she can lay low for a few months.' Standing on the landing, Donavan lit a cigarette. 'And as Sofia said, you two can tie the knot there. If I know Sofia at all, she'd like Calida and Aurelio there when she gets married.'

'When did you decide all this?' Jack asked.

'It's the anise. After all these years I've discovered alcohol makes me think clearer.'

'She might change her mind,' Jack mused.

Donavan flipped the cigarette on the bannister rail. 'She might.' He bent down facing Rafael. 'Be sure to tell her, Rafael,' he said to the boy, 'that you need to get out of

Barcelona, that you want Sofia with you. That'll help, I'm sure.' Rafael hadn't caught all of Donavan's sentence. Miguel translated. Rafael nodded vigorously.

Donavan carried on. 'I'm going out for a while to La Cocina, there will be some mourning and drinking tonight when word gets out about Camillo.'

'You shouldn't be drinking,' Jack said.

'I'm not going to the café to drink, I'm going to find a truck. I'll be back before morning. Get everything ready,' he vaulted over the bannister rail, 'including Sofia. And Jack, don't tell anyone else our plan. The less they know the better, for them and us. I'll see you before dawn.' He disappeared into the night.

Jack sat on the bottom step of the stairs, Miguel had disappeared, but Rafael huddled next to him in a companionable silence. Finally Jack suggested he went to bed. Rafael nodded and disappeared too.

There was nothing he wanted more than to marry Sofia. The words had formed with no forethought or reasoning. Timing had been bad, but he'd the rest of his life to make it up to her. But thoughts of Alice, and then Joe, crowded into his head.

He couldn't allow himself to think the worst about Joe, but the fact was Joe still hadn't appeared. Maybe he'd be in La Cocina, and Donavan would find both Joe and a truck.

Deep in his gut he knew that wasn't the way it would happen.

He needed to write to Alice; he'd do it while Sofia was asleep, and went off to find the anise bottle; he needed some help. The letter took two hours to compose. Before they left in the morning he'd find a departing injured brigader to take it back to England. A place already too far away, like a receding wave in a vast ocean of long-ago memories.

30

Sofia's suggestion to leave for Sabadell signified to Jack the real danger that Herrera posed.

Jack surveyed the lead-grey vehicle Donavan had commandeered. 'Bloody hell, where did you find it? Looks like it predates the Ark.'

'Don't be so choosy, man. Lucky to get it, I had to pull in a few favours.' Donavan wiped crusted mud off the bonnet with the end of his shirtsleeve. 'Nineteen-twenties Ford T, not that old.'

'We'd better get a move on. It's nearly light.' Jack opened the truck's door for Sofia and Rafael, who nestled themselves on the worn front seat. He climbed in too, sitting in the driver's seat.

Donavan tapped on the window and Sofia pulled it down. 'How far?' he asked.

'Maybe twenty kilometres, maximum,' she replied.

Jack put his foot on the throttle, pulled the parking lever down and turned on the ignition switch; the truck, though, only making a half-hearted attempt to come to life.

Outside the vehicle Miguel indicated for Sofia to push down her window again, which she did. 'Take care of Rafael, and yourself,' he said to her, then his voice lowered into a whisper. 'I heard you in the night. Are you ill?'

Sofia stroked his cheek. 'I'm fine, Miguel. Don't worry about me.' She moved her head closer to him and whispered in his ear but Jack couldn't hear what she said. 'Take care, Miguel,' Sofia said, louder, and then shoved up the truck's window.

'I didn't know you were ill in the night?' Jack asked.

'Only a little. I'm fine now.'

He studied her face, aware what could be at the root of Sofia's illness, although Jack didn't see it as a problem. At all. 'Sofia,' he whispered in her ear, touching her stomach. 'We both know the consequences . . . of . . . our love—'

She laughed and the sound bounced through the confines of the truck. 'Jack, stop it! But then she whispered into his ear. 'No, *mi amor*, I am not pregnant. There is a reason I turned away from you last night.'

Despite their emotional closeness the heat on Jack's cheeks burned. 'Ah,' he said. 'That's good to hear . . . at the moment anyway.'

She grinned at him and rubbed his thigh.

'It's your wound that's causing your problems. We shouldn't be travelling yet,' Jack said.

'Come on, let's get going,' Donavan said as he got in the truck, rolling his eyes at their gentle carnal display.

Finally, the engine rumbled to life properly and they did get going. Rafael, oblivious to the adult conversation around him, began singing a song in Euskardi.

It was late morning when they arrived. Jack turned his head to take in the dry, dusty scenery. Mountains rose up in the distance; the odd small home of a Spanish farmer dotted the slopes. He peered upwards at an azure-blue sky. It was going to be yet another hot day.

Surrounding the farmhouse and high into the hills hundreds of olive trees sprouted from the dry earth. Most neglected and only the vines nearest the house looked as if they were being taken care of properly. Despite the melancholia that had overtaken him, Jack couldn't help but admire the desolate yet beautiful scenery. It was a world away from Barcelona, and a lifetime away from England.

He flicked off the ignition and like a sigh of relief the truck heaved.

The house appeared empty, with no obvious sign of its inhabitants. Only a gentle rasping of wind folding through the gnarled trees interrupted the quietness.

Sofia was already walking towards the veranda. The heavy oak door opened a fraction and Jack glimpsed a petite woman. Her hair was thick, although short and colourless. The civil war wasn't being kind to Calida Parrello-Rossello. Despite the shock of her silver mane and a worried face, her complexion was unblemished. Instinctively, he knew she wasn't much more than thirty-five.

'Sofia!' The tiny but solid woman embraced her 'adopted' daughter.

'My God, what are you doing here?' A less worn-looking Spaniard had now joined them at the door. Aurelio. A mountain of a man. Tall and erect. He viewed the truck, Donavan, and then Jack with shrewd eyes.

'These are my friends, Aurelio.' She stepped back nearer to Jack, hooking her arm through his. Aurelio's face softened. 'This is Jack Hayes and Michael Donavan, and Rafael. This is Aurelio and Calida. My adopted parents.'

Like a bear, Aurelio crossed the veranda. 'Please, come in.'

Sofia had disappeared outside with Rafael. Jack and Donavan sat at the kitchen table filling in the story for the couple. About the 'May Days', Sofia being shot, and finally about Joe.

As soon as Calida heard about Sofia's injury she scuttled outside to find her.

Aurelio placed both elbows on the table, his eyes settling on Jack, but said nothing.

'Aurelio.' Jack was finding it difficult to look at this man with his knowing expression. 'Sofia and me are getting married.'

It was a strange situation. Aurelio wasn't her father but he could hardly ask Herrera for Sofia's hand in marriage.

'I wondered which one of you it was.' Again Aurelio's glance took in Donavan and Jack. 'My bet was on you though, Jack.'

'You'd be right,' Donavan chuckled.

Jack continued. 'So we'll be needing a priest.'

'It'll be taking a risk. We're trying to keep ourselves to ourselves up here,' Aurelio replied.

'Is there a priest in the city who you can trust?' Donavan asked.

'Father Rodrigues. Unlike many of the clergy, Rodrigues has no political affiliations. Truly a man of God.'

'Then we can ask him . . . if you approve . . . to marry us,' Jack said.

'I think there might be something you and Sofia may have forgotten,' Donavan interrupted.

'What?' Jack said.

'The marriage banns. I'm sure the legal aspect of marriage here is similar to Ireland. Could take weeks,' he glanced at Aurelio, 'couldn't it?'

Aurelio grinned. 'It could, but it won't. Rodrigues is *disidente*. He will find a way. The only good thing about this war, is that the rules are more easily bent and Father Rodrigues, as well as having influential connections, also has a penchant for bending rules.'

'Mother of Jesus,' Donavan said. 'It's like being back home.'

Aurelio stood. 'Late tomorrow we'll go into Sabadell. The marriage ceremony will be held in the night. It will be better to keep it quiet. Spies everywhere. Families telling on families, brother betraying brother. Nothing is sacred anymore. Spain is broken.'

'Not broken. Spain just needs a little fixing,' Donavan said.

The sun slithered away and, still recovering from her wound, Sofia went to bed early, Calida too. As Jack made his way upstairs he heard muffled voices floating onto the small landing from Sofia's room; he poked his head through the door and saw Rafael sitting next to her on the bed, lovingly rubbing her forehead. Unseen, Jack went back down the stairs.

Donavan and Aurelio were sitting at the kitchen table smoking. Aurelio had opened the red wine they'd brought from Barcelona. Jack poured a glass for himself, pulled up a chair and sat with them. Silence draped the room.

It was Aurelio who broke into it. 'I want Sofia to leave Spain.'

'She won't.'

'She would, with you. You and Donavan could take her to England, to safety, out of Herrera's way. Forever.'

'I'm not going anywhere,' Donavan said. 'I'm here to fight.'

'Michael, you can stay, but Jack should take Sofia away.' Aurelio gulped down the wine.

'She won't leave, even with me,' Jack said.

'Let me tell you about Herrera.' Aurelio stubbed out his cigarette. 'Sofia was three when her mother died. Calida and I worked on Herrera's estate near Bilbao. We had come, as part of the 'package' with Hilgardi, Sofia's mother, when she married Herrera. It was Hilgardi who had the connections with Emilio Mola, not Herrera, but Herrera liked the connection and saw it as a way to go where he wanted to go. In the summer of 1921, Hilgardi was found with her neck broken in the mountains near the estate. The official story was she fell off her horse. But we know differently. Herrera murdered his own wife.'

'Did Emilio Mola suspect this?' Jack asked. 'If it's true, that is.'

'It is true. He may have suspected, but Mola was on his way up. He didn't need a scandal. He swept it away. Mola was busy with his career and didn't want to lose any influence with his superiors. So he kept it quiet, and as good as told Calida and me to do the same. Emilio Mola attempted to protect Sofia. He told Herrera that she would live with us, commanded Herrera to keep away from his daughter. Mola made this very clear, to Herrera, and to Calida and me. Herrera was forced to agree, but resented Sofia, and us. We have told Sofia as much as we could over the years, only what she needed to know – to be able to protect herself.' Aurelio stood up and began pacing. 'Herrera is dangerous. We are here in hiding from him. If anything happens to Emilio Mola, none of us will be safe, especially Sofia. You need to know this. Take her as far away as possible from Spain.'

'Jesus, Mary and Joseph,' Donavan said quietly.

'They won't help,' Aurelio replied, managing a smile.

'No, they probably won't.'

'Sofia means everything to us, Jack Hayes.' Aurelio's hand wrapped around the wine bottle. 'Calida and I are . . . unable to have our own children. Sofia is our daughter in every way. In God's eyes, she is our child.'

Jack placed his hand on Aurelio's, which was still clutching the bottle. 'Sofia won't leave Spain, Aurelio.'

'I know. But worth trying, eh, *amigo*?' He filled the three glasses with the remaining wine. 'It would kill my wife if anything happened to Sofia.'

'Nothing will happen to Sofia, Aurelio.'

'I trust you with her, *amigo*.' Aurelio tipped back his drink in one.

31

The next day they arrived in Sabadell at seven in the evening. It was mid-week and the town was quiet. Unease covered Jack and as he glanced at Aurelio he sensed a similar feeling surrounded the bear of a man too.

'We need to eat,' Aurelio said, his eyes darting around the street. 'It's best we split up and later meet at the church. Father Rodrigues will have finished evening mass by then. I'll find him in the sacristy.' His eyes shimmered. 'Drinking the communion wine.'

'Surely we don't need to split up?' Calida said.

'It's probably a good idea, *Madre*,' Sofia replied.

Calida lifted her eyes upward to a bruised, blue, post-dusk sky.

'Calida, you go with Rafael and Jack.' Aurelio pointed at Donavan. 'You come with Sofia and me. Calida, go to Café Dos Amigos, we'll be at Café Negro y Blanco. We'll meet inside the church at ten.'

Their group fractured into two. Calida walked towards Café Dos Amigos. Jack followed, but then Calida turned and shouted towards Rafael.

'*Vamos, Rafael, deje de perder el tiempo.*' Come on, Rafael, stop dawdling.

The boy was facing the opposite direction, his back towards them. He hadn't heard her and, telling Calida to wait, Jack went to retrieve him.

184

As he approached, Rafael remained with his back to him, peering intently into the small market square. There were no stalls, all having closed up hours ago.

'C'mon, Rafael.'

The boy turned, his face screwed up in concentration but pointing towards the back of the square, now in semi-darkness.

'Someone follows,' Rafael said in English.

Jack looked harder. There was nothing.

'It's a trick of the light, c'mon.'

Rafael waited a few seconds more and Jack wasn't sure if he'd understood, but then Rafael began walking back and towards Calida.

They all arrived at the church at the same time.

Aurelio was right. Father Rodrigues was in the sacristy sipping red wine, and reading a socialist pamphlet. It was impossible to be apolitical in that country.

Jack had expected the priest to be short, old and fat, a sort of Friar Tuck figure, but the priest was tall, even taller than Aurelio, and very thin.

The priest looked up, at the same time reaching underneath his cassock, and Jack glimpsed the sparkle of metal. Father Rodrigues quickly covered up the shiny handgun. Aurelio had said this priest was on no side, Nationalist or Republican. Later the Father told Jack, *it doesn't matter, both sides would like to put a bullet in my back.*

'Aurelio! My good man, what are you doing here, so late?' The priest took in the others. 'All of you.' His expression darkened. 'What's happened?' he said in Spanish.

'Don't worry, Father, everything's fine. But we have an important favour to ask you.' Aurelio's smile appeased the priest's fears.

'And that would be?' He studied Donavan, Sofia and Jack. 'Sofia, my dear, it's good to see you, and you, Calida.' Again he looked at Donavan and Jack. 'Who are these men, Aurelio? I thought you were laying low in the hills. You told even me not to visit. What's going on?'

'Father, we are here so that you can marry Sofia and Jack.'

The priest replied in English. 'My God.' He looked up to the sacristy ceiling, asking God to forgive him his blasphemy. 'Sofia, it is not more than ten minutes since you were a child. Married? Are you sure?' He grinned, his angular face changing completely.

'Your English has improved, Father. You know that I'm always sure,' Sofia replied.

The grin turned into a low rumble of laughter. 'I remember that about you.' His face became serious again. 'I thought you were in Barcelona?'

'We were. But I have, we have, come to stay in the farmhouse for a while.'

'So,' Aurelio boomed, 'will you do it?'

Father Rodrigues smoothed down his cassock, rubbing in a little of the spilt red wine into its golden sleeve, and then began moving towards the sacristy door. 'Of course I will. You did not have to ask.'

Jack hadn't noticed the little bag Calida had been carrying around with her all evening, but realised after Sofia had disappeared into the sacristy, and appeared less than fifteen minutes later wearing different clothes, what had been inside. Gone were her customary trousers and tied-back hair. She walked towards the altar wearing a three-quarter-length cream dress and a garland of Spanish bluebells, which sat on her head like a dainty crown, their colour picking up the lighter violet of her eyes.

The vision of her was pagan and in vivid contrast to the formality of the Catholic medieval church.

Donavan whispered to him. 'Bloody hell, bet you didn't factor this in when you were throwing up over the ship.' Donavan's light laughter carried down into the church. Sofia turned and grinned at him. Calida was already sitting on a pew with Rafael.

Sofia hooked her arm through Aurelio's and they walked to the altar.

The service was short, as they'd planned it to be.

Jack kissed his bride and promised her that after this war he'd never leave her again.

'I know you want to go with Michael to Albacete, and if I were a man, I'd be going too.' She paused. 'But I will stay with Calida, Aurelio and Rafael. We will look after each other. And when you return, we'll decide what we will then do.' There had been no talk between them about Alice since Barcelona. 'We'll sort something out with Alice. Joe may well go home to England, perhaps he already has, Jack. Perhaps that's where he is.'

Jack looked at his impossibly young wife. 'Maybe. Joe was never predictable.'

He truly believed that Joe could well be in England.

Largo Caballero's resignation as Prime Minister of Spain's Republican government on the 17th May 1937 encouraged Jack and Donavan to rethink their stay at the Parrello-Rossellos' home. Caballero's successor, Juan Negrin, believed the only chance the Republicans had of winning the war and defeating Franco was to throw in their lot completely with the Russian communists. It was this unfolding of events which moved Donavan into action.

Jack was surprised Donavan had agreed to stay so long with the Parrello-Rossellos, but he did seem to enjoy the easiness of their microcosmic life up on the hill, and until he heard of Caballero's resignation Donavan had been happy to remain.

But this changed with the news.

Jack discussed the turn of events on a warm evening with Sofia, on one of the last days of May. 'I'll stay if you want me to, you know that, don't you?'

'I know. But I think you should go with Michael. You can take care of him, Jack. He'll let you. There's something about Michael I fear for. A feeling. Go with him. I have Rafael to keep me company.' She laughed. 'I'm going to be a young girl again. I'll enjoy exploring the countryside with him, finding my girlhood again, for a time.'

'And if I don't come back?'

'You mean if you're killed?'

Jack nodded.

'Then I'll turn into an old Spanish lady and wear black for the rest of my life.' Giggling, she nuzzled his neck. 'You won't be killed. I know it.'

The others were up on the hill, enjoying the late evening coolness. Jack turned and picked up his wife and took her up the wooden and noisy stairs. He placed her gently on the bed. She peeled off her clothes and he marvelled at the treasure he'd found in this tragic country. She lay back and sighed as he traced a finger in light arcs over her belly.

'You'll be a fat Spanish wife by the time I return.'

Sofia skimmed her slim hand over her own stomach. 'It's Calida's cooking. I like being fatter.'

Jack kissed the smoothness of her sand-coloured skin. She pulled his head to her stomach and then gently downward. They had known each other for only months but knew each other's bodies as if they'd been together for decades. He kissed her thighs, but slowly moved upward, nuzzling against the gentle rise and fall of her stomach, and then he felt the urgency of her hand as she guided him. Jack found where she wanted him to go and briefly he stopped, looking up towards her. But her eyes were closed, her lips swollen with anticipation. Jack carried on, finding her expectation, which caused his own desire to become incendiary. He worked in pleasure, finally bringing her to a place he wanted Sofia to be, always.

They made love until voices floated upwards and through the open window.

It was June 1st and Jack and Donavan were gathering together their few belongings. Jack had insisted he left the truck with Aurelio; Donavan had begrudgingly agreed. *Giovanni'll never forgive me.*

Father Rodrigues had arranged a lift to take them back to Barcelona. Two of his priests were going to see family there. The priests arrived late in the afternoon, although the small truck they turned up in was in even worse shape than the one Jack had just spent the last two days fixing up. He'd told Aurelio it would probably need oil every day. *I can't seem to mend the leak – just use it for emergencies.*

Calida had packed a basket. 'You must eat properly,' she said. 'And when you return Jack, when all this is over, I want to meet your mother.'

'And she'll want to meet you too.' He hugged her, kissing her on both cheeks.

Aurelio embraced him, doing the same with Donavan. Jack turned to Sofia and was about to enfold her in his arms, but she shrugged him off.

'Keep this embrace for the next time I see you.'

189

He touched her silken cheek with a truck-oiled hand. 'Take care, I lo—'

'I know. Now it's time for you to go.'

Donavan whipped Sofia up into his arms, swinging her around. 'Now, be careful, be good, and be safe, Sofia.' He kissed her hard on her lips.

Rafael pulled Jack away from the others. 'Are you sure everything's going to be all right?'

Jack crouched down, finding the same level as the boy. 'You don't think I'd be leaving if I didn't think everything was all right, do you?'

'No, Jack.'

'Take care of Sofia, lad.'

Rafael nodded with vigour.

Sofia, Calida, Aurelio and Rafael disappeared from sight and Jack's waves lasted a long time after they turned the corner of the narrow road.

He peered up towards the hill. A lone Guernikako, the Freedom Tree, stood at the apex. The sun was high and its silhouette dark against the backdrop of the summer sky; sizzling rays of light created a halo around its portrait image. He rubbed his eyes and the impression was gone.

The tree looked normal.

32

Barcelona

Jack and Donavan had been back in Barcelona for two days, staying there before their journey to Albacete. Only a few people remained in the house. Things had changed since Camillo Berneri's death. To Jack, the building seemed more run down than when he'd first set eyes on it and a sharp snap of despair had run through him on their return.

Miguel though, was still around keeping it all going. He was standing in the kitchen, fingering his latest pottery creation. 'You're expected to report for duty within the next two days. An attack on Brunete is planned.' He placed a vivid duck-egg-coloured bowl on the table.

'Good. Time to get back to work.' Donavan picked up the bowl. 'Nice, Miguel, and a different colour to your usual.'

'Take it, a gift.'

Donavan smiled. 'Thank you.'

Jack was finding it difficult to smile about anything. The thought of Sofia clung to every inch of his mind and he missed her, and not more than once he'd thought of returning to Sabadell and taking her back to England. Donavan would understand.

But days passed and Jack stayed.

'Ha! A near miss, *amigo.*' Donavan had checkmated Jack. Again. Donavan's chess-playing skills were phenomenal.

Miguel appeared in the dining room's doorway. 'So, all set to leave soon?'

'Tomorrow,' Donavan replied.

Miguel delved in his pocket. 'I've been meaning to give this to you, Jack. One of the English brigaders brought it. It's from England.'

Jack made his way to the empty kitchen to open it. In his letter to Alice, he'd told her all about Sofia.

Dreading Alice's response, he unfolded the blue paper.

Dear Jack,

It was lovely to receive your letter. I understand about the Spanish girl you've spoken about.

I don't want to alarm you but I received a letter from Joe. He does not intend to return to England and intends to go to Mexico. I don't know what has happened between the two of you, but I hope it is nothing to do with me.

I have no idea if Joe will ever return, but even if he does I want nothing more to do with him.

The baby and I will be fine. I've called her Kathryn. Magdalena is wonderful. Look after yourself, Jack, and Sofia, and do not worry, I wish you both the best happiness.

Love Alice.

He returned to the dining room. 'The mystery of Joe's been explained.'

Donavan's features contorted with puzzlement. 'Was the letter from your mum?'

'No. Alice. Joe must have written to her. From France. At this very moment he's on a cargo ship making its way to Mexico.'

'You're pulling my leg? So he's not going to make an honest woman of Alice, I take it?'

'Unlikely.'

'You having second thoughts? About fighting, you want to go back to Sabadell, don't you?' Donavan said. 'I wouldn't blame you.'

'No, of course I'm bloody not. I'm going to fight, and then I'm going to fetch Sofia and Calida, Aurelio, and Rafael. Take them all back to England. I'll kill Joe. I swear, I'll kill him. You're right, he must've scarpered after the May Days. How did he manage that?'

'I hate to say it but he has friends in places that we can't hope to visit, and wouldn't want to.'

Jack caught Miguel's eye. 'Did Joe return here after we'd left for Sabadell?'

Miguel shuffled his feet and peered at the floor. 'He came the day after you left.' He said it so quietly Jack had to lean closer to hear.

'What did you say?'

'He came, the day after you all left to go to Sabadell,' Miguel repeated, his eyes not moving away from the stone floor.

Donavan stood up. 'Did you tell him where we were going? I presume he asked?'

'He did ask. I . . . I didn't tell him.' Miguel threw a beseeching look at Jack. 'Jack, I didn't.'

There was no reason to disbelieve Miguel. None at all.

Miguel carried on. 'It wouldn't have mattered if I did though, would it?'

'Bloody hell, man, did you tell him or not?' Donavan leapt from the chair, knocking over a lamp.

'No, I *didn't.*'

'That's it then,' Jack said, picking up the lamp and then putting a calming hand on Donavan's arm.

'But why would it matter?' Miguel asked. 'He's your brother.'

'Miguel, you were here, you know the reservations we all had about Joe,' Donavan said.

'Let's leave it,' Jack said. Miguel had already left the room mumbling something about making food. 'Michael, don't be hard on him.'

'He knows enough to know not to have said anything.'

'Well, he didn't. Say anything,' Jack barked back.

Donavan lit a cigarette and coughed.

Jack walked to the window and stared at the scene outside, people going about their business, going to work, coming home from work. Living and surviving, but the internal conflict of their country constantly dominating everyone's thoughts. Sofia was going to be fine. Joe was on his way to Mexico, where if nothing else, he'd cause no more problems.

Donavan had calmed. 'We need to report in and join our brigade. That's what we're here for.'

Clocking the brittleness of his friend's laugh, Jack acknowledged that there was no way he'd abandon a grey, drawn and knackered Donavan. They'd all lost weight but Donavan's was too noticeable. 'Maybe you should get checked out by a doctor before we leave?'

'You've only been married a few weeks and already you sound like my mother. God bless her.'

'Come on, let's go to Leandro's. I need some brandy,' Jack replied.

Donavan needed no cajoling. Jack planned to find out at La Cocina if there was a reliable doctor nearby where he could take Donavan, as the one who'd seen to Sofia had long ago left Barcelona.

At La Cocina they found a table and Jack scanned the heaving space; the café was filled with drunken Spanish militia and brigaders; the place was rumbustious with excitement. A guitarist played in the corner and a few of the younger women began dancing, tapping their feet and clicking agile fingers.

La Cocina's owner, Leandro, placed two glasses and a half-full bottle of brandy in front of them. 'Something to celebrate – this is on the house.'

'Has Franco surrendered?' Donavan's high laugh was choked by the wheeze it produced.

'Not quite, Señor Donavan. It's General Emilio Mola. He's been killed.'

Jack's chest tightened but at the same time it felt engorged. Painful but not a true pain, only a feeling that it might in the fullness of time turn into something crippling, aggressive and chronic.

'How?' Donavan asked.

'Unfortunately, not by a Republican bullet. Plane crash.'

'When?'

'Late last night. There's talk it wasn't an accident,' Leandro said.

'You mean we are responsible? How did the Republicans manage that?' Donavan replied and not without a little sarcasm.

'No, not us, unfortunately. Rumour has it that it was Franco who arranged the plane to crash. It's common knowledge that Mola was usurping Franco's grand plan to be the leader, the Caudillo.'

'Thanks for the brandy, Leandro,' Donavan said, already fidgeting to move.

'You two celebrate.'

Mola dead. Jack's eyes swept around the bar as laughter bounced from the nicotine-stained walls. The dancers were in full rhythm; the guitarist had begun to sing. Maybe they'd been talking about Mola's demise all day and toasting it fervently because for the Republicans his death was something to celebrate. He might be Sofia's godfather and protector but to everyone in that bar Emilio Mola might as well have had two horns with a fork held tightly in his left hand.

General Emilio Mola – one of the most influential leaders of the Nationalists, aside from Franco himself, Sofia's godfather and her insurance policy – was now dead. Jack loosened his frayed collar.

'This changes everything.' Donavan began coughing ferociously.

'You need to see a doctor. You can't go and fight in the state you're in.'

'You're not listening. Forget me. Mola isn't protecting Sofia now.'

Jack was about to answer when Leandro appeared, this time his face unsmiling. 'What is it, Leandro?'

'My son has just returned. He has some other news. Kitty Markham—'

Jack had planned to visit her before they left Barcelona. Sofia had been upset that she hadn't been able to say a proper goodbye to her friend, but both Jack and Sofia had agreed it was best for all if Kitty had no knowledge of Sofia's whereabouts.

'What about Kitty?' Donavan asked.

'She's been arrested. Taken to Albacete, accused of spying for the Nationalists.'

'Fuck,' Donavan replied.

'She's the mistress of a bloody Republican,' Jack said.

Donavan sighed. 'Wrong Republican, though. I've heard too many rumours of executions for alleged "treason", including women.'

Leandro shrugged, not understanding Donavan's English.

'When was she taken?' Jack asked Leandro in Spanish.

'Just over a week ago.'

And that was the real moment Jack decided to go with Donavan, because he knew Donavan was thinking the same thing as him.

'We go to fight,' Donavan said, 'and we try to help Kitty? If she's at Albacete, then we have a chance of doing something for her.'

Jack gulped back the brandy.

Donavan carried on. 'Sofia'll be safe, Jack. Herrera won't have time to look for her, or the Parrello-Rossellos. He'll have his hands full now, after Mola's death.' Donavan coughed again.

'You need a doctor.'

'There's nothing wrong with my lungs.' He lit another cigarette and took a long puff. 'I'm perfectly healthy.'

That's what the old blokes down the pit would say, days before succumbing to pneumonia and nine times out of ten, dying weeks afterwards.'

Donavan rammed his wool hat on his head. 'As soon as this is over, we both go and collect Sofia, Rafael and the Parrello-Rossellos, and we take them to France. Is that agreed?

'Agreed.'

33

JUNE 5TH 1937

By the time they arrived at Albacete, the home of the International Brigades' headquarters, strategies for the Brunete campaign were already being planned. Jack and Donavan were shuttled from one supposed authority to another. No one knew a bloody thing. The English weren't particularly liked and despite Jack's reasonable Spanish, getting coherent information was nearly impossible. The chaos erupting in Barcelona was depressingly endemic at Albacete too. But one thing was for sure, the Republicans needed every man they could find, and the recruiters weren't that picky.

Food had been scarce during the train journey and although Donavan was now eating next to nothing, by the time they reached the dormitory they'd been assigned, both men were in dire need of feeding. They found a French brigader lying on his neatly made bed, writing a letter. Jack put a hand to his mouth in the eating gesture. The Frenchman looked up, his face expressionless and pointed to the door, which didn't help at all. '*Exterieure . . . gauche et droit*,' he said.

Luckily, Donavan's French was better than Jack's. They made their way outside and Donavan orientated himself.

'The camp's changed around since I was here last. Come on, the canteen's definitely this way.'

They finally arrived at a hastily constructed structure of reused corrugated iron that looked as if with one ripple of wind it'd collapse. They found a table and eventually food. Bread, beans and old bruised fruit, but luckily no avocados. There seemed to be plenty of anise though. The noise levels in the canteen crushed Jack; different languages criss-crossed the large eating area, grating on his ears. The two of them ate quickly, wanting to get away from the mind-blowing sounds but the food, as unsubstantial as it was, picked up Donavan's spirits and Jack was glad to see him put something in his belly.

Jack scanned the heaving room noticing the overheated conversations. 'Seems something's going on.'

Donavan strained his ear towards the next table – a group of French brigaders. 'There's a woman in the camp.'

'Kitty?'

'They haven't mentioned a name yet, shush. My French is too rusty, but it sounds as if she's not been seen since being brought here. They're talking about an American woman, a journalist. It has to be Kitty. Not a good sign that she hasn't been seen.' Donavan rose. 'We should walk around the camp and find out as much as we can. The men'll be bored, we'll find someone willing to talk. C'mon, Jack. Let's find the ammo store. Most boring job in the camp.' Donavan got up and Jack followed.

They strode down a narrow pathway adjacent to the corrugated building of the canteen and although the temperature had dropped as evening fell, it was still too hot. A pungent smell of shit permeated through the thick, humid air. The latrines hadn't been emptied for too long.

'I remember where it is, unless it's been moved.' Donavan puffed ferociously on a cigarette and coughed even more vehemently. 'I heard on the train that ammo's just arrived in the camp, courtesy of the Russians. All happening today,' he finished wryly.

Sometimes you can be lucky and this was one of those times. The soldier in charge of the ammunitions was Spanish but spoke nearly perfect English. He was also dying to chat, and Donavan, doing what he did best, befriended the Spanish soldier. In another life Donavan would have been a diplomat and perhaps that was still to be his destiny. After Spain. Donavan's life path was always going to be different to his own, but Jack didn't begrudge Donavan's education and privilege.

'All we need is one rifle, *amigo*, we need some practice,' Donavan said to the soldier, who was no more than twenty, with greasy hair and a hare lip.

The soldier smiled. 'Here, take two. And make sure you kill more than one fucking Nationalist!' His voice sounded odd with the Spanish accent and a mild lisp.

'Thanks, *amigo*.' Donavan smoothed his finger along its barrel.

The soldier viewed them conspiratorially. 'Just don't let anyone know I've given it to you. No one will notice today . . . too much going on in the higher ranks—'

'Something we should know about?' Donavan asked, intently examining his new acquisition.

'Thought you English might have known. Some problem with an American woman, a journalist that Andre Marty himself served papers on in Barcelona. They brought her here for questioning. They say she is a traitor to the Republican cause.'

'What's the name of the woman?' Jack asked.

'Not sure, but word's out she's Caballero's nephew's lover. Obviously hasn't helped her very much.'

'What they charging her with?' Jack pressed.

His eyes dropped to the floor. 'She's already been executed. Last night. Marty shot her himself.'

'*Gracias*, for the rifle, *amigo*.' Donavan pulled out a few pesetas, pushing them in the soldier's pocket.

'The only reason I can get away giving this,' the soldier nodded towards the rifle, 'is all hell has broken loose. And no one cares about these. The camp is full of foreign reporters, wanting to know why this has happened. Marty says she was feeding fake news to the Americans and English. Marty saw her as a threat.'

'Her body?' Jack asked, thinking of Kitty's curves and smiles.

'Her body is being repatriated. Her husband is on his way from New York, by ship, will be here in a few days. God knows how they're going to explain this.' The soldier shook his head, and shuffled back inside the ammunition shed.

'Kitty was married?' Jack asked.

'New York banker,' Donavan replied.

'You're joking?'

'No, Jack, I'm not joking. She was a rich American with a big conscience. And a superb journalist. Bloody *fascist spy*.' He coughed loudly. 'Sofia's going to be distraught. '

'She loved Kitty.'

'Kitty knew what she was getting into, but that doesn't make this right.' Donavan put his arm around Jack's shoulder. 'Come on, let's practice some shooting.'

Images of Kitty, her voluptuous figure, her dirty laugh. And then the softer face of Sofia, filtered through Jack's mind.

'There's nothing we can do for Kitty now,' Donavan said quietly. 'And if we don't practice,' he waved the rifle in Jack's face, 'your marriage to Sofia might be very short.'

34

Jack and Michael Donavan received their orders on the 13th of June and began their trek to Brunete the next day. Their battalion was moved by train – and for that at least Jack could be thankful. A 250 kilometre journey in the back of a truck wouldn't bode well for Donavan's health. Right up until the last moment Jack tried to persuade him to see a doctor and ultimately, to miss the offensive in Brunete. He wasted his time. Donavan refused all suggestions of help. Even went on to become mates with a burly Scotsman who, when Jack attempted to commandeer the most comfortable part of the train, pushed him to one side, peering suspiciously at Donavan.

'If he's fit enough tae fight, he can sit wi' the rest of us.'

He was from Glasgow and full of information, telling them later about the deserting brigaders, who'd either been shot or taken back to Albacete, where they were put in the prison for insubordination or desertion. Whether true or not, later these stories reverberated throughout the dugouts.

Donavan and the Scotsman talked endlessly about politics and Jack began to hope Donavan was getting better from whatever illness he had, although he continued to tell Donavan he should return to Albacete, go back to Barcelona. But the truth was, it would have been impossible. The commanding officers, paranoid about dissension in the ranks, would see Donavan as a deserter and imprison him. That, or shoot him.

On July 3rd the roll call was given. They were taken to their position and joined the British Battalion already moving towards Villanueva de la Canada. They had been sent as reinforcements after a Republican militia unit had failed to capture the village.

As gunshots, bomb blasts, and the wails of men laced the oppressive summer air, Jack thought of Sofia, although the stark reality was – he didn't have time to think very much. Organisation of the brigaders was even worse than he'd been led to believe.

On July 6th Jack saw again the offerings of a Fascist/ Nazi air force and it brought back memories of the market day in Guernica, and of Paloma. He learnt afterwards that bombs dropped by their own Republican planes caused many casualties during the campaign. But when the German Condor Legion appeared on the horizon that day in July, there was no question as to which country they were from. Like dark bringers of death, giant birds of prey in the sky.

Jack saw the Glaswegian torn in half in front of him as he made an unordered movement towards the town. He saw two young Spaniards picked up by the medical vans. One with his arm ripped from his shoulder. Only a greyish bone jutting out. The other – God only knew what had happened to his legs.

Orders from the top were desperate and badly conceived. The men became confused, then angry. The early enthusiasm vaporised. But the aerial attack was thankfully short.

An American Brigade battalion advanced on the north side of the village of Villanueva de la Canada, while their battalion launched an assault from the south. Jack and Donavan stayed together, keeping themselves (as much as possible), away from other disgruntled brigaders. He didn't want to leave Donavan because despite his protestations of being well, he wasn't. Jack hoped one of the officers would remove him from the fighting unit, but too much was happening for anyone to notice Donavan's illness. Or, more to the point, to care.

Bloody chaos.

The temperature on July 7th in the shade was constantly hitting ninety degrees. Jack and Donavan together with a dozen or so other brigaders lay low on the outskirts of the town. They were unable to move further forward because of Nationalist snipers, sitting strategically in the church tower. The heat was affecting everyone, including Jack, but it was Donavan who truly suffered.

They waited, mad with thirst and itching. Jack had heard about the lice and thought they hadn't been in combat long enough for it to be a problem. However, the heat and unsavoury conditions gave the buggers a head start. The persistent creatures easily found their unwashed bodies and this together with vicious dysentery, which had taken hold too, sapped morale further. Many of the soldiers had been taken to the hospital near Madrid. And many were destined never to return.

For the first time since Jack had mentioned his concerns regarding his friend's health, Donavan himself finally admitted he couldn't carry on.

'I feel really strange. Keep seeing two of the Nationalists when I know there's only one of them.'

'You're burning up, you need to go to the hospital,' Jack replied.

'Can't bloody leave you here alone. Sofia'll never forgive me. I'll be okay. Stop worrying about me.'

Darkness finally fell and Jack was sure he heard everyone breathing a collective sigh of relief. Maybe now they could replenish their water canisters; maybe even get some sleep.

It was perhaps halfway into the night when he heard movement coming from the village; it was Jack who'd volunteered to stay awake. He squinted into the darkness and saw what looked like a villager coming towards their small dugout.

Jack lowered his rifle and checked on Donavan; his eyes were closed but flickering. He couldn't make out if he was asleep or had passed out. Again, Jack peered at the civilian who was heading towards them. He lurched up onto his knees trying to focus into the moonless inky blackness.

If it was a civilian, Jack needed to let him, or her, know he was there, and wouldn't be shooting. He laid his rifle down and stood, shouting softly towards the approaching figure. 'Over here, over here.'

Jack took his eyes away from the figure and glanced at Donavan, who opened one eye. 'What y'doing, man! Be quiet! The Nationalists will be all over us.' Donavan's voice was barely audible.

'I think it's a civilian from the town trying to escape. You stay there.'

But Donavan began to stand and, although unsteady, efficiently he grabbed hold of his rifle using it to lever himself up, and leaning fully on the butt he coughed uncontrollably.

Taking Donavan's initiative Jack picked up his own weapon.

The figure was now close. Close enough for Jack to see the man behind the civilian.

The Nationalist.

Donavan must have seen him at the same time. He shouted towards the civilian, 'Mother of God, get down, move!'

'¡Madre de Dios, agáchese, hágalo ya!' Jack repeated in Spanish.

It was a woman; she was crying, although together enough to knee the Nationalist soldier in the groin and then run for her life, out into the black night and towards the peacefulness of the mountains.

Donavan's face became feral. 'I can't see properly, my vision's double. Shoot him, Jack. Use the fucking rifle and shoot. Now!' Donavan was trying hard to get the breath out from his diseased lungs.

Jack looked at the soldier. No more than eighteen, his eyes soft and brown. And Jack wavered. Only a second he wavered.

Donavan was now in full view of the Nationalist with the soft brown eyes and trying to hold up his rifle, attempting to shoot. It was impossible, Donavan was clearly unable to focus. Jack would shoot the boy with the soft brown eyes. He would, and did, but the darkness of the night made it difficult to get a good shot. Jack heard a yelp of pain; he'd aimed well.

Still holding the rifle Jack squinted into the night, his finger on the trigger and was about to shoot again, and in that second of an eternity, as the soldier aimed his rifle at Donavan, Jack pressed the trigger again. This time bringing the soldier down. But the soldier with the soft brown eyes had already shot Michael Donavan in the gut. Three quick blasts, perfect shots, better than Jack's. Jack threw himself on Donavan. The bullets had entered at close range. In horror, he saw Donavan's hands move towards the wound, his eyes remained open and surprised. He couldn't believe what had happened. Neither could Jack, who had forgotten about the Nationalist.

Donavan had gone down like a rabbit. But the deep guttural sound he made wasn't that of a dying animal – it was that of a dying man. The spluttering, gagging noise he made as he fell to the ground brought pain to Jack's whole body. He turned slowly and knelt down next to his friend, thinking that like the Nationalist he'd shot, Donavan was dead too. But when he lifted his head and as a trickle of thick, pulsating blood left the Irishman's mouth, Jack saw he was still clinging on to a life he had no wish to lose.

'Michael, how are you, mate?'

'Felt better.'

'It's that chest of yours, get you to the medics and you'll be fine. Good as new.'

Donavan managed a smile. 'You sound like my mother. Might be meeting her soon.'

Hot tears streamed down Jack's cheeks. Donavan lifted his hand and wiped them away. 'Aw, mate,' Jack mumbled.

'After this,' Donavan said, trying to breathe, 'go and get Sofia, leave.'

'Don't talk about that now.' Jack sunk down further so his face was as near to Donavan's as possible. 'Thank you, Michael, for everything.'

Donavan pulled him closer. 'I love Sofia.'

'I know you do.'

'No, you don't know, Jack.' Again he tried to find air. 'I love you too.'

'I know.'

'No, I *love* you.'

Had he always known? Of course he had, but it'd never been an issue. Fleetingly, Jack thought of Sofia. She'd known. The liberal, intuitive, and open-minded Sofia. Jack moved his lips to Donavan's cheek and stayed there for what seemed like hours. Donavan attempted to talk again.

'About Joe—'

'Michael, stop. Stop talking.'

'No . . . about Joe. He didn't sleep with Sofia.'

'It doesn't matter.'

Donavan's voice was now so quiet Jack could barely hear him. 'Not interested in women.' Donavan tried to take a breath but the blood that was seeping from his mouth was choking him. Jack lifted his friend's head, trying to wipe away the thick red liquid. 'It . . . wasn't Sofia who Joe had an affair with . . . it was me.' Donavan coughed more blood. 'Probably why . . . he saved my life. But . . . I rejected him. He's dangerous.'

'Stop worrying 'bout all this.'

Donavan's eyes closed. Jack moved closer again and found his lips, kissed him. Donavan smiled, never again opening his eyes. 'You're one . . . on your own, Jack, and . . . I love you.'

'I love you too, Michael.'

Then Michael Donavan died, and a part of Jack died too.

He'd thought the boy with the chocolate eyes was long gone, dead. He didn't know why he thought that. A stupid thought.

The boy had been watching him kneeling beside Donavan.

Watched and waited.

He shot Jack only once in the stomach, timing the use of his last bullet. The already dark world became blacker. Ebony. And Jack knew now how Donavan had felt. Surprised at the imminent loss of your own life. Annoyed. In absolute searing agony for seconds. Numbness.

An image of an incredibly youthful Sofia.

And then nothing.

PART THREE

35

Near Balmaseda

Isabella

MAY 1976

The blood that had begun trickling down Cristina's thigh pre-empted the pain which had caused her face to crease in fear. She wore her red dress that day, and the blood matched perfectly its colour. As she'd fallen to her knees, Tomás rushed towards her, as did Rafael. Hearing the outside commotion Miguel rapidly made his way outside.

'Cristina, my love.' Tomás held her face in his hands.

Gently, Rafael moved him to one side. 'It will all be fine, *niña*. This can happen. It is not serious. Too much excitement.'

'Something is wrong, *Tío*.'

'Shush,' he murmured.

'We need a doctor,' I said. 'Is there one nearby, Miguel?'

'Where you visited Dominica, a doctor lives near her,' Miguel replied, looking at Cristina, her face as pale as the white blooms of the bush we stood beside.

Rafael rose. 'Tomás, you stay here with Cristina and Miguel. Isabella and I'll fetch the doctor.'

Cristina touched the dome of her stomach, fear stretching across her features. 'The baby has stopped moving.'

I grabbed at Rafael's arm. 'We must go.' Rafael seemed to have frozen. 'Rafael?' I whispered.

Finally he moved and within minutes we were in his truck and on the way to Dominica's. We managed the journey in half the time it had taken us only days before.

As we drove I imagined Cristina's baby surviving for a little longer inside its mother's womb. I'd heard somewhere that the baby did not die at the moment of its mother's death. We would go back. If Cristina died I wanted to be with her.

'Stop the car, Rafael.'

He did as I asked and I fell out of the door and in time to vomit into the roadside's glistening mud.

Rafael climbed out and wiped my mouth with his sleeve. 'Get back in, *querida*.'

I nodded and within seconds we'd set off again.

Luckily, Dominica Zubiri's husband was still away. Rafael said little to the kind and resourceful woman in way of explanation of our abrupt appearance, only that Cristina was bleeding. It was all Dominica needed to know. Not even putting on her shoes she ran to the local doctor, who much later I found out had been having an early lunch with his family when Dominica entered their home with only a preliminary knock. He'd pushed his plate away, picked up his bag, and left immediately.

Within fifteen minutes of arriving at Dominica's house we were back in the truck with the doctor. Less than an hour later we pulled up in front of Miguel's. Tomás's black curls were wet with sweat and framing his cheeks like seaweed strewn on white sand when he greeted us in high agitation.

The doctor was inside the house and inside Miguel's bedroom before Rafael or I had made it from the truck.

The doctor told Tomás to stay outside, which the four of us did too. And we waited.

An hour later, the doctor opened the door, indicating Tomás could go in.

'Are they all right, *señor*?' Tomás asked.

'They will both be fine. Cristina has lost some blood, but I have set up a drip. She and the baby will pull through. Has Cristina been upset recently? This can happen with emotional turmoil. She's a sensitive girl. But the baby is strong. Very. He or she will live a long life, of that I'm sure, but Cristina needs a lot of rest.' His eyes swept around Miguel's home. 'Is this the best place?'

'This is the best place . . .' Miguel began but his voice trailed off as he looked at Rafael.

'She is safest here, for many reasons, Doctor,' Rafael replied.

The doctor shrugged lightly, placed his hand on Rafael's arm. 'I do not like Cristina and her baby being in the middle of your battles. This is not right, *señor*.'

The muscles in Rafael's face tightened, only a fraction but I saw. 'Cristina stays here with Miguel, unless you think she needs to go to hospital? If that's the case, then that is different. Cristina can be taken to a hospital in Barcelona.' He glanced at me. 'Isabella?'

'Of course. I'll look after her.' I searched the doctor's features for a reaction.

'No need for that. I will stay another few hours and ensure she doesn't have a relapse. But she will be fine.'

'Thank you,' Rafael said, holding out his hand.

The doctor shook it. 'Be careful, Daguerre.'

Later that night I sat with Cristina, stroking her forehead, feeling her stomach and the small flutters of movement that came from within. 'All will be fine, Cristina.'

She held my hand on her stomach. 'Yes, I think it will. Thank you. Tomás told me about you offering to take me to Barcelona.'

'I care for you.' And I did, because Cristina reached out to something within me that had been buried a whole lifetime.

'And you care for Rafael?' Her eyes shimmered.

'Yes, I do. You get some rest, lovely girl.'

Tomás slipped into the room, took his shoes off and lay next to her. I left. Darkness had descended hours before. Miguel had fallen asleep on the sofa. Making my way outside I waited for Rafael to return from taking the doctor home, not moving from the veranda until I heard the wheezing of his truck. I stood and ran towards him.

'Cristina?' he asked, his voice anxious and weary as he climbed out.

'She's good.'

He took my hand. 'Thank God.'

The rain had begun again and it was turning noticeably cooler. Rafael led me inside Miguel's workshop and closed the door. The smell of ceramics lay heavy in the air but wasn't unpleasant. Silently, he held me, and then pulled me gently to the floor, unbuttoning my blouse, unfastening my bra; he moved his head downward. The tension within me evaporated. I pulled at his trousers and in only seconds I felt him slip towards my centre. And that was all I needed, to have him close, and with me.

The next day my brief sojourn at Miguel's, because that was how I would always see it, came to an end. Cristina, who was much better – the baby moving regularly – was to stay with Miguel. Rafael was to go to Irun.

I was to return to Bilbao with Tomás, and then I'd make my way back to Barcelona where I would write my article. After completing that I'd go to France and see Calida.

Then, to find out if Jack Hayes, my father, was still alive, and if I had a living grandfather too. And discover if I had an uncle. Joe. The little that Miguel had told me about Joe had ignited a fire to my journalistic curiosity. Joe was important in the jigsaw of Sofia's story.

The intuition that Rafael still held something back, I put to one side.

36

Mansfield, Nottinghamshire, England

Jack

MAY 1976

'Bloody too hot,' Jack mouthed to the newly creosoted fence, waiting for the tightness in his chest to subside. He'd forgotten to take his pills again, something Kathryn would ask about when she returned later. His only daughter possessed an obsessive interest in the timings of his medication, which he put down to her job as a nurse.

Kathryn: the light of his life.

Leaning forward in the deckchair, he concentrated on the robust red of the salvias. He hadn't been going to plant any this year but Kathryn had insisted. She loved them, as her mother had done; Jack though, wasn't so keen. Liked the *desolate* did Jack, although this hadn't stopped him from dousing the borders in the middle of the night and feeling like a criminal as he did so. Bloody hosepipe bans, it wasn't as if enough water had fallen before this summer. The country was going to the dogs, infrastructure no better than Spain and it wasn't going to get any better with bloody Callaghan and the Tories in power. He pulled himself up, walked to the flower border and, with brutality, deadheaded the salvias, tossing the gossamer heads onto the parched soil. Slipping his hand underneath his shirt he rubbed harshly at the itchy forty-odd-year-old scar on his stomach. It still bothered him.

Pain and love. And Spain. A place and a time that since being widowed he was allowing himself to think more about.

'Jack, mate, gate's op'en, so knew you were home. Special delivery letter for you.'

He turned to see the postman standing on the patio, his uniform dishevelled, shirt open at the neck, sweat glistening like transparent tiny pearls on his brow. 'You look hot. Want a drink?' Jack asked.

The postman pulled out a bottle of water from his postbag. 'Nah, I'm good.' He took a few steps towards Jack, an envelope held in his hand. 'Postmarked France.' That the postie then went on to pronounce the French city totally wrong was Jack's first thought; his second, he knew no one in France – only Calida – who he'd not seen or heard from since 1946.

The postie handed him the letter. 'Hope it's not bad news.' A smile cracked open on his almost constantly pained expression. They'd had the same postman for fifteen years, maybe more, and the day he laughed with abandon would be a day Jack might never see. 'That time of life. People peggin' it,' he finished.

The postman was a refreshing mixture of directness and kindness.

Jack laughed. 'You're right there.'

The postman unbuttoned more of his shirt and a bush of greying chest hair escaped. 'I hope it's not bad news. D'ya want me t'hang around while you open it?'

'In case it's not?' Jack replied.

He managed a rare laugh and turned on his heel. 'Have a good day, Jack. And let me know who it's from, eh?'

'Will do.'

Jack waited for him to disappear and sat back down. Looked at the envelope. Lilac coloured. Postmarked Marseille. From Calida, must be. He'd often wondered if she were still alive. Obviously she was. His heart quickened in its pace as he scanned the Spanish words. Heat overtook his body, winning the competition with the outside temperature. He loosened his grip on the letter and attempted to hold back tears. The words were Spanish, but after reading it a second time, he was able to translate them inside his head.

Dear Jack,

It has been a long time. Too long, and for that I apologise.

I hope this letter finds its way to you. Neither of us is getting any younger, but there was something inside of me that told me you are still breathing, that you are still alive. I sincerely hope so, Jack. If not, however, whoever opens and reads this letter, perhaps a member of Jack's family, please act on it, I implore you.

But to Jack – we have both lived our lives, and as I near the end of mine, I am filled with the need to share with you what I should have shared many years ago – when you came to visit me in Marseille soon after the war.

You have a daughter, her name is Isabella. She's beautiful, clever and kind, just like her mother.

I told Isabella, from the time she could understand, that her father was a French brigader, and that he'd died at Brunete. I am so sorry, Jack.

I have enclosed Isabella's address below. Contact her. I plan to tell Isabella about you very soon. I only hope that she forgives me, although I strongly suspect she will not. Please, forgive me, Jack. I could not bear for you to take Isabella away from me after the war, as Sofia was, as Aurelio was. Isabella is all I have, but it is time now for you to know the truth, and for me to accept the consequences of what I did.

With my love,
Calida.

Sofia, why didn't you tell me? When I asked you in Barcelona? He knew the answer though.

Jack pulled the deckchair from the slice of sunshine that always settled in a particular part of the garden at that time of day in summertime, and fell into it. *Another daughter.* His and Sofia's daughter. Isabella. A beautiful name. But the news had winded him, as if he'd taken a blow to his solar plexus, and the earlier tightness that was too near his heart turned into an ominous rumble of pain. He waited, willing it to pass, and after a minute or so his body did what he wanted it to do.

He leant forward and held his head in the palms of his hands, his mind flitting to Kathryn. The time had finally come to tell her about Sofia. He'd always planned to leave her the box of stuff he now kept in the garage, so Kathryn could read for herself – after he was gone; although he was aware she'd already had a nose inside before now. As a young kid she'd had a rummage, as her mother put it. Kathryn hadn't read everything though – probably hadn't had time – because as soon as he'd realised what she'd been up to, he'd moved the box from the loft to the garden shed, which he always kept locked, and then only a few years before, he'd moved the box to the garage.

There was, though, one diary that he didn't keep with the others – that one he kept close to him all of the time, either in his jacket pocket or in his locked bedside table.

Holding the letter, he lumbered from the chair, the cotton fabric of his shirt glued to his back. He was unsure if it was the heat or his disintegrating body which made him sweat so badly. Returning inside, he found the tablets on the windowsill, ready. He placed the letter on the counter unit, picked up the multicoloured pills, popped all four in his mouth and took a long drink of water.

Jack made his way back outside. The sun was at its highest. Temperatures predicted to reach ninety. He glanced at the garden; apart from the vivacious bedding plants it really was beginning to resemble the scenery of a long-ago Catalonia. A few vines and it'd be there. His mind catapulted back in time, thinking of rabbit stew and the special gravy. He'd go to the butcher's later and pick up a rabbit, cook for Kathryn – she could take the rest home for her brood. She'd appreciate that, although it would be little consolation for the bombshell he'd be dropping.

After walking to the garage, and rolling up the door, with some difficulty he lifted the box from the floor and put it on the workbench. Waiting a moment, and bending forward, the palms of his hands placed on the front of his thighs, he caught his breath, and then finally opened the box. He pulled out the photos which lay at the top. Only one remained where a pen hadn't been used to scribble out Sofia's face. How old would Kathryn have been when she did this? Ten or eleven. He'd been livid, and the only time in her whole childhood when he'd come near to striking her. He hadn't though, of course he hadn't, he'd rather take out his own eye than hit Kathryn. But he didn't speak to her for the rest of the day. He remembered that, and she'd been distraught. He'd ended up going up to her room after she'd gone to bed; she'd pulled the bedcovers over her head and he'd said sorry but he still hadn't explained anything to her. Just told her he loved her, and her mum. That she'd understand when she got older, that he'd tell her more when she got older. Her head had appeared from the top of the cover and she'd sat up and hugged him. The incident wasn't mentioned again for another year or so.

He stared at the photo, at the one intact face of Sofia. She was standing outside the farmhouse in Sabadell next to him. His heart wavered, feeling the same absolute love he'd felt then, but mixed with guilt when an image of his dead wife appeared. He'd grown to love his wife, but it was never, and could never be, like the love he'd felt for Sofia. He looked harder at the photo, rubbed the image, and simultaneously the familiar pain inside his gut ricocheted through him.

Jack flicked through the defaced images, knowing why Kathryn had done it. Because she'd known his life, and hers, would have been different if he'd stayed in Spain. Kathryn had thought she and her mother had been second best. He leant on the bench. And were they? No. It was the way life had gone. He'd loved his English wife; they'd spent a lifetime together. His existence had been mostly content; he found it hard to use the word happy only because of the 'something' he'd always felt had been missing, as if a part of his heart had been chiselled away. Now though, he knew what that something was.

Jack pulled out the diaries, emptied the box.

There it lay at the bottom, wrapped in tissue paper. Gently, he placed the fragile wrapping with its contents on the bench, and opened it. The scarf looked as it had done forty years before. Its scalding red colour hardly dimmed. In a separate package, tucked in with the scarf, was the dried bluebell flower he'd pressed on the train he and Sofia had taken from Barcelona to Bilbao. He put the flower to one side and placed the scarf beneath his nose, breathed in the musty aroma, although another part of his brain smelt the perfume. He folded the scarf and wrapped it back up in the tissue paper, placed it, together with the dried bluebell, in the box.

He let himself think of melting Spanish skies, of rabbit stew and delicious gravy. The image of Sofia was now faint, a mere outline in a shrouded memory, but the love remained, and as strong as the evening he'd first seen her. Her primary-coloured clothes, jet-black hair, those eyes, the colour of the Spanish bluebell.

He shuffled the photos into a neat pile and placed them back in the box with the diary and again, although knowing the answer, asked himself: *Why didn't you tell me, Sofia?*

37

The butcher had picked out the fattest and freshest rabbit. Jack made the stew, thinking of Isabella. What did she look like? Would she want to know him? Calida had said that as yet, Isabella still did not know about him but she would be telling her very soon: telling a thirty-eight-year-old woman that her father was not dead, and was not French. Why had Calida come up with such a cock-and-bull story? Why hadn't Calida told him in 1946 when he'd gone to Marseille to see her? Would Calida tell Isabella that he loved her, even though he'd never met her? Because he did love Isabella. Already. What the fuck had Calida been thinking? But he knew: she'd wanted to keep Sofia's daughter.

His and Sofia's daughter.

By the time his other daughter arrived, the rabbit stew was ready, and the box was sitting in the living room, the letter on the mantelpiece. The windows wide open letting in even more warm air.

'Hi, Dad, smells as if you've been busy.' Kathryn peered at the Pyrex dish. 'Rabbit? My fave, but not quite the weather for it.' As if emphasising the point, she undid the belt on her nurse uniform. 'Some occasion I've forgotten about?' She gave her dad a hug and he held her a minute longer than normal. She glanced at him, concern in her pale blue eyes.

'I get sick of salads, that's the truth, no matter what the temperature is outside, you still need proper food.' He touched her arm. 'No occasion . . . not really.'

'Enough here to feed an army.' She peered at the dish.

'Thought it'd save you from cooking tonight.'

'You're a star.' She studied him. 'You all right?'

'I'm fine, sort of.'

'What's happened?' She sat down on a kitchen chair, her hands clasped together.

'Come into the living room, love.'

She followed him and stopped dead at the sight of the box. Slowly, she sank to the floor, sitting next to it, knees pulled tight to her chest. He lumbered down too, putting an arm around her shoulders. 'We need to talk, Kathryn.' He looked at the box. ''Bout this.'

She said nothing, got up and perched on the edge of the settee.

'We really do,' he continued, his voice a whisper.

'I know.'

'We should have done years ago.' He hauled himself up from the floor and sat next to her. She was as wound up as a tightly coiled spring.

'Would you have stayed in Spain, Dad?'

'Yes, I would, love.'

Kathryn pulled at her uniform again. Brushed away an imaginary strand of hair from her forehead. 'In a way I'm glad Mum's not around.'

'She knew everything. I told your mum everything. Everything I knew anyway.' He faced her. 'But there was one thing I didn't know.' He got up and took Calida's letter from the mantelpiece, giving it to his daughter.

She unfolded the paper. 'I can't understand this. It's Spanish, isn't it?'

He nodded.

'I recognise Calida's name from . . .'

'It doesn't matter about the photos, love. It really doesn't.'

'I'm so sorry, Dad.'

'You were young, and your mum and me should've talked to you about it properly. I should've talked to you about it . . .'

She glanced at the letter again. 'Who's Isabella?'

He shoved both hands in his trouser pockets and scrutinised his daughter's face. Could he do this? He had to. 'Isabella's my other daughter, Kathryn.' She flinched. God, how could he make this easier?

'Sofia's daughter?'

He nodded.

'How could you *not* know about her, Dad?'

'I've been asking that question since getting the letter this morning.' He watched her reaction and the initial confusion, and yes, anger, had evaporated quickly.

Kathryn's expression finally broke into a semi-smile. His daughter at her best. 'What are you going to do?'

'I'd like for you to come to France with me. Go see Calida. Maybe to Spain to meet Isabella.'

A shadow of a frown appeared on her heart-shaped face. Kathryn looked like her mum and not at all like her father. 'But . . . you need to find . . . Isabella?'

'Best place to start is with Calida.'

Kathryn looked at the letter again. 'Does she give any information about Isabella?'

'No. She only tells me that Sofia had a baby girl, Isabella, in 1937.'

'Dad, why don't you just reply to Calida, asking her to give you more detail. Isabella's details?' She moved towards the living room door. 'Want a cuppa?'

'Good idea.' He followed her into the kitchen. 'Isabella doesn't know about me. Not yet.'

'That was going to be my next question.' She turned to look at him. Touched his cheek. 'It's time for me to know your story, Dad. Yours and Sofia's.'

'It's all in the box. My diaries. Letters, photos. I want you to read them.' All of them but one.

'I'll read everything.' She swilled out the teapot with boiling water, just like her mum had always done. 'Is Calida a lot older than you?'

'Calida? About ten, maybe thirteen years.' He smiled at her. 'You worried one of us might pop our clogs before I get there?'

'Dad, stop it.' She paused. 'I'll go to France with you.'

Relief surged through him. 'Can't think of anyone I'd rather take.' He kissed her wide and high forehead, and Jack reluctantly thought of his brother. Why, oh why, did his wife have to die before Joe? 'Take the box home. Read everything properly. Then we can talk,' he finished.

'Okay, I will. Alan's out with Annie tonight so I'll have time. Thanks for the casserole. I'm off work tomorrow, so I'll be back around ten and we can talk?'

'Whenever suits, love, whenever suits.' He walked her outside. 'Might sun myself, a bit,' he said, squinting into the noonday horizon.

'You'll get sunburnt.'

'I've darker skin than you, love.'

'Was it hot in Spain?'

'In the summer, yes.' He paused, scanned her features. 'I need to go to Spain one last time.'

'Don't say that. Please.'

'I have an inkling I won't live to a grand old age.'

'Don't.'

'I'm just glad you're not cross, Kathryn.' He studied her face. No, she wasn't cross but he knew she was hurt. He saw it and he knew she was trying her hardest to hide it. Jack caressed his daughter's cheek. 'I love you, Kathryn, this changes nothing.'

'I have a sister. I always wanted one.' Her eyes searching his. 'You should write about all this, Dad.'

'That might be your job. In the future.' He knew Kathryn liked to 'scribble' as she put it. Inherited, or imbibed, the need to write down words.

'Maybe, but you could help me?'

He smiled.

She carried on. 'I can't carry the box and the dish. Put the casserole in the fridge and I'll send Annie round for it.'

'No problem.' She was being sensible. That's how Kathryn dealt with things, and Annie would be a breath of fresh air. He loved his granddaughter nearly as much as he loved Kathryn.

As he watched her walk down the path and despite Kathryn's initial pain, he felt lighter than he'd done for years. But Calida's letter, the past, and the worry of Kathryn, had brought on a dragging feeling of fatigue. The ache in his gut had taken a turn for the worse again. He took more painkillers and waited for the ache to go. It didn't.

Deciding not to go sit in the sun he went inside, opened a bottle of brown ale, poured it into a glass, and thought about his daughter reading about him and Sofia, about his time in Spain. A time he'd never spoken about, to anyone, until now.

With Spain and three women inside his mind, Kathryn, Isabella, but mostly Sofia, the sixty-four-year-old Jack fell asleep on the settee.

38

Barcelona

Isabella

Another letter from Calida awaited me on my return to Barcelona. Immediately, I telegrammed her saying I'd be there in a few days and that my best friend, Ignacio, was bringing me. Calida liked Ignacio. Everyone did. In the telegram I mentioned that I too had something of urgency I needed to discuss. I was trying desperately not to be angry with Calida regarding Jack Hayes, but it was difficult. One minute convincing myself she had good reason, the next, blinded by disbelief that the woman I loved most in the world had purposefully lied to me, at the very least omitted the truth.

I distracted myself with finding Jack Hayes. As Rafael had guessed, he was alive, living in Mansfield, Nottinghamshire; a mining town situated in the middle of the country – as Miguel had said. He was married, recently widowed, and had three children. Three. The number seemed so large to me, an only child whose main dream as a young girl had been to have brothers and sisters.

I'd also managed to find out a little about his, and so, my own, family's history. Jack's father was English, but his mother, my maternal grandmother, Magdalena, was

Austrian. She had come to England at sixteen in 1910 as an Austrian Jewish immigrant, widowed soon after the birth of her second son, Jack.

I sat at my desk inside the compact comfort of my Barcelona flat and penned at least eight letters to Jack. I was now looking at the mound of paper screwed-up inside my bin. It was the ninth attempt which I folded neatly and sealed inside an envelope. I looked at it for a long time, and then my eye caught the flimsy piece of paper sitting at the rear of my desk. A telegram from Tomás. It had arrived earlier in the day, assuring me Cristina had made a full recovery and was resting at Miguel's and that he intended to join her and stay a while before resuming his studies in Bilbao.

I walked into my small hallway where a scrap of paper had been pushed under my door. Picking it up, I returned to my study and read Ignacio's neat handwriting. He was a freelance photographer and lived two floors below me. The converted building in the Bario Goticó attracted many who worked within the media. Ignacio was the greatest friend and neighbour a female journalist could have.

The previous night I'd given him a potted overview of my trip to the Basque region. He'd been annoyed that he hadn't been able to come as my photographer – as had I – but Ignacio had been heading towards a job with a regular salary. Juan Luis Cebrián who was moving away from the national newspaper, *Informaciones* –some said with the promise of a massive incentive – had recently set up *El País*. He'd been the director of the new newspaper for only two weeks when he'd propositioned Ignacio. Ignacio played it very cool publicly, although not privately. The night he found out saw us both getting very drunk in our local bar. So by the time I'd agreed to cover the story in

Bilbao, Ignacio wasn't available. He had a proper job. *My mother's beside herself with bourgeois joy*, he'd said. I loved Ignacio like an errant brother.

I made my way down two flights of stairs to his flat and over a bottle of wine and paella his mum had brought over earlier in the day, I told him in more detail about meeting Miguel, about the existence of a father I'd never known I had. A grandfather who was probably still alive. About Tomás, Cristina. I didn't say much about Rafael, but I didn't need to. Ignacio had kissed me on the cheek, saying something about how now he had a proper job and I had a proper life. We opened a bottle of ancient champagne and talked about politics and the world. That's what Ignacio and I did.

The next morning Ignacio knocked on my door. He had his first assignment with *El País*, and it happened to be in France, and was why he was able to drop me at Calida's.

'Time for Calida to come clean with you,' he said. 'We leave in an hour.'

39

Marseille, France

The familiarity of the flat French countryside relaxed me as Ignacio drove to Marseille. My restless limbs became still and I thought of Calida, the slight but nevertheless sturdy woman who had single-handedly brought me up, although since learning about Jack Hayes my feelings towards her had shifted. But, I owed Calida so much, she'd done everything she'd been able to do for me. *Well, nearly everything*, Ignacio had pointed out somewhere in between Portbou and Perpignan – *apart from telling you that you have a father.*

I tried to remain open-minded and it had been Rafael who'd instructed this approach, and thinking about him a sliver of electric ran through my body. Despite Calida's omission of truths, I wished Rafael were here with me so I could introduce the man I had fallen in love with to the woman who I respected like no other. The feeling of wanting to please her, the teenager who didn't want to disappoint her, the young woman who wanted to impress the strong and intelligent Calida, was never far away. What would she make of Rafael? *She would adore him.* Only as I was sitting in Ignacio's car did I remember the 'urgent matter' she wanted to discuss with me. I guessed it must be a financial issue, something to do with her house.

'Why don't you sleep a bit?' Ignacio interrupted my thoughts. 'We'll be a while yet.'

'I can't sleep, too much going on.' I tapped my temple. But I did sleep, on and off, and by the time I woke we were within an hour of Calida's farmhouse on the outskirts of Marseille.

The road turned into a lane, and then a bumpy track. Overgrown bushes scraped the side of the car. I opened the window wanting to smell the air; the summer's flowers that were erupting all around, the aroma of a childhood so long gone.

'What's your plan?' I asked. He'd been driving for hours. 'You should stay for the night.'

'I'll come and say hello to Calida, but then I have to go. A deadline, Isabella.' He laughed jovially. He loved his work. 'Have to be in Nice as soon as is humanly possible.'

'I understand. Calida will have food though.'

'Christ, I hope so. I'm starving.'

Calida was standing in the field that surrounded her home. It looked as if she had gained some weight, but not much. Her long grey hair flowed in the wind and she wore a smile that told me how much she loved me. This was going to be difficult, and it was unfortunate Ignacio had to leave soon after dropping me, as his forte in life was in diffusing awkward situations.

Calida walked back towards the house, and we pulled up beside her. Getting out from the car I fell into her open arms.

She held me away and scrutinised my face. 'What has happened? Something has. I see it.' Calida was a woman who always did many things at once. Still holding my hand, she peered inside the car. 'Ignacio, what has my lovely Isabella been up to?'

'Changing the world, both hers and ours.'

'*Maman*, don't listen to him.' I hadn't told her about my trip to Bilbao, it had happened so quickly, I hadn't got around to it.

Later, I was sure, she would wish I hadn't taken the assignment. It had changed my life, and hers, forever. Guilt spread through me, because although desperate to know why she'd lied to me all of my life, I still loved her and shivered at the thought of the inevitable confrontation.

'It's so long since I've seen you,' she said, 'so a change is all the more obvious.' She glanced at Ignacio. 'But Ignacio, remains the same.' She ruffled his long and blond hair, then rubbed the darker sideburns, looked disapprovingly at his outrageously flared trousers. 'You're staying with us?'

Ignacio took on the expression of a dazzled rabbit. The thought of being caught in my conflict with Calida was something that would inject a frenzy of discomfort through his laid-back personality, and although he was concerned at what I'd told him, about Jack's visit so many years ago, he was fond of Calida. He didn't want to get involved, but on the other hand understood that I had to find out. *You need to know the facts before you see your father*, he'd said. To go into a story without them was an obscene thought for Ignacio, and to Ignacio it didn't matter that this wasn't 'a story', but my life. To my best friend and neighbour everything was a story. To Ignacio, life was a story. He wouldn't want to be around when finally I confronted Calida but would want to know every minute detail afterwards.

He hugged Calida. 'A flying visit, I'll stay for your food, though.' He looked at his watch, descending into exquisite distress. 'I have to be in Nice as soon as I can get there, then our plan . . .' Ignacio glanced at me; his nervousness at my predicament with Calida, and fear of getting caught up in it, was probably only obvious to me. 'Is that I'll come and pick Isabella up on the way back to Barcelona . . . in a few days.'

Calida's face fell. 'Only a few days, Isabella? It's been so long since I've seen you.'

Her strong but ageing body slumped into the old lady she was. I dreaded our conversation and embraced her. 'I have to leave with Ignacio . . . and I have to go to England soon.' I studied her expression as if she might know why I was going to England, but of course she wouldn't know, although I saw anxiety in the contours of her face.

She took my hand and stroked the skin of my palm, just as she had done when I was a child. 'There is something of importance I want to talk to you about, Isabella. I was going to wait until we'd spoken of other things. It's so long since I've seen you.'

'Is this what you mentioned in your letter?'

She nodded.

We would talk after Ignacio's departure.

Ignacio had jumped in his car an hour before and Calida and I were sitting outside in her overgrown but beautiful garden.

'Garden looks good,' I said.

'Yes, a little out of control.' She smiled. 'Remi's arthritis is getting the better of him at the moment. He hasn't been here as much as I would have liked. Think I need a younger model.'

Calida did well keeping up with everything. Five years ago she had sold a large part of her land and was now living off the proceeds. It had taken me years to persuade her.

'You'd miss Remi too much.' Calida and Remi were both in their late seventies. Remi had been odd jobbing for Calida for thirty years, and I was certain they enjoyed more than a shared interest in roses.

She laughed out loud. It was an ill-kept secret. 'Talking of love. You look different. And I haven't been around this many years not to suspect the reason why.'

'I *have* met someone.'

'Tell me.'

'First, *Maman*, you tell me what you need to speak about.'

'Later. Who have you met, Isabella?'

This was as good a way in as any. 'My recent assignment in Bilbao . . .' I went on to tell her about the Civil Guard and the mercenaries, the discord within the separatist movement, leading finally to my meeting with Rafael.

'Why is nothing ever simple for you, my love?' She didn't ask for names, and I hadn't yet mentioned Miguel's, or Rafael's.

'I think nothing has been simple for me from the very day I was born, *Maman*.' I stood and pretended to smell a rose in the hanging basket. I turned and looked at her. 'I love you, and I owe you more than I can ever repay. You've had a hard life, especially the first half of it, and I have no wish to upset you. The man I have met, a member of his family, knew my mother.' I paused and it felt a cruel lull. 'He told me about Jack Hayes.'

Her face turned the colour of the ash that fed her roses.

'It is what I wanted to talk to you about, Isabella. What I wanted to tell you.'

Anger leached through me then and I couldn't suppress it. She attempted to move closer and I shuffled away, but the distress crossing her features caught me in the stomach. I couldn't hurt this woman, no matter how much I'd been hurting since finding out about Jack Hayes. She continued her silence and I waited for her to ask about Rafael, or about the man who had told me. She did not. Soundlessness wrapped the air between us.

'Tell me now,' I said finally, trying hard to dampen an anger that was rising like boiling milk in the pan.

'Aurelio wanted me to tell you, and I probably would have done if he had lived. I didn't want to lose you, Isabella. I didn't want Jack to come and take you away from me. You're all I had. You are Sofia's daughter.'

'Jack did come to France, didn't he? There was never a French brigader?' I thought about the wasted time of looking for a potential French father, and the milk boiled over. 'You made sure Jack could never find me, because he didn't even know I existed. All through my youth I searched for a man who didn't die at Brunete and who didn't exist.' I rose from the chair and paced the terrace. '*What* happened in Sabadell, Calida?'

She lifted her shoulders imperceptibly. I saw her pain, and it was too much, and I loved her too much to do this to her.

'Sit down, *Maman*,' I said softly.

'So much happened. So much. I wanted to shield you from everything, everyone.'

'And my grandfather?'

'Your grandfather? He is dead. Why should I have told you about a man who is not worth even remembering?'

'He is still alive, so I'm led to believe.' I watched her. She didn't know.

'Herrera, alive? This cannot be.' She leant forward in the chair. 'Isabella, your grandmother's marriage to Herrera was arranged, it was a common occurrence then. Hilgardi had no wish to marry the man who her father had suggested but despite her natural rebelliousness, she did. To disobey would be seen as dishonouring the entire family.'

Calida carried on and I thought it was a relief for her to finally talk to me about things she'd held inside for so long. 'Herrera's madness was always there. It was Emilio Mola, Sofia's godfather, who recognised his instability – as well as Aurelio and me. Emilio developed a special love for Sofia. He took it on himself to protect her, especially after Hilgardi's death.' She paused for breath. 'There were rumours, strong rumours, that it was Herrera who killed his own wife . . . your grandmother, but when your mother came to live with us, with the blessing of Emilio Mola, we did not tell her this. We never told her. There was no reason for me to tell you about Herrera, Isabella. I thought he was dead.'

Observing Calida's desolation I began to despise myself. She carried on. 'I had hoped he was dead.' She got up, stumbling a little as she did so. I rose quickly, grabbing her flimsy arm to steady her. 'I'm fine, Isabella.' She touched my shoulder. 'Let's walk through the field.'

I heard the gravel in her voice, noticed the stoop in her posture, the lines scored into her cheeks, which had deepened since I had last seen her. How I could be so angry with her and yet love her so much at the same time? We walked into the warmth of a summer field in France. I calmed down and waited for Calida's explanation. What had happened had happened. We were where we were, now.

'This is the truth as I know it,' she began. It seemed that as she unburdened herself, Calida lost the stoop and walked in a way that told me she had done what she'd thought was right. 'Something terrible happened in Sabadell. It was the decision of Aurelio and I that we left Spain, without finding out what had happened to Sofia. A woman from the next town had found you, brought you to us, a scrawny baby. She would tell us nothing. We all had to leave, to save you, to save ourselves.'

'But did you know Sofia was dead, Calida, did you know?'

'Aurelio searched for Sofia for a week, day and night. Time was against us, we were in danger, all of us.' Calida searched my features. 'We had to save you, Isabella. In the end we had to make the decision to leave. For France.'

I inclined my head. 'And the day you received Jack's letter?'

'I will never forgive myself. I love you, Isabella.' She wiped a tear from her eye. 'I didn't want Jack to take you away.'

'Did you discuss *anything* with Jack that day when he visited?'

'He told me he'd been captured at Brunete, that he'd been very ill, and that he had been taken back to England against his wishes. When Aurelio and I left Spain, we had thought he was dead. Until I got his letter . . .'

'And you said nothing about me?'

She shook her head. 'I wrote to Jack. A few weeks ago. I told him about you. I received a reply from him. He wants to come and see you.'

'I'm going to England, Calida. I'm going to see my father.'

'Do you forgive me?'

'What I understand is this. You have loved me as a daughter. Taken care of me all of my life. In one way I can see why this happened, in another, no, I don't understand.' Watching her broke my heart. 'But, I forgive you, Calida.'

She stroked my face. 'Call me *Maman*, don't stop calling me that.'

We walked back to the house. She had forgotten to ask the name of the man I'd fallen in love with. For her it was now inconsequential; other events pushing my news to one side.

I had no wish to find my father at the expense of my relationship with my living mother and I poured the boiling milk down the sink.

Ignacio picked me up as he'd promised, and full of the assignment he'd been on. He made a big fuss of Calida and we left in peace.

'How did it go?' he finally asked in the car.

'It's all going to be fine.'

'Good, and your plan?'

'I posted a letter to Jack. Calida wrote to him only a few weeks ago telling him about me. So odd. Maybe it's because she is getting old.' I turned and looked at him. 'Maybe she thinks she is going to die soon, and guilt was biting at her. I don't know, Ignacio. I have to forgive her because she won't live forever, and I love her. I told Jack he didn't have to agree to see me if he didn't want to.'

'Hope he doesn't turn out to be an English shit, my friend. Hope that wasn't the real reason Calida kept the knowledge of him from you.'

'He has replied to Calida. He wants to meet me. And I am open to anything now. A father I didn't know existed, a mad grandfather. The mysterious death of my grandmother.'

'More intrigue?'

I told him about Herrera and Hilgardi.

He replied, 'That's some heavy shit.' He took his eyes away from the road and looked at me, smiled. 'And a new lover who's heavily connected with some of the most dangerous men in the country. Yes, my darling Isabella, you don't do things by halves, that's for sure.' His smile slid away. 'You've been holed up with Calida, you may not have heard.'

'Heard what?'

'The police chief of Guipúzcoa, Melitón Mancera, has been killed. Car bomb. Basque extremists have claimed responsibility.'

'My God, this'll crack open the wound.'

'Daguerre, will he have been involved?'

I hadn't told Ignacio everything, but I had told him that Rafael wanted to leave his organisation. Wanted badly to leave. 'No, he did everything he could to stop something like this. It's one of the reasons he has stayed in the organisation.'

'You're playing a hazardous game, *mi amiga.*'

The rest of our journey was mostly silent. I thought about Jack Hayes, my mother, Calida, and Mancera.

And I thought of Rafael, and how he made me feel as the dance made me feel.

Alive.

40

Jack

Jack had spent the previous evening with Kathryn. In the end it had taken his daughter more than a week to read everything inside his box and come back to him. But now, she knew all about his time in Spain – as much as he did anyway – apart though, from what he'd written in his secret diary.

To his relief she'd been calm, almost a bit detached, although understanding Kathryn well enough to know this was only a front. Her parting words, *Oh, Dad*, were muffled by the tears that settled like raindrops sitting on glass in her eyes.

She didn't mention his marriage to Sofia. She didn't mention Alice, her mum. She didn't mention Isabella. But already Jack had had calls from both his sons, so he knew she'd told them, and Kathryn sharing was Kathryn being okay about it all; that's what his sons had told him in the reassuring way that both of them seemed to have with Jack. He wanted to believe them, although he'd been unable to sleep thinking about Kathryn's quiet distress.

He heard a loud knock, put his mug of tea on the floor and got up from the settee. The postman was earlier than usual on his morning delivery. Not even eight yet. He opened the front door.

'Another foreign letter. You're a dark horse.'

Jack took it. An ochre-coloured envelope with a Spanish postmark, not French. It wasn't from Calida. He rubbed the high-quality paper hard. 'Thanks.'

'Was the other one bad or good news?'

Jack was still staring at the envelope and didn't reply.

The postman carried on. 'Sorry. I'm being too nosey.'

'No, you're not. It's fine.' He looked up and caught his eye. 'It was good news.'

'Glad to hear it. Must get on.'

Jack didn't notice him make his way down the path. He opened the letter with the door still wide open, stroking the matching ochre-coloured writing paper as he did so, the font staring up at him, as if flowing off from the page; words that would stay imprinted inside his mind, probably forever.

Dear Jack,

I know this letter may come as some surprise and in a way, I hope it does, and that you were not aware of my existence. I believe you were not, and are not.

My name is Isabella Adame. I am Sofia's daughter, and I believe I am your daughter too. I was born in December 1937. Calida and Aurelio Parrello-Rossello took me to Marseille soon after I was born, fleeing Franco. Calida is still alive.

I am a journalist and was in the Basque region, on assignment, when I learnt of your existence. I met a man who told me about you. I had no idea, Jack. I will not go into too much detail, as I am certain this news will come as a shock. I know you came to France after the war looking for Calida and Aurelio. I know Calida did not tell you of my existence. If I had not met the man in Balmaseda, I would not have known about you.

I understand if you have no wish to contact or see me,
but I would very much like to meet you.
   I look forward to your reply.

All best wishes,
Isabella Adame.

Jack's breathing had initially slowed as he read the letter, but by the end his breaths were rapid, as if he'd just taken the stairs. He stared at the words and then folded the letter gently and placed it back in its envelope, like he would a religious text. Finally, he returned inside, closed the door and made his way to the living room.

Calida hadn't told Isabella yet, that was obvious, and the coincidence of it all hit him.

'Dad?'

He looked up, startled; he hadn't heard Kathryn come in. She looked as if she'd slept as little as he had.

'You all right, Dad?'

'I thought you were on a morning shift today, love?'

'I called in sick.'

That was unlike Kathryn. He patted the settee for her to sit next to him, holding the letter. 'From Spain.'

'Isabella?' she asked tentatively.

'Yes. It seems Isabella didn't find out from Calida, but from someone else. Someone who I think lied to me all of those years ago, but I don't know the truth yet. Not until I've spoken to that person.' He handed her the letter.

She read it quickly. 'Isabella mentions no names?'

'I think I know who she's met.'

'Miguel?'

He smiled at her, forgetting that she'd read everything. 'I'll write back today, post it this afternoon.' He took her hand. 'Do you mind me giving Isabella your number, seeing as I don't have a phone? It would be good if she could call me?'

'It's fine.' She got up, paced the living room. 'I'm sorry, Dad.'

'About what, love?'

'That you never knew. It's tragic. For you, and her – Isabella. I had a mum. She never did.' Kathryn crossed her arms over her chest.

'She had Calida. Calida loves her, and so much so that Calida didn't want me to take Isabella.'

'I'd have grown up with a sister.' He watched as she wrung her hands together. 'This'll change things. I don't know how I'll feel. Because it feels as if I'm betraying my mum.'

'Only do what you're comfortable with, Kathryn. Your mum understood . . . about everything. Your mum was my best friend as well as my wife.'

'I'm already jealous of Isabella. So stupid.'

'I love you, Kathryn.' He paused. 'And I loved your mum.' He had the capacity to love his two daughters equally, and incommensurate of the time spent with them. Innately, this was something Jack understood. 'I have more than enough love for the two of you, Kathryn. A man, a father, can do this.'

She nodded. 'I know. Enough love inside you to feed the world.'

'Steady on love . . .'

She grinned and walked towards the living room door. 'It's true, though. Cuppa?'

'Love one but I've run out of milk. Milkman taking a day off, I think.'

She grabbed her handbag. 'I'll nip to the shop to get some.'

And Kathryn left.

Despite her jokes he knew she was hurting, of course she was. He was also aware of why that hurting had a sharper edge than it might have done under different circumstances.

A mild twinge in his chest.

Still more he had to tell Kathryn.

41

Barcelona

Isabella

1976

When I arrived back from my trip to Marseille a letter awaited. I'd thought it was from my editor with an offer of more work. It was not. It was from my father.

Dear Isabella,

I have received your letter. I did not know about you, if I had, I would have found you. You don't have to come to England, I am well enough to come to Spain.

You asked if I would like to meet you.

Isabella. I think I have been waiting to meet you for nearly forty years.

We do not have a telephone, but please find enclosed a card with my daughter's telephone number. Her name is Kathryn.

I look forward to meeting you.

Jack Hayes.

The words hit me in the same way missing a step in the dark did, taking away all sense of equilibrium. I sat down on the hall floor's cold tiles and stared at the print of Picasso's *Guernica*, which hung pride of place in the large hallway. A present from Calida. It hung next to Ignacio's father's photographic image of the 1937 massacre. His father had been a photojournalist during the civil war and it was he who had given the world the images that would become iconic. The civil war that was a long time in the past, but a war still living inside people's minds. Like Jack's. Like Miguel's. Like Dominica's mother.

Reading the letter again and again, I felt as if I knew him. I did forgive Calida for not telling me about Jack because now all that mattered was seeing him, knowing him. Like a giant jigsaw being assembled inside my mind, I saw pieces fitting in an abstract and profound way.

This was my life.

I sent a return letter, explaining I planned to visit England.

That day I called Kathryn.

I spoke to a woman with a thick accent which I had trouble understanding. My sister. My English was good, but not so good with regional voices. Kathryn suggested she pick me up from Heathrow Airport, and we would both stay in a hotel nearby for a night. She planned to bring Jack's diaries and journals, which she thought I should read before meeting our father. I had folded on the other end of the phone thinking this wasn't a good sign; but then Kathryn reassured me it was her idea, and not Jack's. She mentioned something about Jack's health, then I remembered what he had said in the letter, *well enough*, and an image of a frail old man came to mind, together with a scenario where meeting an unknown daughter might be too much.

Already I worried about Jack.

Ignacio was lying on my bed, shirtless; it was a hot summer. He watched me with an amused grin as I fumbled inside my wardrobe, throwing clothes onto the floor. Finally, he rolled over, lurched off the bed, and pulled a thick jumper from my suitcase.

'Darling Isabella, you won't be needing this.' He placed it back in an open drawer. 'The English are having the hottest summer on record. Take the stuff you would normally wear here.' He pushed me onto the bed, and ran his fingers over the clothes, stopping occasionally to pull at a dress. He yanked out four and then picked out three pairs of trousers from a drawer, several tee-shirts and four pairs of shoes from the depths of an untidy wardrobe. 'I'll leave the underwear to you,' he said with a grin.

It was now my turn to lie on the bed. 'Thanks, I appreciate it. I can't concentrate.'

'Thinking about Jack?'

'And Rafael, Tomás . . . Cristina. Kathryn.'

'What's the plan, with you and Rafael? When will you see him again?'

'He's in Bilbao. Things aren't going well since the Mancera killing. He's making moves to leave the movement properly, leave the Basque region.'

'And you?'

'Me? I will think about what I'll do after seeing Jack. '

'A functional question, I know, but do you have enough money for all this? I can lend you some if needed.'

'Ignacio, you're a doll. Rafael has transferred some to my bank account. He told me to stay in England for as long as I need to.'

'True love. I'm envious.'

'You'll find true love, my friend. Now you have your career sorted you can concentrate on your love life.'

He lifted his head and picked up a stray sock, threw it at me. 'You definitely won't be needing these.'

I laughed and we both descended into an amicable silence, but broken within minutes by the screeching sound of my intercom.

'It's probably Señor Soto, with food. He thinks I starve.' Señor Baltasar Soto lived next door, and had been a journalist. I think the deal was that he brought me food in exchange for my stories from a world he had retired from twenty years before. Our arrangement worked well, and I adored him.

'He never brings *me* food,' Ignacio whinged.

'You have a mother who does that.' I got up to answer the door.

Rafael stood in front of me. Thinner. Older. He wore a panama hat that covered his long hair. As I opened the door wider he took it off. I was sure his hair had greyed and the lines around his eyes intensified. The sight of him, and his absolute sorrow, made my heart falter in its constant rhythm.

'Hello, *querida*, can I come in? It's too hot today. I dislike Barcelona. I am dying for a cigar, but won't allow myself one. So I thought if I came to see you, Isabella, I could assuage at least one of my cravings.' His face broke into a brilliant smile.

I jumped into his arms. 'Should you be here?'

'No, I should not. I have had to make the most convoluted journey to ensure no one has been able to follow me. I shouldn't have come, shouldn't be allowing you to be involved.'

'Who would be following you?'

It was a stupid question. If Rafael were doing what he had said he would do, regarding moving away and disconnecting from 'the movement', there would be people wanting to know where he was going, what he was doing. There had been an incident only a few years before, when a suspected Basque activist had been persuaded by the Spanish Cortes to give information about his involvement. They had promised protection. The protection promise had been either untrue or ineffective. The man had been shot in his bed, inside a third-rate hotel in Madrid. If the government weren't willing to afford a decent hotel, it was rumoured, then their promised protection was suspect too.

Rafael slumped against the door's frame. 'I shouldn't have come.'

I pulled him through the entrance. 'Yes, you should. And another day later I wouldn't be here. I fly to London tomorrow.'

'Ah, *querida*, good. Did you get the money?'

'I did. I feel like a kept woman.'

The sadness, the underlying anxiety I'd seen in Balmaseda when there was mention of Jack Hayes, and of me visiting England, appeared. As then, I wanted to question him, yet something stopped me, as if it were a line I should not cross. But I knew he wanted me to go, find Jack, to find a part of the puzzle that was my life. So why did I have the feeling that Rafael was hesitant about my visit to England?

He pulled me to him and I smelt the heat from the Barcelona streets, a faint odour of new sweat, a hint of Miguel's home, burning wood and anise. He licked my lips, kissed me, his tongue teased.

After a long moment we pulled apart, and I heard Ignacio clear his throat.

'Who's this?' Rafael barked.

For the first time in the years I'd known Ignacio I saw him flinch. Men know each other better than we can ever know them. I'd mentioned Ignacio to Rafael in Balmaseda.

'Rafael, this is Ignacio Daza.'

Rafael viewed Ignacio with detachment then glanced at me and beamed. I heard my neighbour's sigh of relief.

Catching Ignacio by surprise, Rafael shook his hand. 'Ten years, I hear you've known Isabella, and you never proposed? You are a very stupid man, Daza.'

'Perhaps,' Ignacio replied. 'But Isabella and I are the best of friends. And you, Rafael Daguerre, *you*, make sure you look after her.' Ignacio glanced at me. 'Time for me to go, *amiga*.'

'You don't have to,' I said.

'I have work to do.' He nodded towards the bedroom. 'Think you're ready to go.' It was his parting shot.

Rafael shook his head in the amused way I'd seen him do so many times at Miguel's. 'Good to meet you, Daza.'

'You too, Daguerre.'

Ignacio left.

'I don't belong in your life,' Rafael said quietly.

'Because of Ignacio? There's nothing between us.'

'I know that but you would be better off with someone like him.'

I pulled him further through the hallway. Towards the bedroom. Ignacio had packed my case and placed it on the floor. I pushed Rafael onto the bed.

'*Querida*, we must talk.'

'Must we?'

He pulled me on top of him, holding my face inches from his. 'Things are moving beyond my control, if I ever had any control.' He moved me gently to his side and I traced a finger along his neck, cheek, and finally towards the scar.

'After I've seen Jack, can we make our decisions then? About us. Everything?'

'It isn't just about us, *querida*. It's about Cristina, Tomás, Miguel. In Irun after I left Miguel's, I practically begged them not to carry out the Mancera bombing. I have tried to keep quiet my deep misgivings about where the movement is going, but by opposing the Mancera bombing I have indicated my position. Succinctly.' He paused. 'And . . . I did tip off the government about the bombing.'

'Rafael . . . and they did nothing?'

'An anonymous tip-off so they took no notice. I should have given my name, because the radicals will find out what I have done anyway.'

'Oh Rafael—'

'Do not worry, *querida*. The cards are already falling but I know what to do to stop them. I am in control.'

I wrapped my arms around him. 'The man who ordered the break-in to your house. He would know that you knew. What's the game?'

'I pretend I don't know. He pretends he didn't do it. We all pretend I am loyal to him. The movement has turned into a political game. And making things worse is the stronger involvement of the foreign mercenaries. And the man I squabble with,' he smiled sadly, 'is making contact with the mercenaries himself.'

'I don't follow.'

'They can be bought, like any other commodity.'

'You mean he's thinking of hiring mercenaries?' I understood where Rafael was going with this.

'There is some "loyalty" within the movement. Killing your own doesn't sit well. Eases the conscience if an assassination of one of your own errant members is done by someone else.'

The hot room was suddenly cold.

He continued. 'It would be a last resort, this is true. There is something else, *querida*. I've met with Bernardo García.'

'Ah.' García, the ambitious lawyer, the youngest ever to sit in the National Assembly. A liberal, a reformer. Hot-headed, I'd decided on my meeting with him, many years ago now. But he was also intelligent and passionate.

'He is looking into many things and is becoming more ardent since Franco's death. Looking into the "lost" civilians from the civil war, the war crimes committed during that time.' He paused, nuzzled my cheek. 'The secret faction that is forming, silently and insidiously within the government, who see their job to coordinate the mercenaries, potentially using those mercenaries to do the government's "dirty work." Many foresee a dirty war against the Basque activists. A secret war, and waged by the government itself.'

I propped myself up on my elbow. 'Bernardo García. I met him briefly when I was investigating the illegal adoption cases during Franco's time.'

He nodded. 'A crusader, and I suspect he has his eye on bigger things. International injustice is what motivates him. He begins in Spain but wants to take on the world. He is ambitious. I like him. More importantly, I trust him.'

'How much information does he want from you? *What* does he want from you?'

'Everything.' He smiled wryly. 'He knows I'm *uncomfortable*.'

'He's aware you opposed the Mancera bombing? That it was you who alerted the government?'

'Yes, he knows it was me who his government ignored. He also knows what the government's long-term plan is – to contain the Basque activists, but to contain them using its own form of violence.'

'The government plans to pay the mercenaries? Allow mercenaries to fight the government's war?'

'You know, *querida*.' He stroked my stomach. 'As much as me.'

'Have you met with García recently?'

'He's here in Barcelona. '

'You've already seen him? That's why you're here?'

'Seemed like a good idea. And to see you.' His fingers moved towards the inside of my thigh. 'You remember me telling you about my brother-in-law, Cristina's father?'

I moaned at his touch. 'Of course.'

'García is investigating that incident, amongst other things. That's another reason why we met.'

'Go on.' I grabbed his hand and pushed it further to where I wanted it to be.

'García believes Cristina's father was murdered by a mercenary, ordered and paid for by the government. For García, this is the tip of an iceberg. If he can prove it, he is thinking of taking it out of Spain and to the European Court of Human Rights.'

'He wants your help?'

'I want *his* help. I want justice for Cristina's father. And I wish to be free from the movement.'

After coldness the temperature in the room was now becoming unbearable. I slipped from the bed and moved towards the balcony, opening the doors wider. The heat fell into the room with the vigour of schoolchildren scrambling out the classroom at the end of a hot afternoon. I closed the doors, pulled the shutters; the room fell into darkness. And I lay back down next to Rafael.

'And you want García to help you get out the country, with Cristina and Tomás?'

He looked at me through the room's dimness. 'Yes, and the baby.'

'Where will you go?'

'America.'

'And me?'

'Go and see Jack.' He fingered his scar. 'And let's see where we are afterwards. I've persuaded Tomás and Cristina to go to France for the time being. To safety.'

'Calida. They can stay with Calida. She would love it.'

'You sure?'

'Absolutely.' I slid my hand underneath his shirt, feeling warm skin. 'I love you.' I could wait no longer and moved down the bed, kissing his stomach, taking in his essence, and then moving upwards I held his hand near to where we joined and within seconds the world slowed as my weary body was replenished.

For a few hours, enclosed within the hot walls of my bedroom, both of us forgot the world outside, and all who inhabited that world.

42

Jack

Waiting for Kathryn to return from the shop with milk, Jack acknowledged he really needed to tackle the subject of Joe. She'd had a lot to take in from his diaries, but still she hadn't mentioned Joe. Much more information about Joe was in the diary he kept locked in his bedside table. It'd been so long since he'd looked at it, although the small key to the drawer was safely tucked away inside his wallet.

Joe. His brother.

Kathryn was fastidious and probably wanted to mull over her questions, of which Jack was absolutely certain there'd be many. And some about Joe.

'Think there's a milk shortage. None in the corner shop,' Kathryn shouted from the back door.

'We'll have it without, love,' he replied, walking from the living room into the kitchen to join her. 'I've a lemon,' he said, his face straight.

'We've never had lemon in our tea, Dad!'

'First time for everything.' He flicked on the kettle and then ferreted around in the cupboard and found some garibaldis.

She laughed at the paper doily he placed on a plate; he'd found a stack of them in the back of the cupboard

256

that had escaped the clear-out after her mum's death. He wanted to make his daughter laugh.

She picked up a biscuit. 'You know, Dad, you really should think about writing a book.'

'Get away with you. Anyway, I'm sure it's been done. There were hundreds like me, thousands, who went to Spain.'

'But not all with such a rich tale. It's like Anna Karenina.' She took a bite of the garibaldi. 'Tell me more about Sofia.'

Jack sat down and recounted other incidents that weren't in the diaries, and expanded on some of the ones that were. He didn't mention the last remaining notebook. Not yet.

Kathryn was thoughtful and silent, and Jack began to fret. He'd been tempted to not give Kathryn the diaries and tell the tale himself so as she wouldn't know about his marriage to Sofia. But he couldn't because that would have been betraying Sofia. And he felt he'd already done that. A daughter between them and he'd never known.

In the silence which swathed the kitchen he again asked himself: why hadn't Sofia told him she was pregnant when he'd asked her directly sitting inside the old truck? Of course he'd suspected that she could well be, but he'd trusted her implicitly and had believed her completely when she'd denied it. She hadn't told him because she'd known he'd never have gone to Brunete with Michael Donavan, knowing she carried their baby. Sofia had wanted him to look out for Michael. When Leandro had told him and Donavan about Emilio Mola's death, he would have gone back to Sabadell then and taken them all away. But it had been news of Kitty that had stopped him.

What could Donavan and he have done to save Kitty? *Fuck all*, as it turned out, although at the time he'd really thought they could help her. That's the thing about youth;

it saw no boundaries or obstacles. Jack saw the buggers everywhere now.

Kathryn sipped the lemon tea and grimaced. 'Now I know where that deep unhappiness comes from, about Spain . . . and about Joe.'

On the few occasions in her adult life when she'd even mentioned Joe, Kathryn had never alluded to any connection, as if the connection didn't exist.

'I did despise Joe, for what he did.' He took her hand. 'To us, the Republicans, and to your mum.'

'Dad, do you think Joe might have told Herrera where Sofia was – in Sabadell?'

He shrugged tired shoulders but the brutal pain of Joe and what Jack had always suspected his brother might have done swept through him. 'I've tried not to think about that for the last forty years, that's the truth.' He'd thought about it most days of the life he'd lived since the last time he'd seen Miguel – that winter in December 1937, when he'd finally made his way back to Barcelona from Franco's concentration camp in Burgos. And when Miguel, standing in Camillo Berneri's house, had informed him that he'd told Joe where Sofia, Calida and Aurelio were hiding. Sabadell.

He studied his daughter. There were no flies on Kathryn but he wasn't ready yet to tell her that part of the story. Instead he went on to tell her about when in 1946, after the war, he'd travelled to France to find Calida, and then afterwards to locate Miguel in Spain.

She only shook her head in sadness. 'I think it's time I went to see Joe.'

It was then Jack's turn to shake his head. Kathryn had always been able to read in between life's lines.

★

A week later, and in the early evening, Alan, Kathryn's husband, came over to tell Jack that Isabella Adame had called and would be on the morning flight into Heathrow the day after tomorrow. Kathryn had agreed to take a few days off work to pick Isabella up, and Kathryn's plan, *if it was okay with Jack*, Alan explained, was for her to take Jack's diaries and journals to give to Isabella. Kathryn and Isabella would stay in a hotel near Heathrow that night, giving Isabella time to read them before meeting Jack.

It seemed a good plan. Kathryn had thought through all the details. She was a good girl, and always had been. His two daughters would then know as much as each other about his time in Spain.

Almost everything.

43

England

Isabella

A woman who looked the same age as me was waiting in Arrivals holding a large sign with my name on. I walked towards her pulling behind me the suitcase that Ignacio had all but packed.

Kathryn. My half-sister. She was shorter than me, and her hair a dark blonde. As I got closer I noticed pale blue and wide eyes, and her heart-shaped face. I saw no resemblance at all to my own features.

I walked towards her. 'Kathryn? I'm Isabella Adame. Thank you so much for meeting me.'

'Your English is very good.' Her voice was low and soft. She crouched down and put the sign on the floor.

'I've travelled a lot to England with my job.' The words spilled out and I wanted to pull Kathryn to me, kiss her cheeks but I held back. This was England, not Spain, and despite the social, and to a large extent, emotional revolution, which had occurred in the UK during the sixties, I knew through previous visits the British were as rigid in their sentiments and emotions as they had been for centuries. Britain joining the EEC hadn't knocked down any of their emotional bridges, and I was sure that the UK's reluctant inclusion into Europe wouldn't change anything any time soon. Ignacio had been taunting me for days about my 'British' bloodline.

Kathryn stood with one leg crossed against the other, but with her arms free of the sign I shook my sister's hand and a tiny smile appeared on her extraordinarily pretty face.

'You look just like your mum, Isabella.'

'I do. I know.' I paused. 'Do I look at all like Jack?' It was then I saw Kathryn's awkward façade slip away.

'You're a mixture of both parents, I'd say. I look nothing like Dad.'

I searched for hostility or bitterness in her tone. I don't think I found either but then again I was aware of the difficulty in reading the people of this country.

'What does Jack look like?' We'd begun to move away from the throng of incoming passengers.

'He's still handsome.' A slip of a smile. 'Tall, like you. I have some photos I'll show you later?'

'Thank you. It's good of you to pick me up. I appreciate it.'

'It's no problem.'

'I'm sure it is. It's good of you.'

She smiled properly then. 'This is a bit awkward, isn't it?

'A little, yes.'

'You speaking English makes things easier.' She swung around, nearly bumping into an irate tourist. 'Although Dad's Spanish is quite good.'

We were now outside the airport terminal and the warmth took me by surprise.

She carried on. 'I've booked us into a nearby hotel. I hope that's okay?'

'You did mention it. Of course it's okay.'

'I've brought Dad's journals and diaries, photos, some letters, as I said I would. They're in the back of the car. I've only just read them myself.' She watched me. 'I thought seeing as you're a journalist, it'd make things easier. They're well written. He'll tell you everything himself, though.' She looked up, distracted, scanned around, working out how to find her car.

'This way, I think.'

She peered at me with a puzzled expression.

'I've flown into this airport several times,' I explained. 'Normally I hire a car too. I know the car park well . . .'

'I've actually never flown anywhere. I've never even been to an airport.' A mild pink appeared at her neck.

'Lucky you! Travelling stinks.'

She turned to look at me. 'We've had very different lives.'

'But one common denominator now?'

She nodded.

Kathryn found her car, which would have been hard to miss; a metallic-lilac-coloured Hillman Hunter, and we began the short journey to the hotel. The conversation darkened only once when we touched on Jack's wife's, Kathryn's mother's, death, and which had occurred less than a year ago.

It was then that Kathryn dropped her bombshell. And it was then when I realised what an incredible woman she really was.

At the hotel Kathryn retrieved a box from the boot of the car and we walked to my room. She handed the box to me.

'Shall we meet in the bar later, for a bit of food?' she asked.

'Let's go and have a cup of coffee now? I'm not that hungry. Would you mind if I stayed in my room this evening. Read what you've given to me?' I searched her face and was certain I saw some relief.

'Good idea. It's already late. And to be honest, I'm looking forward to an early sleep, and having a big hotel bed to myself.' She laughed. A proper laugh.

'You're lucky. A husband and a daughter. Your husband sounds lovely on the phone.'

'Alan is. He really is. I *am* lucky, Isabella.' Tentatively she put her small hand on my arm. 'I'm glad you found Dad. Read his diaries and you'll know him a little before you meet him.' She paused. 'Your mum sounded amazing, Isabella. I'm . . . so sorry.'

'I think she was,' I replied, looking beyond Kathryn at the hotel guests milling about in the small hotel foyer. 'But sometimes and more so recently, I sense that my mother might still be alive. There is that possibility . . .' And perhaps there was that possibility. Rafael, and Miguel, had both agreed there was a chance. Small, I understood that, but their positivity that this could be a viable scenario had seen my hope soar in the past weeks, although until now it was a hope I'd kept well veiled.

'She could be.' Kathryn smiled with tentativeness.

'Come on,' I said, sensing my words had made her uncomfortable. 'Let's go and drink coffee.' Her smile opened up, perhaps because I'd dropped the subject of Sofia's fate so easily. 'And I'd love to hear about your daughter.'

At the mention of her child Kathryn's smile transformed into a beam. It was the one thing in my life that brought on the inner and complete loneliness – that I'd never met anyone with whom I wanted to spend my life with, have children with. Then I thought of Rafael.

Kathryn and I drank coffee in the deserted hotel bar and she told me about her family and her job as a maternity nurse. We agreed to meet for a late breakfast the next morning and then head up to Mansfield.

★

I stayed up most of the night reading. Jack had a way with words that made me both laugh and cry. Inside my mind I now had a clear image of my father, and my mother, and was able to fill in the considerable gaps Miguel had left. I also comprehended Kathryn's earlier hesitance when I spoke of the possibility of Sofia still being alive. Jack and Sofia had married in Spain, a revelation that brought me great joy, but was undoubtedly uncomfortable for Kathryn, and more so if Sofia were still to be alive, somewhere. But I revelled in the fact that Jack had loved my mother, and she him. Completely and utterly, and I acknowledged that this disclosure was, and always had been, what I'd wanted to hear: my parents *had* been in love and I was a product of that love. It's all I'd needed to know as a child and was why, even though I'd really tried to forgive Calida, I was having such difficulty doing so fully and unreservedly. Although reading Jack's diaries and seeing Calida as she'd been then, knowing her love for my mother, took much of my angst and insecurities away, as well as the last part of me which was unable to fully exonerate Calida.

But as I lay flat on the bed staring at a bland white ceiling, mental numbness spread.

It was not only Calida who had withheld the truth from me.

Rafael had known my mother. And he had not said a word. The room shrank in size, the ceiling above moved downwards as if about to touch my body, crushing me.

I turned onto my side on the hard hotel bed, thin and lifeless pillows pushed underneath my neck, sneezing occasionally at the dust that fizzed around the bedside cabinet as I attempted to switch off the lamp. Sleep, though, never came that night as I questioned what Rafael knew from the days in Sabadell, after Jack and Michael Donavan had left for Brunete. The period of time when my mother disappeared.

By not telling me he'd been in Sabadell with my mother, Rafael had betrayed me.

The small world that I'd constructed over the past weeks collapsed as easily as a sandcastle in a swift incoming tide, flattening rapidly, destroyed completely, all traces of it gone, as if it had never existed. Why had I opened up to him? Why had I allowed him into my life, my heart, my very soul? Before I finally fell into an agitated sleep I swore I would not forgive Rafael Daguerre. I could not.

Although unlike the sandcastle on a beach, obliterated by the waves, the evidence of Rafael would remain with me forever, and visible forever.

44

I was packing the diaries back in the box when Kathryn knocked on my door.

'You look tired. A lot of reading last night?' Kathryn was bright-eyed, her pale skin luminescent. She appeared much more relaxed than the day before.

'I am a little tired.'

'Have you read it all?'

'I have. I'm a fast reader, it goes with my job.' I managed a smile; managed to hide the pain ploughing through me.

'Right, then,' she said brightly. 'Let's make tracks.'

Ignacio had been right: it was hot in England. Sticky and humid, and with little sleep I didn't feel well. However, the day I was to meet my father, the sky, and for the first time in weeks Kathryn reported, was a dark pewter grey. Halfway to Mansfield the clouds gave in to their weight. I peered through the car window barely recognising the brown scenery of a country that the last time I'd visited had been so green and plump. Fat droplets of rain, like fragile translucent berries, bounced off the windscreen. Kathryn and I hardly exchanged a word until she pulled into a narrow street with silver birch trees planted on the grassy verge that followed the road along.

She slowed down and stopped outside a small bungalow. The tightness which had begun on the aeroplane in my upper back, crept quickly through my whole body.

'This is Dad's place.'

I saw a figure walking down the neat and tidy driveway. A thought fluttered through my mind: would Jack lie to me too? *No, his diaries were not a lie.*

His hair was a sorrel-brown, although at the temples it was streaked with white. I'd imagined him handsome, and he was – perhaps not handsome in the true sense of the word – but attractive in a tough, unpolished and unprocessed way. Like Rafael. As Jack approached I looked down to my resting hands that lay palms upwards on my lap. The skin at my wrist pulsed at an alarming rate, and warm perspiration covered every inch of my body.

I glanced up and as I did so, Kathryn got out the car without saying a word and took several steps back. Jack walked to my side of the vehicle and then it was as if my heart stopped and time was suspended. Throughout my childhood I'd imagined this moment – meeting my father. I'd always envisioned it happening somewhere in France. When I was very young, the meeting would be in Paris and my French father was important, because in my mind's eye he was extremely important, perhaps a doctor, a surgeon; maybe a military man, a Général de Brigade, at the very least a Lieutenant-Colonel.

Jack opened the car door, his eyes settling on my face. The lines around his green eyes showed a man who had laughed a lot but the furrows of his brow showed a man who had worried more. My English father looked so much kinder than the credit my imagination had bestowed upon my French father.

Still without saying a word, he held out his hand and helped me from the car, and as I took his hand I saw my own trembling. Standing, I could gauge his height. A good three inches taller than my five foot nine. Close to him, I smelt a hint of soap and cologne I liked but didn't recognise. The smell indicated comfort to me, a comfort for which I'd been searching a lifetime.

'Isabella.'

'Thank you for seeing me.' I had no idea what to say, or how to say it. He was a stranger but as I scrutinised his face I saw fragments of myself. His features different to mine, set in a contrasting way, and yet somehow similar. I knew no one to whom I was directly related and so it wasn't something to which I gave much thought. I looked like my mother, and this I knew from the few photos I had of Sofia. But studying Jack I guessed his genes might well have had a significant influence on what occurred within the depths of me.

That was what I liked to think the day I met my father.

He held his arm out, indicating I hook mine through, which I did. I turned towards Kathryn, who'd retrieved the box from the boot and quickly made her way up the path. She returned empty-handed.

'Dad, I've left the box by the back door,' she said.

'Thanks, love.' He hugged his daughter and I saw the love, and I was pleased.

He turned to me, asking in a whisper, 'Have you managed to read anything?'

'All of it,' I said.

'Lots of questions?'

'Many.'

'I'm going to leave you two to it,' Kathryn said. 'I'll come back later, I have to make sure our house hasn't imploded, or exploded, whilst I've been away.' She giggled and this pleased me too, seeing this other side of Kathryn, a side exposed by her father's presence.

She drove off, swerving wildly around a young boy playing on his Chopper further down the road. The English bike was popular in Barcelona too.

'Come on, I've just boiled the kettle.' He paused a moment. 'You do look like your mother.'

'You loved my mother.' It wasn't a question but a statement, and one I felt comfortable voicing simply because Jack's diaries had made me feel as if I'd known him before I actually met him. His writing was concise but emotional, and written with depth. A style my editor admired in my own. I watched his body loosen. *Oh yes, he had loved my mother.* Of that I had no doubt. If I had come to England for nothing else than to see this, my father's love for Sofia, it would have been worth it.

'Ah, I did. More than anyone will ever know.'

My guts pleated inside. 'This is difficult, isn't it?' Too aware I echoed my words to Kathryn from the day before.

Jack shrugged broad shoulders. 'No. Not for me, and I hope not for you.'

He ushered me through a door and into a small and tidy kitchen, a white Formica kitchen table dotted with small red strawberries as its pattern sat against the end wall. A dying red hydrangea resided in the middle.

Glancing through the window, he screwed his eyes into the sunshine that filtered through; the earlier rain had lasted less than an hour. 'Everything seems to have happened at the same time. Beautiful rainbow in the south.'

I peered through the window too. 'It is a gorgeous rainbow. I'm sorry about your wife, Jack. Your children must miss her, especially Kathryn?'

'Yes, they all do, but especially Kathryn. It's hit her hard.'

'Last thing she needs is me.'

'I thought Kathryn would be angry but she isn't. Take a seat.' He pointed to a chair.

I sat down. 'And your other children?'

'My sons? I've told them, they're fine too. Intrigued more than anything.' Jack pulled a dead flower off the hydrangea and threw it into the sink. 'There's a lifetime to talk about, isn't there?'

'There is.'

'Shall we start with how you found out about me, because I'm guessing it wasn't from Calida. And tell me about you, Isabella. I *need* to know about *you*.'

How do you fill in a whole lifetime? But I tried, keeping to my career, my life between eighteen and now. I would wait before I got to Calida.

'I can't believe someone hasn't snapped you up,' he said, pushing a tight white curl away from his temple.

'Oh, they've tried, I just never found the right one.' I glanced up at him. His eyes such a striking green and the light from the kitchen window bringing a twinkle to them.

'Something tells me that might have changed?'

Was I that transparent, even with someone I didn't know? My life *had* changed, but I could not speak about it now, not yet. Not after finding out about Rafael. And Miguel, he'd kept it from me too. 'You are . . . *perspicaz*.'

I wanted to tell Jack about Rafael, but despite his warmth and wanting to be completely open with him, I would not. Too many years of keeping everything inside. He was my father but I did not know him, yet my feelings were almost like that with a lover who you have only known a short time; you see love, smell it, almost hear it whisper from the skin of people who naturally comprehend who you are. Innate understanding does not come from linear time, as does not real love, either sexual as with Rafael, or familial as with Jack. Both come from within, from the lining of a soul with which we are born. Understanding

270

and love grow, although both can also appear spontane-ously when they are authentic.

Rafael had betrayed me by withholding the most impor-tant of truths. Why had he not told me he'd known my mother? I had felt *his* love, smelt it. Felt safe within it. He'd had plenty of opportunity to tell me the night before I'd left for England. *Why had he not*?

'*Perspicaz* . . . insightful,' Jack said, bringing me away from my thoughts.

'Kathryn said your Spanish is good.'

'I'm a bit rusty now. I have a – what do people say – a knack for languages.'

'Your mother . . . my grandmother, was Austrian?'

'She was. You've done your homework.'

'Homework's part of my job, but it's all in your diaries.'

'Learning Spanish, and German, which I did during the war, was easy for me.' He shook his head as if his gift was nothing.

I too spoke other languages easily; perhaps a gift inherited.

'Come on,' he carried on. 'Tell me about you, Isabella.'

'I went to the Basque region on a job. My contact, Tomás, is engaged to a girl who is the niece of a Basque activist, who I interviewed.' I had no wish to mention Rafael yet but it was time I mentioned Miguel.

'Yes, I gathered as much from your letter.' He undid the top button of his shirt. 'Is there more?'

I waited a second. 'I met Miguel.'

A dawn of understanding filled his expression. 'Miguel?'

'The Miguel from your diaries. Yes.'

'I've so much to tell you, to add to what I wrote down all those years ago. When I met your mother, a war was raging but that wasn't the problem.'

'What was?'

'People. Other people. Families.'

'Herrera? Your brother, Joe?' I hoped Jack could fill in the detail of Severino Herrera. My grandfather.

'Yes, both. Come through, Isabella.' I followed him into the sitting room. Framed photographs filled every surface. I wanted to look more closely at them but felt it too presumptuous.

'Kathryn has quite some importance in the story,' he continued, seeing my questioning expression. 'A thread of the story includes Kathryn . . . and Isabella, there is a little more to my story that wasn't included in the diaries you've read, diaries which Kathryn's read too, as I'm sure she's told you. There's another notebook – one which no one has read.'

'Jack, whatever you think is right.'

I didn't tell him that I was already aware of Kathryn's importance in the story. She had already revealed the truth, but imploring me to allow Jack to tell me. *It's Dad's story, not mine. I shouldn't have said anything. Can you do this for me, Isabella?* At the time, inside Kathryn's lilac-coloured car, it hadn't seemed like a big ask. Now, though, it did. More secrets and omissions. Sitting there with my father I accepted she'd been right in her request, and Kathryn confiding in me had been a huge thing for her – and a compliment.

The mention of Jack's other diary had thrown me, although in my hotel room the night before I'd guessed there was more; there had to be. The final penultimate piece of the puzzle.

The course of events in Sabadell after Jack and Michael Donavan's departure, and what had happened to Jack after he'd been shot.

'I hope one day you might call me Dad, Isabella,' Jack said, breaking into my thoughts.

Again I smelt the cologne he used. 'I hope so too.'

He ruffled the top of my head, just as Calida had done when I'd been small. 'You fancy a walk? Get some hot, fresh air?'

'Good idea.'

We walked through brown, sun-scalded fields and talked mainly of my life. I told him the story of Calida and Aurelio. Jack said little about this, only occasionally nodding. I told him about the day I remembered him coming to the farm-house in France. And that was when he did stop walking, finding an old rock to perch on. I attempted to protect Calida, explain why she had kept it to herself, and lying to him on his visit.

'I can't believe Calida kept all this from you, and me.' I heard the rattling deep in his chest, noticed the way he rubbed at his stomach. 'I understand, in a way, why she didn't tell me. But I can't bloody forgive her. Do you?'

'I do,' I replied. 'I have to. What would my life be if I lost Calida's love? It would make my whole existence pointless.'

Sweat dribbled down both his temples. 'Come on, let's go back. It's too hot.'

45

Kathryn was sitting in the kitchen when we returned, nursing a glass of fruit juice. She wore a dress, the hem sitting high on her thighs, with a pattern of tiny strawberries on the fabric, similar to those on Jack's Formica kitchen table. She looked so comfortable, so a part of the space, the house, Jack's life, and a sudden rush of homesickness ran through me. I wanted to be eating paella sitting on my lounge floor with Ignacio, drinking cava, talking about music, the perfect way to cook rice, about my 'inadequate' wardrobe, as Ignacio called it, and not think about Rafael.

'Ah, Kathryn, we've been out for a walk,' Jack said. 'I didn't expect you back until later.'

'I wanted to come. To be here, Dad.' She glanced at me and I thought I saw a hint of guilt in her expression. 'When you tell Isabella . . . about me.'

'Aw, love.' To me, he said, 'Please sit down, Isabella. I'll make a cup of tea.' But before turning to put the kettle on the stove, he placed a protective arm around Kathryn's shoulders. 'You start, love. Start the story.'

And then Kathryn talked while Jack and I listened. She directed her monologue mainly towards her father, telling him, explaining to him. She went back to when she was a teenager, when she'd found the box and Jack's diaries in her parents' loft.

Jack said nothing as she relived her find and I followed his silence, thinking back to the morning when Kathryn had revealed the moment which had shaped her childhood. Underneath the table she touched my leg, took a sideways glance at me, and the benign complicity between us wasn't a bad thing.

Kathryn's real father was Joe Hayes. Jack's older brother. My uncle.

She was my cousin and not my half-sister.

Kathryn had discovered that Jack was not her father when she was twelve. However, none of this had been discussed until Jack and Alice had finally told her properly, admitting the entire truth to Kathryn on her sixteenth birthday.

As the Hayes family had reeled from the grief of Alice's unexpected death just under a year before, Kathryn's real father had returned to England. Joe was an old man with health issues, coming back from forty years in Mexico to make use of the British National Health Service.

Joe turning up had caused huge ripples of discontent and resentment. Things had escalated when Joe had got in touch with his daughter, asking her to go and see him in the nursing home in which he'd placed himself. Kathryn had refused. And Jack had had no intention of seeing his brother but he'd hoped Kathryn would, thinking it would do her some good. As Kathryn spoke, I understood why she had no desire to meet a father who'd ignored her existence from birth – from before birth.

I then told her how Calida had kept Jack's existence a secret from me, how I'd spent years trying to find out about a French father who had never existed. In those moments, in Jack's kitchen, Kathryn and I bonded in a way I'd never dared hope was possible.

'I'm so sorry, Isabella.' She glanced at her father. 'I'm glad though to get everything off my chest.'

I understood the English phrase. I had the greatest desire to get the problem of Rafael off my chest too.

I would, soon.

Jack got up and kissed her on the cheek and touched me on my shoulder. 'We'll talk about Joe later.' He looked at me. 'You'll have a lot of questions, Isabella. Ask away.'

It was three in the afternoon when my questions began; Jack answered all of them, Kathryn helpfully adding details. My questions were about my mother, the war, the International Brigades, and many about Joe, because Joe was definitely bringing out the journalist in me, whilst Michael Donavan prodded the storyteller. I found Jack's account of his friend charismatic and so interesting, and I cried a little when Jack began recounting the part of the story when Donavan died. My editor would be ecstatic with the amount of material I could use from my personal life.

We sat in Jack's sitting room well into the night and as the ticking clock's hour hand moved towards eleven, the three of us ate tongue sandwiches and drank tea. Eventually, light-headed but with a good exhaustion, the three of us decided it was time to sleep. I slept in Kathryn's old room and Kathryn slept in her brother's. For Jack, having both his daughters under the same roof made him happy, and I tried to ignore the brown rings encircling his green eyes.

Refreshed, the next morning after breakfast we carried on talking. I understood the outline of Jack and my mother's story but there was always something that surprises, and my father's anecdotal additions added more depth, bringing calmness and serenity regarding my mother. Jack made Sofia come alive to me, and I owed him everything for that.

He fleshed out the skeleton which Miguel had reconstructed and added muscle to his own written memoirs. Getting to know Sofia allowed me to know myself. The burden of silence surrounding my mother for my entire life was lifted, and this elevated me, as if a piece of my soul had been found and slotted into place.

Throughout, Kathryn and I interrupted Jack to ask questions about the other people in their story and Kathryn let go the fact that the story was about Jack and a woman who had been his first love, his first wife.

Still, I hadn't mentioned Rafael; Rafael, who knew more than anyone about my mother's final days. But he had not even told me he'd been there. Rafael and Miguel must have been aware that Jack would tell me everything, and yet they'd both wanted me to come and find Jack.

I thought about our trip to see Dominica Zubiri and the bones of her aunt, the baby. Rafael did everything for a reason. Had he taken me to meet Dominica to prepare me? But prepare me for what? Both he and Miguel had given me some sliver of hope that my mother could still be alive; I knew this was a wild hope, but Rafael had been with Sofia after Jack left for Brunete, so perhaps in his subconscious there was something that led Rafael to believe there was hope that Sofia was still alive? Again though, as in the hotel bedroom the previous night, anger bubbled through remembering my last meeting with Rafael – when I'd given him everything from within myself. He'd said we should always be honest with each other, although he had not been honest with me. People I loved and who surrounded me had lied. Calida, and now Rafael.

Attempting to put thoughts of Rafael to one side, I concentrated on the part of the story I needed to find out more about whilst here in England. And that was Joe Hayes.

My mother's disappearance was still a mystery, to both Jack and me, and now was the time to find out everything. About my grandfather, Severino Herrera, and Joe.

What really happened in Sabadell after Jack had left?

What had happened to Jack following Donavan's death? The diary entries had ended abruptly at Brunete – Kathryn had mentioned this too.

Jack picked up what must have been by then, a cold cup of tea, and his gaze moved first to Kathryn and then to me, as if he knew what I was going to ask next.

'There is one notebook that I don't keep in my box.' He pushed himself up and disappeared, returning five minutes later with a battered-looking black diary.

He placed it on the floor. 'I want you two to read this together. No one has read it before. I haven't read it since coming back from the war in 1945.'

Kathryn and I stared at him.

'Go on, now. Both of you read it together. I'm going outside for a bit to water the bloody flowers.' And that's exactly what he did.

Kathryn placed the diary on the dining table and pulled out two chairs. 'Come on, better do as we're told or we'll get no supper tonight!'

I grinned and sat down next to her, and together we began reading the final part of Jack's time in Spain.

46

Jack's last diary

FEBRUARY 1938

After the boy with the brown eyes had shot me, I was taken to a disused monastery in Burgos, now a concentration camp, San Pedro de Cardena. I remembered nothing of the long journey, which was probably a good thing, a fellow prisoner had told me. That prisoner also told me I'd 'died' at least twice on the journey from Brunete, and I became some sort of mascot to the other foreign prisoners within de Cardena.

The first weeks in the stone building I spent swimming in and out of a disjointed consciousness, knowing pain but not feeling it. Thinking sometimes I was dead but knowing I wasn't, only knowing because of the sweaty Nationalist soldier with the wide, fat face, thick moustache, bulging stomach and devilish breath. He was the one who took away my clothes, gave me no food and very little water, and when he did bring the murky, foul-smelling liquid, thinking of the dysentery that had taken so many, I didn't dare drink it.

I spent those weeks wondering when the true torture would begin.

And that seemed to be the torture itself. The waiting; that together with the real pain from the gunshot wound which was infected and still open. The moustached Nationalist finally allowed me treatment in what was laughingly called by the other prisoners, the medical unit. After that, he allowed me to keep my clothes, although retained my fear by regularly taking me outside into the fetid heat of the winter Spanish sun.

The first time the fat-faced soldier did this, my hands bound behind my back, blindfolded, I thought for sure it would be the end of my life.

In the dusty and medieval courtyard, like a picture of a biblical Hell, where even the sound of birds and bleating amphibians were silenced, I heard the splitting, unique sound of rifles being loaded and the execution squad shuffling their feet. I heard the bullets travelling over my head like giant mosquitos. I tried not to flinch, but flinch I did. A visceral reaction to oncoming death. I only understood the fourth time this occurred that they never intended to hit their target. The fat soldier would take off the blindfold and lead me back into the rat-infested monastery, my stomach retching in unison with the soldier's laughter that always accompanied this ritual.

Living conditions were inhuman and that I'd survived the initial wound from the clash with the brown-eyed boy was a miracle. I'd believed my redemption at the firing squad was a miracle too, until I discovered that many of the international prisoners were more fortunate than their Spanish counterparts. The foreigners' lives were spared simply because they were ideal candidates for the Nationalists to exchange for Italian and German prisoners who'd been captured by the Republicans. By the fifth 'execution', I understood this, but it didn't stop me from being petrified. I didn't think I'd leave the hellish camp alive.

I was released on the 20th December 1937. My life was a swap for three Nationalist soldiers. I found a friendly priest who agreed to take me as far as the outskirts of Barcelona. The priest didn't ask me about my final destination; he only helped me in being able to get there.

When we said our farewells on the outskirts of Barcelona we both understood we'd never see each other again. The priest managed to find a Republican friendly farmer and his family, and left me with them. It was this farmer who persuaded me to stop off at the hospital before carrying on to Barcelona, and Camillo Berneri's house.

The nurse who'd carried out the triage reminded me of Sofia, and for the two nights I spent in the hospital and during fitful sleeps, I called the young nurse by the name of my wife.

The doctor told me, you're lucky to be alive. He also informed me that the stomach wound was serious and would need proper treatment. I told the doctor I couldn't stay, patch me up as well as you can. The doctor did as he was asked. I promised on my return to England I'd seek treatment, pretending I didn't hear the remarks between the doctor and the nurse who looked like Sofia, if he lasts that long.

My experience during the weeks in Burgos and then the journey to Barcelona were unreal. A nightmare. Reality, the past and the present as mixed up as the country of which I was now part.

The only thing I focused on was Sofia.

By the time I found myself in Barcelona, my body was broken, my spirit crushed. The only thing keeping me on my feet and orientated was the obsession to return to Sofia.

When I entered the heart of the city I finally connected again with the world, although immediately sensed the subtle change in Barcelona's pulse; too fast but at the same time weakened, a feeling of distrust and anger pervaded, the people like a pot of under watered and neglected flowers; souls struggling for subsistence and too accepting of a fate that lay before them.

I learnt quickly that the Nationalists were moving further north towards Bilbao.

It was past six in the evening when I arrived, exhausted, at the familiar street. I was utterly unprepared for the consummate sadness as the house came into view.

I still couldn't believe Donavan was dead and had stopped myself from thinking of the gentle Irishman − having to − to survive. But now my mind returned to Michael Donavan. Then to Joe.

Joe. Bloody hell, it didn't make sense.

I looked at the house, at peeling paint and rusting metal, and wiped my brow; the humidity still penetrating, even in December.

Thoughts of England, my mum and Alice pummelled at my brain. I had to let my mum know I planned to leave Spain. With Sofia. I'd sort something out with Alice. She'd be nearly due now and I counted inside my head, but even simple arithmetic was difficult. No, the baby was probably already in the world. Maybe Joe was back in England; him and Alice already married. I forced myself to stop thinking; it hurt too much. Nothing was making sense.

I'd find a way to get to Sabadell, pick up Sofia and her adopted family, and get them to France.

My wife.

Slowly, I climbed up the steps. I nudged the door open. The coldness of the hallway hit hard. I stood there, taking deep breaths. The house smelled the same. A gentle aroma of garlic and mustiness hit my nostrils and the familiarity calmed me.

'Hello,' I said softly.

Silence.

'Miguel, are you here?'

A faint rustling. I made my way up the staircase, remembering every noise the old wood beneath my feet was capable of making. I stopped at the room I'd shared with Sofia, pushed the door open and peered inside. I padded to the wardrobe, opened it and Sofia's essence engulfed me. I fingered the primary-coloured scarves that hung tidily on the back of the door and pulled one out, placed it underneath my nose, inhaled and rubbed the silk fabric. Her favourite, a scalding red. I was surprised she hadn't taken it with her.

I didn't know why but I thought Aurelio might have used the old truck to come to Barcelona to retrieve the remainder of Sofia's belongings. I didn't know why I thought that, my thinking wasn't linear.

I didn't feel right.

I had no time to be ill.

Wrapping the scarf up tightly, I put it in my pocket, and continued to stare at Sofia's clothes. Later, I'd fold them, put them in a bag and take them to her. This thought catapulted my mind to Sabadell. If I couldn't get a lift there then I'd walk. It wasn't that far. A day, two maximum. If I walked though, I wouldn't be able to carry very much. I'd buy Sofia some more clothes, maybe in Paris, where we'd visit before going back to England. My thoughts circular. England.

A movement in the doorway and I turned.

Miguel. He looked terrible but I probably did too.

'You're back,' Miguel said.

'Are you all right?' Stupid question.

Miguel's body didn't move, but his eyes roamed furtively around the room. 'Is Donavan here?'

Donavan.

No, not here.

'No, Miguel. He's not.'

Miguel cupped his small chin in his dry and cracked hands. 'Is he dead?'

I took a step forward, clumsily putting my arms around the Spaniard. 'Killed at Brunete.'

'Were you there?' His voice only a fraction more than a whisper. 'With him?'

Yes, I was there.

'I was.' I tried to pull Miguel further into the room but he held back.

'Jack. Come downstairs—'

Fingers of desolation curled around me. We made our way down the stairs and I followed Miguel into the dining room. I sat on a chair and the fingers turned into muscular arms squeezing tight. The room was cool but still I found it difficult to breathe.

Miguel stood by the window. The late winter sun still making its way through the pane of glass. He turned. 'You don't look too good, Jack.'

'No. Nor do you.'

A twist of a smile. 'I had a visitor a week ago.'

Miguel's image was blunted by the low sun. I squinted. 'Who? Aurelio?' He had been. Aurelio had driven the godforsaken truck to Barcelona to pick up Sofia's stuff so she had her favourite clothes to wear. Then I remembered the wardrobe. Her clothes were still there. Even sitting in the musty dining room I smelt her spicy fragrance.

'A priest,' Miguel carried on.

I pulled the top of my shirt open, feeling the beads of sweat drip down my breastbone. 'Father Rodrigues?'

'Yes, that was his name.' Miguel again turned towards the window. 'It's Sofia.'

Jack's heart dropped onto the floor. Please God, no.

'She's disappeared.'

'Disappeared, not dead. She isn't dead—'

'The priest thinks she's dead, Jack.'

My heart ceased to beat, yet I was still alive. If I were still alive then Sofia would be too. 'What's happened? They're all still at the farmhouse. That's where they are. Rodrigues, what does he know?'

'Sofia is dead, Jack. We're sure she is.'

'Are they all still at the farmhouse in Sabadell?'

'Sofia is not. She disappeared. Aurelio and Calida were still there, but the priest is organising for them to go to France, Marseille. He's brought Rafael back here.'

'Going to France? What about Sofia? Disappeared. She can't be dead. I need to find her. I have to go to Sabadell. Speak with Aurelio.'

'They'll be gone. They can't find Sofia's body. It's dangerous for them, Jack.'

'What happened? I need to go to Sabadell.'

'I think Rodrigues is already on the way to France with Calida and Aurelio and—' Miguel glanced away. 'I don't think he wanted to tell me too much, he said he'd already told me enough.'

'Calida and Aurelio would never leave Sofia,' I said. 'Never.'

'They have to leave the country. They had to go.'

Calida and Aurelio would not leave Spain without good reason, and not without Sofia. An image of my wife filled my consciousness.

I tried to re-form my thoughts. 'Rafael's here? Let me see him.'

'He's not talking. He's unwell, Jack. The priest says he hasn't spoken since Sofia went missing, and he's still not talking.'

'I don't know what's happening, but I'm going to find out. If Sofia's dead, where's her body? What the fuck is going on?'

'Jack, they've gone.' Miguel sank to his knees. 'They had to go.'

'I want to speak to Rafael,' I shouted. But then the room began to shift, change shape. I couldn't focus. Sofia dead. I might as well be dead too.

And then I passed out.

I slept for twenty hours. That's what Miguel told me as he placed water and bread on the table next to the bed. I didn't believe Sofia was dead. Her noble and laughing face was in every corner of the room. I couldn't and wouldn't comprehend she no longer existed. But I'd known. Known as soon as I'd entered the house. I wished more than anything in the world I'd died at San Pedro. Without Sofia there was no point to my life. None. She was my life.

'Who killed Sofia, Miguel? Where's her body?' Just saying the words caused me to sink back down into the bed.

'The priest doesn't know what happened. No one does. But he had some interaction with Nationalists, and they weren't in the Sabadell area, Jack. Not as a military-recognised unit, when Sofia went missing.'

'What do you mean, recognised unit?'

'A group of Nationalists had been spotted in and around Sabadell, before . . . Sofia's disappearance. But they weren't an authorised unit.'

'Who were they?'

'I don't know,' Miguel replied.

'Did the priest know anything more?'

'He said the leader was probably an officer. He wondered if they were Nationalist deserters.' Miguel wasn't looking at me. 'The priest just wanted to get Calida and Aurelio out of Spain with the . . .'

'What? With the what?'

'. . . with all their things.'

'Send Rafael in to see me.'

'He won't speak. I told you.'

I got up, trying to ignore the dizziness, but fell back onto the bed. I'd talk to Rafael later. 'I have to go to Sabadell and find out what happened.'

'The farmhouse has been burned down. There's nothing there. This is war. You have to accept Sofia is probably dead.'

So that was it. Everything that had happened and that was it? 'If there's no body, no one saw or knows what happened, then there's hope. I'm going to Sabadell.'

'Jack, you're not well, even if there was something to find, and I don't think there is, the war is taking everything, everyone. You're not well enough to do anything yet. And, there's something else.'

What else could there be?

Miguel continued. 'Another Englishman, a brigader, came about three or four weeks ago. He brought a letter from England for you.' Miguel left the room and came back with the unopened envelope. 'I said I didn't know when you'd be back.'

Or if I'd be back

'I'll let you read it in peace. Jack—'

I looked up. 'Yes?'

'I think you should get a doctor to look you over, you really do look terrible. What happened to you?'

'I don't want no bloody doctor. I'll be fine, another sleep and I'll be fine.' I ignored Miguel's last question. I didn't want to talk about Burgos. Ever again. To anyone.

'I'm going out for a while. I won't be long.' Miguel touched me lightly on his arm. 'I'm sorry.'

I wanted to tell him that Sofia was my wife but the words were buried before uttering them. Rafael would have told Miguel that Sofia and I were married, but maybe he hadn't, because Rafael wasn't speaking.

Miguel hovered, still not leaving. 'Have you heard from Joe?'

'No, why?'

'After you left for Brunete, Joe came back. I thought him coming back was good, that you'd all be pleased. I always liked him. The thing is, Jack . . . I did tell him. Tell him you'd left Sofia in Sabadell. I'm sorry. I know Donavan didn't want me say anything and I don't know why I did. But I liked Joe. I'm sorry.'

Joe knew. My flaky brother. My untrustworthy brother. My brother who seemed to possess no ability to know right from wrong. My brother who was covered in an inexplicable envy and anger directed at everyone around him. I swallowed, holding down the acidity in the back of my throat. I swallowed back the pain.

Joe. He'd revealed Sofia's location to the most dangerous man in Sofia's life. Her father, Herrera. I wanted to kill my brother, and would have done so if he were there.

I would have killed Joe. I knew that.

I lay back on the bed and said nothing. I was angry, empty and hollow.

I was broken-hearted.

'I'll see you later,' Miguel said quietly.

A light but intermittent pain fluttered inside my chest. How would I manage the journey to Sabadell?

I opened my mum's letter, dated August.

3rd August 1937
Dear Jack,

I haven't heard from you and I'm so worried. I have received a letter from Joe – he's in Mexico. He didn't enlighten me on what he was doing. He assumed you would be returning to England and will marry Alice. I have replied to him but heard nothing.

Alice has had the baby. A little early, but thank God she's fine. Alice's parents, as you can imagine, have only made things worse. Alice is in Springfields – you may remember it. Out of town, secluded. A mental institution. We're hoping she will get back to normal as soon as possible. I am looking after the baby, and George Wrigley is helping a little financially.

When are you coming home, Jack? We need you.

I know you told Alice about the Spanish girl. Maybe now you have her out of your system – love is fickle in war, in a foreign country, as I'm sure you know.

I wait for your reply, Jack.

Much love, your mum.

I threw the letter to the bottom of the bed but eventually retrieved it and read the words again.

Poor Alice. My God, a mental institution.

Sofia was dead. How long had I known? The answer came swiftly because it had lain in my subconscious.

Soon after we had turned the corner from the farmhouse near Sabadell.

289

After I saw the tree on the hill.

But I had to find her. She wasn't dead. No, Sofia wasn't dead.

My mind twisted and wriggled, trying to hold on to what was real. The Parrello-Rossellos would never have left the country without Sofia. If they'd left, then Sofia was dead.

Sleep overtook me but my dreams were as demented as a wakeful mind. Sofia in the church where Father Rodrigues had married us. The crown of Spanish bluebells so beautiful, although they began to change in front of me, becoming a crown of thorns. I watched from above, as if embedded into the church's high and ornate ceiling, as blood trickled like a miniature red lava flow down Sofia's forehead. At the end of my dreams and in half-wakefulness I questioned if any of this had really happened.

Perhaps I was still in England. Maybe meeting Alice for a picnic so she could read my poems. Going for a pint of brown ale.

Maybe Sofia was only a figment of the most romantic part of my imagination: a character in a poem or a play.

None of it real.

On Saturday 8th January 1938, a brigader who I'd met at Leandro's café came to the house and insisted on taking me back to England. I was too ill to argue and Miguel encouraged it too.

The brigader took me to Gandia, a small port near to Alicante, very near to wine-growing country. Together we boarded a British warship, *The Sussex*, which took us as far as Marseille, and then an ambulance transported me to the airport, and back to England.

They told me that I was extremely ill and disorientated but like the journey to Burgos, I remembered nothing.

The two weeks I spent inside a ward in a Hampshire convalescent hospital would be forever irretrievable too.

By the time I felt myself, Alice, her baby and my mum were accompanying me back to Mansfield.

47

Isabella

Kathryn and I had read Jack's diary together, she turning the pages, and me saying to her every minute or so, *go on*. When we'd both finished I took a sip of cold tea and turned to her. Tears glistened.

'Are you all right, Kathryn?' I asked, taking her hand.

'I'm fine. I just wished Dad hadn't kept this to himself and for so long.'

'I think there was the right time for him to share this, with you, and with me.'

She nodded and as she did so Jack returned to the room.

He pulled up another chair and sat next to Kathryn. 'Don't be sad, love. Some things it's better not to share.'

'Did Mum know?' Kathryn asked.

'She did. She knew everything, love.'

And Kathryn's eyes filled again. Jack turned to me.

'Joe was involved somehow, wasn't he?' I said.

'I tried to think he wasn't but—'

'I'm ashamed I share his genes,' Kathryn interrupted but toughness cradled her voice.

Wanting to change the direction of the conversation, I asked Jack, 'Why did you never go back to Spain, after that last visit in 1946 to see Calida?'

'Life took over. I had to think of Alice and Kathryn, and

our sons came along quickly. I was busy with the union work at the pit. And it was obvious to me, although I didn't know why then, that when I visited Marseille, Calida wanted nothing to do with me.' He caught my eye. 'War does funny things to people . . . Calida had a very bad time.'

I inclined my head. This was something I'd always known.

'Tell me about Rafael,' I said, finally, although feeling a cramp in my stomach.

He watched me carefully. 'Rafael? Miguel's nephew?' My newly discovered father was not stupid. Jack searched my face. 'Why do you ask about Rafael?'

Kathryn moved closer to me, as if she knew. A woman's intuition.

'He is the man I told you about. The man I've fallen in love with,' I said softly.

'Rafael?'

I nodded.

'My God.'

'Neither Miguel, nor Rafael mentioned anything to me about Rafael being in Sabadell,' I said.

Jack stood and rubbed his stomach. 'Rafael went through a lot during the war. He was so young. You shouldn't judge him too badly.'

'Do you think he knows something more about my mother?'

'That question has been with me for forty years, Isabella. Rafael didn't speak at all after he returned from Sabadell.'

I dug index fingers into my temple. 'Rafael, and Miguel, have both implied that there is a slim possibility that my mother could still be alive.'

I watched for his reaction. He did not believe this was even a remote possibility, I saw it in his eyes and in the way his shoulders slumped. He didn't answer. There was no need to.

I pushed on. 'Have you ever tried to find Rafael?'

He sat back down on the sofa. 'Soon after Alice died late last autumn, I visited the Basque region to look for Rafael.'

Kathryn suddenly became alert. '*Did* you, Dad?'

He grinned. 'Skegness?'

'When you said you were going there for a week to be alone?'

Jack nodded. 'I tried to find Rafael, but he was pretty much untraceable.' He glanced at me. 'Which is understandable seeing as what he's doing now.'

'He's not what you think he is,' I said.

'You sticking up for him, eh?' His face crinkled.

'Things aren't always as they seem.'

'No, they're not, so hold onto any judgement about him.'

'Touché.'

Kathryn cleared her throat. 'Someone needs to go see Joe.'

'Not me,' Jack said.

'You, Kathryn?' I asked.

'I think to start with, it should be you, Isabella,' Kathryn said. 'You have a way with words. You call the nursing home he's put himself in.'

'I think I may just do that.'

48

The next day I rang the nursing home in Nottingham. A thick, gravelly voice answered the phone.

'The Lodge, how can I help you?'

'I believe you have a Joe Hayes living at your residence. I wondered if it might be possible to speak with him?'

'Joe Hayes is with us. Yes, he can take a call, especially in the morning. At his best in the mornings. The Parkinson's doesn't kick in properly 'til the afternoons.' She paused. 'You a foreigner?'

I grimaced. 'Spanish. Could I speak to him, please?'

Franco had suffered with Parkinson's towards the end of his life. It was a shame the disease hadn't taken the fascist earlier.

'He's out in the garden. Who's calling?'

'A friend of his daughter's. Isabella.'

I waited five long minutes.

'Joe Hayes speaking.'

The tone was clipped, as he tried hard to form his words. I only guessed this because of what the nurse had unprofessionally revealed about him.

'This is Isabella Adame.' Silence.

Finally, he replied. 'They said it were a friend of Kathryn. Adame, you said?'

'Yes. Sofia's daughter.'

'You know Kathryn?'

'Yes.'

'I'm not talking to you until Kathryn agrees to see me.'

'I want to talk about your time in Spain during the 1930s.'

'Jack refuses to see me, I bet. That's fine. I haven't any desire to see him either. I only want to see my daughter.'

A daughter he'd abandoned for a lifetime.

'She will come *if* you agree to see me.'

'I'm better in the mornings.'

'Would tomorrow suit you?'

He grunted a yes. 'I know a lot. And I'm willing to tell that lot, if Kathryn comes to visit.'

'You abandoned her.'

'Better off without me. We all know Jack made the better father.'

'She never had the chance to choose, did she?'

'It was a long time ago.'

'It was, and now it's time to talk.'

'I did what I did, there's no turnin' back. I'm sorry for how it turned out. But Jack al'as knew how to wind me up—'

I needed to get off the phone. 'Ten tomorrow morning?'

'That's fine with me.'

I arrived at the well-presented nursing home just before our appointed time. The sky had unfolded but, despite the dampness, Joe was already in the garden sitting underneath a substantial gazebo with a tartan blanket spread over his lap. His skin was leathery and dark, reminding me of heavily varnished timber. A newspaper lay in his lap. He didn't look up.

'Hello, Joe.' I tried to feel some empathy for the old man, but was unable to conjure anything up.

At last he lifted his head. 'You really do look like Sofia.'

Joe pushed the newspaper to one side. 'There's a chair over by that tree.' He pointed.

I dragged it towards his and he pulled the tartan fabric towards his chest. His hand shook, a pin-rolling movement.

He caught me looking at the tremor. 'Why I came back.'

'For the British healthcare?'

'Yes. And to see Kathryn.'

'Have you ever met Kathryn?'

'Once, at my mother's funeral.'

'Magdalena?'

'Your grandmother, eh?'

'Did you speak to Kathryn . . . then?'

'No, she wouldn't have anything to do with me. Jack was there. He kept us apart. Interfering Jack. Always in my bloody face.'

'I've looked up the fees to this residence, it's expensive. Can you afford it?'

'It's none of your business.'

'I think it is my business.' And it was. What I suspected Joe had done was all done for money.

'I don't want Kathryn's money. Don't need her money, if that's what you're implying.'

'Why did you go to Mexico?'

'A shipload of the Republicans went to South America after Franco. Nationalists went too. They took their money and scarpered.'

'And were you a Republican or a Nationalist?'

His eyes darted towards the large patio back entrance of the nursing home, evading my gaze. 'Does it matter?' he finally answered.

Joe was as slippery as a jellyfish. 'Why did you go to Mexico?' I ploughed on. 'To get away from Jack? Alice? Your responsibilities?'

'England wasn't for me, that's the truth.'

'What did you do for a living in Mexico?'

He shrugged.

'You must have worked, to survive?' I was beginning to understand how he had survived.

'I had enough money. Still do.' He peered up at me. 'I don't need my daughter's money.'

'Where did the money come from?'

'And there's the question you've come here with.' I remained quiet. Waited. 'A large sum of money was placed in my bank account in the autumn of 1937.'

'From a Nationalist?'

'Yes, from a Nationalist, of sorts.'

'So you did *go over*?'

He remained silent.

'A Nationalist gave you money for information?' I pressed. 'What information?'

He shuffled in his chair and not for the first time that day I wondered why he'd really agreed to see me and answer my questions. Because I knew there was going to be a reason.

With what looked like an effort, he tilted his head upwards, as if it were too heavy for his neck. 'The location of the pregnant Sofia.' The words came out quickly, falling over each other, as if he wanted them banished from his lips. As if he didn't want to share them. But he had to give me something because he wanted something.

I swallowed. 'You knew she was pregnant? Why did you do it?'

'For the money . . . and to teach her and Jack a lesson.' He paused a moment. 'And Donavan.'

'Because Michael Donavan rejected you?'

He flung the blanket to the ground. 'I didn't have to worry about him. Killed at Brunete.'

'What else do you know? Do you know about Jack being in Burgos?'

He nodded. 'I know everything that happened.'

'And do you know what happened to my mother?'

'I didn't know, or about Jack being in Burg . . . os.' He stumbled on his words. 'Not until I saw . . .'

'Saw who?'

Silence.

'Who?' I pushed.

'I want to see Kathryn,' he said

'Who told you Jack was in Burgos?'

'Herrera.'

'It was Herrera who paid you?' It wasn't a wild guess.

'Herrera told me what'd happened to Jack at Burgos, and to Sofia . . . in Sabadell.'

'Herrera knew what had happened to . . . my mother?'

'He knows everything.'

'Knows?' As Miguel had suspected, Herrera wasn't dead. I tried to work out how old my grandfather must be. Late-seventies. Joe hadn't answered. 'Herrera's alive?'

'Yes, unless he's died recently. A tough old sod.'

I looked him in the eye. 'What happened to my mother?' I was so close, close to finding out. This repulsive man sitting in front of me possessed the key to ease the ache inside my heart of the not knowing, and the anguish within Jack's heart too.

'I need a glass of water.'

I sighed with exasperation, and deep sadness. I got up and went inside. A nurse handed me a glass. I said my thanks and made my way back to the garden.

Giving it to him, I sat back down. 'Tell me.'

'I didn't mean it to end the way it did. I just wanted to show Jack, Sofia and Donavan that they couldn't make a fool of me.'

'They weren't doing that. My mother and father fell in love. That's all they did. And Donavan had nothing to do with anything.' I looked around the garden trying to find something to fix my eyes on as I was having a hard time fixing them on Joe. 'Donavan didn't love you. You had Alice waiting for you. She was pregnant with your baby.'

'I felt trapped. Contrary to what everyone thinks, I did bloody go to fight for the Spanish Republicans. I believed in their ideology. Then.' He looked towards me, expecting some sort of reassurance. I said nothing. He continued. 'After Jarama—'

Now I did have to interrupt. '*Did* you do a deal with the Nationalists? Is that how you got out alive?'

'In a way. I used Sofia's name – as I'm sure you know she was Emilio Mola's goddaughter – thinking it would help me, having a Republican prisoner with connections to the highest. Better bargaining power, you see. They would exchange me for a Nationalist prisoner held by the Republicans. It happened all the time. They sectioned me away from the other prisoners for a couple of days. Then Herrera came to see me. Offered me freedom in return for *continuing* information.'

'I thought he'd given you money?'

'He did later, after I delivered the prize.'

'The prize being Sofia's location. Miguel told you where she was, didn't he?'

'That's right.'

'So in between you returning from Jarama and then disappearing again after the Barcelona May Days, you were feeding information to the Nationalists?'

'Yes.'

Unconsciously, I moved my chair a little further away from his, disturbed at the velocity of hatred for this man. My uncle.

He peered at me with rheumy eyes. 'Miguel told me Sofia was pregnant.'

'Did Herrera know?' I asked, hearing my voice's clipped tone, aware of the pressure building inside my cheeks. I could not cry. I would not cry. Not in front of Joe.

He nodded. 'Yes. I didn't know what he was going to do.'

Sickness engulfed me. 'What was he going to do?'

'I only found what he intended to do when I went to see Herrera, after my mum's funeral. I didn't know until then.'

'*What* happened in Sabadell? To my mother?'

He shrugged. 'That's for you to find out, Isabella Adame.'

In that moment I wanted Joe to be dead, I wished him dead. *Hold your nerve. Don't rise to his bait.* 'How much money did he give you for information about my mother?'

'Enough to live well in Mexico. And warned me not to return to England, to talk to no one about my time in Spain. I did as I was told. No way would I mess with him.'

I wriggled in my chair, only wanting to leave. 'Why now?'

'I'm going. To Hell, probably. Who knows? I want to see Kathryn before I die. How do you know so much?'

I remained silent.

'Jack doesn't love you. Did he even bother finding out that you existed? I was always surprised he left Sofia in Sabadell. Alone.'

'There was no reason why he shouldn't have done. Sofia should have been safe there if you hadn't told Herrera. It was *you*.' I stood up. I had no intention of giving him the satisfaction of asking more, no way I'd beg this reptile to help me. 'Where's Herrera now?'

'I'll tell you if Kathryn comes and sees me.'

I knew Kathryn would come, because we'd discussed it but I wasn't about to share that with Joe.

'I won't tell if she doesn't come,' he carried on, his face breaking out into what would have been before the Parkinson's had taken hold, a smile.

'I'll find out.'

'Not without my help.'

'We'll see,' I said.

'When Kathryn comes, because we both know she will, I'd like her to bring a photograph.'

'Of who?'

'Michael Donavan.'

There were several photos of Michael Donavan but I had no intention of relaying Joe's request to Kathryn. 'I'll see what I can do.'

'Will I see you again?'

I looked directly into wet, desperate eyes. 'I very much hope not.'

Turning, I left.

Outside, Kathryn was waiting for me patiently in her lilac car.

'How did it go?' She leant across the seat and pushed open the car door wider for me.

'I think you were lucky that Joe left both your mum and you,' I said, getting in.

'He was never going to be the Dalai Lama, was he?' She grinned.

'He knows where Herrera is, but won't tell me until he's seen you. I can find Herrera's location but it'll take me a while—'

'I'll go and see Joe.'

'Oh, Kathryn.' I leant across and embraced her petite form.

We drove back to Mansfield in anxious silence, the car windows open allowing the warm wind to flow thorough;

the day was hot. When we arrived at Jack's he was hovering near the front door.

'I'm going to see Joe, Dad,' Kathryn said. 'I'm going now. But only because he has information that we need. No other reason.'

Jack half grimaced and half smiled.

'We've only just got back, Kathryn,' I said.

'I wanted to bring you home. Here with our dad.'

She turned on her heel and made her way back to the car.

Jack turned to me. 'Both of my daughters with attitude. I like it.'

Waiting for Kathryn to return was purgatory. Jack had gone to rest in his room and I heard him gently snoring soon after lying down.

When Kathryn walked into the kitchen a few hours later she looked different. Less tense, a victorious smile hovering on her lips.

'All done. Herrera's in Cuba.' She pulled out a notebook. 'Address and some details about him.'

'Thank you.' I touched her arm with my hand and she rested her own over mine. 'You didn't stay and chat, I take it?'

'No, we didn't chat. He's not my dad, Jack is.'

'He absolutely is.'

Concentration devoured her face. 'My dad's diaries and journals, photos.' I looked into her eyes. Blue, like Joe's, but Kathryn was the total opposite to her biological father. 'I used to have reoccurring nightmares that Sofia would come and take my dad away from me, my mum, my brothers. I somehow guessed Sofia was pregnant. That there was a baby. Somewhere.'

'Why did you think that? And how could you have guessed about me?'

'It seemed obvious from what Dad reported. Sofia being sick. Dad's clever but like most men doesn't see what's in front of him.'

'My mother told him she wasn't pregnant, and Jack . . . believed her.'

Kathryn's expression softened even more. 'Yes, you're right.'

Kathryn had known about me long before I'd known about her. And she'd read a lot more of her father's diaries as a young girl than Jack had ever realised.

49

Kathryn and I spent the next hour talking as we waited for Jack to wake. It was near to five when we heard rapid footsteps making their way up the concrete pathway of Jack's house and the back door opening without a knock.

'Alan!' Kathryn jumped up from the kitchen chair. 'What's happened? Is Annie all right?'

An average-height man panted inside Jack's kitchen. Kathryn's husband looked as I'd imagined; soft, kind eyes, attractive, and so utterly and beautifully normal.

'Annie's fine, love. I've just taken a call at home.' His gentle caramel eyes found me. 'I'm sorry, Isabella, we haven't met, but I know all about you. Someone is trying to contact you, from Spain.'

'Who?' I said, my heart plunging inside my chest.

'Rafael Daguerre . . . There's been a bombing, on the Basque border. Rafael asked that you call him, as soon as possible. I'll run you back to our house so you can use the phone.'

I grabbed my bag and followed Alan through the kitchen door and thoughts of Rafael not telling the truth about having known Sofia deserted me.

Alan led me through a hallway and house that wasn't that different from Jack's. In the dining room of Kathryn's home, her husband picked up the phone and dialled, indicating for me to sit, which I did, pulling out a chair from underneath the table.

'He said he'd wait for your call,' Alan said.

'This call will be expensive.'

'Don't worry about that.' He handed me the receiver.

I dialled and the ringing tone ended. 'Rafael?' I mouthed.

'*Querida.*' His voice was crackly and I could barely hear. I shoved the receiver closer to my ear. 'It's Tomás and Cristina . . . They were on their way to France, to Calida's, both of them, Isabella.'

'*Dios mío . . .*'

'Tomás, at the last minute . . .'

The line crackled again and frantically I moved the receiver to my other ear. 'I can't hear you, Rafael . . .'

Suddenly the poor connection improved and I heard him carrying on. '. . . Tomás said he would follow Cristina to France in the next few days. Cristina, she was a lot better . . . she didn't mind driving to France alone.' His voice cracked on the other end and it wasn't the phone's static. I could not bear this for him.

'*Was?*' Real pain gripped my stomach, fear rippled down my spine like freezing water over rocks.

'The Citroën blew.'

Cristina. Beautiful, vivacious Cristina. I thought of the doctor in Balmaseda, and what he had said about her baby. *He or she will live a long life, of that I'm sure.* It seemed that fate would not let go of Cristina's baby's soul, that nothing would keep away the grim reaper from claiming it. My heart exploded inside my chest with sorrow, disbelief, and grief.

'The mercenaries and our government?' I asked after long moments.

'I think not. Our own. My own. They thought I was going too, to France. They thought I'd be in the car.'

I was silent.

'Are you still there?' he asked.

I heard the desperation in the voice I'd grown to love. I wanted to help him, but I could not. 'I am.' Then I heard Rafael's tears. They cut through me. 'I'm coming home, Rafael.'

'How has it gone with Jack?' he asked, finally.

'You know how it's gone. This isn't the time to talk about it.'

'*Querida*, we *need* to talk. It was better coming from Jack.'

'No, Rafael, it would have been better coming from you.'

I pushed away the thought of a future without him and drowned.

'I'll be there waiting for you at the airport, Isabella.'

I put the phone down.

Alan gave me a glass of brandy and then took me back to Jack's. I walked into my father's sitting room. He and Kathryn waiting. I had to talk, to tell someone, I could not hold this in, tired of holding everything in.

'You all right, love?' Jack said.

'Course she's not all right.' Kathryn pulled me to her, embracing me.

'What's happened?' Jack asked gently.

'I told you about Tomás, his girlfriend Cristina? She is dead, along with the baby she was carrying. A car bomb.'

Kathryn held me tighter.

'Love, I'm so sorry,' Jack said. Kathryn released me and gently pushed me towards Jack, who enfolded me like a bear.

With my father and my newly found 'sister' I allowed myself to cry. I cried for Cristina, her baby, my mother, and even for Rafael. Because as Jack's arms held me tight,

I knew there was something that Rafael could tell me. A thing he knew which he had never shared, even with Miguel. With no one.

I walked to the sitting room's small window and looked out to his tiny but well-kept garden, bruised and singed by the English summer's blisteringly hot sun, and I remembered Cristina. Her laugh, her pretty face, the way she stroked her widening stomach, of how she had told me she'd known she was pregnant before the doctor had confirmed her future motherhood. *Girls just know, Isabella.*

Fixing my eyes on the silver birch tree in the corner of the garden I attempted to think things through. Because of the danger surrounding Rafael, and what was essentially his 'defection' from the separatist cause, and because of the contact he'd made with Bernardo García, there was no way Cristina would be able to have a public funeral. And, there would be no body to put in the coffin.

The effervescent Cristina didn't exist; she was only inside our minds now. A beautiful ghost.

Cristina's death made me examine my life in fast-forward, and in seconds my existence flashed before me. My stoicism, and my hardness, which I'd spent years acquiring to survive my job, left my consciousness as quickly and brutally as Cristina had so needlessly been taken from this world.

I thought of Rafael, of how much I loved him. There would never be peace. No happy ending.

How could I have ever imagined there could be?

Twelve hours later as I flew over the Pyrenees and twenty-five thousand feet above the world, I wondered if Cristina and her baby's soul passed anywhere near the plane taking me home.

50

Castelldefels, 20km southwest of Barcelona, Spain

Rafael, Miguel and I, together with Tomás and his mother, made our way up a spiral road that took us up the El Garraf mountain in Castelldefels.

The five of us had stopped for a lunch that no one ate in a town that was, these days, a burgeoning holiday resort. It seemed incongruous that for an hour we were surrounded by carefree tourists with sun cream smeared across pink faces and wet patches visible beneath pretty sundresses after morning swims in the turquoise sea.

At the top of the mountain sat a castle and a small church. It was Rafael who had organised Cristina's coffin to be brought up the mountain the day before, and Rafael who'd arranged a tight-lipped priest to carry out the service. The church overlooked, a thousand metres below, the Balearic Sea.

Throughout the tense service my dominating thought was that Cristina did not lie in the coffin, and that the flowers deluging the top covered an empty space below. But it did not stop the tears I made no attempt to halt.

It didn't stop me from thinking about the baby that would never be born. Cristina would have made a perfect mother.

Tomás sat next to me and as the priest ended his short and pithy speech I watched my friend crumple. The darkness of his hair already bleached grey at the temples. The pain and grief engraved on his face showed Tomás as ten years older than his nineteen years; it would never leave, as I wondered if he would, mentally, ever leave this church on the top of a mountain with a perfect vista of the sea.

His mother tried to console him but it was an impossible task. Perhaps time would heal, and even in the depths of my own despair I knew it would, but not for a very long time. And as I scrutinised this boy of whom I'd grown so fond, I recognised it was up to Rafael and me to ensure he did nothing in the near future to join his love.

Rafael took my hand; we both sensed this was our role, and for that role we needed to be together. For Tomás, it was my duty to level and make peace with the man I loved. Still loved. I caught sight of his scar that shone red in the warmth of the church, angered by the heat, the sadness of the funeral, and my disillusionment with Rafael lessened. Tomás's life was more important than my hurt. Cristina would not want me to hate Rafael, to abandon Tomás. And I would not. I would not lose myself.

We'd decided to bury Cristina's coffin in the small graveyard adjacent to the church, although it seemed wrong, her final resting place being in a region in which she'd never lived. But it was for the best, and on this we all agreed. When I say all, I did not include Tomás, because as well as stopping eating, Tomás had stopped speaking too. Tomás nodded at all the suggestions we made, unable to articulate his own.

Thirty-nine years before in Sabadell, Rafael had lost the capacity to speak too. It was time for the seven-year-old boy to open his heart. We needed to talk, not only about what Jack had told me, but also about the reality of what was happening within the Basque movement, and his agreements with Bernardo García. My speculation was that the Basque radicals had organised the car bomb, not directly, but it was they who wanted to be rid of Rafael, and his family. So now the clock was ticking and it would only be a matter of time before they reached their target.

The bell of the church began its funeral melody and we moved towards the burial plot. I took hold of Rafael's hand and squeezed it tight, and the priest said more words at the graveside to which I hardly listened. I looked at the church and the statue of an angel that guarded the entrance of the cemetery, and remembered Jack's diary, and Paloma Fuente. Such a waste of life and still happening. Would it continue forever?

The coffin was lowered and we waited for Tomás to throw a handful of soil onto the top. But Tomás stood, seemingly frozen in a snatch of time. Rafael stepped forward, bending down and scooping up a handful of earth; it was Rafael who threw soil, his eyes red, his body shaking. And I loved him. Death intensifies love.

Tomás walked slowly to the mouth of the grave, and Rafael moved quickly forward, anticipating Tomás throwing himself onto the top of the empty coffin, and I acknowledged that with the destruction of Cristina and her baby, and looking at the disinterested priest who represented the God we were sending Cristina towards, my faith was annihilated too.

Rafael and Tomás's mother held him between them, and they returned to the car.

Miguel handed the priest a fat envelope of cash.

'God works in mysterious ways,' the priest said to no one in particular, looking inside the envelope as he spoke.

'I think,' Miguel said as he placed an arm around my waist, 'that God isn't working at all, at the moment. *Adios, Padre.*'

Miguel shuffled me towards the car. Before we got in he faced me. 'Faith has good and bad times. It is not constant. Perhaps God is constant, but we mere mortals are not, we fluctuate and change, like the wind on a stormy day. You will see all this differently on another day, in the future. And Isabella . . .'

'Yes?' I said.

'Allow Rafael to speak to you.'

'Why didn't you tell me, Miguel, that Jack had come to find you in Spain after World War Two?'

Miguel's head dipped downwards. 'I heard he was looking for me. I was building my house in the valley then. I'd no wish to see anyone from the civil war.' Finally he lifted his head, found my eyes. 'I assumed that Jack had been to see Calida and Aurelio in France at the same time he came looking for me . . . and that he'd known about you since the end of the civil war. When Tomás mentioned you, when I first saw you, I thought you knew about Jack, your English father. I had no idea.'

I shook my head in sadness. 'You knew Rafael was there in Sabadell, Miguel. You knew Sofia was pregnant, and yet you didn't tell Jack when he returned to Barcelona from Burgos and the San Pedro prison? You knew Calida and Aurelia had taken a baby, me, to France. Why didn't you tell Jack then?'

He plunged both hands into his pockets. 'The priest, Rodrigues, begged me to say nothing. I worried about Rafael. I didn't know what I was doing—'

'You had time later, when Jack returned to Spain in 1946. You purposefully avoided him.' I was trying hard to understand.

'I know, and for that, for everything, I am truly sorry.'
He glanced at the cemetery where we had just laid Cristina's
soul to rest. 'It seems I am being punished.'

'Miguel—'

'I felt guilt that I told Joe where Sofia was staying. I felt
guilt that I didn't tell Jack about you, then, in Barcelona
in 1937. Then when he came back to Spain after the war,
I avoided him . . . because I felt guilt about what I hadn't
told him. I am sorry for not telling you about Rafael
being in Sabadell. But now it is Rafael who must tell you
everything. Allow him to tell you.'

He stroked my cheek, and I moved away a fraction. He
continued. 'By 1946, I only wanted to be left alone. I have
no answer for you, Isabella, regarding me. But Rafael, he
has never spoken of the time in Sabadell.' He sighed and
looked into the car at Rafael. 'It has been held inside him.
He loves you, loves you enough to finally allow himself
to remember.'

'Love needs honesty.'

'Love needs understanding, *niña*.'

Tomás, his mother and Miguel took the train back to
Bilbao from Barcelona the next day. Rafael stayed with
me at my flat. Luckily, and only because the last thing I
needed was the perceptive questioning of my neighbour,
Ignacio was away on assignment.

As soon as we closed the door I went straight to the
bathroom to have a shower. When I returned to the
bedroom Rafael was sitting patiently on a chair. He had
moved it next to the balcony doors, which he'd opened.
The sound of guitar noise drifted through; it was the usual
busker who seemed to live on the street below, and playing
my favourite tune. I wondered if I would ever dance again.

313

'So, Severino Herrera lives in Cuba?' he asked.

I towel dried my hair. I'd already told Rafael about my visit to see Joe, and about Kathryn. 'It would seem so, Rafael. I have to go to Cuba.' I had already decided.

His sigh was long, loud and exasperated. 'We'll talk later about this.' I felt his eyes following my movements. 'I have spoken with Calida, and she is expecting Tomás and his mother. They need to be out of the Basque region for a good while. I know though, that Miguel won't go anywhere, and I'm hoping that his location is still secret, but in case it isn't, I insist Tomás and his mother go to France.'

'Good.' I unravelled the towel and shook my head. 'Calida will be pleased to have them.' Calida would have loved Cristina. I could not blame Rafael about Cristina. But Sabadell was a different matter. It wasn't the fact that he had been there; it was that he hadn't told me, even after the most intimate of our moments together.

But we'd had to talk about other things, like Tomás and his mother going to France. And Herrera. I scrutinised him. His face gaunt, a sadness sketched across it, and which I still wanted to erase. He sat back in the chair and my desire to kiss him overrode any compulsion towards anger. With Cristina's funeral over I'd begun to find some clarity. Rafael's grief and horror, and guilt, was impossible not to sympathise with. I thought back to what Miguel had said. Yes, I loved Rafael and my sympathy and empathy was unequivocal.

As if knowing what I thought – Rafael would always know what I thought – he held out his arms and beckoned me.

I shook my head.

'Then sit, *querida*. It is time I told you my story. The story of your mother.'

'Why didn't you tell me in Balmaseda?'

'Months ago, when I realised who Tomás would be working with, when he told me your editor had contacted him to be your guide, the memories gradually came back. For the first time in forty years, they returned. I allowed them to return. I asked him to bring you to me, to Miguel's.' His eyes shimmered then. 'I knew you would bite.'

I sat down, dropped my head forward and brushed my hair, and then flung it back and looked at him, unable to stop the smile. 'No, you didn't.'

'I did, *querida*.'

'Are you saying you had no memory before?'

'Of what happened in Sabadell? No, I did not. I blocked it out. When the priest brought me back to Barcelona, and back to Miguel, I couldn't speak. I was seven years old, Isabella. Miguel tried to find out what had happened, as had Calida and Aurelio. But I said nothing, and over the years I buried it so deep, it was irretrievable. I knew about you, I read your articles, your name opened up so many memories and thoughts, but I avoided knowing anything about you. I pushed the knowledge of you away – until your editor contacted Tomás. I never said anything to Miguel about . . . Sabadell. Miguel knew you existed, but knew nothing else. He was surprised when I said I hoped to bring you to meet him. I think he hoped that finally I'd remember. Then you came, Isabella. Then I met you. I didn't know what to tell you, so I said nothing. I took you to see Dominica Zubiri, and after that I thought I would tell you. Then—'

He stopped talking and rose, placed a hand in the small of my back, and despite the gravity of our conversation I only wanted to feel him close to me. God, I only wanted him. I didn't move his hand away and he pulled me to the bed, and together we fell onto it. He stroked my stomach, my breasts, and continued to talk.

'Then we made love, *querida*. And everything I saw and heard came back to me and I had no wish to sully anything. But I wanted you to see Jack. Perhaps I was a coward by leaving it to Jack to tell you. And for that I am truly sorry.'

He rolled onto his side, his lips so near to mine and I felt his breath on my face, the smell of his body. 'I saw you come into this world, and I swear, I will not allow you to leave it before me.'

'You saw me . . . being born?'

'Listen.' He kissed me gently, turned onto his back. 'And I hope there will be a part of you that forgives my silence, concerning your mother, Scilla. Sofia.'

He began recounting his and my mother's story, his eyes never leaving the whiteness of the space above.

Beginning on a hill in Catalonia.

51

Sabadell, Spain

The Skinny Boy's story

December 1937

It was December 1937 and Jack and Michael Donavan had been gone for over five months. We had no idea what had happened to them. There had been no news, but if I said anything about the possibility of them being killed, which sometimes stupidly I did, Sofia got very angry with me. She was always positive and refused to believe anything could happen to either of them, although we both knew the Brunete campaign had finished by the end of July. Sofia assumed they had gone off to fight in another offensive. I had heard Calida and Aurelio discussing the same subject late into the night; they both believed Jack and Michael had been killed.

The weather was changing slowly, getting colder, but Sofia and I spent most of our time up on the hill. The age gap between us did not seem to matter. By that time her pregnancy had made her cumbersome but she still tried to climb the same trees as me. She was different in Sabadell, different from the capable Sofia in Barcelona. 'You shouldn't be climbing trees, Scilla, what if you fall and hurt the baby?' I said. She laughed and half-ignored me. Her concession was to climb only to the first or second branch. I had taken to calling her by the name of the Spanish bluebell flower, Scilla. Her eyes so matched the colour of them, and became more of that lovely violet the heavier in pregnancy she became.

We would stay out all day, even as winter began to take a proper hold. Calida would pack us lunch to take up the hill so as we didn't have to walk all the way back down.

Sometimes, I heard a rustle, sensed someone else nearby, although I had heard Calida and Aurelio talking about the renegade Nationalist soldiers in the area, and my imagination, and fear, was strong. I said nothing to Sofia though, not wanting her to think I was a cry-baby – that was the last thing I wanted her to think about me. She was so fearless in everything she did. She was a girl but I wanted to be like her. I admired her and put her on a pedestal so high that all I could do was gaze up towards her. Admiring her, loving her.

One day, December 4th, a day milder than the preceding ones, and bored with our hill we decided to go investigate an old uninhabited farmhouse on the other side of the valley. The journey took us along the same route I'd taken with Calida a few days previously, accompanying her to a neighbouring village looking to exchange clothing she had made, for meat. On that trip with Calida I had heard rifle shots. The cracking sound blasted into the quiet air of the peaceful countryside. Calida had pulled me towards a cluster of vines and pushed me down into the ground. We lay there for a long time, hearing voices of men coming closer. The renegade Nationalist soldiers. I remember not daring to breathe; not moving a muscle. When finally Calida and I allowed ourselves to move and when we could hear them no more, we dared to extend our limbs. Slowly we made our way to the dirt track.

And we saw.

The soldiers had made a sorry attempt to bury the bodies. Arms and legs jutting out at strange angles, sometimes a face that had died in horror and surprise, was visible from crumbly dry soil; no rain had fallen for weeks. That was probably why they did not bother to bury the bodies properly. It was too much hard work, that and because they did not care. I was aware of what was happening in the war, but this was non-Nationalist territory. Calida and I finally arrived at the next village, where she did not exchange a thing. The truth was: people wanted meat more than clothing.

The day Sofia and I went to the other valley and farm-house, Calida had forbade us from wandering too far away from our home.

Anyway, eventually we found ourselves at the farmhouse. Sofia's pregnancy, although advanced, was compact. She was not huge but it still took us a while to get there. We went inside and dusted off an old wooden table. Only one chair was stable enough to sit on so I used the rope I'd found in the corner of the kitchen to hold together one of the other chairs, so we could sit together and eat Calida's lunch. Sofia looked tired and I told her she should have a siesta but she said she just needed something to eat. She had sat back on the chair after eating and in the strangest position, she managed to fall asleep.

Guilt began to gnaw at me – her baby was due soon – I shouldn't have allowed her to walk such a way. She was much older than me though and knew what she was doing.

I sat watching her and didn't want to wake her up. She looked so peaceful. I decided to go outside and find her some flowers, make them into a pretty bunch I could give to her when she awoke. I wanted Sofia to sleep. I wanted her to be happy and healthy.

I put my jumper behind her neck and went to find the flowers, but it was December and there weren't many to be found, only the yellow winter jasmine which deluged the ground around the farmhouse's track. I picked some but wanted another colour to add to the bunch, and so off I went on my journey to find a different flower, hoping for a blue, like the bluebells she so loved, although knowing no such flower bloomed in December. I walked, maybe half a kilometre, picking coloured weeds and bits of grass, lost in my thoughts. I admitted defeat with ever finding a blue flower and made my way back.

Halfway up the track to the farmhouse, I heard loud voices coming from the building. Men's voices. I froze. Dropped the flowers and then I heard a woman's voice too. A high-pitched sound, and distraught. I moved quickly behind a jasmine vine and crouched down. They were only ten or so metres away. I hid my head in my hands but then thought of Sofia sleeping in the old farmhouse.

I peered outwards and they came into view. Three soldiers with a woman in front, a rifle butt pushed between her shoulder blades. I looked hard. It was then I recognised the soldier at the rear, sauntering along, recognising him from a photograph I had seen. Hot tears washed down my face. I wanted to run back to the farmhouse and warn Sofia. But I dare not. I was so frightened. I waited until they passed, and long enough for them to reach their destination. The farmhouse.

I knew it was where they were heading. It was as if I had known all day. I thought of Jack, and my promise to look after Sofia. But I knew that I couldn't because terror

320

wiped away everything. I watched from a distance as they entered the old farmhouse and then I began to move towards the building. I *had* recognised the officer, the leader, and knowing who it was – Sofia's father – stopped me from trying to run to the farmhouse to tell Sofia. I was a coward.

Sofia must have woken up when they kicked down the door. I can only imagine her fear. I recovered some courage and made my way to the outside of the farmhouse. They must have thought I would be in there too. They must have followed us, or known where we were heading. We had spoken to a farmer on our way there, telling him our destination.

I made my way to the window at the side of the house where an old wooden barrel sat. I would be able to stand on it, see, and hear.

And see and hear I did.

I climbed up onto the barrel and peered inside, through the broken window. Sofia was still sitting at the table; my jumper had fallen on the floor. The officer was talking. One of the other soldiers stood by Sofia, he was ugly, rubbing her shoulders, and then he swept his hand through her hair, almost tenderly. A feeling of hot and petrified abhorrence whipped through me.

'So at last, my dear anarchist *daughter*, we meet again. I've been waiting,' Sofia's father said. I had heard hushed talk about Severino Herrera. 'And not only a *daughter* I have, I hear, but also a *grandchild*, and not an English bastard *grandchild* but I also hear, a legitimate one. I'm pleased about that.'

'Have you been following me?' Sofia replied quietly.

'I know everything. You should know that. You have no protection now. Mola is dead. Jack, that's his name, isn't it? Has left you to go and fight in a war that is already over. A war in which you chose the wrong side. You are too much like your mother, headstrong and with no Catholic values. With no reverence for your own father, just as your mother had no respect for her own husband. And look what happened to your mother'

Sofia lifted her head and I recognised the defiance in her posture, as did Herrera. He didn't like that.

'What happened to my mother?' she asked obstinately.

'Ah. What really happened? What really happened is your mother fucked someone else and so I killed her. She thought Mola would protect her, but he couldn't.'

Herrera stamped the stone-tiled floor hard with his boot. 'I bided my time with Hilgardi, as I have done with you.' He stopped talking and his eyes swept over the room. 'Where's the boy?'

Sofia did not falter. At all.

'He's gone back. He didn't feel well. I told him I would have a sleep and follow him on.'

Sofia looked at Herrera, turned her head to look at the soldier, and finally turned towards the petrified village woman they had brought with them and who stood in the corner, silent. 'Why have you brought her?' Sofia pointed at the woman. 'Let her go.'

'She's here to help.' It was then, and for the first time, I saw a shred of fear pass over Sofia's face. Her hand moved to her swollen stomach.

Herrera carried on. 'It's neat, your fatness.' He moved towards her, shoving the soldier out of the way. 'Time for your baby to be born, Sofia.'

'Clear the table and lay her on it,' Herrera said to the kinder-looking of the two soldiers.

Disorientated, the soldier stepped back, as if frozen. The other soldier who was burlier, and his features much harder to read – the ugly one – then spoke.

'Leave it to me. I'll do it.' In one movement, he cleared the table of our lunch debris and then picked Sofia up. He laid her on the surface, flattening her body. She did not say a word. Remaining silent was her last and final weapon. By then, the first soldier, the kinder one, I thought, had recovered himself, undoubtedly knowing his own fate if he did not comply. He was the one who held Sofia, as gently as he could; I remember that, as his gentleness was so incongruent with what they were doing. Herrera ordered him to tie her hands, and legs, to the table. Sofia could remain silent no longer.

She began to cry, so hard she cried. 'My God, what are you doing? Please stop this. Please, Father.'

But it was futile. Herrera had already passed over the line. He felt invincible. I saw it. And he was.

I was still at the window, not caring if they saw me or not, and wishing myself into Sofia's mind. I hoped she knew I was there. I like to think she did. Inside my head I called her *Scilla*, the bluebell flower she'd worn in her hair when she had married Jack.

I think Herrera must have already discussed his intention with the ugly, burly soldier. Sofia stopped moving, and began moaning.

For the first time, the woman spoke. '*Jefe*, she's going into labour, for God's sake, let her go.'

'Having the baby? It wants to meet its fucking *riojo* mother, does it? Well, we'll help it along.' Even from the window I saw the saliva settling at the sides of his thin lips. He nodded towards the ugly, burly soldier. They had both moved forward. The burly one pulled a large knife from underneath his uniform.

And then it happened, almost too quickly for me to realise.

Sofia screamed. The woman screamed.

Herrera shouted at the other kinder soldier to hold Sofia firm. The horror of the event mirrored in the soldier's face. He'd begun to cry.

I fell backwards off the barrel and vomited. I tried to be silent and wiped away the sick and made myself get back up to watch. I thought about running back to the house, finding Aurelio, but there was no point. It would all be over by the time we returned. I hoped they would leave as soon as Herrera had relieved his hatred, and then I could help Sofia and her baby.

But they stayed.

As did I. My fear paralysing me.

I watched as the ugly soldier pulled the baby from its resting place. The woman from the village cut the cord and took the infant.

Took you, Isabella.

The woman made for the door, watching to see if Herrera would stop her. He did not.

She shouted, 'The baby is dead, the baby is dead, allow me to leave and bury it.'

She risked her life and left the farmhouse with the baby.

With you, Isabella.

Sofia had remained almost motionless so as you would have some chance of survival. Sofia thought you had died because the woman had to make all the people in the room believe you were dead, Isabella.

I thought they would leave and I would be able to comfort Sofia.

They didn't leave.

Herrera had not finished.

It was then that I thought Sofia, who was now semi-conscious, could see me at the window. I like to think she did, but if she did, she would also know I'd done nothing to save her.

They untied Sofia and together the two soldiers carried her outside. By then I had hidden behind the barrel. They wrapped an old blanket around her, and the three soldiers made their way up the hill. Herrera a few steps behind. He looked so nonchalant. So calm. So insane.

Sofia was still alive then, demanding they let her go. I heard her quietly saying her baby's name, *Isabella, Isabella*. She had somehow known you would be a girl. She and Calida had been talking for weeks about what they would call you.

I thought they were taking Sofia out towards the ditches with the dead Republican bodies. I thought they were taking her there to bury her. If Sofia wasn't dead by the time they got there, I knew they would shoot her. I prayed to God she would be dead by then. But they didn't head towards the ditch, they carried on walking up the hill, the hill where Sofia and I had played hide and seek. It seemed such a long way. I did not think they had seen me. Only later did I realise Herrera knew I was following, and obtained a perverse satisfaction from it.

I loathed myself in those moments as I walked up the hill, realising how useless I was. How full of fear I was. A void existed in Herrera's soul where human morality was supposed to live. Herrera had no boundaries and was devoid of any love or empathy for human life.

They finally reached the top of the hill. Sofia still clawing at a life she wanted to continue living, still defiant. I watched. I was numb. I had vomited twice more coming up the hill, imagining her pain, her loneliness, the grief.

There was a lone tree at the very top. It had always appeared ghostly but regal, standing alone from the others.

A monolith on the apex of our hill. The tree of freedom. Its branches were long, a thick trunk, with no lower outgrowths.

The two soldiers – the kinder one had long since given up on being rebellious – helped the other place Sofia up against the tree, holding her a few inches above the ground. Using the rope they'd unravelled from the chair in the farmhouse to keep her upright.

Darkness was falling. Now, surely, they would leave and then I could release Sofia and go find Aurelio. But they stayed.

Then Herrera walked towards the tree, and Sofia.

'You always thought you were more than you are, living with peasants, the Parrello-Rossellos and embracing a life that was never intended to be yours. You and your mother both embarrassed me, stalled my career.' He touched her face then. 'I could be Franco. I could be him, but for your behaviour, you are a blasphemous communist.'

Herrera – utterly deluded with who he thought he could have been.

Sofia opened her eyes. 'I feel sorry for you, Father, because you have no idea about love. About honour.'

Sofia then fell into unconsciousness.

All the time on the hill, I thought Jack would come. I don't know why I thought that. It was a hope. Of course he did not.

This horrendous act against another human being had nothing to do with the technicalities of the war being played out all over Spain. It did though, have everything to do with the mentality a war brings with it.

Sofia was dead.

I did not run. I stayed. I waited. As day turned into a paradoxical beautiful dusk, I watched the kinder soldier dig a hole and place Sofia in it, only a few metres from the auspicious tree. Herrera and the ugly soldier had left. I did not know where they had gone and I did not care. The kinder soldier finally got ready to leave and shouted.

'You can come out now.'

I looked towards him, not attempting to hide any more. He said nothing, only shrugged in desolation and surrender, and then he left the hill too.

I crawled on my belly to Sofia's grave. I kissed the soil and said *sorry*. My apology uttered because even then I knew I would never be able to tell anyone what I had seen.

I made my way back home and met Aurelio halfway. The woman from the village had already given you to them. The woman told Calida and Aurelio nothing of what she had seen. She had a family she had no wish to see butchered. After leaving the newborn with them, you, Isabella, she disappeared.

Aurelio knew Sofia was dead. He and Calida were in agony to know where her body lay. But I could not tell them. Even Father Rodrigues could not get it out of me.

It was Rodrigues who arranged their passage from Spain, and it was he who took me back to Barcelona, to Miguel. I did not speak for five years. To no one, not even Miguel.

I grew up and I pretended to myself I had forgotten.

But it was always there.

The fear. The terror.

Always there, Isabella.

52

Rafael finally stopped talking. We had not moved at all and I felt as if I'd never move again. I would never be able to tell anyone how I felt when Rafael described Sofia's final minutes in this world and a part of me wished he had kept his silence, but only a small part, and the part which had futilely hoped that my mother was alive somewhere in the world; the segment of me that still held a fraction of my childhood when Sofia was never dead, only disappeared.

'I knew about an *Isabella Adame*,' he said after minutes of silence, 'but I pushed it to one side, thinking it could not be you, but of course I knew it was you, that you were that baby. I read your articles. That day, when I returned to Calida and Aurelio's farmhouse, I saw Calida holding you, like a precious jewel. Aurelio told Calida that they had to find out about Jack, if he was still alive, to let him know about his child. But they did not find Jack. They did not seek out your father. And from what you have now told me, Calida had no intention of Jack knowing.' He stroked my forehead, his hand resting on my brow. 'Do not be hard on her. She had lost Sofia, and she wanted to keep you. Calida and Aurelio were desperate to find out what had happened to Sofia, and I could not tell them.' He found my eyes. 'They left Spain to save you.'

My anger towards Rafael had evaporated, how could it not after the story I'd just heard? But, resentment still gnawed at me that he, and Miguel, had given me false hope about my mother. Gently I took his hand away from my forehead and looked at him. 'I know this, but, Rafael, you led me to believe there was a chance, I know slim, that Sofia could be alive. Why did you, and Miguel, do that to me? Why?'

He placed the palms of his hands over his face, stayed in that position for minutes. Finally replying, 'I was still lying to myself, I am so sorry. And Miguel, Isabella, Miguel went along with what I said. Miguel didn't know what to do, so he did and said what he thought I would want him to do and say.'

'My mother's death. How am I going to live with that?' I moved onto my side, facing away from Rafael and curled into a ball.

How was I going to live with it? Jack had told me about a woman who was so alive, so vibrant, and that had made me happy, content, and able to cope with a void I'd always felt. But Rafael's revelations threw an unwanted light into the dark unexplored corners of my soul. The truth of my mother's murder and the unquestionable identity of her murderer.

'I do not know, *querida*, but I hope with every part of me you will allow me to help you heal.' He sat up and moved his legs over the side of the bed, leant forward. 'I will take you to where Sofia is buried. To the tree.'

'We must inform the authorities first, Rafael.'

'And the same thing happens as what happened to Dominica Zubiri's aunt's remains?' Cynicism lacing through his voice.

I nodded. 'But it must be done.' I stroked the thick greying hair on the back of his head and at my touch I felt his relief. 'Sofia has waited forty years to be found but there is something I must do first, before we find my mother.'

Rafael sighed and swivelled back onto the bed. 'We will need some help with what you anticipate, because I know your thoughts, Isabella. Since you told me about Joe's information regarding Herrera, I've already begun investigations.'

'This is not your fight. I have to go to Cuba alone.'

'This *is* my fight. I was there. I loved Sofia. She was like my older sister. No, not even that. Sofia was my older friend. I did nothing.'

'You could do nothing.' I moved thick hair away from his forehead, revealing the scar.

'I dared do nothing to help Sofia.'

'But you did dare. You stayed. You were seven years old.' I touched the scar.

'Do you love me less?'

'Less because you didn't tell me before? No.'

'Less because I'm not the man who you thought I was.'

'You are a man who is more than I had thought. What happened in Sabadell has made you who you are. It shaped your path.' My decision was made about the man sitting on the bed. I had forgiven him.

'The wrong path. See where it has got me. Even García was unable to stop what happened to Cristina. I worry, *querida*, that I have done the wrong thing.'

'In asking for Bernardo García's help? No, this is the right thing.'

'I've already spoken to him about Herrera. It has been known for years he didn't die during the civil war.'

I pulled a pillow behind my head. 'Go on.'

Rafael went on to tell me about Severino Herrera. Now nearly eighty and living in Cuba since he left Spain in

1938. A man who was a hardened fascist taking the favours of a communist, Castro. Herrera had laid low in Cuba during World War Two. After the Cuban Missile Crisis, Herrera began exporting cigars to North America, but in more recent years expanded into drugs; a new venture for him, but he was doing well with it. The young, ambitious García knew everything about Herrera, and was doing all he could to collate enough evidence against him to have him extradited back to Spain for the war crimes he committed during the civil war. García was on a mission; he and a small team within the National Assembly – outside official government policy – were determined to bring justice within Spain.

'How long has García been investigating?' I asked.

'Since he catapulted himself into a reasonable position of power, more so since he's been looking for glory, a career on the world stage.' He smiled. 'I like him though. García truly seeks justice for the innocents of the civil war. He is aware of the proposed *dirty war* within the government and its secret collusion with foreign mercenaries to tackle the Basque problem. And, he is the only government official of stature genuinely sympathetic to the thousands who disappeared during the civil war.' He caught my eye. 'Like Sofia.'

He went on to tell me that García was now fully aware of the events surrounding Dominica Zubiri's aunt's murder, and about Sofia Adame.

I was not the first person Rafael had told his story to about what had occurred in Sabadell. García had been told first. When I'd met Bernardo García, I had marked him out then for great things, and like Rafael, I'd warmed to him too.

Rafael told me the plan they'd formed inside a bar in Barcelona, over cognac and a handshake. García would get the man whose extradition he coveted – Herrera – and hence gain a higher profile within his government. Rafael would be able to put his own ghost to rest regarding Herrera, and also take García's help in ensuring that he could exit the movement he so wished to leave. Already, García was moving on Rafael's information pertaining to the Basque radicals. Rafael and García had obviously discussed me, postulating that bringing Herrera back to Spain, and to a court of justice, would help bring me peace.

Both men assumed this was what would make me happy.

But those were not my thoughts after listening to Rafael's story.

'What is García's plan?' I asked.

'Someone has to go to Cuba, find out more about Herrera before García begins to make the diplomatic moves for his extradition. Things are delicate.'

'Delicate?'

'Castro wants Herrera out of Cuba. Herrera is causing trouble, he is a loose cannon. García has suggested a meeting with you. I think I might have an idea what he wants to discuss. And I don't like it.'

'He wants *me* to go to Cuba?'

He nodded.

'And what does he offer in return?' Not that payment mattered. I'd planned to go to Cuba anyway and García's request would make it easier.

'Complete protection. New identities. A new life, in a new country. You, Tomás and me. In America.'

'It will be that bad for us, won't it?' After Cuba, I would go anywhere to be with Rafael.

'I'll disclose everything to García about the organisation I helped form. He suspected the tip of the iceberg. I have, and will, show him all of it.' He watched me. 'This has moved more quickly than I'd thought. You're implicated now, Isabella, and not just for the obvious reasons.'

'When can I meet with García?'

'Tomorrow at Tibidabo.'

It had been a long time since I'd been to the fairground at the top of Tibidabo Mountain.

'I loved it there when I was younger.' As a student journalist I'd visited the old-fashioned funfair, for the view over Barcelona as much as for the rides.

He smiled. 'Better times?'

I dipped my head and pulled my knees towards my chest into a tight ball, rocking rhythmically.

53

We stood at the perimeter wall of the fairground that overlooked Barcelona.

'Beautiful view, isn't it?' Rafael said.

'It is.'

Tibidabo held a magical and surreal quality, with its old-fashioned rides, the incongruity of fairground music slamming against the mountain's silence. I pulled my scarf tightly around my neck against the fierce wind, and then looking at my watch I felt a light tap on my shoulder.

I turned. 'Señor García?'

'Señora Adame.' He leant forward and kissed a freezing cheek. He was a good-looking man, distinguished for someone so young, for García was an easy ten years younger than me. His hair was full but greying, cut stylishly, and as chic as the suit and overcoat he wore. The finest cashmere. On the top of Tibidabo mountain I was convinced I saw a light of invincibility illuminate his shape; his power I'd glimpsed on our first meeting a few years before had matured. His dominance shone as a bright, uncompromising light.

'I am sorry we meet again under such circumstances, Señora Adame,' he said.

'Please call me Isabella.'

He stepped closer. 'Words cannot express my sorrow about Cristina, and your mother. We *will* bring Herrera to justice.' He eyed me. 'Properly and legally. But first—'

'First you have to get him back to Spain,' I finished for him.

He nodded. 'You are the perfect person to go to Cuba. You have the experience. I have been working on an alias for you.' He scrutinised my expression. 'I can cut through the small talk. Is that right?'

'Always.'

'Excellent. You use the name Daria Martinez, I believe? For the purposes of a trip to Cuba, as Daria, you work as a freelance writer for the American magazine, *Women and Politics*, which sympathises with the Cubans regarding the US trade embargo. '

He pulled out a box of peppermints, offered me one. I declined and he slipped the sweet into his mouth and carried on. 'I don't want you meeting Herrera on this visit. It's too dangerous. We don't know what he knows. Use your alias as a cover to find out as much as you can about him. That's what you're good at. I don't want you making any physical contact with him. I'm certain he hasn't lived in a vacuum all these years. He may well know you exist.'

Rafael tried to catch my gaze, moving his shoulders upwards and managed a sideway glance at García.

'We can have Herrera extradited to Spain, Isabella,' García continued. 'I've been in dialogue with Castro's aides. We can do this properly, with the backing of our government, with the backing of Amnesty International and the International Criminal Court. Castro has no desire for Herrera to stay in Cuba. Cuba is moving towards recognition within Europe and, in the future, America. Castro's tired of being cut off from the States. Herrera and people like him are making Castro's job difficult in gaining entry back in. Therefore Castro doesn't want to be seen harbouring a 'war criminal', especially a fascist one like Herrera. But

Castro can act only secretly. He treads a fine diplomatic line. Although Herrera has,' he looked at Rafael, 'left a wide trail. It's not only Sofia, there were many others.' He now watched me. 'We *can* get Herrera. And we *will*.'

'I will go to Cuba with Isabella,' Rafael said.

García shook his head. 'No, she goes alone. You have a price on your head, Daguerre. Stay in Spain, for now.'

'It's better I go alone,' I said.

'Will it be safe?' Rafael asked García.

'Nothing is ever guaranteed, but yes. As long as Isabella doesn't make contact with Herrera directly.' He turned to me. 'You only talk to Herrera's designated representatives, Isabella, is that clear?'

'Very clear.'

'And all questions should remain related to the trade embargo between the States and Cuba. That is your cover story, Isabella. The Cuban government knows about this investigation. It baulked at the idea initially, but the "magazine" promised a fair assessment of the situation in Cuba. Castro doesn't know it is you. To them, you are Daria Martinez.' García's smile was thin. 'Categorically, *no* contacting Herrera. And one more thing.'

'*Sí*?' I said.

'Mancera, you remember?'

'Of course I remember Melitón Mancera.' I glanced at Rafael who nodded at García.

'It was Mancera who tortured your father at Burgos,' García said. 'Sadly, now, we cannot bring him to trial. Rafael's old friends have made sure of that.'

I leant against the wall surrounding the fairground. 'Is there no end to my parents' pain?' Rafael gathered me close. 'I do not want Jack to know this. It will serve no purpose. Mancera is dead.'

336

'I agree,' Rafael said.

García smoothed down the lapel of his coat. 'Will you go to Cuba?'

'There was never a question,' I replied softly.

'Rafael will coordinate.' García turned, popping another mint. 'I will see you both soon.' He turned and within minutes the crowd swallowed him.

Rafael took me by the elbow. 'Let's go and get coffee.'

At the café table a masked actor came to perform, his painted-on, laughing, yet semi-tragic face peered at us.

'*Por favor, no hoy*,' Rafael said.

Disappointment was apparent underneath the actor's make-up. I pulled out a five-hundred-peseta note and gave it to him. Rafael crossed his legs. 'Generous.' He smiled. 'I don't want you to go to Cuba, but I know you will.'

'García wants this and he might help you, us, in acquiring obscurity. We need his help.' I sipped the cooling coffee. 'Tell me, Rafael, if you'd known about Mancera being at Burgos with Jack, would you still have tried to keep his itinerary away from the man who ordered your home to be ransacked?'

'I would not have changed my actions. To have Mancera in a court of law would be enough for me. It would be enough for Jack too.' He looked at his watch. 'It's time we left.'

A sigh of wind blew through my hair, strands caressed my cool cheek, and I did not reach to brush them away. The fairground sounds followed us into the silence of the mountain and for a long time afterwards, the hollow tin-like noise echoed inside my ears.

After leaving Rafael at Tibidabo I didn't see him again for a week, and during that week inside my flat, I began making my own parallel plans for my trip to Cuba. I called

337

my editor, who without asking too many questions – my editor could smell a potential story hundreds of miles away – shared all of his contacts, which would enable me to organise a different strategy once I was in Cuba.

A week later, I met up with Rafael at an obscure hotel in the business district of Madrid. I did feel some guilt that I was going against García's carefully thought-out plan, and against Rafael to a large extent. If Rafael suspected my alternative agenda he would never allow me to go to Cuba, or would definitely insist he went with me. I couldn't risk that, on many levels; Rafael would hamper me, clip my wings, and, I did not want Rafael exposed to the man who had effectively destroyed his early life; I loved him too much. It was in that moment of clarity I recognised I had truly forgiven Rafael.

García joined us soon after Rafael's arrival. Inside the room, which García had reserved, the more detailed plans for my trip to Cuba were made; *Daria's* updated identity and papers, including a passport, were given to me. García stayed for two hours going through the plan and protocols. He'd left nothing to chance. I listened intently, a wave of guilt at my duplicity passing over me and for a short time I thought of ditching my own renegade plan. But my wavering confidence soon returned when I thought of Herrera, and what he had inflicted upon my mother. His own daughter. I wanted an eye for an eye.

Rafael and I stayed in the hotel room for the rest of the afternoon and made love as we had never done before. Deep, passionate and sometimes frenzied, as if both of us were trying to make up for the ugliness and betrayal threading its way through both of our lives.

García had told us to leave separately. It was Rafael who left first. He would make his way back to Bilbao and then on to visit Calida in Marseille to check on Tomás. He would then fly on to England to see Jack – to tell my father what he had told me about the day at the farmhouse and on the hill in Sabadell. Jack deserved the story first-hand. Rafael and I both agreed.

After Rafael left I fretted about bombs and travel; García's protection would always be limited – the Basque radicals were easily capable of upgrading its bombing activities to commercial flights. And the alternative plans I'd made would be ramping up the stakes on all sides.

As I showered my mind returned to Herrera. The mental image I possessed of him wasn't pleasant. I convinced myself he had no idea of my existence and that I'd died in the arms of the village woman. Died the moment I'd been wrenched into this world, away from my mother.

Stepping out the shower, I dressed, ordered coffee, drank it and then left the hotel.

I walked to the metro, heading towards the Atocha train station, and as the last of the city workers made their way home the usually heaving Madrid streets emptied. I slowed my pace realising I'd be early for the return train to Barcelona. And it was then I noticed a man standing in a shop doorway. As I looked in his direction he avoided my gaze, staring intently at the gum-stained pavement. I stepped up my pace and carried on towards the metro, only looking behind once. The man had taken off his hat. The heat, although dying as the summer came to an end, was still strong. He was a few metres away, sweat glistening on his bald head. I felt the dampness begin to pool underneath my armpits as memories of Tomás and Cristina outside the house in Balmaseda came back; the man with the motorbike, his bare scalp. I shot a look to the side of him, half expecting to see a motorbike nearby.

When I glanced back, he had gone. Perhaps I was tired, making things up. That was what I told myself, as I had no intention of mentioning this to García, or Rafael. I didn't want to give them any reason to stop my trip to Cuba, any reason to suspect my alternative arrangements.

That was the very last thing I wanted.

54

Mansfield, England

Jack

When the telegram arrived from Rafael telling Jack he'd be visiting England, as well as being happy that at last he'd see the young lad again, Jack also experienced a strange peace he'd be meeting the man who'd fallen in love with Isabella. Jack had felt his Spanish daughter's inherent unhappiness, as he'd sensed too her deep love for Rafael. He wanted Isabella to have the calibre of love that he, shamefully, admitted to only having known for such a short time with Sofia. Thinking of Alice he disliked this thought, and himself.

Jack was more than aware though, that there was another reason why Rafael had taken the trouble to come to see him in England. It had something do with Sofia and Sabadell, and it was this that encouraged him to take a double dose of the heart pills. The gnawing emptiness and futile frustration he'd experienced for years was only half explained in the appearance of Isabella.

From the day he'd received Isabella's letter he'd always known there was more: the missing link surrounding Sofia's disappearance. Her death.

Jack checked his watch. Kathryn had driven down to Heathrow to pick up Rafael. They were due now. He opened the kitchen door and allowed the late summer breeze to float in.

The scorching summer of 1976 was coming to an end.

Rafael Daguerre filled Jack's kitchen with his presence. Jack would never have recognised him, not from the young skinny boy he'd left in Sabadell. Kathryn said her hasty farewells, saying she had to get Annie somewhere, although he couldn't help but notice her mild flirtatiousness with the good-looking Spanish bloke who seemed to occupy the kitchen's entire space.

They made no small talk, got straight down to the big talk. Jack thought about asking him if he wanted a tongue sandwich, decided not to, and gave him a homemade mince pie and a cup of tea instead, indicating Rafael to sit down at the table. Rafael seemed too big for the chair, and the table; the house.

Jack began foraging around for his Spanish. '*Lo siento que no me encuentro.*'

'English will be good, Jack,' Rafael said.

Jack smiled. 'I'm sorry I didn't find you before. I did go to Spain after Alice, my wife, died. I came to find you.' He watched the younger man. 'I came to find you because I thought there might be something you could tell me.'

Rafael pushed the pie to the side of his plate. 'There is, Jack. Isabella thought it better if I came and told you myself.'

Jack didn't ask, *why now?*

As if reading Jack's thoughts, Rafael said, 'I buried what happened. I buried it deep inside. I didn't tell Miguel. I told no one. I am so sorry, Jack.'

Rafael began the story of what had happened while he and Donavan were at Brunete, and later when Jack was in

342

San Pedro. Rafael told him about Sofia's pregnancy, how she'd settled in Sabadell, gone back to her childhood a little with a seven-year-old boy.

About the day inside the farmhouse on the side of the valley, and up on the hill afterwards.

Jack didn't interrupt him at all because he was unable to speak.

Rafael stopped talking, rose, and got himself a glass of water. He drank it slowly, placed the glass on the table, centring it neatly in between the strawberries. Jack cleared his throat, and Rafael rubbed at the scar on his forehead. Jack pulled his chair closer to Rafael, lifted a hand to his broad shoulder and rubbed it, as he'd have done with one of his sons during the times when they'd been teenagers, and came home with a woeful tale they'd no wish to share with Alice.

Rafael looked at him and Jack saw the skinny boy.

'I'm sorry for *you*. Go on, lad,' Jack said quietly.

'I didn't tell Isabella the full story, and changed it a little for her, the ending. But I'm going to tell you, Jack.' Rafael wrung his hands and gazed at them, then lifted his eyes to Jack. 'Herrera came back, after the soldier had buried Sofia's body.'

Jack's own body tightened and at the same time icy coldness covered every inch of his skin. He began to shiver in the heat of the dying summer.

'But before Sofia died it was your name she called out, Jack.'

Jack heard his own gasp.

Rafael moved close to him. 'I'd remained behind the bush. I'd urinated inside my trousers, the vomit had dried hard on my shirt. The acrid smell of my own body continues to be a reminder of that day on the hill. Then Herrera turned away from where Sofia lay, newly buried. I said a

343

prayer, knowing my life would too, soon be over. *Come out now, boy.* I did not move. *God, you stink, a peasant, a riojo, who can't control himself. Come here, boy.* He grabbed me with the only clean part of my shirt. *I'm not going to kill you, boy . . . as much as I would like to I want you to remember this, and for it to be a lesson to you. If you ever mention what has happened here, I will find you, and your pathetic family, and I will kill you. And remember – I will always be able to find you.'*

Rafael took a breath and carried on. 'Herrera shot me but he knew the pistol was empty. Then, he smashed my forehead with it. I don't know how I found my way back to Aurelio and Calida.'

Gently, Jack touched Rafael's scar, and Rafael finished his story at the point Rodrigues had taken him back to Barcelona.

'I'm so sorry, lad.' Jack gulped back the tears for the woman he loved and for the boy of whom he'd been so fond. He thought he could cry forever. *But of course we don't cry forever, only inside.*

'I've spoken to Isabella,' Jack carried on, focusing on the present, on his and Sofia's living daughter. 'And she tells me she's going to Cuba, to investigate Herrera. Do you think that's a wise move?' More than anything he needed to stop talking about Sofia.

'I do not know, but I think that doing it this way and through García, and with his protection, it will be safer. She would have gone anyway.' Rafael smiled grimly. 'She's a journalist. It's what she does.'

'She would, that's true. But *you* need García's help?' Isabella had explained to him about García during the phone call he'd taken with her at Kathryn's. Jack saw the lay of the land – Rafael and Isabella assist García, and in return the Spaniard helps them.

'I do need García's help. Isabella and I both need his help. To disappear.'

'Tell me about García,' Jack said.

Rafael gave Jack the details of Bernardo García and what he hoped to achieve. Of a plan where Isabella would help García in obtaining Herrera's extradition by teasing out information on a trip to Cuba, information that would be pertinent to García.

'You should have gone with her, Rafael,' Jack said. 'She'll make contact with Herrera, of that I'm bloody certain. When did she go?'

'Early yesterday morning. I can get a flight direct to Cuba from London.'

Jack got up and opened a kitchen drawer, pulled out a piece of paper, and gave it to Rafael. 'This is Herrera's address in Cuba.'

Rafael put it in his pocket.

It was Alan who took Rafael back to the airport and an hour after they'd left, as Jack lay on the settee thinking about Sofia, Kathryn let herself in.

'Dad, you look terrible. What did Rafael tell you?' She perched on the edge of the settee and kissed his forehead.

'I'll explain later. Sit down. I thought you were at work? You look upset, love. What's happened? Is Annie all right?'

'Joe's died.'

What a bloody day. He took a while to reply. 'How do you feel about it?'

'I don't feel anything.'

'When did you hear?'

'A few hours ago. I was at work when the nursing home called.' She watched him closely. 'How do you feel about it?'

'Nothing. I feel nothing.' That though, wasn't true. If Joe hadn't told Herrera about Sofia's location, she wouldn't have died that long-ago day in Sabadell. How did he feel? He hoped his fucking brother rotted in Hell, that's how he felt.

'Are you upset at all, that you didn't see him, Dad?'

Jack shook his head, only hoping that he wasn't on his own way to Hell too. Because there was no way he could stomach being in the same place as Joe.

PART FOUR

55

Cuba

Isabella

My stomach moved disconcertingly backwards towards my spine as the plane landed on the runway of Cuba's José Martí International Airport.

I walked the short distance through customs, missing Baggage Reclaim. Hand luggage only. This was no holiday; I was at work and this was like any other assignment.

García had arranged a chauffeur. *Safer*, he'd said.

Perhaps not quite like work.

I'd made my own final secret arrangements in the two frantic days before I flew out of Spain. Everything was in place, and because of my editor's practical and discreet help, I was hoping for a smooth run. Neither García nor Rafael suspected a thing regarding my off-piste plan.

I stood outside the main entrance. Humidity was high. The ground was wet. I looked upwards at the sky but no clouds remained, any evidence of recent rainfall swept away neatly by a mild but persistent wind.

Joe's instructions to Kathryn had been explicit. Herrera's villa would be found on the outskirts of a fishing village, Cojimar, six kilometres east of Havana. In the warmth of the Cuban sun I shivered, thinking of a man I wished dead.

I'd been in contact with Herrera's *PR* people only the day before and of course without García's knowledge. They were expecting Daria Martinez for a friendly interview, but now that interview was to be conducted at Herrera's villa. With Herrera himself.

Severino Herrera wanted to be seen as legitimate, a saviour to the Cuban communists. An old fascist in bed with communist Cuba. García had set up the whole magazine scenario with the professionalism I would expect of him, and which had made my covert plan consummately easier. *Daria's* magazine had the ear of Gerald Ford, Herrera thought. Dangerous Herrera was, but like people the world over, I'd only needed to flatter his ego.

A small blue car which had pulled up beside me took my attention. The driver was well dressed and didn't suit the dilapidated vehicle he drove.

The man wound the window down. 'Señora Martinez?'

'*Sí.*'

'Señor García's friend?'

I slipped into the back seat.

The journey was short, which was a relief as the car had no air-conditioning. I saw my reflection in the rear-view mirror, sweat bubbled unflatteringly at the apex of my cheekbones.

The driver spoke. 'We're nearly there. This is the Habena Vieja area.' I tried to catch his eye in the mirror but he was concentrating on the road. He carried on. 'A nice part of the city.' He turned his head and decided to expand, as if he were a tour guide. 'The government is renovating it, anticipating the increase in our tourist industry.'

I remembered what García had said about Cuba's desire to become more integrated within the capitalist world. As if knowing my thoughts the driver added, 'Tourists are important, especially to Castro, a man who soon plans to become President.'

Castro was still First Secretary of the Communist Party of Cuba, a post he'd taken in 1961. There were strong rumours that by the end of the year he'd be giving himself the title of *President*. I suppose he hoped that by appeasing the West and the capitalists, by encouraging tourism in Cuba, they would be more accepting of his title.

My driver drove slowly and finally we entered the deep core of ancient Havana. The atmosphere and feel changed immediately. It possessed a crumbling magnificence, an elegant but fading beauty. We passed by gorgeous plazas, and these in turn were surrounded by engaging narrow streets. It cried out a tired but compelling ambience and inadvertently, I fell a little in love with Cuba.

The car pulled up outside a weary-looking but charming building. 'This is your hotel.' He turned his head, not smiling.

Instead of attempting an exchange with him, I got out the car and viewed my home for the next week. García had purposefully chosen a downmarket hotel.

'*Gracias*,' I said. I hadn't asked his name.

He didn't help me with my small case, his body moulded to the driver's seat.

'I will be here. All the time.'

'What about sleeping?'

'In the car. I'll see you tomorrow, Señora Martinez.'

The hotel was more of a pension and it only took me a few steps to reach the reception. An old, emaciated man greeted me. The smell of cigar hung in the air around him.

'*Buenas tardes*, Señora Martinez?'

'*Hola*. One room?'

'Yes, at the back.'

'Thank you.' I moved closer to the aged wooden counter and nearer to the man.

He moved like an old dog from behind its domain, and a stronger smell of cigar moved along with him. He indicated where I could find the stairs and then waddled back to safety.

The bedroom was tiny with the one large bed leaving no space for anything else. It was even darker inside the room than the staircase. I flicked the light on. No window.

Unpacking a few things my stomach grumbled and the feeling of hunger surprised me. I washed my face and went out straightaway to find some decent food.

The blue car and the 'chauffeur' hadn't moved. A well-thumbed book was propped up against the steering wheel. He looked up as I made my way from the dirty canopy of the pension entrance, nodding as I walked by.

As I walked, I took in the early evening of Havana; cigar smoke, mixed with the strong aroma of mariposa flowers, which were outgrowing the many pots and window boxes of each small home I passed. I stopped to admire the single Cuban orchid, a fragile white with a hint of violet-blue deep within its petal root. Looking upward, a great ceiba tree overtook the width of the small causeway. The ceiba produced the best oil for soaps. It was Calida's favourite. I took a deep breath of the sweet air and continued walking, through the old Havana streets towards the restaurant old cigar man from the ension had recommended.

Should I have come clean with García, and Rafael? Allowed García to do his job, as he wanted to do it? But for me this was the perfect opportunity. I *had* to meet Herrera. And do what? I didn't know, but the compulsion to see him face-to-face was a compelling enough reason in my own mind that it needed no explanation. I swept away conflicting thoughts as the round and convivial restaurant owner's wife pulled out a chair for me.

56

As promised, the chauffeur was waiting outside when I emerged from the pension early the next afternoon. My meeting with Herrera, which I'd arranged without García's knowledge, was scheduled for two o'clock.

The chauffeur scrutinised me. '*Buenos días.*'

'*Buenos días*,' I replied, about to ask his name but he still hadn't offered it, and I didn't pursue. 'I believe you know where Señor Herrera's villa is located?'

He looked at me in his rear-view mirror. '*Sí.* I know where the butcher lives.'

'That's our destination today.'

He turned. 'I was led to believe that is not the destination, on this visit, *señora.*'

'A change of plan.'

His gaze now on the road. 'García's instructions are very specific regarding Herrera.'

'Bernardo García isn't here. I want to go to Cojimar. If you don't take me, I'm sure someone will for American dollars.'

Again he turned. 'It's not a good idea, *señora.* Herrera is not a good idea.'

'I'd prefer if you took me.'

He banged his palms against the steering wheel, but then twisted the key in the ignition and the engine sprang to life.

'Thank you.' I watched the back of his head as we moved away. I'd thought of arranging my own transport but I knew if I'd done so, and this chauffeur was as obedient as I'd suspected García's employee would be, García would very soon have been alerted to my counter-plan.

He drove slowly out of Habana Viejo and not until we left the city did he speed up. Only twenty minutes later we approached the small fishing village of Cojimar. Here again, he slowed down. It was a pretty place, with a hoop-shaped bay that enclosed the village; a turquoise, frothy sea surrounding the small beach.

The driver was now making his way to the other end of the village and out the other side. 'Not far now.'

It was more humid than the day I'd arrived. Opening the car window, I let in the oppressive air; hot drafts pummelled at my face. I closed it quickly and fixed my eyes on the road ahead.

Then I saw what I knew immediately was Herrera's villa. A massive terracotta-coloured wall surrounded it, while bright red electric gates guarded the front. The car pulled up outside. I didn't know what to expect – some sort of guard, something, but it seemed a normal residential home.

'You need to ring the intercom.' He looked at me. 'Let's stand outside the car, won't be as stuffy.'

I half-smiled. We got out simultaneously. He examined me, and I him. I waited for him to make another attempt to stop me seeing Herrera. He didn't, and I wondered how much he knew.

'I'll wait for you, *señora*,' he said. He lit the biggest cigar I'd ever seen and coughed. 'I only smoke when I'm worried.'

'Thank you,' I said. *Should I ask my driver's name?* 'I'm only interviewing Herrera. I'll be no longer than an hour.'

'And if you are longer?'

'I won't be. I promise. It'll be fine. I'm a journalist.'

'I know.'

I walked away from the car, pressed the button on the large metal pad of the intercom system, and waited.

'*Sí?*' A loud voice answered from the metal.

'Daria Martinez.'

The gates opened and I turned, giving a small wave to my chauffeur.

I walked through to a large courtyard; a beautiful and modern house ran three quarters around its perimeter. An obese but well-dressed man came towards me, late forties I estimated, and puffing hard on a cigar. I studied the *Havana*, as opposed to the man. It looked similar to the one my driver was choking on outside the gates.

'*Buenas tardes*, Señorita Martinez.'

'It's very good of Señor . . .' I paused briefly, 'Herrera to see me.'

A benevolent smile opened out his thick features. 'Yes, he is interested in your magazine.' He examined me as a buyer would at an equine auction. 'And you, I believe.'

I nodded but didn't answer. As I followed my stomach tightened with every step.

The atrium of the entrance hall belied the simple elegance of the outside of the house. Opulent and rich. Definitely vulgar. The man and the cigar took me left and into a small room, perhaps an office.

'Señor Herrera will be with you shortly,' he said.

I waited, glad of the massive fan rotating at full speed on the high ceiling.

And then Herrera entered.

He walked slowly.

He used a stick.

He appeared ancient, which he was. Easily eighty. An old man. Looking at him was like looking at the Nazi war criminals years after they had been imprisoned. Another generation, such as myself, could possess no comprehension of their past, their crimes. But I knew what Herrera had done and my already tense muscles hardened further, although I hoped that to Herrera I appeared perfectly calm and relaxed.

'Señorita Martinez? How can a woman so beautiful be still unmarried?'

I prayed García had done his job well.

'I have my work,' I said, smiling.

'Ah, yes, so I understand. Would you like some refreshments?'

I wanted nothing to eat or drink. 'That would be very pleasant. '

Herrera shot a glance at the man who had greeted me, his whole body rotating to enable his head to turn. 'Rico! Refreshments, make yourself useful.' He, painfully it seemed, turned back to look at me. 'Please sit. Let us begin. I get very tired later, so let's be efficient.'

Herrera began with my 'connection' to President Ford; he really did believe my magazine possessed the right connections with the US leader. We talked for another half an hour. He appeared relaxed. He appeared to be enjoying himself. This worried me, and disquiet gnarled at my insides. But I was there and I had to carry on and I persevered with my performance.

A gap opened up in the flow of questioning. Herrera's emaciated frame sank into the ornate chair, swallowed by its gilt enclosure. His face changed and his shallow smile disappeared. His eyes glazed, like pebbles on a stream's floor.

'Señorita, you look very familiar.'

My heart slowed. A mirror hung on the wall opposite my chair and I found my reflection. I *was* Sofia's daughter; the resemblance there for the world to see. For Herrera to see.

'Do I?' I pulled my bag slowly towards my chest, hoping that I hid my accelerated heartbeat. 'I don't believe we've met before. I would remember.' I checked my watch and my intricate preparations dissolved in seconds. 'I think I may have kept my driver waiting long enough. I've everything I need, *señor*. I'm sure I can write a "sympathetic" article for you.'

'Can you?' He shuffled in the grotesque chair.

'Yes, I can. Of course.'

'You're not here with the American magazine, are you, *señorita*?' Old, rheumy eyes pierced.

'I really don't understand. I ought to at least check on my driver.'

'No. Please stay.'

'I wish to leave.' I heard the perfect pitch of my voice.

He smiled. 'Rico, check on the driver!' It was a rasping shout.

Rico opened the door, a tray of savoury food in his fat hands, looking at me with expectation. Quickly, he put the tray on the nearest table and peered at his employer. 'Check he is still there, *jefe*?' he asked.

'Yes, check he's still fucking there.' Herrera glanced at me. 'Why can't everyone be as bright and clever as you and me, eh?'

He was enjoying himself. 'I really don't know,' I said.

'It *is* Isabella, isn't it?'

I stared at the shrivelled form.

He continued. 'You disappoint me. Or were you aware I would know who you are? Is that why you're here? You are too courageous.'

Did I know he'd know? No, I did not. García had arranged everything. But he hadn't arranged everything. It was I who'd organised the meeting with Herrera. Someone

358

had betrayed me. I thought back to the man with the bald head in Madrid. I hadn't told Rafael, or García, about him, perhaps not my best decision, but to have done so, I wouldn't be here now. The radical Basque activists' connections spread far and wide. Could it be possible they had a connection with Herrera? The fear I felt had nothing to do with what could happen to me; I only thought of Rafael, car bombs, disgruntled and corrupt government officials, who were all in a position to erase Rafael as easily as they had obliterated Cristina.

The room was quiet apart from the buzzing fan. I looked at Herrera and surveyed my whole life in moments, a life of which he had snatched away such an important part. My mother.

'You should not have come,' he croaked. 'I was prepared to leave you alone.' He moved in the chair. 'I've known about you for some time. You don't think I could have done something, before now? Of course I could. I chose not to, granddaughter. But now you have sought *me* out.'

'How long have you known?'

'It's irrelevant. The question is − when did *you* know about me? Not until recently, I imagine, or you would have been here before now. It wasn't Joe Hayes − I know that. No balls.' A sly smile crossed his face. 'Rafael? Must be Rafael. I am surprised what he's turned into. The skinny *riojo*. Who would have thought? Has he told you, Isabella? What happened the day in Sabadell?'

'He has told me.' I watched him as I fingered the leather of my bag.

'So scared, he shit himself, did he tell you that? Did your boyfriend tell you that? Sofia lasted a long time . . . wilful to the end.' He continued to search my face. 'Does Rafael still have a scar on his forehead? I meant for him to carry the day with him forever.' He didn't wait for my reply. 'Sofia was a prostitute, like her mother . . . perhaps like you too.'

I tried to compose myself. 'Who told you it was me coming here today? Someone told you. Who?'

He didn't answer. Only smiled.

I imagined him up on the hill. I imagined everything, and the things Rafael had not told me. *Oh, Rafael*. And then a thought passed through my mind; why hadn't Rico searched my bag? Because Herrera was confident I would not be stronger or more resourceful than him. Fat Rico was perhaps standing outside. I would die in this place, and yet my raging fear subsided like an ocean tide.

Herrera watched me. 'Just you and me. As it always would be.'

In one movement I catapulted myself towards Herrera. God knows what I thought I would do, what I could do. And I wavered. He was an old man, I could do nothing. I couldn't kill him. My own grandfather. Why had I come? Still no one had entered the room and in a manoeuvre of a man half his age, and as I procrastinated, Herrera launched himself at me. And I waited for Rico.

But Rico didn't come.

I pushed him off and he fell to the floor; it really was as if Herrera had found a sliver of his youth. He sprang up and fumbled beneath the chair he'd been sitting on, pulling a hidden emergency handgun from the seat's underneath wooden carcass. I was unable to move, frozen in situ, my lithe dancer's muscles paralysed.

Herrera's gun was aimed directly at me. I only thought of Rafael, of what I'd found and what I would lose again so quickly. Herrera held one arm steady with the other, and then my grandfather fired his gun.

I closed my eyes and thought I had died, a flash of Jack's story at Burgos passed like a reel of film inside my head. But Jack had survived. Then the sound of splintering of glass. Herrera had shot the mirror, not me. I lifted my hand to my cheek and my finger was red with blood from the tiny shards of the mirror's glass that had sunk into my skin; I was not though, dead. Herrera appeared as if he'd frozen too and I gathered myself quickly, looking at him, his expression blank and unseeing.

Finally, movement returned to my limbs. Herrera lunged towards me gasping, his lips turning blue, and as I fell to the floor Herrera collapsed, falling on top of me. I punched at his face, I set my knee into his groin as hard as I could. And then I felt him tighten, convulse. I pushed him from me with disgust more than fear.

Clutching his chest he fell to my side, grunting on the floor. I managed to stand.

My God, the bastard was having a heart attack.

In a pretty fishing village near Havana, I watched my grandfather, my mother's murderer and torturer, clinging to his final breaths. Herrera's eyes were still open. He wasn't quite dead yet. I heard voices outside, many different voices. I was not worried what Rico would do to me. I didn't care.

I glanced down, but shifted my eyes away from his contorted face, looking at my patent cream stilettos. I stepped closer to his body. 'Who told you I was coming?'

He remained silent but still conscious.

I leant over him and pulled his right arm outwards, at a ninety-degree angle from his body. I bent my right knee and lifted my foot high, my stiletto a poised knife. I thought of Sofia's death.

He screamed and gazed upwards, as though it were me who was insane. 'My God, what are you doing?' His voice almost inaudible. 'Rico, Rico!' he rasped. 'Where the hell are you!'

I held my leg in that position for a few seconds, listening to his pathetic cries, but then, slowly, I lowered it.

Yes, where was Rico? It was a question I was asking too. I waited for the appearance of Rico. No Rico.

'*Who* told you – about me coming today?' I asked again.

He reached up to touch me with his free hand. I recoiled. He remained silent.

'Who told you I was coming?'

Nothing.

Again, I lifted my foot, although knowing I couldn't see it through.

His twisted face peered up at me, his hand moved. I hadn't retrieved the gun. Herrera grabbed at it and then quickly aimed it at me. *Why had I been so stupid*? I believed that would be my last thought. I squeezed my eyes closed. Waited. But then the noise of more shattering glass, and almost simultaneously, the sound of Herrera's second attempt to kill me. But I still breathed.

I opened my eyes to see Cuban police officers pouring into the room. The window had been smashed. Glass filled the floor and loud but controlled voices heaved through the room. All slowed.

The third gunshot that day did not come from Herrera's gun and it was not aimed at me.

One of the officers shot Herrera in the chest. A clear and clean aim at his black heart.

I was barefoot when a policeman led me outside, somewhere in those last moments I'd lost my stilettos. I saw Rico, and others, being led to a large vehicle. The policeman leading me said nothing but held my arm with an unsaid kindness. By then I had an idea of what might have happened. Bernardo García hadn't told Rafael, or me, the whole story. García's negotiations with the Castro regime had been very firmly in place. Like all politicians, García had only told us the bare minimum.

It was then I saw Rafael.

The late afternoon rain had come, and it had come ferociously. The enormous and prolific raindrops blurred my vision, but I saw Rafael's concerned face, and as movement returned to my limbs, I ran to him.

Behind Rafael stood my chauffeur. His cigar long gone.

'Are you all right, *querida*?' Rafael asked, so quietly I could hardly hear him through the noise of sirens. 'There's no time to explain now. I'll explain later.'

'I'm sorry.' I watched as more heavily dressed Cuban police fell out from yet more cars, carrying guns. 'It's over now, isn't it?'

'Fernando, take her to the car, keep her there.' He spoke to the chauffeur who now had a name. Rafael turned to me again. 'This episode is over, yes.'

Fernando pulled me away. 'It'll be okay.'

I squinted into the distance. Rafael spoke into a walkie-talkie and I saw the paleness of his usually suntanned face, the vermilion redness of his scar. Every move he made was athletic, considered. I closed my eyes.

I'd been way out of my depth.

57

Fernando drove us to a slick hotel in the centre of Havana. Rafael and I spoke briefly about what had occurred in Herrera's villa, but then fell into silence in the back of Fernando's car. I rested my head on his shoulder and it wasn't until we arrived that he spoke again.

'That, *querida*, was not as we had planned it.' He tried to look stern.

'Did you know?'

'That García was already in dialogue with the Cuban government? No, not until I spoke with him before I flew to Cuba, after I saw Jack.' Rafael sighed. 'García didn't tell us everything.'

'But García sent you here?'

'Yes, but, *querida*, it was Jack who knew what you would do. I should have known too, but I have no wish to clip your wings.'

'Herrera knew I was coming, Rafael. He knew it was me. García has an informer in his circle.'

'The leak might not be coming from García's office, although it might have originated there.'

'From the radical Basques?'

He nodded.

'I saw someone in Madrid who could have been the man in Balmaseda, Rafael.'

'You should have told me.'

'You would have stopped me coming.'

'I would. Why did you do it, go to see Herrera, what could you have done?' His face ruptured into a smile that he did the utmost to suppress. 'Kill him?'

I thumped his arm, although with a smile on my own face. 'I had to see him.'

His smile evaporated. 'But your life, was it worth your life?'

'I knew I'd be okay.'

'No, you did not,' he said quietly. 'As soon as we return home we're meeting García in Madrid.'

'Was Rico, the others at Herrera's villa, involved?'

'If they hadn't been, you wouldn't be here now. I'm pissed off with García, but he "layered-up" and ensured your safety as much as possible. García and Jack know you better than me.'

'Rafael.' I rested my index finger on his scar. 'I love you.'

'And I love you.'

For two days I remained in the hotel while Rafael liaised with Castro's closest advisors, as well as with the chief of the Cuban police.

Prior to my arrival in Cuba, García had already made a semi-deal with the Cubans regarding Herrera's extradition. The Cuban government had wanted more information on Herrera's criminal activities before he left Cuba's *hospitality*, and this had been my, *Daria's*, job. The Cuban government had said it was so they could *deal with it in a legal way*; García though, more than aware it was so they could secretly take over Herrera's lucrative businesses. But that had suited García — who'd only wanted Herrera.

García was annoyed at Herrera's death. He'd wanted to put him on trial, if not in Spain, then within the legal system of Europe. García was a lawyer first and foremost, and saw Herrera as the beginning of the beginning. With half a smile I explained to Rafael that if Herrera hadn't been shot by the Cuban police I really would have killed him. Rafael had grinned, saying, *using your two-inch stilettos?*

Three inches, I'd replied.

It was important to keep the humour.

A tight-faced García met us at the Madrid–Barajas airport. His chauffeur whisked us straight to the Audiencia National in the centre of the city. The summer over, the streets were again full. It took us over an hour, and for the first time in years I managed to admire the sights of my capital city as the car crawled through its clogged streets.

García led us up the beautiful staircase and down a wide corridor, carpeted in lush berry red. He then steered us into his elegant and vast office. When I'd visited García at the National Assembly building several years previously, and at the dawn of his career, he hadn't occupied such a grand space. He was moving upwards at a phenomenal rate.

García sat down behind his desk, tucked away to the side of the room. He took in both Rafael and me, his expression that of a parent examining their naughty children.

'What the fu . . . were you thinking, Isabella?' He shuffled uncomfortably in his chair.

'You weren't fully honest with us, Bernardo,' I said.

'You didn't need all the facts.' He leaned back, stretched, and placed his hands behind his neck; I thought in an attempt to look relaxed. Which he was not. 'We have too many leaks.'

Rafael interjected. 'We know that. You are going to have to sort out your department. I am not feeling very safe, Bernardo.'

366

García sprang up and paced the floor like a hungry lion. 'It was Rafael's idea to go to Cuba, Isabella. If he hadn't, I don't know what would have happened.'

'The Cuban police didn't know?' I asked.

'That you planned to see Herrera in person? No. This is a goddamned mess. I can't believe you did it.' He glanced at Rafael. 'This was supposed to be covert. Now the entire fucking Spanish government knows. Herrera's men, including Rico, had been informed. They were aware of our "operation", they were on our side. My diplomatic *adeptness* has to now cope with an extremely pissed-off Castro, and an exceptionally annoyed American CIA. *And* the smart-arse remarks of my own opposition here in Madrid.' He sat back down, defeated.

'You were playing parallel,' Rafael said. 'You should have told me.' Rafael's anger and frustration filled the room, competing with García's.

García carried on. 'The CIA is interested in Herrera. He's been exporting illegal cigars into the States for years, but more pertinent to the US government, he's also in the last fifteen years, been a prolific exporter of the best cocaine. *Also* in his spare time, he was a busy octogenarian, he has been the saviour of many war criminals, from Spain, from Germany and Russia – moving them around the world, mainly to South America. The CIA has been *very* helpful with my interest in him.' He lit a cigarette and drew on it strongly. 'They weren't so happy though, about what happened in Cojimar, Isabella. It's made their job more difficult. And ours.'

I rolled my eyes towards the frieze of angels, which stared down at me from the high and beautiful ceiling.

Now Rafael spoke. 'García had enough evidence regarding Herrera's perverted activities in Spain during the war to have him put away, Isabella.'

Rafael was attempting reconciliation with García, and I could see why but still I pushed back.

'He was not honest with us, Rafael. We need *all* the facts, not just the cherry-picked ones.' I set my eyes on García.

García sighed. 'Bringing Herrera back to Spain, alive, we would have been making a direct statement to the world about such *war criminals*. Sofia was not the only victim. Herrera was a compulsive homicidal maniac. It's only coming to light of his involvement in the murder and torture of many International Brigaders during the civil war.' He took a sip of what I was sure was brandy. 'It was Herrera who ensured Jack Hayes's interrogation and torture in Burgos, Isabella. Herrera was Melitón Mancera's superior. Jack was only set free because of the Nationalist need to barter for the Republican's Nationalist prisoners. Herrera wanted Jack dead. The only reason Jack survived Burgos was because of the barter, without that, Herrera would have ensured Jack's demise.'

I sat by the ornate window, tears stinging my eyes.

García said more gently, 'Exhume Sofia's remains and bury your mother. It is time. Leave everything else to me, Isabella.'

58

Barcelona, Spain

22ⁿᵈ OCTOBER 1976

I sat at the end of the large table that the owner of Los
Caracoles, my absolute favourite place to eat in Barcelona,
had kindly made ready for us all. It had been Bernardo
García who had managed to persuade Señor Caracoles to
close the place for the afternoon. It turned out he was a
big supporter of the young García, as well as being an old
Republican.

I crossed my legs and attempted to repress the nausea
gathering in my stomach, which worsened every time I
detected the faint smell of chicken. I'd been feeling unwell
since returning from Cuba. It seemed to be worse today,
but I put it down to nervousness and the organisation of
getting us all to Barcelona at the same time.

To distract myself from the rumblings inside my stomach
I surveyed the people in my life closest to me, and this
included Bernardo, because it was he who had made all
of this possible. A dichotomy of feelings ran through me;
uplifted to see everyone gathered together, but sobered
because of the reason.

We were all congregated so that tomorrow we could
make our way to Sabadell, to the hill, and to the tree, to

369

retrieve my mother's bones. I was happy that finally I was able to put Sofia to rest properly but at the same time so sad I had not found her alive. There had always been a part of me that believed there was a chance I would – the part of me that was still a girl, still naïve, still hopeful and optimistic.

I'd had to fight García and Rafael regarding the final resting place of Sofia. Neither wanted Sofia's funeral service in the city, arguing that we would be easy targets for Rafael's enemies. I dug my heels in deep and insisted Sofia would not be ignored in death. I was determined her final resting place would be in the city she had loved; the city in which she had been so loved. Both men acquiesced more easily than I'd thought they would; although my win explained García's agitation and Rafael's obvious anxiety.

My line of vision rested on Ignacio, who had interrupted his assignment to be with me and had travelled up from Seville early that morning. He was sitting next to Bernardo and in deep animated conversion. It was right he was there, because more than anyone he understood my sense of non-belonging – and coming from a tight-knit family Ignacio put great store on these things. I'd also asked Ignacio to record photographically the impending day in Sabadell; it was important to do so and I knew he'd be discreet. I could think of no one better for the job.

It had been Rafael who had got in touch with Jack, telling him the outcome of my trip to Cuba and asking him if he would like to travel to Spain. Of course I knew there was no way Jack wouldn't be there, no way at all. Rafael had also suggested that if Kathryn would like to come with him, it would be something I'd love. I wanted Kathryn with us, and I knew Jack would too. Both had arrived two days ago.

On their first day in Barcelona, Jack, together with Kathryn, had taken Rafael and me to Camillo Berneri's house. It was a building I'd been aware of for many years, a beautiful piece of architecture in the centre of Barcelona, but of course I'd never been aware of the precious history it held. It was a private home now and so we were unable to go inside. Jack had perched on the steps where he had first glimpsed my mother – Kathryn sitting next to him, holding his hand. I could envisage Sofia walking up the street and seeing Jack, and I thought of the first time I'd seen Rafael; although it had been the second time he'd seen me. The first being in the dilapidated farmhouse where I'd entered the world. Had Rafael and I felt the same as my mother and father had felt on their first meeting?

I liked to think we did. I would never find another like Rafael.

Calida left France for Spain, travelling with Tomás by car. They picked up Miguel in Balmaseda, all three taking the short journey to Barcelona together. They'd arrived the day before. I'd anticipated my reunion with Calida would be difficult, and in many ways I dreaded seeing her. But she had taken in Tomás and when I scrutinised the boy who had lost everything, I forgave Calida. Tomás had gained weight and although still looking desolate, he was now at least engaging in conversation. I'd known Calida would be good for Tomás; known because she'd been through so much, seen so much. She would be the one person who could not only empathise with him, but actually help him move away from the darkest of places. The previous evening it was I who had explained to Calida the course of events inside the farmhouse and on the hill all those years ago. Together, Rafael and I decided on filtering the detail; it was too much, and part of a past that had sucked too much from her. We did, though, tell her about Herrera's involvement. I think she had always known.

Calida's coldness to Rafael was hard for me to watch, but I understood it was a reflex defence at the decision she and Aurelio had made – taking Rodrigues's advice and help, and fleeing Spain. I did not need Calida's explanation anymore. She had been given a newborn baby – me – and I'd been her first concern. What caused me the most sadness was not Calida's discomfort with Rafael, but her iciness with Jack; although I understood this was her guilt showing. She was sitting at one end of the table, Jack the other, and next to me.

I relaxed back into my chair and took in each person sitting at the table. All together to exhume my mother's bones and to pay our final respects to Sofia, the mother I had never known, although through Jack, I had come to know her. A young woman who had taken on her shoulders the politics and disunion of the era in which she'd lived; a woman ahead of her time, who had lived for a cause she'd believed in, and perhaps even died because of it. A woman who had rebelled, and lived with her convictions, who had found love, and given it in equal measure. The only solace I gained from her final hours was that her silent suffering, as they'd ripped me from her belly, had not been for nothing.

After Rafael and I had left Jack and Kathryn at their hotel after visiting Berneri's old house, we'd returned to my flat, and whilst Rafael stood on the balcony having an illicit cigar, I had reviewed my life. A life not left wanting from what I had done, only from what I had felt. That was until the last few months in which I had experienced true anger, and true love.

I had a new life now and thinking of my father's descriptions of Sofia's ebullience and vitality, her liberalism and dogged optimism, of Rafael's description of her first and final sacrifice for me, I owed her something more than what I was. I had wanted to kill Herrera – my mother, I was sure, would not have had the same desire. And as I turned my head and glanced at Jack, observing his innate kindness, I acknowledged that although my father would have killed Herrera to protect Sofia, he would not take a life for pure revenge. As Rafael would not either.

Despite the occasion, and unlike what seemed like the long-ago lunch in Castelldefels, the atmosphere at the table in Los Caracoles was airy. It was Ignacio who was truly helping what could have been a sombre afternoon along. His assignment in Seville concerned the corrupt behaviour of the local mayor, he told us, who, riding the wave of new building construction in the city due to the upsurge in tourist activity, was taking bribes from wealthy developers. García had been born in Seville, and knew of the mayor. He gladly gave Ignacio titbits that otherwise my photojournalist friend might never have found out.

Tomás had begun to chat with Kathryn, although Tomás's English was only marginally better than Kathryn's Spanish, but the barrier of language helped Tomás emerge from the dark place he still visited regularly. And Calida was finally talking to Rafael. It was only Jack who seemed removed and distant.

'Are you all right?' I asked my father.

'Course I'm all right, love,' Jack replied. 'I'm glad Kathryn came.'

'I am too.'

'You'll stay in touch with her, won't you, after I've gone?'

'Gone?'

'Dead, Isabella.'

'Don't say that.'

'But you will?'

'Of course I will, but you're not going anywhere soon.' I took his hand. 'I might have to leave Spain, if I go with Rafael.'

'*If*?'

'I'm still not decided.'

'What you talking about, woman? You love him, he loves you. Don't mess up . . . Like me.'

'Stop it, Jack.' I took hold of his hand.

The afternoon turned to early evening and the owner of the restaurant began roasting chickens on the rotisseries which resided on each side of the entrance. The rotisseries, and the chickens, were Los Caracoles' trademark. The restaurant was getting ready for the evening public. Jack made a joke about taking a rotisserie home with him to cook his rabbits; I think it was only Kathryn and I who got the joke, and maybe Rafael and Miguel, but Rafael was distracted and not listening.

I lifted my arm to the nearest waiter to get the bill but as I did so, a wave of discomfort pushed through me again as a soft smell of chicken made its way to my end of the table. In that moment I was glad I'd only eaten bread and Caracoles' delicious tomato salad. I scraped my chair back violently.

'Not feeling well, love?' Jack asked as I pushed past him, although noticing his nod towards Kathryn, who immediately rose from the table too. 'Kathryn, go with Isabella.'

She nodded and led me away towards the restaurant's caverns where the toilets were located. We made our way down the staircase in silence, Kathryn holding on to my arm.

'I'll wait outside in the hallway,' she said softly as I closed the door. I made my way immediately to a cubicle

374

and vomited into the toilet. Afterwards, I put down the lid and sat on it. God, I felt terrible. I took a few deep breaths, wiped my lips with my handkerchief, got up and then washed my hands and face in the tiny basin. Staring into the mirror that hung asymmetrically on the wall, I leant forwards against the sink.

Finally, I made my way back to Kathryn who was waiting patiently.

'I am so sorry,' I managed. 'I think I may have an illness.'

She smiled. 'I think you may have, Isabella, although I don't think it's terminal.'

I turned to look at my cousin, a maternity nurse, my own smile spreading. 'No, I don't think it is.'

'Come on, it's time to leave. Get ourselves ready for tomorrow. Señor Garcia is settling the bill.'

We returned to the others.

It was my father who spotted us. He grinned, stood up, and took me in his arms.

59

Sabadell, Spain

On one of the coldest autumn days that Spain had seen for years and four decades after my mother's murder, it was finally time to find Sofia.

It had taken me a few weeks to organise the necessary documentation; protocol and legalities dictated that the mayor of Sabadell had to agree to the exhumation of Sofia's remains, but he didn't do so easily. García, making himself as unpopular as ever with *trumped-up bureaucrats*, as he called them, vetoed the mayor's decision to disallow the exhumation.

This stubbornness was García's speciality. It's what got things done and over the coming years, what mythicised him. García was not a flamenco dancer but he possessed the magical quality of the duende, that understated power of the soul, the ability of behaviour that was able to conquer and understand all.

I danced to capture the duende; García lived his life in such a way that he seized a part of its essence every day.

For Bernardo García, my mother's exhumation was only the beginning. He intended to orchestrate the excavation of the 'lost' bodies which he believed were dispersed all over the country. His vocation was to eradicate the ghosts of Spain and his enthusiasm was not only because of his connection with me and hence Sofia, but also because he wished to oversee a justice he truly believed had not been carried out regarding the victims of the civil war. Despite what I thought of him; ambitious, focused, hard, García was a true and authentic *buscando protagonist*, tenacious and fastidious, and obsessive in how he went about achieving his aims. But conservative politicians, and many at the very top, were becoming alarmed at García's popularity and drive. Rafael and I both saw turmoil ahead for him.

A small digger had been moved up to the top of the hill the day before.

Two cars took us to our destination. Rafael, Jack, Tomás and me in one car. Kathryn, Calida, Miguel and Ignacio in another. It was cold, grey and trying to rain. I looked towards the hill as we approached; it was probably the same road Jack had travelled on his way back with Michael Donavan to Barcelona all those years ago. As we got nearer, I squinted towards the hill, then at Jack. His utter sadness and confusion eclipsed anything I could feel.

And then I saw it. The tree.

It did indeed look like some sort of apocalyptic monolith perched on the top. Just as it would have appeared then. I didn't think anything had changed. Rafael squeezed my hand and a wedge of hope for us settled deep inside.

Both cars stopped and we all got out.

'How are you feeling, *querida*? Rafael asked me quietly. 'Your stomach, has it settled?'

I touched my belly. 'It has. I'm fine.'

He nodded and squeezed my hand.

I stared at the tree, and the digger, which had done the harder work; its driver waited for us.

'I've gone down as far as I need,' the digger's driver said. 'The remains are now nearly at the surface.' Glancing at Rafael, he carried on. 'Do you want to finish?'

Jack stepped forward. 'I'll finish.'

Despite Jack's age and weakening heart, he looked strong. Kathryn walked with her father, only releasing his hand as he went to bend down, his long legs resembling a Z. Slowly, Kathryn crouched down next to him, not to help move the soil but just to be there. It didn't take Jack long to gently scrape away the Catalan earth.

A grey piece of bone and then gradually, Sofia's entire skeleton was revealed. The dense clouds parted and an ethereal ray of a near-winter sun caused the bones to glint and shimmer, giving them the appearance of something jewel-like. As Dominica's daughter had seen by the river.

The operator of the digger offered to take over; Jack mouthed, *no,* and continued, painstakingly placing the bones in a coffin that had been brought in a separate car. And then Kathryn, first looking towards me for approval, did help her father move the remains of a woman who, if she had lived, would have taken away the father whom she adored.

Jack finished and the hole was empty.

I did not move but when the skull was finally excavated, I turned to Rafael and he held me tight against the drizzly rain, engulfing me inside an embrace explaining his love. Sofia would soon be laid to rest properly. It was my turn then to step forward as Bernardo García passed me the huge wreath of Spanish bluebells. Only a man like Bernardo could find a florist who was able to source the out-of-season flower. They displayed a glorious bloom when normally they would be only bulbs in the ground. With them I made the place where my mother had lain for so long into an ocean of violet.

Jack pulled the red scarf from his pocket. He looked to me, a question on his features and I smiled and loved him. He put the fabric to his face, inhaling deeply, and for minutes he held it to his cheeks. I glanced at Kathryn and in a snap of a moment I saw her sadness for my mother, and heartache for her own. Finally, Jack let the scarf fall. It floated softly, opening out into a cochineal vastness and landing in an almost perfect blanket over the surface where my mother's body had been buried for so long. I turned my head away. Jack leant against Kathryn, his face grey and drawn. The tears streaming down his cheeks relentless and I worried for how much longer I would have a father. I wanted to hold him in my arms, but I did not; he had Kathryn, and she needed to be there for him. Instead I allowed Rafael to enfold me.

There had been no words spoken. I took a container from my bag, opened it and poured the contents onto the top of the scarf; the dried Spanish bluebells that Sofia had worn as a headdress on her marriage to Jack. Calida had finally admitted to me that my box of dried bluebells were not from Sofia's childhood in Bilbao.

Calida's sobs echoed through the noon air.

'Shall I fill in the hole, Isabella?' Rafael asked.

'Yes, time to fill it in,' I replied in a whisper. 'Can we cut down the tree?'

'Of course, *querida*. You all leave now. I will stay.' Rafael glanced at the man with the digger. 'Will you cut down the tree?'

'Consider it done,' the man replied.

'And plant another, in its place?' I said.

'Again, as good as done, Señora Adame.'

I wanted to say a prayer to God but no prayer came and, as if knowing my dilemma, it was Calida who took over.

All crossed their chests except Jack and me.

We left. The others I sensed, feeling this signified both a beginning and an end, although for me the beginning

379

was too far away. But I promised myself that Spain was moving forwards and towards a different and vibrant era. It was time for the next generation to sweep away the ghosts of the civil war and its aftermath, and to ignore the apparitions that snaked around us. It was time to progress.

We walked down the hill and I relished the soft pressure of Rafael's hand on the small of my back. I placed my own on my stomach, so sure I felt a flutter of life, and thought of Cristina. *Girls just know.*

As we made our way to the awaiting cars, the sky fissured and the clouds cleared fully and the sun shone. It was then when I saw the rainbow. Each colour so vibrant, so defined.

I *felt* the presence of my mother, Jack's Spanish girl, and I continued walking.

Historical Note

By the time the 1970s was underway, ETA – *Euskadi Ta Askatasun* – Basque Homeland and Freedom – a separatist movement within the Basque region of northern Spain, was rapidly moving away from its peaceful roots, becoming ever more extreme and violent. Rafael Daguerre is utterly fictional, but his actions, and those of Bernardo García, who is based on a non-fictitious character, are centred around real events that occurred during the early years of ETA. Events that follow through to the present day.

With its desire for a clear national identity and the ensuing escalation of violence, which rears its ugly head with power and the human predilection for basic fundamentalism, the rise of ETA during the 1970s is mirrored today in both current modern global right-wing extremism and conflict.

The aim of the Basque activists was to gain autonomy from the central Spanish government in Madrid, and was woven tightly with the events of Spain's civil war (1936-1939) – in that they hoped for a freedom, which they felt Franco's victory in 1939 had denied them. Many Basques had fought hard against the Nationalist rebel, General Francisco Franco. And it was at Guernica, in the very heart of the Basque region and the subject of Picasso's most famous work, where the world witnessed the shocking treatment by Franco against his own people. The links between the

Basques, ETA and the civil war are much closer than they first appear.

The Spanish Civil War itself, both during the conflict and afterwards, was a war, and political campaign, which people today still have difficulty comprehending. It is only with hindsight, and using the backdrop of the contemporary wider European canvas, that historians are able to analyse events during that period, although that retrospection, by the very nature of fiction, is denied to the characters that live within in the novel – except perhaps the older Jack.

In 1936, Franco rebelled against his own democratically elected Republican government. Ordinary Spanish people immediately and organically took up arms against Franco, forming the partisan military group, POUM (The Workers' Party of Marxist Unification). Towards the end of 1936 the International Brigades was formed, volunteers of which travelled from all over Europe to fight alongside POUM in Spain against fascism. As international aid for the Republican government remained stagnant, and as fascism grew in Europe (a Europe already seeing the steady rise of Hitler and Mussolini), Spain's Republican government relied more and more heavily on communist Russia for help to defeat General Franco.

By the spring of 1937 there were essentially two conflicts within Spain; the first between the Republican government and Franco, the second, between the Republican 'Russian friendly' government, against POUM and the International Brigades.

A parallel can be drawn within the Europe of 1930s, which was seeing the power of the fascist state becoming indomitable, with modern politics today: the rise of uncontained and fanatical right-wing extremism.

As with any war or political dissention, in any time, in any country, the story is often not about victory or defeat but about the aftermath; the lives that are changed irrevocably, about the love that is found, and many times lost. About fear, grief and betrayal. But also about forgiveness and redemption. About not looking backwards but peering forwards, untethering ourselves from notions of revenge and hate. Taking up hope, faith and trust.

Isabella and Jack's stories are intertwined because of their familial relationship, but also because their tale embraces two conflicts, separated by time and brought together by history itself.

Acknowledgements

This book has been a long time in the cooker and so there are many people to thank. I will though, keep it relatively short and, I hope, moderately sweet.

My gratitude to Miguel Soto, born in Madrid, December 1925. After becoming a refugee, a young Miguel fled to England soon after the Spanish Civil War. He worked for the BBC World Service, before locating to Geneva where he was a translator with the World Health Organisation.

Miguel's descriptions of Spain and his early life prior to, during, and after Spain's civil war really did fire my imagination. I'm so sorry that he's not alive to see the book that would always be dedicated to him, although I know his widow, Farida, will take joy in its publication.

My thanks to the Johnson family who introduced a teenage me to all things Spanish, although it's the matriarch of the household who truly inspired – Isabel Carmen Adame Hernandez, known as Carmen – who was born in Benamahoma, Spain on October 2nd 1934.

After coming to England in her twenties, Carmen worked as a nurse in the NHS, but she was also a gifted seamstress – a skill she'd learnt growing up in Spain. My over-riding memory as a fifteen-year-old is of Carmen knocking up an outfit one Saturday afternoon for a party that night, pinning the black and silver lurex material to my body, and then miraculously and rapidly transforming it into a gorgeous dress at her sewing machine. Later, and on a trip to her homeland, she taught me how to interpret the sense and feeling of the Flamenco. Carmen really is a true legend.

To my ace writing friends who really do keep me going in the real world. My mentor, friend and consummate literary professional, Essie Fox and my lovely mate and colleague, Laura Wilkinson. David Evans, Claudia Cruttwell, Jan Beresford, Sally Spedding and the wonderful Jools Banwell.

A special thank you to Sarah Ward who championed me at the imperative moment, seeing me through that penultimate draft.

Huge thanks to Andrew Johnson and Michelle Flood for their friendship, support positivity and practical help with so many things, and not only writing.

Many thanks and respect to my editor Olivia Barber for seeing my story as I saw it, and pointing me in the right direction in making it a better book. A big shout-out to my copy editor who has done a great job. Any faults will be mine.

Thank you to my agent, Camilla Shestopal, for her guidance, serenity, and hard work.

My biggest thanks though is to my fabulous and patient husband who over the years trekked to Spain with me whenever I needed to 'do a bit of research.'

And my gorgeous, clever and erudite daughter, Rhiannon, who grew up with this story, which is beautifully appropriate, as I think I grew up with it too.

Love you both.

Printed in Great Britain
by Amazon

39268155R00223